MOTHERS SWAM

DOMINIC GRAHAM

Copyright

To my Family

CONTENTS

PART 3

PART 4

AUTHOR'S NOTE

With regards to languages other than English: while I have used historical personal and place names, I have tended to use modern Romanisation; I write, 'Daegu,' rather than 'Taegu,' which is, I think, closer phonetically and so not in effect anachronistic. However, a Japanese character may refer to the same city using the contemporaneous Japanese name, 'Taikyu.'

At times I have been unhindered by the Hangul Revised Romanisation, to try and best represent Korean as it might be heard by a novice ear.

My intention throughout has been to create both an authentic and enjoyable experience of the languages. I hope that this comes across in the writing.

***

Thank you to Lee Youn-jin and Kim Shin-woo for your help and advice on Korean.

PART 1

CHAPTER 1

A man stood and looked out from the Korean coast. Waves lapped the cliff face below, slow and reluctant to reveal their force against rock which knew it only too well.

The sea stretched out, and the man wondered whether it was possible for any of those same drops of water to have been there, then. The wind shifted and he felt his mood turn resilient, just as his shoulders sank into him and his back braced against the new cold.

The temperature of the water on a given morning; the cover of the clouds: on such things could the tide of a whole life seem to depend.

The man acknowledged what had happened at that place, and what had been forgotten often too gladly. He looked down to the rock of the peninsula beneath his feet and felt the blustering air rush past him: mirrors of eras past; reminders that everything was remembered and accounted for.

He stood on that Korean coastline, looking out at the tranquil view, and acknowledged that there was an insult worse than many others.

It pulled on wounds of pain and suffering, of stolen hope. Of rape.

CHAPTER 2

The rolling waters reached out for the horizon. There they met a wall of steel. Heavy and imposing, it seemed metal buttresses may well have sunk down from those grey battlements and embedded in the rock sea floor. Battleships they were called. From the shore they were a haze, perhaps a dream, or a mist taken on menacing form.

***

Small feet kicked at the tide; the child, two years old, not much more; scarred. Close enough to newborn for water to seem natural; the year breathing alone, enough to panic at his isolation. He reached out with short arms, and gasped in ever shorter breaths. Tears began to overtake the urge for air, and dangerous gulps neared the lapping waterline. Still his legs kicked against the shoreline current.

The waves rolled back and forth, and the child with them. Perhaps he could have swum under, and held his breath as newborns can, but even in his child's mind he somehow knew that he might not reach the surface again.

***

Sun-a swam in the waters she had known all her life. Her friend Hae-ja dived under a wave, then emerged beside her in a splash, arms thrown to the sky. Sun-a screamed, splashed water in return and sprang away with a strong stroke.

They were fishermen's daughters and best friends, and Sun-a felt it in the water around them as they swam. She cast a brief glance to shore, seeing their outer clothes along the pebbles and rocks, and turned back to the leaping chains of water and fun. In the back of her mind the clothes remained as they lay, and she viewed them, young enough to discard them on the shore, carefree, and old enough to know that no man must see them swim.

Hae-ja screamed in delight, then swam after her friend. Sun-a dipped below the water and kicked high with her feet to propel herself down. A smile beaming across her face, she arced underwater before emerging with a cry and a burst of laughter she could not keep in.

Hae-ja turned in the water, and they giggled together as they doggy paddled against the gentle current.

"Have we been missing too long yet? Do you think anyone will notice?"

Sun-a scrunched up her face. "I'm not sure." She looked up to the clouded sky with a brief squint. "I don't think the sun's moved that much. Do you?"

"Maybe a little bit. Maybe we should go."

"Yes, maybe we should."

With a shared smile that they both understood perfectly, they sprang away and began to race the short distance back to shore.

***

Gloom rolled over the Korean waters underneath an overcast sky. Wind ripped off the sea and tore at the foliage on cliff-top trees.

Sun-a looked around her frantically as she paddled at the waters to stay afloat. She was cold, and her wet hair took the shape of her scalp, making her shiver. She looked again to the battleships on the horizon, closer than they had been before. Looming, and impossibly tall out of the water. She felt them tower over her, though there was an expanse of sea between them.

Screams sounded from inland and Sun-a twisted against the tide to face them. Tumultuous waves swelled about her, and it was all she could do to keep her mouth above water. Neck strained and arched, she kicked harder, but the sea seemed to have grown more viscous, and its weight pulled at her like cooking oil. Every kick was through silt, and for the first time in her life she knew she would drown.

She gulped in air, and threw out an arm to rake the surface of the sea. She pulled it back to her frozen, naked body. Then flung out another weak arm.

She moved through the water.

Stroke after stroke she clawed into the East Sea, while hidden below, her legs kicked relentlessly to keep her head above water.

Sun-a staggered onto the rocky beach of the Korean coast, across rough pebbles; she pressed into shoes, looking at the tree line. Hae-ja's pile of clothes had long since gone, and she hurriedly grabbed her remaining garments from the ground, beginning to move. She threw her long skirt around, wildly beneath her arms, reaching for the threads on her back; she pushed her arms into her blouse and tried to tie the cord at the side, as she ran and shivered and climbed the coastal path to leave the beach behind.

***

The battleships waned and faded, perhaps a mirage.

Young Sun-a and her lifelong friend Hae-ja ran laughing into their village home, hair and clothes soaking wet. They carried the fishing nets that their fathers had asked them to fetch too long ago. Caught around their heads and arms, they tried to untangle them, with hushed whispers that would go unnoticed, and unpunished.

With the nets almost unpicked, the girls drew up at Hae-ja's home. Deok-hae emerged from the low doorway with a stoop, and straightened to give a shake of the head. Hae-ja grinned at her mother and asked anyway:

"Mother, can Sun-a sleep at our house tonight?"

"And what would be the point of that, our daughter, when she lives twenty steps over there? Besides, only a fool is disappointed by the sight of her very own bed."

Sun-a's mother, Gyeong-hui, looked over from where she squatted before a mat of drying fish, chillies and cicadas, and beckoned her daughter. As Sun-a and Hae-ja untangled the netting between them amid bent heads and secret whispers, Gyeong-hui shared a smile across the village square, with her own best friend since childhood: a happy, motherly exasperation, which marvelled at how they had come to have daughters of their own, and was secretly only too glad their young girls followed in well-worn footsteps.

Hae-ja freed her hands from the netting as if it were cobwebs, and folded and dropped it into Sun-a's arms. Crossing the village to her own home, Sun-a placed the freshly tangled netting on the ground and sat down beside her mother, and younger sisters.

"You'll turn into a fish if you spend any more time in that ocean."

Sun-a nodded, stuck her tongue out at Yun-jeong, and picked up a cicada from the mat. Now dry, its wings plucked off easily in her fingers, and she turned it around, considering its tiny body.

Gyeong-hui looked across, told Yun-jeong and Cho-hee to both put their tongues back in, and handed her eldest daughter a sharp knife. Sun-a took it, expertly picked and dropped a fish, and sliced it along the belly. With economical nics and cuts she carved out its innards, threw the guts onto the pile, and unthinkingly readied the next fish.

Sun-a heard her grandmother humming inside the house, looked back and gave a wave into the darkness. She could just make her out, on her stool, where she always sat in summer to keep out of the sun.

Her father came around the corner of their one storey home, with its baked, crumbling walls, rustled her hair and carried off his nets.

***

Sun-a ran alone into the village as dark skies rumbled in the distance. She slowed, and looked about her.

***

Sun-a lay beneath the shelter, hidden beside the clearing. The ferns and foliage blotted out the stars, and she could hear the rain drumming its unpredictable rhythm above her.

She put a hand to her stomach and left it there.

CHAPTER 3

S un-a took slow steps into the village she knew so well.
Everything was still. No animal or bird or insect made a sound, as if all had heard a summons, and they had decided she was not worth telling. She felt isolated, worse, left behind. For the first time she understood that the absence of action was not always the same as peace; she felt the feeling stay with her as she walked, horribly, like it might never go away.

As she moved on with hesitant footfalls, she saw a figure, Hae-ja's father, Chi-won. He leaned beneath the roof of his house and beat his closed fist against their cart, which lay propped against the wall; slowly, too slowly to break it, so that the wood shook a little. Sun-a stepped on, seeing more of his face, and that he cried, bitterly, though she could barely hear it.

Sun-a realised she had stopped and that she quaked. She could feel the unsteadiness in her legs, and willed them to keep walking, right on past to home, as if she had heard and seen nothing. But then Chi-won kicked out wildly at his precious cart, again and again. He needed it to carry vegetables, and firewood, and... Sun-a couldn't understand. And then he saw her, and she wished she was ten paces further on.

Her best friend's father turned, and looked at her, right in the eyes, like no one had ever looked at her before, like she had never considered it possible that eyes should need to look. He murmured her name for someone else's ears but hers, and Deok-hae emerged to stand behind him. She stood and stared, with hair ragged and unpinned, and face whiter than skin was meant to be, and eyes that looked with that same feeling, which she could now say she recognised.

Sun-a's stomach turned. She met the stares, hoping they would turn to smiles, and her stomach dropped. It kept dropping as if her insides had fallen into a bottomless pit.

She ran past her friend's parents, trying not to let them see her cry. "Mummy," she choked as she neared her home. Her sister was there, Cho-hee, the youngest of the three girls, as normal as ever, entwining flowers in a chain, by the wall that caught the morning sun.

"Younger sister, where are mother and father?"

The face that looked up was different to the very same features on all past days, and Sun-a felt a horrible, sickening unsteadiness, as if all the world was at sea, or as if she had run from the waters onto the wrong beach and this was not her world at all. She was swept in a sudden panic – longed to sprint back to the sea and surface a second time; but then her mother was there, straightening her back as she cleared the doorway. And her father too. For the brief time it took a spine to unlock, Sun-a felt the extreme of fear swap seamlessly to hope, that all was well. Then she looked upon her mother's face, full, and knew that everything was truly wrong.

Gyeong-hui carried a heap of folded blankets, which stopped only beneath her chin. "Sun-a," she said with tones that confused relief, joy, and nausea.

Sun-a looked to her father, who stood before the doorway, shoulders wide, blocking it. And she wanted to cry, for his face completed the nightmare.

"Mother, what are you doing?" Sun-a asked.

"We're leaving."

"Why?"

"Your father is staying here, and we are going to your uncle in Yeongcheon."

"But I don't want to leave."

Gyeong-hui snapped aside, "Cho-hee, why are you sitting there?"

Sun-a did her utmost not to meet her father's unflinching gaze, and stared at the woman who was her mother. "Yeongcheon? No, I can't leave. I don't want to marry a farmer."

"I don't care what you want! Do you know what you've done?"

Sun-a looked between her parents, and tears flew down her cheeks. "No," she said.

As her father turned his back and walked out of sight behind the house, Sun-a sought words she did not know. She could hear her grandmother humming a tune, inside the house, something frantic, too fast for her – see her shadow, small squat shape on the stool; she tried to put it out of her head. Surely something could be said. Something to salve. "I'm going to marry a fisherman. I don't want to marry a farmer. We both are."

"You will listen to what-" Her mother's voice cracked and the blankets spilled, as she put a trembling hand to cover her face.

An ominous creak drew Sun-a's attention. The family's cart rolled out from beside the house, pushed by her father, with the mood of a man bringing back a body from a storm at sea. Sun-a knew it was for her, and she cried out to her mother in desperation.

"But I promised, mother; I promised Hae-ja. We're going to marry fishermen and live in two houses on the cliff, and be friends for-"

Then her father spoke.

"Child!" He shook his head. "Hae-ja won't be marrying anyone."

"They'll return," her mother said, addressing her father. "The factories-"

Sun-a turned to look to her best friend's house. Where was Hae-ja? She looked back to her own home. Where was Yun-jeong? Where was she?

"Where is Yun-jeong? Where is my younger sister?"

The girl who had swum for too long spoke to her father's hunched shoulders. She looked up from beneath wet, plastered hair, her cheeks salted red.

"Dad. Where is Yun-jeong? Where is my younger sister?"

He looked at her.

"You let your sister take your place."

The tears caught in her throat and began to strangle. She managed to gasp, and saw through a floating salt-water wall that her father had turned away. By the time her hands wiped across her eyes, his shadow was disappearing into the recess of his home.

***

"She can't stay here."

Her mother hurried from the house with all of their clothes folded over her arm, and dumped them into the cart. Her father barged out, so angry. She had never seen anyone so angry, not even when the storm had smashed the boat and threaded the net through itself, back and forth, so that she had spent an afternoon trying to unravel it. His face was red underneath and his neck and arms and back and legs stuck in lines with the things under the skin sharp and tight and stretched.

"She can hide by the cliffs just fine. As she did."

Sun-a nudged back where she sat so her spine was against the mud wall of the house and her legs folded to her. She saw her youngest sister looking up from where she squatted and played with a stick on the dirt; her eyes were wide like circles.

"And if they return? Because they will. What if someone tells, a rumour? Or a sight of her?" Gyeong-hui asked – asserted.

She held her gaze against her husband's. His stance looked like he was about to lash out and hit her across the face, but he stood there, held in it, and it boiled there as she went on:

"Tomorrow, or next year-" Gyeong-hui suddenly felt how exposed she was in front of the house, her back to the yard. She glanced over her shoulder and regretfully saw Deok-hae bending to a knee and picking up vegetables from the ground. Keeping her voice down, she forcefully asked, "And what will they think then? What will they do to you or me who kept her hidden? We could lose everything, the house... everything. They think no one will complain in the countryside."

He was shaking his head, but she continued:

"She will be old enough to work, or marry. If we wait, it looks more suspicious, like we were keeping her from them. Either she joins the others, or-"

Sun-a saw her mother look over at her; she wasn't sure what her face said. "She mustn't, go with them. We'll stay with my relatives-"

Gyeong-hui paused and wiped a hand across her forehead.

"I'm not going to hide her," she heard her husband say.

Gyeong-hui considered Jin-gyu as he turned away: rage given up to rounded shoulders and drooping arms. The realisation made her sick stomach fall away even further in disbelief. The man was broken, no good to them. For how long? Heartbroken, and foolishly, cowardly thinking that was the same as giving up.

CHAPTER 4

Sun-a held her side of the cart, Cho-hee the other, as their mother dragged it across the village square. It was early morning, too dark to set the boat out for fishing, dark still for a long time. They left the dim light of the lamp near their home and were out into the black night. Sun-a was scared; her parents had been scared, she had seen it. She could hear Cho-hee breathing quickly and full of fear, slightly ahead and on the other side of the cart, and in concern tried to hold and quieten her own breaths. She could barely see her feet lift from the black ground. Her grip was tight on the timber side.

They had left her father and her grandmother. She turned – perhaps it was still a clear view to the house. Grass and branches appeared briefly in the darkness; her home was gone behind the low hillside.

Cho-hee had told her, Yun-jeong had 'gone for work'. Japanese soldiers had been to the village. She had known that the boys, held in doorways behind their parent's arm, watching them pack the cart, might labour for the Japanese one day. She had stood near her youngest sister, and heard through the shade of the doorway, her mother say to her father, "even if they take her far, our daughter will come back." The night was black around them. Her mother said nothing, but pulled them on along the dirt track that led to their village, and for the first time led away.

Her eyes began to adjust to the night and the faintest moonlight. She saw the cherry tree that she had often thought of since that day as a little girl – a blackened shape. Her father had let her accompany him as far as the blossom, as long as she had promised to hold the cart side at all times, and hurry straight back with some pink flowers for her mother. She had been so excited, and honoured, and had walked all the way home with a beaming smile, a trail of cherry blossom marking her path.

The tree passed by. She hated the journey now, and ached to return to the days when permission was given and gratefully received.

Cho-hee looked to her elder sister in the darkness, with a face of worry, which could barely see over the timber side. Their mother's steps had slowed.

The cart was turning and her gripped hand with it. Sun-a shuffled her feet as her mother span the cart to the right. The wheels strained against ruts, and then Sun-a found her arm moving upward.

"Keep quiet. Not a sound."

Yet she could hear her mother breathe hard as the cart climbed. Branches and leaves brushed her side, unseen, and Sun-a flinched and leaned aside from bushes, which seemed to cover their path.

"Hold tight, our daughters."

Gyeong-hui heaved the loaded cart along the rough path, trusting where she had remembered it to be. Not suited to the cartwheels, but their route away from the nearby crossroads.

She looked fixedly ahead, trying to pierce and see through the darkness before the features became solid beneath her. She pulled the weight of the cart as steadily as she could, keeping the wheels revolving, but quietly. And ahead the ground fell away, and she slowed and braced herself against the handles.

Gyeong-hui paused, listened, and waited at the edge of the road. She looked back, to the hidden shapes of her daughters. "Step down carefully," she said at a whisper. "We will cross the road here. Don't speak until we've climbed the other bank."

Sun-a's step dropped, and she held on to the cart side as her foot searched for the slope. She hung on, finding the cart firm and bearing her weight; and Cho-hee's too, hands gripped and face held just above the level of the side. Sun-a's feet stumbled beneath her onto a flatter surface and the cart creaked onward, bearing them all. She sensed the space had opened out; the bushes were no longer there, and there was a different kind of quiet.

The cart crossed the smoother road, its wheels quietly disturbing the gravel. Gyeong-hui looked aside as she pulled them onward, but the night blanketed the way to the crossroads. Ahead she saw the first impression of the opposite bank rising, and between grass and plants saw the track start again. She readied herself to turn and drag the cart up the small cliff. Then she heard the voice:

"Who goes there?"

Darkness remained. Gyeong-hui froze at the sound. Only then did a faint torchlight move eerily through the scene. It lit up a strange distorting oval as it passed over leaves and dirt and road, then flared toward them and blinded her in the darkness.

The Japanese voice repeated: "Who goes there? Where are you going?"

"We're travelling to relatives."

Sun-a held tightly to the cart side. They had stopped. The man was walking towards them; the light he carried moved unsteadily, jumping, revealing and then disappearing the ground. She squinted and averted her eyes.

"This way to the check-point."

The soldier backed away and beckoned. Gyeong-hui was motionless, hands tight on the cart handles. Finally, she moved and the wheels began to grind on the spot. She pulled the cart after the soldier, her first steps face down, everything deadened. Terror was there, as she ploughed on, and she glanced back quickly to her daughters. They walked, holding the sides of the cart.

"Where are we going?" Sun-a asked.

"Hold onto the cart, and do not look in his eyes," Gyeong-hui said, low and urgent.

Sun-a peered forward, and as the mountain slopes drew back their bushes and the leaves they held over the track, she saw the crossroads widen out. To one side sat a truck, lit by its front lamps, green and brown and oily black. Another Japanese moved from the side of the truck. Smoking, with a gun hung from a strap. Sun-a looked down at once.

Gyeong-hui heaved the cart onward, head down like a mule. "Don't look up."

Out of the corner of her eye, Sun-a saw a cigarette ground by a boot into the dirt. She swallowed nervously and fought the urge to raise her eyes.

She felt the tug on her hand fade and slowed her steps. She glanced up for the tiniest moment, then back down to the dirt. The soldier who had led them was close. He moved to her mother with arm outstretched. Sun-a heard broken, stuttering Japanese that cut off in a dry throat.

Gyeong-hui swallowed for spittle and tried again, using only basic Japanese: "We're taking the country road."

"All vehicles stop here."

"I'm sorry, I didn't know. We're taking the country road."

The Japanese soldier stepped closer and leaned over the cart. He looked from the gathered belongings, to Sun-a, and Cho-hee.

"Where are you heading?"

Gyeong-hui delayed, caught between feinted difficulty in understanding and a fearful search for what the answer should be.

"Sir, to Yeongcheon. To visit family."

"Why so early?"

Gyeong-hui looked away to hide her panic.

"Sir, we go quickly. The country road."

"A night by a ditch, still."

Sun-a listened to the foreign sounds. She sensed the desperation within her mother's voice. She could hear the strain. Her mother was afraid, and she had rarely heard it. Afraid of what? Sun-a knew that all the women practiced their Japanese for such situations. She had sat alongside while they talked of where they were to go, and the road they were taking. She had always known it was important, to stop a woman getting lost. Surely her mother said the right words.

The soldier leaned by her a second time, and she could smell his sweat as his chest passed her ear. She tried not to smell, nor to let her eyes flicker aside while his hands lifted the blankets, and his face tilted to peer beneath.

Gyeong-hui would not allow herself to look back, though she craved to answer her fear.

"That's a lot of provisions for a visit," the soldier said in surprisingly good Korean, and Gyeong-hui felt a cold swell from her stomach up.

"Sir..."

The tall soldier stood back and looked down. Gyeong-hui lifted her head, slightly, so that a glance could, for a moment, see the dark eyes above the uniform. Though she knew she should not, she could not bear to hear the verdict, blind.

"On your way."

Sun-a's hand moved away from her, and she had to suppress a smile as she tightened her grip on the cart, and walked her feet alongside. She did not know what it was that lifted the corners of her mouth, or why she felt such a lightness that she could almost drift up off the road itself, untouchable by anyone; but to have not smiled for a day and a night suddenly felt the most ridiculous of things. It was as if she had been the foolish girl in some grown-up joke, the meaning of which she was too young to understand, but which would shortly be explained to her.

"Hold on."

Gyeong-hui froze, as if her muscles had been waiting for the word, complicit and forewarned of what was to come. She pivoted her head, on hunched, taut shoulders, feeling it was the last thing in this world truly under her control. Briefly, she saw her eldest, and that pretty face grow pale and drawn as it searched for assurance from the mother who had always given it, and she swept her gaze on.

Her eyes danced across the dirt, until the sound of footfalls became tall black boots at the top of her vision.

"Is there a problem?" the voice said in Japanese.

The checkpoint guard replied. "No Sir, I am sending them on their way."

"Where to?"

She heard the tones of equals in spite of their obvious ranks – two men well accustomed to each other, in discussion, in debate of their fate.

"Family in Yeongcheon."

"Family is important. A mother who does what is best."

Had Gyeong-hui understood none of their language, the sarcasm would still have been clear. As it was, she had been raised in Daegu before her marriage, had known nothing but Japanese rule, and had understood fine. She looked away and continued to feign ignorance.

The ranking soldier considered Sun-a with a growing smirk. Gyeong-hui sensed his focus without needing to look, and fought the impulse to raise her eyes.

"How did we miss this one?" the officer went on. "Translate."

His subordinate bowed. "Yes."

"To care for her young is a mother's prerogative, but so too is to let them fly the nest."

Gyeong-hui swallowed as the words met her ears, not once, but twice, then willed her voice to give away nothing.

"Without a doubt, Sir. In fact, my eldest is to marry. It is a great blessing to a mother to see a daughter so."

The checkpoint soldier translated from her Korean into Japanese, his authority now reduced to the role of messenger. More words were spoken, and this time Gyeong-hui was forced to wait, to blank all comprehension from her face, for the soldier began his Korean with reticence as if unwilling to speak the sentence. Finally the Korean took form and structure, and for the second time the words landed upon her without her consent. As was her horrible part to play, she feigned emotion and faked her expression in all the right places, as if hearing the words for the very first time:

"These are changing times, I concede, but it is perhaps a little too strange for a bride to be dragged aside a cart through the night, with her family in tow. She who travels for love finds a thousand miles just as one mile, yet here she seems a dour bride, not at all as happy as you would have us believe."

Sun-a stared at the ground as the words were translated. It was about her. She felt her breath quickening, though she could not be sure why.

More Japanese, and before it finished, more Korean: "All married women are not wives."

Her mother spoke in a panic, and Sun-a looked up in surprise at the terror that seemed to explode around their cart in an instant. She saw her mum with eyes raised, looking from soldier to soldier, hand leaving the wooden frame to gesticulate. The opposite of what she had told them to do.

"An innocent girl, Sir. She saves herself for her husband."

The first soldier – the one that could speak Korean – did not stand back as before, but stepped forward with a stride that made Sun-a slide away on the dirt. With his back to the other soldier he said in a strong voice:

"Be on your way then. Your relatives won't want you lost in the dark."

"Thank you, Sir," said her mother with eyes wide, white and strained.

The cartwheels began a turn in the mud, and the second soldier moved with a start, his face tight with sudden anger. He pushed his way past his friend and barked out words Sun-a could not understand.

The words touched Gyeong-hui's ears, again against her consent. She did not want to hear.

"Stay where you are! I am not as wholly convinced as my colleague!"

Sun-a put her foot down, to find that the cart had not moved with her. They had stopped. She span, back to the old wood as the barking man rushed her. At the edge of her vision she sensed her mother raise a hand to cover her mouth, as if to muffle a scream. Yet there was no sound, apart from the heavy crunch of boots on dirt, and the snarl of foreign words.

Gyeong-hui could not bear it. She looked away. Yet still the words kept coming.

"I see no smile. No blush in the cheeks for married life to come! Are you inflamed girl?"

Sun-a heard only growled, sharp sounds. The man's animal face was directly in front of her, closer than it should have been. Its eyebrows rose, as if expecting something from her, and so she looked to her mother, whose hand now trembled and whose face gave no answer, and then back to the soldier. His expression was there, right at the tip of her nose, close enough to bite, making her recoil against the wood, and she would look anywhere else. Her eyes darted for a way past the horrible, blocking shape, and found in a corner the face of the tall soldier. Her eyes pleaded, but he did not translate.

The man went on, quieter this time, his breath smelling horribly of whatever he had had for dinner and hitting her in the face. She wanted to turn away and breathe clean air, but somehow knew she must remain where she was and wait for it to pass.

Gyeong-hui heard. The words had been for her anyway.

"No mother should suffer an ungrateful daughter become an ungrateful wife."

His nasty gaze was on her mother now, with those eyebrows asking another question. And then he laughed, and Sun-a knew for certain this was no adult joke that she was yet to understand. There was no humour at that crossroads. None at all.

Her mother dropped, with hands clenched so tightly they were streaked white and red, as if she meant to drop to her knees. Yet she seemed to stick halfway down and rock there, knees bent, desperately trying not to collapse all the way.

"Please, I beg you. The sun is soon rising and we must hurry."

Sun-a heard a low rumble, which became the grind of a truck slowing.

The tall soldier turned away from her, something like sadness on his face, and ran over to the vehicle just arrived at the crossroads, hand raised, shouting short-tempered words, which it seemed to Sun-a the truck driver did not deserve.

Gyeong-hui rocked on her haunches, hands draping the dirt. It could not be happening. How could it be happening? The day had started with drying vegetables on their old mat, her middle child smiling, looking up at her, and Sun-a playing with her neighbour's daughter. She had kissed her husband goodbye, then seen him walk through the early morning village, away to mend the boat. She had played hand-clapping games with her youngest, then... She had seen and heard, and seen her eldest run back, late, hair wet and straggling, and... No. How could this be happening?

"She will do well for the Imperial Empire."

Sun-a could back away no more. The Japanese man placed his hand upon her arm. Sun-a looked down at it and saw the shadowed fingers clasp, and felt the pressure through her clothing.

"Mother," she said.

The grip moved, and Sun-a moved with it.

"No! Please no!"

The truck was waiting at the crossroads and the other soldier was turning from it to look. Sun-a saw her mother stumble and rise, and take steps toward her – but knew they were too small to ever get her there in time. Still, she reached out with her free hand, as far as it could stretch and her spine could arch. Then the back of a hand grew oddly large in her world, and she found her head snap aside, before she heard the smack and felt the stab of pain deep inside the flesh of her cheek.

Sun-a screamed, and heard her mum scream with her. As vision returned, she only then realised it had been gone for some moments. And as her head swung back the way it had come, she saw her little sister, Cho-hee rooted by the cart, staring at her in the blackness, with her mouth a small open circle, about to ask a question or sob quiet sobs. Sun-a felt a strange sensation of shame as she shared the gaze of the sister she was supposed to protect, and that it wasn't right for someone so young to see this.

Before the thought could settle, her whole form twisted and she found herself dragged across the crossroads, arms held high above her head. She kicked out with feet that raked the ground. Her body lurched as a heel dug in, but a sharp pain in her shoulder spun her weight aside and dislodged her anchor. Kicking, kicking, frantically, she was dragged, screaming out the air in her lungs, "Mother, mother!"

Up she went and into the open cabin of a truck, where she landed hard on a seat. Her mother's voice seemed distant, though its scream was shrill. It seemed so hopelessly far away that it made tears well in her eyes.

"No! You already have one of my daughters, you don't need two! No! Please let her go!"

Her mother was crying.

She saw, through the yellow glare of the window, the outline of the cart, and two figures.

Another voice – that of the tall soldier, though the truck cabin hid him from her. She did not understand what was said. She waited, half on the seat, seeing the truck door move, the soldiers outside, the night and the glare. The one who had dragged her stilled and the half-open door too; he replied, snarled, hidden sounds. The tall guard, she could see his outline, straightening – "Yes," he said; a Japanese word she knew. But then he stepped back; she saw his figure pass the headlights in front. The door moved slightly, outward, and then slammed shut.

***

The checkpoint soldier hurriedly waved the waiting vehicle through; he crossed promptly to the cart and placed Gyeong-hui's hand back upon the handle. With a heave he pulled for her, and set the cartwheels moving.

"You're blocking the crossroads. Hurry on."

The cry of Sun-a shrieked out.

Gyeong-hui looked at the Japanese soldier, her mind seemingly running with seconds' delay. She nodded something barely recognisable as a nod, and trudged with the inertia of the cart.

"Mother, are we leaving my elder sister?" Cho-hee asked.

Gyeong-hui did not turn to answer and so did not see Cho-hee look back to the truck, or the despair on the young girl's face.

She dragged the cart forward, on legs that felt like seaweed. She wanted to scream out and cry all the sorrow that she had never known one day alone could bring. But she could not; she had to think of her only daughter.

Finally, Gyeong-hui looked back, and saw the truck, cut off, isolated in the darkness; no sign of Sun-a. The guard who sent her away, backed off, still facing her, and smaller behind him, the other stood watching. She turned away and carried on along the dirt road.

Cho-hee held on tightly to the cart her father had once built. She noticed that her hands hurt, and when she looked down saw the skin over her knuckles sharp, like she had never seen it before. Nevertheless, she dug in her nails to make sure she did not slip.

***

The glare from headlights flared at their eyes. It cast everything with an off-colour yellow, and made the black night in between vehicles seem like falls into plunging abyss. Sun-a saw through squinted eyelids, vehicles, and bustling soldiers, and rifle butts being prodded into confused, shuffling girls. She turned from the circle of noise and discomfort which surrounded her and let her vision depart on the back of the poor woman in front. Engines revved and orders were shouted, but she kept her head low.

A Japanese soldier walked close by and forced her attention up. He barked orders as if they were supposed to understand, and then pointed with his gun to the back of a truck which reversed towards them. The large vehicle stopped with a glare of light, and Sun-a found herself looking up at the night sky in search of darkness. Yet even there the glaze of horrid yellow washed out the stars and made the cold and black into something that hurt her eyes.

She looked back at the old three storey house – the biggest building she had ever seen – which leaned over the square. In its many windows, curtains were drawn and she could see silhouettes of men standing, or walking, and some bright yellow spaces that were missing theirs. She turned to face the back of the woman in front, and wait in line.

Metal sounds. Echoes, patters like slow rain, caught her attention. Soldiers and orders hurried out on the square in Daegu, and she saw other lines and groups of women, heads and skirts outlined in yellow haze. The metal strikes were footsteps and knees, she saw; women clambering onto other open-backed trucks; grabs of the arm and shoulder, and prods of barrels and rifle butts. She tried to see, and shuffled forward, and kept trying to squint and see. If they could run, run, all the way back home, however far-

Sun-a glanced back to the leaning house, toppling more than those others around it, and wondered if her sister might be inside. She took tiny steps forward, only peripherally aware of the angry soldier's stare that passed over the slow line, and realised as she had countless times already, that this hopeless search was the one hope she had left. Then, as before, she felt sick with self-disgust that she should wish this on anyone else, just for the embrace of a loved one, or a smile on a face she knew.

The soldier brought her back, with a sharp shout that pierced the din. Her line began to move quicker as scared girls sought not to be at fault, and Sun-a with them. She saw faces ahead turning to see the angry orderer, then promptly hung low upon newly learned instinct. Some belonged to women, beautiful but for the dirt and mud, or plain as you would see in any village, or even near ugly. Girls, perhaps. Women. She could not seem to tell the difference any longer. And then the thought struck, that could she be sure others did not look on her the same.

Two places ahead, a woman struggled her way onto the back of the truck, and before she was up, the woman in front was climbing and looking about for a place amongst the cram of girls between metal sides. And then Sun-a knew it was her turn and she tried to reach a foot onto the truck floor, though she wasn't tall enough to do it. Yet somehow she was managing, and arms and hands were helping her up, though there was little kindness on the faces that looked down.

She was lifting up into the air, and finding her place, as the last girls were packed on and the tailgate snapped up to crush them in, when she saw her face. Yun-jeong, the middle of the three, her younger sister, sitting hunched to her knees on the next truck. Sun-a felt her lungs fill as her mouth gasped, and she raised a hand towards her family. But there was no need, for Yun-jeong's eyes had grown wide with wonder and astonishment and then with joy, as they had laid upon her own.

Yun-jeong pushed herself from the truck floor to see better through the crowd, and Sun-a smiled, and neither of them paid heed to the warning growl of the engines. Side by side they rolled for precious seconds, before their trucks turned separate ways out of Daegu. Their gazes turned to final ghostly looks of horror that both would never forget, and they pulled apart like the two wings pulled apart from the back of a brittle cicada, which it had long been clear could never fly again.

Sun-a slumped against the body of the woman beside her, who had been packed so rigid that she barely moved. The village girl slid down, but there was not room for her knees to fold under her, and so she remained, stuck, half-way to collapse, pinned amongst her kind. It was over. Hope was over.

The truck carried them north from Daegu, into parts of Korea that Sun-a had never ventured.

CHAPTER 5

25th August 1939

Mick waited at the end of the line for the women's room, with a clear view of the door. It dispensed pretty girls at regular intervals, and replaced them from the queue that never seemed to shorten. The girls shuffled one by one in their dancing dresses and heeled shoes, and Mick craned his neck in search of Miranda, but Daisy Finch appeared instead, straight onto the arm of David Hutton and away. Mick tutted to himself. He was quite comfortable in his present location, but equally could feel the clock ticking.

"There'll be no dances left by the time the chain's flushed another dozen pulls." Eddie had voiced what he'd been thinking.

"It's not dancing I'm after," Mick replied. "Pete at the bakery calls it a preamble."

"As in amble around, like walking?"

"Like walking. When you don't even know which direction you're heading."

Mick mimed an upper-class waltz for a second. He dropped down to his stance and grinned. Eddie grinned back, but the smile disconcertingly fell off his friend's round face and was replaced by something earnest. Eddie nudged him with one of his small shoulders, remembered to check for eavesdroppers, then quietly went on:

"If you're thinking that... There doesn't have to be a ring on her finger, or even in a box in your top pocket, but you've got to have given it some thought."

Mick stood up a little bigger and looked down into the hall. He could see couples sweeping by, one after another through the picture-frame rectangle at the end of the corridor. Beside him Eddie changed the subject:

"We going to the Baseball Ground tomorrow?"

"Course. We're not working men for nothing, right?"

"Uh. See if we can hold onto the top spot this time."

"Dix, Crooks, and with what they paid for McCulloch; I've got a good feeling about this season."

"Don't you think they ought to call it by what it is? Not been a base there for forty years."

Mick nodded, half hearing, still looking tall to the dance floor.

"It does no harm."

He glanced aside to Eddie and thought he looked about fifteen. More girls tottered through the women's room door and swung onto the dancehall corridor, skirts twirling with the motion. Mick watched them all the way, face practised at showing no emotion, just ambivalence. Eddie tapped him on the shoulder and stood on tiptoe to his ear. As soon as the girls were far enough away Mick bent down to hear his friend's well-intentioned but likely daft comment. He'd thought for a good year or two that it was time Eddie grew up a bit.

"Haven't you got to think, that's someone else's wife you might be fondling?"

"She's not married to anyone."

Eddie shrugged.

Mick sought a light-hearted reply in his increasing annoyance. "What's this talk of bases, anyhow? You trying to get us conscripted?"

Eddie laughed a bit, and Mick grinned at his own quick wit. They planed their faces and straightened their backs, as three slick-haired lads from their own school year sauntered toward them: Thompson, Radcliffe, and Gaunt.

"Either of you two seen Bob's bird around?"

"Who's he courting?" Mick asked.

"Chubby girl. Annabel... or Beatrice. Something like that."

Eddie frowned. "Those names sound nothing alike?"

"What's it to you Eddie Edkins?" chipped in Radcliffe.

"Teddy."

"I was talking alphabetical." Thompson pulled a face and cast mocking glances to his chums. "Is he trying to sound like the bear, or what?"

"It's a President's name. They've just finished dynamiting his face into that hill in America. It was in the newsreel."

"Maybe he fancies himself a great xylophone player!"

"Xylophonist!"

The three laughed, hands expanding to the famous band leader's waistline, more hands miming the beaters. Thompson snorted in hysterics, and managed to say, "I could see you tinkly-tinkling away in your bow tie."

Eddie looked to Mick for back-up.

"We've not seen her."

"Oh right," said Thompson, emerging from his banter and insult. "Hey, Mick I heard you poked Hayward's sister."

Mick delayed, before replying with a casual shrug. "I heard much the same thing."

"True then?" asked Gaunt.

"What kind of fellow would I be if I told you rabble?"

Thompson patted Radcliffe on the shoulder, and the three lads wheeled off with backward steps in the formation they had, which looked like a march they must have practised hanging around Gaunt's street corner.

Radcliffe called back, "There's no shame in not having the bottle on your first attempt. Me, I'm fizzy as a Dandelion and Burdock."

Thompson and Gaunt laughed, and pointed and jeered as Radcliffe mimed his fizzy drink.

Mick didn't think it was funny. He waved a dismissive hand at them, together with a noise that joined in the fun and one of his grins. He turned back to Eddie, the smile already dropped.

He thought for a moment, then said definitively: "Got to keep these things quiet or I'll never get anywhere with Miranda."

His small friend raised an eyebrow, a disbelieving one, and curled his lip, like he thought he was a gangster.

"Oi, I don't call you Teddy."

"I'm thinking we should start it off. I like it." Edward stood up straight and nudged his head in the direction of the comfort room.

Mick turned to face the queue, annoyed at himself for having lost his concentration, and feeling unsettled.

The two women, eighteen years old, in pretty dresses and wearing plenty of blue eye shadow, exited the ladies' door.

"You'd think they pissed two to a stall," quipped Mick quietly. Then, standing to attention he held out his arm. Eddie did the same, so that when the girls seemed to float up to them in their bobbing dresses, Miranda could link her arm with Mick's, and Beverly with Eddie's, all without missing a step. They pivoted as if they too had rehearsed before that small, crowded corridor, and it felt truly great – and they began their stroll to the dance floor.

"What a dreadful queue," commented Miranda.

"We're sorry you had to wait so long," followed Beverly.

"Patience is my middle name," said Mick.

Beverly looked to her date. "What's your middle name Edward?"

"John."

Beverly sent Miranda a disconcerted look, not altogether well disguised.

Miranda asked plaintively, "Do you and your friend dance, Mickey?"

Mick supposed that the girl on his arm knew the answer to that question very well, but he didn't mind the ruse one bit. He simply smiled, and felt very glad to have such a beauty at his side at the Derby ballroom. He led her to the dance floor.

Eddie hesitated for a moment, then opened his mouth to speak. Beverly nodded before he could get any words out, and they followed their friends onto the polished wood, well smoothed by a decade of swivelling heels, of waltzes and foxtrots.

Mick felt a bit of history there as they danced. The way the floor looked under his polished, twisting shoes. He had a notion of the young men and women of each previous year, now married and settled into the safe pattern of family life, now sitting in front rooms about the town with their wirelesses on.

Young men proudly led young women in two-by-two artful procession, rising and falling and spinning. He danced with his girl in the middle of it all, but he felt himself bigger than the lot of them, somehow scarily so. At the edge of them, all was a whirl of dresses and smiles and nervous expressions at the most important counted beats of life so far – on which their whole future seemed to rest. Colours and pleats flew and pulled back, and sailed out in fans of unfolding fabric, designed to ignite that very moment. It made him dizzy and he tried not to see it. Everything seemed uncomfortably fleeting: the moment like the spinning, whipping dresses. The thirties didn't seem permanent all of a sudden, as if the decade was indeed about to turn, and wouldn't go on spinning around that dance floor, year after year, and he with it.

***

Mick sat with Miranda on the stone steps that led down to the lapping waters of the River Derwent. The current was so still below them, it seemed not a river at all.

Mick looked at the girl beside him in the darkness, beauty picked out perfectly in thin lines of white by the cast-off glow of streetlamps. With the town and its light behind them, they were perfectly alone.

"I'm not that kind of man, Miranda."

"I know. It's just... that I heard this rumour. Mick Bowler... and... had his way with... Do tell me different. What kind of man are you?"

Mick found his response was not on the tip of his tongue. For a moment he was reluctant to lie to her, but then felt oddly unsure what the lie would be. Well aware that a hint of hesitation could cost him, and riled at himself, he quickly began, "I'm the kind that-"

"The chip shop was about to close, but we got there just in time."

Eddie and Beverly hurried through the pools of light on the pavement and took the steps quickly, Eddie trying to balance their already open newspaper of fish and chips, with Beverly clinging to his arm and laughing.

They looked to have had a good time. Mick sent a glare to his friend for the untimely interruption, but it went unnoticed in the dark, with the smell of fried potato and vinegar turning Miranda around with a delighted cooing sound, and the excitement of hungry tummies setting the mood.

Miranda patted the step beside her, and Beverly plumped down, out of breath.

"Oh, he is a funny one: you should have seen him in the chippie. Have you two been alright without us?"

"Just fine," said Miranda, leaning shoulder to shoulder with Beverly, and hiding a shared look between the two of them, which was followed by a girlish laugh.

Mick grinned and received his bulging, well-packed newspaper. He could feel the heat and dampness wrapped inside the ink and stories, and gladly unwrapped it beside his girl. The smell was delicious, and he stationed it half on his leg and half on Miranda's.

"Don't move, or it'll fall."

"Oo, thanks," Miranda said, dipping in with delicate fingers for a well-chosen chip, which she held poised between finger and thumb, and bit in between her conversation.

"Thanks Ted," said Mick, and meant it, glad now that his less than serious frown had been drowned out. "You're a life-saver."

"It's getting on for curfew, Mizzie, we'd better eat fast," said Beverly, and then seeming to recall an earlier thought: "Oh, I do think you'd look wonderful on a boat Eddie. Don't you Mizzie? He might join the navy."

"He'll what?" blurted Mick.

"You'd look grand, I reckon," affirmed Miranda, leaning out to wish Eddie her best. Mick struggled to keep the fish and chips balanced.

Beverly leaned out in symmetry, to ask, "What about you, Mick?"

"What about me?"

He caught Eddie's grin and wry raised eyebrow, which asked him not to let the side down.

"Oh, I've not given it much thought."

"Oh you are funny, Mick," said Miranda, nudging her shoulder up to his.

"You can wave us off from Portsmouth if you like," said Eddie, a brave and selfless note sounding in his voice and in his posture.

"Oh, so it's the seas for you too, Mick?" asked Miranda.

"You would make a good officer, Teddy, I'd vouch for that." Mick replied. "But you know, I don't..." He looked across and saw Eddie and the girls watching, expectant. He about turned. "Captain of your own destroyer, hey Ted?"

Eddie nodded confidently, and Mick continued. "I expect I'll be in the R.A.F. I could see myself at the controls of a fighter, taking it to the Germans."

Miranda said, as if she'd been waiting for the cue, "I'm sure you'd make a fine pilot."

Mick knew the importance of backing up a friend, like he knew Sunday school stories, but something rankled in him. He felt an overwhelming urge not to joke about such a topic, and to set things straight, because it was too far-fetched, after all.

"But come on gang, what are the chances, hey? Really? I don't care how crazy them Germans are, they aren't going to want a second round against us Brits. They know what happened the last time."

"You're probably right, Mickey."

"Us Brits could take on the whole of Europe if it came to it. Even the world, I reckon. Empire and all that. Hitler wouldn't dare. It'll never happen."

Eddie looked downcast, even in the shadows that kept his features mute, and Mick could sense his urgency to draw a line under what had been, until then, a successful conversation.

"Whatever happens, I'm glad you'll be safe here," Eddie concluded to his girl.

"That's sweet of you, Eddie."

****

Mick strolled with Miranda past Chester Green. Her arm was through his, the summer sun still not done setting, and the air was as comfortable as it could get. He had waited three days before casually popping into the small tailors at which Miranda worked, and asking her out, though he had been itching to go the morning after the dance. By the terraced houses they walked, hearing the shouts of children playing, and of mothers calling them in before dark. It had been a very enjoyable evening so far.

Over the road the huge square of the Green rolled out beneath the tall oaks and ashes. Terraced houses stretched along three of its four sides, and the Union Foundry, with its great arched windows, spanned out in the distance opposite them, just visible in the dusk; the tall tower of the church stood near the corner of the Green, toward the town. It was pretty, thought Mick. He felt proud to hail from such a place and to be able to court there.

Abruptly he stopped, and turned into Miranda's path. Taking both her hands, he said, "Just you wait here – and I'll be right back."

With that he ran to his front door, which wasn't locked, and he was inside in a flash with a brief wave and smile behind him.

Miranda stood outside, elbows almost touching in front of her, hands nervously clutching her handbag. The night seemed to have darkened even in their last few steps, or perhaps the solid row of houses had obscured the last pinks and purples of the sunset. She looked about her, not wanting to seem amiss, saw the diffuse warm lights in front room windows, and heard the faint crackle of wirelesses in the still air. It was a pleasant summer evening, but she couldn't help thinking she should pull her cardigan tight.

Mick ran down the stairs, two or three at a time, while simultaneously trying to cushion each footfall. He loped around the foot of the banister, down the hallway, and leaned into the front room with a hand swinging on the doorframe. His free arm he kept tucked by his side, and the flask it held nestled into his lower back.

"Ma-Dad," he said. "I'm off out."

Pam looked around from her armchair, knitting temporarily paused mid-stroke.

Harold, snoozing in the adjacent armchair, adjusted the glasses on his nose, and observed. The newspaper on his lap rustled as he pushed back out of his comfortable slump.

Pam looked at her son with a disconcerted expression. "You just got in."

"Back later."

Mick pulled himself out of the living room doorway and turned, face to face with Miranda. She smiled apologetically, then briskly looked to the slowly closing door, whose narrowing angle thankfully presented only a view of the dining room table, cabinets and ornaments toward the back of the house.

"Good evening Mr. and Mrs. Bowler."

Pam startled in her chair, and looked to the doorway. There was no one to see. She glanced quickly back to Harold, who was looking atop his glasses frustratingly slowly. Pam leaned back as far as the cushion would squeeze and saw a glimpse of blonde curls and a pretty feminine face.

Mick pulled Miranda from the doorway and guided her quickly to the front mat, with a flustered half-smile on his face. He ushered her onto the low step outside on the street, and closed the door behind them.

The front door clicked shut and there was silence from the hall. Pam looked to the lace-curtained front window and waited, watching the panes by the frame. No one stepped into view; she looked aside to her husband.

"Who was that, Harold?"

"Not important, or we'd have been introduced."

Harold picked up his paper, as Pam pulled a face and looked back to the window, in case her son's shape might still appear. "We raised him better than that," she said.

Mick could recognise something like hurt or confusion in Miranda's expression, which had been unable to hide itself fully, so off-guard had it been taken. On instinct and alarm at plans awry, he sought to disarm it with what he always presumed was his charm. Taking her hand, he led her across the street, with a skip to his step, and smiles over his shoulder. And he saw her face already brightening. Then recovering a bashful smile.

"I should like to have met your folks, Mick."

"And you will. And I shall like you to. But the time has to be right, doesn't it?" Miranda nodded, and he went on, while leading her across the road and onto the now darkest green grass. "I just didn't fancy them spoiling our fun. Besides, you look so beautiful, and I didn't want to waste a minute."

"I should like you to call on me, next time. And you know, my Ma, will likely open the door."

Mick nodded. He turned on his heels and gave a sharp tug on her arm. Her steps tottered, over-balanced as he'd intended, and she gave a little whoop of delight. Mick stepped into her fall and they were dancing.

She was gazing up at him, wondering how it could be that she waltzed without having taken hold, and thinking herself the most fortunate girl in the town, with all Chester Green her ballroom.

The grass turned black beneath them as the stars showed themselves above, and the lights of living rooms all around seemed to be a ring of floodlights focused on just them two. Mick wondered at how he had done it, and said to himself that charm it most definitely was.

To Miranda he said, "Come on, I want to show you somewhere."

He took her by the hand, at a run, across the Green. She couldn't help but cry with delight and the romance of it all, as she tried to hold her dress down against the breeze.

CHAPTER 6

Their footfalls brushing grass seemed the only real sound, now that children were indoors. Radios drifted their voices and songs into the air, but they were only a background buzz from another world entirely. Mick led Miranda by the hand, across the black grass and under the low branches of tall, spreading trees.

He ran ahead to the path at the side of the Green, turned and bowed gracefully with a sweeping arm and the other folded behind his back. He stood up straight, laughed, and brought the metal flask from behind him. He took a short swig, swallowed, holding his face against any ill effects, and offered it to Miranda.

She approached coyly, considering him flirtatiously with her eyes, and tentatively took a drink. He saw her features marked out in the fuzzy night-light, like a skilled artist would sketch - lines and charcoal. She gasped almost immediately and handed the bottle back on the end of a straight arm.

"This way," said Mick, warmly, and escorted her onto the church grounds.

He took her past the white stone war memorial, visible in the dark, glowing. He and his friends had counted several times the seventy-five names engraved on it from the Great War, when there had been nothing much else to do. They walked beyond the tower, to where the church building cut out at a right angle; he stopped at the large arched window, which faced toward Derby at the furthest point of the Green. The deserted graveyard spread out to their side beneath huge oaks. There were few graves, for as people knew the law had been changed not long after the church had been built; now people got buried on Nottingham Road.

He rested his back against the large stones of a mossy buttress. She stood adjacent to him, looking out, not leaning. The last light of the evening, or perhaps beginning moonlight, scattered silvered patterns throughout the darkness; it remembered the faintest impressions of colour and shape from the dark stained glass window and shone across her paled blonde hair, hints of reds and blues and oranges. He followed her gaze across the ground to the trees, now seeing an ochre, yellow, oddly violet hue in the night: light from across the Green, or thrown gauzed from the town somehow, fell across the few headstones, and peppered branches of leaves and long blades atop the black grass. They took in the display, and Mick heard her as she got her breath back.

"Pretty, isn't it?" he said, aware of the understatement as soon as the words left him.

Miranda nodded, and Mick took a drink from the flask. He offered it, but she gently shook her head to decline.

"Do you like it at the Works? That's a good trade my Pa says."

"It is, and with a decent wage."

Miranda's tone changed involuntarily, feminine true feeling raising and trembling her voice: "You'll do your family proud."

Mick saw her expression was one laid bare, growing cherry red in the unusual cast of light.

"I mean, the family that you will have."

He could hear the opportunity in her words that had been running out of air, and her nervousness that had been too afraid to breathe again lest the words catch in her throat.

He rounded on her. Stepped in front of her. And she straightened up against the church wall. He moved closer.

He said, "You know I like you, don't you?"

Miranda nodded, wide eyed, and pushed back into the wall, her hair bunching up against the windowsill. Mick gently kissed her.

He moved a fraction away, and looked into her eyes, moist and beautiful and now on the other side.

"I was always hoping you'd ask me to dance, you know? But you never did."

"Well, I'm glad I got my act together in the nick of time."

Mick smiled, moved his head a motion forward, and kissed her again. She kissed him back, with growing intensity. He moved a hand onto her waist.

"Was it my dress that you liked? Ma took me to Clarkes for it, though I did the alterations myself."

Mick listened and kept his focus. "I did think you looked lovely, but more than that, a fellow just realises what's important."

Miranda smiled and gave Mick a daring little peck on the lips. For a moment she almost bounced on the spot with delight, and then Mick pressed up close, and kissed her as passionately as he could. Slowly, he moved his hand toward her breasts.

The sound of friction and scratched moss and old stone. Mick's eyes opened to see her sliding aside, and too late felt her warmth and pressure leaving his body.

"I can't."

"It's alright, Mizzie."

"I really can't."

She was shaking her head, standing away against a buttress, belonging to a different night altogether. Mick felt shock at the sudden change, and how easily and unnoticed everything had slipped away from him. Panic at a moment lost welled and threatened to show through his composure, and he rallied against it, to regain lost ground, to backtrack to the moment just stolen.

"I know it's fast, but times are changing. Whatever we might say, we both know there'll soon be a war on. We can't think like we did before."

As calm as he could pretend, Mick moved over to Miranda and took one of her hands in his.

"Sometimes it seems like the world's going crazy. But not that crazy," she said bashfully, eyes downcast.

Mick nodded in apparent understanding, but really defeat.

"Are you scared?" she asked.

He smiled confidently and took a hopeful step forward. "I don't scare easily."

He stepped forward again. Direct. He kissed her again, and she didn't object, though he could feel the tentative move of her lips. He pushed on, unsure whether he could save the situation, then felt relief as she relaxed into it. He moved his hand up to her breasts.

Her eyes flicked wide open, but she didn't object, not with words. She stared at him, their faces so close, and he wondered if he should stop, but kissed her anyway. She said nothing; her lips barely moved. He closed his eyes, discomfort gripping its hands around his stomach; she would surely close her eyes, and go with him. But when he glanced open, her black pupils were large and staring at him, surrounded by pools of bright white. His stomach tightened, and he wondered if he should move back, then felt his hand under her breast, and felt both a rush of success and the purge of nausea as a belt seemed to tighten by notches around his gut.

He pulled back, and his hand came with him. "What's wrong?"

"I can't."

'You can." It came out by default. In truth he no longer wanted to. It seemed another man, he of just seconds before.

"I can't marry you, Mickey."

"Oh?"

Mick looked around him, one side to the other. Something wasn't right. He looked at Miranda. Still she stared at him.

"I'm leaving town," Miranda said. "I'm going to my Auntie's house near Crich. They won't be gassed there my mam says." The words, one after the other, formed a row of sounds that he knew must be words, yet they met him cold and somehow foreign. Was he hearing right? His awareness seemed to slip from his consideration, and he felt a rolling motion like at sea, as if he and the words could not stay on an even keel. He looked behind him, saw the empty graveyard, dark, as before, daubed as before with unearthly colours. And his girl went on: "Why do you look so surprised? I told you. I wrote to you."

His stomach had dropped, slipped its noose. "You wrote to me?" he asked, hearing fear transparent in his voice.

"I wrote to you all the time."

Mick took a step back. Breath came out of him in little puffs of disagreement, under frowns. He looked wildly around him; the flask dropped to the ground, making a dull, tinny thud.

"Mizzie, I... You're a wonderful girl, and I... I promise I'll come see you, every leave I get."

She hadn't moved. Her eyes hadn't left him. Then she replied. "Well, I won't be there."

Mick's breaths were rapid. He daren't turn away from her, so stepped back, and again, blind onto the open grass.

"Don't be like that," he all but pleaded.

"I won't be there. I'll be dead."

Mick wanted to scream. Bathed in the yellow-violet glow, he stared at her. His mouth hung open, empty of smooth words. He wanted to cry, then to scream. He wanted to grip his head in between both hands, and wrench this away. But Miranda began to move toward him, white, wide eyes never leaving him to blink. A woman possessed.

"You shouldn't say things like that."

"Why not?" Miranda stopped on the grass, pretty in her dress. "I ran away to find you."

'What?"

She stepped closer, and Mick saw her pallor unnatural, her features gaunt as they hadn't been.

Her expression changed for the first time in an age, so that Mick felt sweet relief to see it. Her large eyes seemed to want to weep, though they were frozen as saucers in her pretty face, and she whispered to him, "like my letter said. Your mam answered the door, but she'd never even heard my name. You'd returned to the barracks again, had your leave. So I went to my folk's. My pa shouted, but I cried for you. My eyes were still wet when the bomb fell through the roof. Ripped me apart, it did."

The night was darker, dropped suddenly from elsewhere. There was a noise: a low, deep, reverberating rumble. It seemed to come from everywhere. Mick hastily backed away in the blackness, across the slick grass. The thud reverberated from his spine to the teeth embedded in his jaw, and he found himself flat against the stones of the graveyard wall. His body was numb, as if a hundred points become the funny bone. Suddenly he did not feel sure which way was up, or across, or down; he was just pinned there, on the stone, with dark grass, and pale shadows like carved surfaces falling back between him and a girl in a dancing dress.

"I haven't been to war. The dance... It's not right Miranda." His voice whimpered like that of a child.

Miranda grinned horribly.

"The look on your face, Mickey. I thought you didn't get scared."

Mick knew which way was up, and which way was right, and which wrong. His head almost cleared. Whatever had happened there, he had to get away, and get back to his house, just a minute away across Chester Green.

Reality stopped him. He looked aside to see the war memorial trembling, its colour and shape beginning to blur. He swung his gaze above Miranda, expecting to see the church tower shaken in the grip of an earthquake: heavy stones breaking and falling; mortar billowing in clouds, pieces dropping through, arcing down toward them. Yet the tower stood, though it shook for its full height against the night sky. It stood, impossibly, unmoved. The booming rumble was becoming a roar against his ears. He looked to ground. Beneath his feet, and across the empty graveyard the black stretches of grass had lost their blades into an oily sea, a pit. And yet his polished shoes stood distinct over the gleaming, see-through black floor.

He looked with terror back to Miranda, and saw that she too was blurring with vibration, her every strand of pastel colour on that dark night, fraying and shredding into thousand upon thousand of thin, torn strips.

He stumbled from the graveyard to the shelter of a heavy stone buttress, and reached out a hand to the covered moss. Everything was a blur, shaken beyond form. Miranda was with him, and speaking, and he turning, to face her.

"Don't you remember?" she said, leaning close. "Your mam told you. She saw my face in the paper – the girl who might have been introduced. Sent the letter you never received. It's folded, in the bag under your head."

Mick looked into her wide eyes, so close he could kiss her. His face creased so that it might cry, but the fear was terrifying, overwhelming. "What's going on?" he screamed, loud over the din, for all was noise. "Stop it Miranda!"

"In the bag under your head," she replied, calm, emotionless.

"No!" he bellowed, or roared, and gripped his head between his hands. Staggering back, pulling on his skull, he fell against the church and found with shock, firmness, supporting his back. And all around the tremors threatened to pull reality apart.

***

Mick's eyes flashed open, wide and bloodshot white. His arms were raised, hands pressed against his ears, compressing his skull. The tension of muscle against head sent soundless waves reverberating around his inner ear, with a high frequency tremble, like a pressed seashell about to explode. But it was background noise under the roar of semi-automatic rifle bursts and single aimed shots, which cut through the din like offbeat percussion, deranged drum rolls.

He was staring he realised, not yet fully awake. He needed to wake up. A string of bullets ripped into the dirt diagonally above him. Their pit-patter into the soil echoed against his back. Puffs of vapour-soil popped out of the earth, and Mick tilted his head and saw the smoked plumes of minute buried dragons above him. He looked back to the fight, and was awake.

Gulliver stumbled on loose ground in front of him, face screaming, hand reaching, looming large in the adjusting range of Mick's vision. It grabbed the pack strap through which one of Mick's arms was threaded – as always when at rest, with the pack contents a hard pillow – and wrenched his shoulder from the concave of the dirt escarpment.

"How can you bloody dream?" he shouted.

His friend leaned back with his weight, and Mick was pushing from locked knees, and on his feet. He punched his loose arm through the flailing strap, and felt the pack heave down with gravity as if weights had dropped from the sky to topple him back where he had slept. He hunched against it, took control of the mass, then grabbed Gulliver's backpack to stop the man overbalancing for his efforts. He saw him righted, turn and move off, and without need of thought was already running, and diving for a shallow ditch to join others of the platoon.

He was a soldier. He saw his mud-spattered uniform of the British army, and knew the weight of the fifty-pound backpack of provisions, kit and ammunition, stuffed to bursting; his Lee Enfield rifle was in his hand, with its strap around his neck, and his throat-slitting knife dug at the side of his leg from his belt. He glanced left as dirt flung up further along the trench and machine gun bullets pounded dirt clouds from the top of their cover. On his arm, one third encased in dried mud, was the two chevron mark of his corporal command.

20ᵗʰ January 1942

On either flank of the ditch, British soldiers returned fire into the jungle. A mass of branches and leaves and strange foliage, and entwined stems, impossibly knotted, barred the way ahead. But figures could be seen moving amongst it all, lit by muzzle flashes, sounded out by shouts and bellowed orders and panicked fighting.

Mick fired over the ridge. Then ducked low.

Behind him more of his section were straggling through the jungle from positions further back. Men floundered, and skidded on their bellies on the slimy dirt, propelled by the weights on their backs. A soldier, Monty, dropped as a bullet took him in the neck. Mick yelled orders, and pointed exaggeratedly his commands. Men dove and returned fire, and ducked for cover, and scrambled to stay alive in the onslaught. Gulliver shouted, spittle spraying the Burmese ground, and fanned his section wide. The lieutenant was further down the ditch, overhung by trees and roots and obscured by the lie of the ground. Men were dying and fighting there, and the silver fizz of bullets was flashing like momentary lightning through the mist, or smoke, which hung in a cloud beside them.

A shape came down amongst them. Close quarters, and took a bullet. Mick's knife was slammed into the man's chest, and then he was pulling the blade out, his other arm struggling for dominance with the enemy's pointing rifle. He pushed the dying man back, pulling his rifle from him and firing up at one o'clock, at the shadow that lurched and then became a dying man as he fell over their heads into the dank-water, foot of the ditch.

Mick raised his head, looked, and fired into the jungle at a Japanese soldier, close enough for his features to be seen: his face recoiled in horror, but his attack carried his fall forward, and he dropped unseen into the foot-tall undergrowth carpet. Mick picked out another target, fired one shot, and a second, adjusting for the prediction of a next step. He didn't see any sign between the ferns of a third being taken. Again he called out orders, then said the same by hand signal to the last men appearing to the rear. He screamed to the men to his immediate left and right – Lance Corporal Clifton, Private Monk – and the three of them stood and opened fire, strafing wildly, ferociously across the forest wall, making muzzle flashes drop and blink out.

He sensed Buckley in the clear air beneath, able to get his head up; the man reared the Bren gun from the ditch, its weight swinging down like a wild beast pinned; two spikes dug into the wet earth at either side. The gun team aimed, held the next magazine ready. The light machine gun boomed suddenly, fast, repeated explosions. Mick ducked low into the ditch, rifle again readied and waiting, watching the jungle cave-in in a dozen, two dozen places, ferns sucked away, folding and disappearing at their centres; the green wall leaning back, wanting to pull up, retreat.

More sections arriving in the lull over his shoulders. Signals sent. The Bren stopped to silence. The men emerging from the jungle had understood and did not quell or stall their advance. They leapt on over the ditch, boots digging at the ridge top, turfing soil on those who waited a fraction too long. All who sheltered were up, and spinning, up and over, out of the ditch into full view of any surviving enemy gunners, and charging them down.

Mick barred his teeth, fired and ran. In seconds he was kicking through greenery with raised boot, not knowing what lay two feet on the other side. He saw a dark face ahead, and shot him in the chest, dead centre; bolt-action back, copper casing in the air, breech already shut, locked, and fired again. Reload. Barely missing a stride he drew his knife, hacked the fronds and vines and stabbing branches with one hand, held the rifle readied in the other, and all the time watched for a glimpse of he who would try to kill him first.

He glanced to either side and saw, as expected, the other six men of his Rifle Section in strong formation – with one man, Monty, dead, back by the ditch. Far down the line amongst trees and undergrowth he saw the survivors of a section hacking through the mist and the forest. Ahead of him the jungle seemed to shake and waver from side to side as it rebounded from the fleeing shapes pushing desperately through it. Mick nodded and Monk and Carroll each took a grenade from their belts, removed the pins and hurled them high through gaps of foliage ahead. As he and his men hit the dense green deck, Mick saw in the periphery of his vision, a dark green oval loop through the air from the sergeant's position, while to his other side Gulliver's section staked ground with boots, crouched and machine gun set, to ensure no one could get in behind.

The booms of ordnance pounded the jungle in quick succession. Clouds of yellow dust filtered by shreds of spinning leaves came drifting through the meshed forest. The air was already crowding for space and the dust seemed to sneak through the atmosphere so that no one saw he was breathing it until it was muddying his vision yellow. Mick signalled his orders and led his men on, through the camouflage. They could barely see each other as they advanced, nor could be seen. They each depended on him, on his lead; each was capable in his own right, yet it was he who set the direction.

As the dust-storm in the jungle subsided to the mushy floor, shots rang out from both sides. The Japanese were retreating, backs to him, wild shots flung over shoulders, just glimpses in between branches and moss.

"Hold the line!" he called, and heard his words repeated in different voices throughout the formation. "Watch for Gooks offside!"

CHAPTER 7

14th July 1942

Indian soldiers walked beneath a white pillared veranda in Commonwealth uniform. In the shade of the porch, British soldiers played cards at a wicker table, relaxed back on chairs dangerously pivoted on two legs, some men showing the wounds and bandages of survival. The heat was too stifling for banter and competition, so they considered their hands quietly, while sweat refused to run in rivulets down their faces, and somehow hung there, as if vertical was off by forty-five degrees - like their cane chairs.

The overgrown English lawn tried to cover the dirt around the building. It led, patchy and threadbare in places, up to a rockery of palm trees and rambling bushes - the plants of the subcontinent, gone wild, the gardener now clearly putting his hand to other tasks.

The sun was dazzlingly bright on the paving stones beyond the shadow of the porch, from beneath which Mick watched. He was glad to have shelter for a moment, though it merely meant the heat was stifling rather than unbearable. No structure could keep the humidity away.

The meeting they had engineered was about to take place. Along a wide, crisp corridor through the General Headquarters, of offices, Operations, Radio, came the two field officers. The shade of the building's interior appeared almost balmy in contrast to the glare of the veranda. He pulled himself up, ready to salute.

Beside him, Gulliver said at barely a whisper, "That's him."

Orde Wingate was unmistakeable. They had been told he would be passing through. He was reportedly a harder man to find at a desk than at walk, but had at least sat long enough to read and sign their requests. The man beside him was Major Bernard Fergusson, also hard to miss with the monocle held at one eye.

"Ah, here they are," Ferguson said with a Scottish accent; "two NCOs."

Colonel Wingate nodded, accepted Mick and Gulliver's salute, and then exchanged handshakes. "Your names?"

"Sergeant Michael Bowler, Sir."

"Sergeant Arthur Gulliver, Sir."

"Right. With the 2nd King's Own Yorkshire."

Gulliver spoke up. "Yes, Sir."

"Which one of you was in Norway?" the Major asked.

"I was, Sir," Mick replied, standing as straight as he could.

"You transferred regiments to get to India. And now again? Restless?"

"Sir, I simply want to be where I can be of the most use."

Orde Wingate said, "And you are fully aware of my operation, of what you have volunteered – been recommended for?"

Mick answered. "Yes, Sir. I think I speak for myself, and Sergeant Gulliver, when I say we are fully aware of what the field may entail, Sir."

"Field in this case meaning Timbuktu swamp. Sergeant Gulliver?"

"Yes, Sir. I am prepared."

Wingate surveyed the sergeants. He nodded to himself. "Glad to hear it."

Ferguson addressed them: "You will be working on jungle tactics and survival for the next six months, under the command and tutelage of Major Michael Calvert."

"Thank you, Sir," the sergeants replied.

"You will be transferred to the 77th. In effect forthwith. Your commendations are impressive: newly commissioned and highly respected NCOs, and I don't doubt you will acquit yourselves admirably."

"Thank you, Sir," they each said, hands at salute. Then to Wingate, "Thank you, Sir."

Colonel Wingate and Major Ferguson departed promptly, leaving Mick and Gulliver's salutes behind.

Gulliver looked to his friend with a mightily pleased grin. Mick tried to respond in turn, but felt a weight pulling down the corners of his mouth.

****

Indian palms grew wild on rough open land, and copses of old spreading teaks led to the structure of the Army Headquarters; small plantations of mango, jackfruit and papaya marked out fields and roads. Mick stood at attention on the cantonment parade ground amongst the rows of men. Outside the white post and black railing boundary wall the town of the British base was quiet. Further to the north was Jhansi, a small city, yet like most in India, it seemed, a sprawling cram of a place, with a stained smell of spice. To the south was central India's jungle. A readiness pressed in the humid air as they waited.

Orde Wingate stood before them, his face patched with eczema, taut and thin on a short, uniformed body that seemed unsuited to its profession, and yet was proven in it. To either side, flanking, yet separate enough to make Wingate's position protrude, were General William Slim, and General Archibald Wavell, Commander in Chief of all India, as well as other officers whose names he had been only recently given.

Wingate held his hands behind his back and looked out over them, the newest army brigade. Mick could sense the rank and file out of sight behind him, as though those ranks possessed a weight that made an impression on the field. Most of the British in the army were battle-hardened, battle-weary men; men who had formerly been as far as Blackpool or Minehead, but who had since fought on one continent before being moved to the next, and might expect to fight on another if they survived. Beside them were Gurkhas and Burmese, veterans of the fight against the Japanese, as well as some brave new recruits from the slopes of Nepal.

Mick stood, level in line and waited. A fly buzzed about his head, threatening to land on the sweat, but he remained rigid, unflinching. The sun burnt down, and he stood, seeing the glare of orange Indian dirt around him, and felt how strange it was to have come to be there. A picture surfaced, of before, which he always carried, of the living room back at Chester Green. He wondered what his mam would think of him, what she would say. Or his dad; but he'd never said much about anything.

They saluted. General Wavell began to speak, with the same authoritative clipped southern vowels that Mick had at first found so tricky. A memory of ice and white and gunfire, and orders given. Then being stationed in Scotland and sitting in the barracks, a collection of letters resting on his leg.

"-and so gentlemen, I shall address you as the best and the bravest, for this brigade requires the utmost rigour of which his Majesty's army is renowned. Colonel Wingate..."

"Thank you, General Wavell." Wingate turned from the top brass, and addressed them in his distinctive, off-kilter way of speaking:

"Welcome to the 77th Indian Infantry Brigade, soldiers of Britain and her Empire. To be frank, as in war we must, we are to trek behind enemy lines, exist in the jungle entirely unnoticed, and to launch numerous unexpected attacks from whence attacks could not possibly come. This is Long Range Penetration Warfare – which has already met with success in Palestine, Ethiopia and further afield. We, the 77th shall take it into new terrain."

He paused momentarily and surveyed the brigade again, sweeping across hundreds of individual faces he seemed already to know to the man. He went on: "77th Brigade, needless to say we will not operate as other divisions do, but will work as eight strong columns, each with the capable men that will be necessitated: rifle company; heavy weapons; reconnaissance platoon; sabotage; transport. Our aim is to disrupt the Japanese, cut off their supply lines, outmanoeuvre, and halt their conveyance, and in co-ordination with covert airdrops and the other divisions of the Indian theatre, to turn the tide in the east. Training shall begin at once, under the tutorship of 142 Commando and the Bush Warfare School."

Without a concluding remark, Wingate stepped away and turned to his superiors, so that the salute he gave could have been for them, or for the ranks of soldiers he had finished addressing. The commanding officers of the operation took their haphazard cue and moved before the men. They began to shout the orders which were readying a new type of warfare.

Mick waited for the order, to salute and call his command. The end of summer would be spent living in the jungle, in preparation.

***

The ground was full of misgivings underfoot. Solid earth was followed by damp sponge; a tree root rolled under his boot, really a broken branch covered in moss, diving away. He kept his feet, kept his rifle ready for war. His eyes and their tendons worked overtime in his head, picking out threats on the floor, scanning the near ground, glancing every which way about the tessellating green, looking for the merest slither of shade misaligned.

The trail of men and beast stretched in a long arc through the rainforest before petering out into the trampled ground of some animal migration: perhaps they had been elephants, their tank-like forms invisible after mere paces of jungle undergrowth; or some herbivore frighted to stampede at the sight of panther; or men with guns marching. The mules carried the burden of the supplies, cumbersome packs bulking from their sides. He and the other men too struggled under great weights, with the fabric over metal frames not doing anywhere near enough to hide the drag of backpacks from grooving their shoulder muscles. They pushed on, knowing that they could not think of discomfort when what they felt was only the beginning of days and weeks of worse.

***

13th February 1943

The troops waded from the jungle into a low river. The column widened with relief, and sore feet rejoiced all around at the soft splash of water and the sudden cold that swamped boots and socks. Mick walked aside his men, mindful of the brief seconds of care-free banter that made a moment's too much noise. He kept aware of the undergrowth that flanked to either side in his peripheral vision, instinctively observing its folds, trenches and spurs of green, as if it were topography mapped from above. He also saw Wingate in the near distance, over rank after rank of layered slouch hats and unwashed splatterings of hair, through a reed forest of bayonet blades, as he led the division down the centre of the river. The colonel slowed his steed as other officers rode their mounts alongside, and Mick observed the conversation take place across the front rank.

The march slowed. Mick waited. He noticed the water moving around his booted ankles, pulled by the current regardless of the towering obstacles in its way and the splashing, explosive strides before.

They had reached the point on the map. Mick spoke quiet orders, which filtered through the ranks under his command. The high spirits of refreshed feet remained, but the mood had changed; postures buoyed, but stony faces set. Hands were held still in acknowledging waves; heads nodded; the column began to peel away and leave the Northern Group. Mick saw Gulliver far ahead marshalling his own command onto the new course.

"Platoon march! East." Mick called, low, a rare raised voice. The two dozen men under his command parted from the main artery, just as other camouflaged sections also began to branch away. Orders given, Wingate took the thinned group on, down the river, away from them, making his path its arced course, as if the waters had been laid down as a convenient jungle road for that very purpose.

Mick saw the platoons alongside, the mules, baggage, Vickers machine guns, disappearing into deeper jungle, and then the ferns and trees and green that reached out to the river dissolved him too. The columns were to reconverge in the months ahead, radio contact and enemy encounters all being well.

The sounds of the Chindwin River were soon gone, replaced by crunching, snapping, careful footsteps and the calls and hoots of birds and monkeys. In a parting in the dense rainforest to his left he caught sight of a pair of eyes, watching. Not for the first time. Yellow eyes, framed by the hopeless camouflage of orange and black stripes. The tiger was observing, as he was, and looked wary rather than ready.

"Tiger, left," he said quietly. Scared heads turned in succession down the line as the message reached them. Yet no soldier would fire. They had been trained better than to let their rifle sound in unknown territory. If it attacked or stalked them then that was different, but for the time being their tactics were the same.

Mick turned away as the tiger fell behind, obscured by foliage, hidden, till that moment at least, where it had been. It was appropriate, he thought. They too were out of place in this world of greens. But they had to make it theirs. They had to become the top predator, or let the Japanese roam wild with the Germans, and not just here, but wherever they so chose on the face of the world. An odd overlay drifted through his mind of a Japanese face on the massive, rotating, striped shoulder blades of a tiger, with a gun in its paw, pacing slowly across the mowed grass of Chester Green.

Mick shook his head physically, and mentally threw the picture away. He focused on the ferns that slapped back at him and the branches which made him duck his head, and marched into the jungle.

CHAPTER 8

Machine gun fire grated through the jungle, like the call of some foreign animal, lost in the impossible terrain. It snarled again and again, in two second bursts; every which way he glanced to track it showed the same trembling leaves, swaying branches, each view a distorted mirror of the other. Single shots boomed out, with echoes all of their own, louder than could be.

Mick advanced with his platoon. They used the cover, just as it was used against them. Ear cringing bursts of machine sound shocked from the depths in front, and to the side and from directions that were not easily placed. The roars leapt, and were gone before a man's two ears had realised to adjust. All was chaos, and sliding mud and loose soil, and screams, and bellowed orders. Sometimes he could place the accent to England, Yorkshire, Japan, India, Cornwall, and sometimes the man standing beside him screamed in words that a translator would have missed. And then he was moving again, giving orders, hearing his own voice like it wasn't in his own head. Staccato fire, and leaping flames, and a rat-a-tat-tat that was so fast he only heard its munition drum-roll once faded and already lost.

Many had been lost: sometimes a body under foot that appeared as the next step brought perspective over a low bush or spring of some kind of grass; sometimes a collapsing figure in Jap uniform that made his heart swell with justified hate. Sometimes a colleague and countryman that might have been him.

A mule wheeled, disorientated, and he reached for its bridle, with his rifle kept pointed at the dense jungle. The poor creatures couldn't comprehend how they had come to be there, how their spines ached, and their sides chaffed with Chindit supplies. He rested his hand on its neck while soldiers moved through, encroaching on the next dense wall of vegetation. Sometimes, in a battle, separated, mules would just fret and spin in the mud, braying silently at jungle wall after jungle wall, vocal chords cut for war. Mules took bullets and went toppling. Sometimes they ran, and crossed Japanese lines and perhaps were shot or captured – sometimes perhaps headed back to India. He supposed many went in circles that would see them unclaimed and wandering for weeks ahead, lost in the jungle. Bullets landed into water bottles and provisions, and left soft impressions on thin skinned ribcages of mules unaware of their providence. Many of the hardy animals stayed their course though, and held their churned ground and waited for the good cause.

Mick charged forward, firing, spotting human movements amongst the wall of nature in front of him. Through the towering undergrowth, seeing depth emerge and fall back. His platoon cut through alongside. They stilled. He signalled for quiet and they listened, for footsteps, breathing, anything to track.

In place after place, unknown before to anyone, he had fought battles, and skirmishes had caught sides in surprise. Bodies had fallen and been left there unburied. It was untried warfare, behind enemy lines.

Mick fired, and held his ground, and worked with the platoon, leading the platoon. Strategy amidst the all-surrounding dense green.

All was sound, and terror, and glimpses and glances. And all too much to comprehend, only to be thought back on as images and did-that-happens, and half-real sensations, which were reality and his memories.

***

Mick stood, work complete, and looked out at the train tracks from the last foot of cover. Two of the commandos he and Gulliver had trained with walked off the embankment, detonations double-checked.

"Now have to wait it out a while, Sergeant."

Mick nodded.

The two men stepped into the line of the jungle beside the railway. A hundred yards away a team of sappers crouched around boxes and rolls of wire at the primary site.

Suddenly all was quiet. The team in the distance, shapes, detached; the reddened iron running sharp to the point where the banks of forest washed over it. Mick felt for an instant that perhaps he was the only human in the whole of a wilderness jungle; then he heard the faint whine of high frequency metal. He looked to the wires, which ran from the small rectangular packages secure against a sleeper, turning a right angle on the embankment top under the stones he had pinned them with. The thin black lines followed the track, before passing over pressed-down blades of grass and fronds to the detonator at his feet.

Early. An extra engine to the scouted schedule.

The sappers grabbed equipment in a distant, slow blur; barely seen moves, wire still rolling out, figures labouring, cutting, priming; in reality a frenzy of fast action.

No sapper would reach the secondary position. Mick dropped flat into the undergrowth, then told himself he would not move again until he held his head down to the ground.

The shriek of tensing metal rang out louder. The tracks could almost be seen vibrating. Mick saw their shape and mould and imprints, their rivets and craftsmanship, and their weaknesses. Fire of the workshop, the darkness, the brightness of sparks from molten metal, chains rolling overhead. And the track on its low bank, with a wall of green vegetation bright in the sunlight opposite him. The horrible hum he had heard so many times, and never disliked before was wailing now. A bayonet-charge war cry of the Japanese. He placed his hand on the detonation trigger. His shoulders hunched, his calves tensed; every muscle readied for the compress into the grainy dirt.

The train was visible now. The detonation team were into the forest. Someone shouted. They shouldn't have done that. The train was too close to stop, but every half moment of surprise might count.

A rush of breaking vegetation far to his left. Infantry taking cover.

Boom.

Mick ducked on instinct. The train hopped through a cloud of dust, and landed with a tremendous grating pound, misaligned on its steel slides. Shouts resounded. Carriages went askew further down the line, near the middle of the train.

Mick watched as the massive steam beast kept coming. Arms and the rims of Driver's and Fireman's hats showed from the sides.

The Japanese machine hurtled on for seconds more, even as its middle bulged off the rails like a moving snake's, confronting the vegetation wall that ran alongside the embankment. Ploughing with force and pace down its metal artery, even as it fell. The link between provisions and soldiers, tanks and fuel, bullets and machine gun turrets. The only conduit through the wild rainforest.

Mick hated the train, with its round closed-eye face and its churning steam and its shrieking roar that rocked the steel tracks just feet from his own face. But he was composed and a soldier, counting, waiting, timing, and connecting the detonation current to the wires to the track.

He was down with his face squashed against the dirt, beneath the brim of his hat. The boom echoed forward and back, bouncing and compacting the air above him. Everywhere was echoes. The eye that wasn't in the dirt flicked up, and felt the shockwave squeeze its white.

He raised his head, enough, and saw dust and smoke and sheared metal, and ghostly, then immediate, through it burst the engine. It dropped forward, vast weight falling to the crater where the tracks no longer were. Behind the blast he saw the carriages rise and baulk like the segmented, insect back of some monstrous, mythical worm. Possessed by supernatural horrors, it dove, as if it thought itself from Jules Vern, and might tunnel into the earth.

A huge cloud of flung dirt, steam and fire exploded from the bomb crater, and the wide snout of the beast lurched up and out of it. Toward him.

His arms pushed him up; his feet swivelled, grinding root and dirt, and turned; his head twisted, his voice box yelled out; and his heart pumped arms swinging wide, and contorting, stretching torso. His legs exploded out, away from his cover.

He was flying. Smashing through branches and undergrowth, letting them snap back in his face and snap off. He felt pain and cuts, as if they were not there. His bush hat, brim down, deflecting, strap yanking tight beneath his jaw; he looked back, and at once straight ahead. The train was chasing him down, careering off angle, free of its tracks, charging toward the tree line.

Mick ran as fast as he had ever run before. The mission was a success, the railway blown up, the train and its cargo derailed. Now survive.

The beast-engine snorted steam like it might explode with rage as it stampeded after him, bounding in great, creaking, thundering lurches. He glanced and saw uneven ground, hidden by green, unearthed, shovelled clean by the single, black, metal jawline. The flat, riveted face bore down expressionless, closing. He leapt over undergrowth, not seeing the ground until he was landing and hurtling over it. Roots and earth caught and ripped out and trailed the air behind him, blood bursting through his temple. A glance: if it was possible the engine seemed to sheer off the land and follow his flight. He veered away, but through the trees saw the shadow of overturned, chain-linked carriages, crashing into the pike-like defence. The splitting sound of the palisade snapping and breaking and struggling to hold. He shouted his own cry amidst the roar of sound, darting away, through great leaves and flashes of greens he could not see, not knowing if the monster would lurch and bring him down at the heels. Jungle whipped and tore at him but could not slow him. Running until the crashes of pursuit faded and he was clear.

Mick slowed and stopped dead. He heaved painful breaths. So grateful not to have fallen and disappeared on that ground. His hand went to his side and padded his trouser pocket. Through the coarse fabric he felt the imprint of folded paper. It was still there, and the thought made him breathe a second sigh of relief. He felt a fool for it, but he would not be sorry to be glad. He had stowed the letter there since the return to the jungle – this operation made the proximity of his backpack not close enough. He did not know why he carried it so; he suspected he could have reached a conclusion, but he would not let himself think on it.

Mick turned, his breath back under control. He disappeared into the jungle.

***

They were further still behind enemy lines.

Mick ran from the cover, crossing the dirt track atop the ridge. His platoon moved alongside and in support, of one purpose. The turret was before him, immediately now, and his adrenalin fired. He increased his pace with a burst, rose from his crouch, and leapt. With his right foot he pushed off the turret wall, propelling himself up alongside the Japanese guard. The enemy's back was to him, the young soldier unaware, watching the scenery.

It seemed like he hung in the air. In one fluid motion he pulled on the head and cut across the throat fast. He felt the pressure, the resistance of living skin, from the knife, to his hand. He fell the two feet to ground, and let his knees bend to quieten the dull thump. A glance saw the second Jap in the turret, also slumped, and the machine gun untouched.

It was a horrible way to die – though there were many more horrible. To watch your own life spill away down your bib, just as you felt it spill away from your mind. The symbolism matched the reality: perhaps that was what made his legs feel weak, like walking down a hospital ward always had. But it was effective, and soundless – it cut the voice, the air and the veins. It was wise, if they were presented, to go for the joins. Like striking a platoon where it buttressed against the next. Where the arteries and veins dared to run exposed.

Mick looked down the ridge and saw one of Gulliver's soldiers stepping down from the turret wall to leave a Japanese man sitting at an uncomfortable horizontal. To the other side he saw much the same. A struggle still in progress, but then a Japanese uniform looking the wrong way, now dead.

"Ruin the gun; we can't take it."

His lieutenant consulted with another soldier in the turret, and they began to decommission the grounded weapon.

As sergeant he climbed the soil packed rampart for a good vantage. The Japanese had planned their posts well. A village below, tracks, cleared forest, farmland, squares of rice. To his far right, Gurkha rifles, moving out down the trail; his platoon in formation around the jungle edge – Dawkins, watching the forest, a man five years older than himself. He'd been reluctant with respect at first, but now held his position. The team right-back, Mick sometimes thought.

The sound of breaking machinery: the intricate details that would waste many man-hours to repair.

"Let's go."

Mick jumped down. Half the team began to leave the field. Half the team heard the sound.

A low, ominously deep rumble was slowly shaking the forest. That frequency meant something big.

"Cover!" Mick commanded.

Impossible, it was already in view. A tank gun, and the daunting bulk that held it from the ground, swung slowly into line of sight. The forest, the ridge, the lie of the land, had masked the sound somehow. Behind it, cars, a convoy, driving solidly along the dirt track. Branches and undergrowth smashed and flattened as the tank followed the dirt track, and a debris flanked road collapsed open in its wake.

Throughout the platoon, feet lifted to run. Before a boot could set down, a crack of near explosives hurt ears, and made figures hunch involuntarily right along the track. The tank shell went over heads and blew a small hole in the long space between platoons.

The sound of returning fire: Gulliver's men, closest, strafing at the slow, crunching train. And every platoon in the mission was hurling itself into the cover of the Burmese jungle.

"Go! Go!"

Mick urged his men on with sweeps of his arm. Into the jungle. They moved deeper, perhaps forty feet in, completely lost in the camouflage, then cut ninety degrees, heading parallel to the track. The convoy was slowing, news no doubt beginning to filter down the line. The lead tank began to wind down, its engine growl changing with its gears. But they were past it already, the turret fanning where they had been. More engine sounds and vague shapes of vehicles glimpsed through the trees – reconnaissance cars compacting, overlapping into two, three undergrowth lanes in the confusion.

"Fire!" Mick yelled, and before his mouth had closed a blistering volley began. Leaves shredded, rocked where they hung with perfect holes drilled dead centre. Out on the path, the closest car veered as if it could evade the bullets from its flank. Mick saw through gaps, its driver hit, red blotted, and the steering wheel spinning. A man in the back reached desperately to the front seat, clambered, and stamped his foot down, unable to kick through to the pedals. The car charged toward the slowing tank in front; a reaching hand on the wheel avoided it, almost. A corner of the bumper clipped a rotating track hard and the power of the many, bound wheels heaved the car into the air, and toward the ridge, where it seemed to hang, tilted in mid-air with its cargo of dead and alive soldiers. The car went over the ridge and dropped.

Mick kept firing, focusing along his rifle sight, taking aim, part of his mind recalling a brief scenic view from beside the machine gun turret. A distant explosion from below ground shook them – he kept moving, picking targets, and the ground tremor faded into the vibration and noise of fired bullets and shoulder recoil.

Mick gave orders, which passed along the crouched, stalking ranks. His team kept low, heading north through cover as the convoy panicked, engines now again revving, desperate to head south. The Chindits firing. Circling back, where they weren't supposed to be.

A step aside gave a long view of the dirt road as it curved away on the safe side of the high ridge. He saw the Japanese convoy, moving on as if unchecked, a stomach turning, great train of cars with eyes scouting the jungle, lorries with canvas sides – and a glimpse inside one as it turned the curve, packed with men.

The train of vehicles slowed once more, this time each carriage with like mind. Arms raised from the backs of cars and on disembarked men, who took up positions behind the cover of vehicles, while others received orders to step toward the tree line. Index fingers pointed, and aimed, at him, and to his left and to his right.

"Back. Fall back!" he shouted as a whisper.

Soft footfalls, then quicker strides, and the platoon was moving at speed, punching through vegetation and making a way where there was none. Behind them the whir of a mechanised turret as its huge gun swivelled to point after them.

Boom! Again he ducked on instinct, but the ground rushing beneath him stayed ground. Far to his left he heard the roar of impact, and ground now airborne. He ran on. Always running. Yes, always running it seemed.

Gunfire cracked out in a dozen places to their rear. The impenetrable jungle whizzed with bullets.

He hurdled a log, skidded on and over mud that only boots could have pressed – surely their own advance. Rushing through low hanging tendrils and leaves the size of palms and torsos, and striated greens that lashed as ferns – all flying past in blurs. His breathing, his heart pounding.

"Come on!" he called, not sure if his soldiers could hear him, then focusing and picking up trails of flight puncturing to his left and right, and beyond. The vehicles could not follow them. They could regroup. He needed to ascertain if ground troops were in pursuit. Yes, needed to regroup.

As he told his legs to slow, Mick saw the dark greens and browns grow lighter ahead, almost yellow. Suddenly he was through, burst out into an open clearing, back with their packs and laden mules. Yet somehow, he sensed, the stationed men were not as they should have been, and he looked up, to see the clearing around him.

Men he knew – some he had trained – fell under his rising gaze. Encircling them were Japanese troops.

Other survivors burst into the clearing behind him. Shouts resounded, in English and Japanese. Two dozen Japanese rifles pointed, jabbed and swayed. Mick looked over his shoulders, and screamed orders not to fire.

A Japanese soldier pressed his trigger. A muzzle flash. A Gurkha was hit in the forehead. His eyes flashed white as his eyeballs rolled back with shock and speed. Mick screamed again:

"Don't fire!"

He held up his rifle, and his other hand, palm open. In surrender. To his right Gulliver's voice cut through the melee as well, repeating the command.

Mick looked to the Japanese, skimming uniforms, insignia, the lines on faces, and the steadiness in eyes. His gaze settled on a likely commander. The man glared back at him and barked in foreign tongue. Mick held the line of sight, never letting it fall, while bending and placing his rifle on the ground.

He rose tall once again, hands raised. There were insurmountable forces on the ridge; doubtless ground troops making their way through the jungle, following their stampede tracks; and now they were outnumbered to their face as well. In his peripheral vision he had seen ranks of Japanese soldiers. Perhaps three deep, with other figures back in the jungle, mired with tree trunks and green.

"Put down your weapons!" Mick called.

Gulliver had spoken the same command. The sergeant was off to his right somewhere, and there had been pain in the voice.

The Japanese commander crossed toward him, his narrow eyes enlarging by the step. Mick held that gaze as he must, and so saw little of the rifle butt as it swung round and clubbed the side of his head.

The stare of equals was broken and Mick was collecting dizzy thoughts with the jungle mush inches from his nose. He put a hand to his head and felt the stickiness of blood, then knew he must get to his feet. The speed at which he did so had implications.

He stood as straight as he could manage, though the world he saw seemed to be off kilter. Try as he might he could not seem to correct it. He once again sought the hard face of his opposite number, and locked onto the black almond eyes. Blood banked against his eyelid and it flickered to close, but he forced his stare, resolutely. Must not show defeat. Must not drop that gaze, that line of sight, of dignity, that could keep them alive.

But the Japanese officer looked away with barely a consideration, and walked to the right, into the space where the bodies lay. Mick's stare followed him, as he stopped several feet from the dismal line of surviving soldiers. For the first time Mick saw their state: battered, bloody, chests still heaving on top of gasping lungs. Gulliver was there, hobbled on one leg, the other bent and caked in blood between knee and thigh, his weight supported by an arm around the private next to him.

The commander looked the sergeant up and down and then in a kind of rage, forcibly dragged the two men apart. Gulliver wobbled for a moment, then fell. His ruined leg crumpled beneath him, as if its bones were not all connected.

The Japanese commander screamed at Gulliver in Japanese. It sounded like an order. Then as calm as could be he took a step back and made a gentle lifting motion with his hand. He wanted Gulliver to stand.

Mick's stomach dropped. Gulliver was not going to be able to stand. He tried. His strong leg, took the weight, and pushed off the Burmese ground, but the other leg floundered in the humid air, and other unseen injuries worked against him.

Gulliver was half-way to standing when he fell – collapsed into a heap on his side.

Two other Japanese soldiers hurried forward, propped Gulliver up, and sat his torso upright on top of uncomfortable pressed and folded limbs. They stepped aside.

The Japanese commander spoke the command again: the same order, by its sharp rhythm and length.

Gulliver did not attempt to stand. Instead, he just sat as straight backed as he could, held his head up, and met the cold stare of the Japanese man.

Apparently satisfied that his conditions had been met, the commander aimed his rifle and shot Gulliver in the forehead.

Mick's friend from the King's Own, died in the clearing beside other dead men and mules.

Mick gasped, but muted the sound, and closed his mouth. He stood lopsided and met the stare of the commander with the one eye that was not setting in dried blood. The man turned from him, dismissively, and gave orders to his soldiers, which saw them binding the able-bodied survivors, hands behind their backs.

Mick did not blame his opposite number. It was war, and men died in war. But he hated him for everything he was: for being the fascism that wanted to control populations; for being the love of power that wanted to do the controlling; for standing there with it running through his veins, looking through his eyes. For being it, and for making them give their lives on jungle floors to stop him. Mick had not been a religious man, but as he was led off, a prisoner of the Japanese, he asked with conviction, for God to curse that man, and generations of his family.

Implications dropped down upon them from the jungle canopy. Beaten shoulders slumped. Surrender – and it settled. Their war was over, at the very best – and it settled, and weighed heavily. Victory would not be of their doing. Mick trudged on, down Japanese jungle tracks that they had previously monitored, but never walked. Up in front he saw the back of the commander. For the hours and days that followed, he starred at the back of that head, for the few moments when the narrow eyes would meet his own. Must not drop that gaze, that line of sight, of dignity.

CHAPTER 9

An inch of salt water sloshed around their feet - although it was hard to be sure, in the dark, and with the motion of the sea banishing all sense of spirit level. It was as if the Japanese egged them on, to commit suicide by thirst and weak will. To deplete the numbers if they but could.

His back ached so completely that it seemed some other sensation and not an ache at all. He crouched, close to but not against the icy cold iron; at times letting his spine rest upon it, turning onto either shoulder blade when the temperature spread through him like permafrost. Somehow, the metal could be colder than the water which gave it its cold. He longed to sit, but would not slide from the cramped squat. Just to fold his soaked and battered boots, still carrying the mud of Burma, as a seat under him, would flood wet, rotting socks with acid salt. To rest an arm into the sea floor, would see it never dry. To sit, bottom and legs awash in the sickening tide within the prison, was an equal to suicide, to pneumonia, and shaking to death on clanging metal sides. The only way he could sleep, was to crouch; it was hard to know, but he didn't think he had slept the whole punishing voyage. Waking was darkness, and the creak of metal frame, and moaning of diseased, freezing men; it was an extinguished world, black and shards of light, and dreams were much the same. As he moved ever toward starvation he felt his body shuttered, windows boarded, like a house on a dark night, with dark rooms indoors. Yet somewhere beyond the prison, they were moving, through daylight, surrounded by sea to a new destination.

He swallowed dryness and wavered. Someone talked to his left, not in the thin light from the gaps by the hold roof, and therefore invisible to him. The ship rolled and the saline floor did too.

Before the ship had been other prisons, and before them a long walk through the jungle that not all of the survivors taken prisoner had survived. When they had slept they had been given no shelter. When they had drunk they had been given no clean water. And when they had been hungry they'd eaten nothing.

As was well known amongst the British soldiers, the Japanese detested the surrendered. Mick often wondered in the iron box, how he was still alive, and had not been shot outright in the jungle. At times the question and the images, the memories, had drowned his mind for hours, days. Some of the platoon he had led had shared a similar fate; others not. Some of them were sitting in one of the camps they had briefly been dumped in; some had been moved on, to where he didn't know, and had only seen the backs of heads as they were marched out; some were on this transport across some ocean or other, and some were dead.

He thought of Gulliver and wished him well, purposefully avoiding the question of God which accompanied the perhaps futile gesture. Then came a surge of envy, that his friend had escaped the worst of it. Mick apologised in his mind, and felt his hunched crouch weaken from the despondency. His war was over, or would be after several months of labour, or torture, or a firing squad when he got off this cursed ship. One of those was preferable at least to the worst outcome. It was what soldiers could not consider, even when battles were turned against them, and retreat followed route, followed tactical retreat: that they would lose. Now, in this ship's hold he considered it often.

As a soldier he had fought and fought, and known that so long as he kept fighting, and that the man next to him in the trench or jungle or mortar crater kept fighting, then they could not lose. If only ten men were left in the entire British army and he was one of them and they were fighting, and seeing their bullets riddle the vile enemy, and hearing the crack-crack-crack of the machine guns from their position, then the war was not done with. Defeat had not occurred. The war went on. And if he died in that last battle, then well, he'd never have known one way or the other. And so, like this, a soldier could logically get by, and pass a whole war, never truly considering defeat. Its consequences.

But he had not died. He had lived on, in squalid, embarrassing confinement. It was possible that the British Empire would not win the war. They all took it as a given that right and goodness would prevail. But it was not a given. It was very possible that they could lose. They could even have lost while he was slumped with impossible back ache, lost in blackness, and he was yet to learn of it. They could lose while he sat in some prison camp for the next ten years, and if no gloating Jap guard deigned to boast in his face about it, he would know nothing, only suspect the morbid truth which hung in the air about his head.

His stomach squirmed, though there was nothing in it. All dry, and salted by the sea-ammonia air. He felt his back against the metal; pushed himself up a little, realising he was drifting too far.

Mick looked to the depths of the floating chamber, at the scores of soldiers, crammed in, some along the walls, many standing, slowly turning like asylum patients. They took it in turns, their slow procession around the metal walls, and into the middle. An attempt at order and a unit's discipline. Like musical chairs played in terror, and awful resigned agreement. But then someone would break, and men would push and fight like animals; then they would still, and mumble curses and apologies, and all begin sliding around the metal walls again. It would soon be time for him to stand and take his turn in the middle.

He looked across the barren faces, most blacked out in darkness, and saw the soldier who occasionally spoke to him, persisted in speaking to him, glance his way. The Scot. He didn't want to talk, and let his gaze drift on, over more staring, morose faces, until he wasn't seeing, but was taken by introverted thoughts, and a dark, depressed sense of something he must consider.

The worst of all of them. A pretty face, now hopeful, now dusted with rubble. Of her. Blonde hair. Now lit by streetlamp from overhead, now somewhere beneath the spongy turf he regularly imagined - had brought to mind so often he would have been surprised if reality were any different. The guilt. War and hate and determination and the scale of the disaster set about the world were as nothing.

The man who sometimes spoke, though Mick seldom replied, brought him temporarily back to salty, stinking reality.

"Quiet Man, how's it going?"

Alistair MacCallum considered the Quiet Man in the darkness, noticing his slump that as always refused to submerge in the sloshing water. He expected no response, but liked to remind the forlorn, brow-furrowed man that he still existed. Never got his name out of him.

MacCallum turned to the defeated soldier beside him, who went by the name of Colin and was English like most of the poor bastards. He spoke louder than was necessary, so that those who weren't often spoken to could get a remembrance of what it was like.

"They're taking us east, north-east you know? Hard to tell, but the way the sunlight sneaks in - must be north-east. That means the Philippines, or further north after a time to China, or to Japan. Deeper into the nest, wherever it turns out to be."

The defeated soldier who had once been called Colin, said in his now grated voice: "Anywhere but Changi. Rotting in the prison we used to run. The further away from Singapore the better."

"Where do you reckon, Quiet Man?" MacCallum asked, in his distinct Scottish drawl.

MacCallum waited some time for the tall man now crouched and hunched. He saw him shrug.

Someone unseeable on the far side of the hold said, "What does it matter? Makes little difference. No escaping when the viper's nest is a few thousand miles one way, and a fucking big ocean the other."

MacCallum nodded, although he suspected his own face was lost in darkness from the other man's view. He looked back at the Quiet Man, who he could tell had been listening. He wondered what his thoughts were on the matter, but he didn't want to piss anyone off too much. He didn't even know what regiment the Quiet Man had been with - most fellas told you that much like rote before they themselves knew they were answering. Even the ones with glassy eyes, who thought the darkness hid them always and that they needn't bother to pretend to look out anymore. But the Quiet Man wasn't one of those; he kept to himself, with his own thoughts, but he still looked out. Didn't even curse and F-word like most of the captives when they changed position and shifted weight from one dead leg to the next, stretched the old one out and cursed some more.

MacCallum mused to himself, why the word for 'loveless sex' was most men's curse of choice when life went to shit. He, like many, had spent a lot of his time – before he met his Susan – going mindlessly after that very thing, which he had spent his life simultaneously cursing. They must all have hated it, all along.

He wondered what Japanese men said when they wanted to curse their worst. Similar? They were men, and going by what he knew of the Japanese, it must have been something worse. But what could you say worse than 'fuck' and its derivatives?

***

Some harbour somewhere bustled with equipment, small unsteady cranes, and cargo being unloaded and loaded. He and the prisoners of the cargo hold, filthy and off-colour, waited in an orderly queue at two open-backed lorries. Several soldiers stood and watched, but no one was running, so hopeless was its cause.

Rifle butts were jammed into smalls of backs, and the hamstring backs of knees, making it impossible to walk, just as the order was given and demanded. Mick clambered onto the back of his lorry and looked up at the blue sky for the few seconds it took for his eyes not to be able to take it. He looked down at the metal floor, scattered with a few bits of straw and stained with the dried puddles of rain that had fallen without canvas to hold it off.

His form slumped, his eyes closed and he felt too tired to think of anything – not where he was, and not where he was going.

***

Alistair MacCallum walked around the large oval dust bowl that was the parade-ground cum firing-squad-end-place cum exercise yard. Beside him walked Mick the Quiet Man, Jihar the Indian, Breck the Australian, Colin the Farmer, and a new arrival to their hut who went by the name of Frank. MacCallum and his friends talked little. They were on Formosa, and the green of the island was all around them – everywhere but the trodden-down dust of the camp. It had been a mire in the rainy season. Above them, over a strait of sea was China, and to each side were oceans and reaching hands of Asian lands. He could feel his place on the open map, hemmed in, trapped. His world was on the full scale, with the war raging all around them – he supposed, and believed – in spite of the enclosed monotony of each and every day. There was the daily path to the lake, which somehow seemed a disconnected place they transplanted to, to slave and then return from; there were the wooden huts, imprisoned by a square fence; and around it the three-hundred-and-sixty degree limit, encircling them: jungle-covered, rising and falling low hills for half the turn and the flatter land where the river was for the rest of the circle. They were near the capital, Taipei – they'd been paraded through it on first arrival, to forced, standing crowds of emotionless-faced locals. The prison camp was called Taihoku.

They'd been there near three months. A dozen had died in that time. They worked hard each day, early morning until the sun would soon have made it difficult to see their way back. They were building some kind of garden, extravagant memorial park, and were cutting out a huge lake from scratch, with picks and shovels. MacCallum couldn't see why anyone would get enjoyment sitting in a park, knowing hateful hands had scoured out every contour for you. He wanted to make the place vile; to make it as ugly and sick as hell; so it turned the stomach of every Japanese soldier who sat in it. But it was hard to do: God-given land had a way of promising to be beautiful however you sculpted it. Yet he knew they wouldn't get the chance – he told himself. The war would be done by then.

Back in their damp hut, miserable hours later, each man on his own slatted shelf that splintered through uniform, MacCallum watched flickering Japanese lights between the wood-board sides. He'd talk for a bit, seeing as no one else would. He liked the sound of his own voice. He knew that. But he thought that the others were glad for at least some interruption, though they never said.

He addressed Frank, as yet without a suitable moniker. "You ever in Singapore, Frank?"

"Yeah. Got the crap beat out of us in Malay."

"Anywhere near the Muar?" asked the Australian.

Frank shook his head. "The Leicestershires were at Jitra. We were trying to stop them reaching you."

"You from Leicester, then?" It was the Quiet man. Those who knew him, turned to check, to be sure.

"Yep, how about you?"

"Derby."

"Ah right. Derby. Been to Derby. It was alright there."

"Yeh."

MacCallum saw the Quiet Man turn on his side on his bunk-shelf, away to the wood wall.

"You were on Singapore at the end?" Frank asked MacCallum.

"With the Argylls." MacCallum lay back, with a hand behind his head. "We were fighting them back, same as you were. Led by Colonel Ian Stewart."

"I know that name."

"Ay, you should. A fierce commander. The 'Jungle Beasts,' us Argylls were. Holding the slanty-eyed bastards back, slowing them. I was at Slim River."

No one said anything, but MacCallum knew they'd heard of the horrors. He left the pause that the name always deserved.

"The 11th Indian was being cut down like a scythe through wheat, I tell you. It was a bloody mess. The Japs came at us so quick. Their tanks were charging us down like a bull stampede and we didn't have any anti-tank defences. No word they were right on us. Cut us in two. We fought on and held them back. Groups of us separated in the jungle, giving them hell. Made it over the railway bridge with seconds to spare. You should have seen us, running for our lives, sweat and blood and jungle, and us sprinting with it. Tanks chasing us down, but we got across that bridge before it blew."

MacCallum's bluster stalled and his tempo simmered down, as it always did at this point. "Didn't stop them in the end. Some of us made it to Singapore. Some of us, perhaps still in the jungle. Maybe still. Although a year and a half is a long time, but I wouldn't put it past them."

MacCallum laughed, but he knew there was little humour in the sound.

Mick the Quiet Man had turned to face out into the hut. He looked up to MacCallum's bunk.

"Colonel Stewart. I think I saw him once."

"When?"

"After Singapore. In India. Lecturing on jungle warfare."

"He'd know a thing or two about jungle warfare, alright."

The hut paused.

"What were you doing there?" asked MacCallum.

The Quiet Man had returned to his own thoughts. MacCallum could see, in the shadow of the shelf above, the darkened expression on the young man's brow, and knew that he was gone again. The Quiet Man.

***

Mick and his hut-mates trailed slowly around the camp grounds. They were thin, always hungry, and the thirst was threatening to choke his throat. He'd shown the others how to harvest ants from the nests beside their hut, yet leave plenty to keep the colonies going. They were given rice, but not enough for half a meal. He was surviving, holding on to some weight; keeping some strength in his arms and legs, through digging the colossal lake and the park to honour the Japanese soldiers.

The tropical sun shone with intent, even in spring. They walked on in looping circles. A low dust cloud hung in a ghostly yellow-brown tail around and behind them, like from a comet, made to travel at crawling pace.

They were talking about football versus cricket. Jihar was passionately defending cricket as a game of skill and purpose and excitement. His English was excellent, and twice as fluent when talking about cricket. Breck was also in support, and passionate about Australian football, while the others, and Mick, were against. Colin said, "How can you have a game where you could win or lose if it rains?" An unarguable point Mick thought. Jihar said that "Cricket is like war: victory and defeat, life and death, often do depend on the rain. More often than not, than on tactics or valour." Everyone went sombre after that. MacCallum picked things up after a while in defence of football, with its beauty and movement and pace and excitement, and said, "No, football is like war, with attack and counter attack, and the importance of holding your position on the field, lest someone get in behind you, or a winger flank you and put a ball into the box." Breck said, "There is no offside in war," but MacCallum continued his defence and somehow talked about the superiority of Scotland, and the faults of England.

They were on their fourth lap when one of the large gates in the tall wire fence opened. Guards lined a path to the exit, while others walked quickly to the assembly point and shouted out the familiar Japanese sounds to line up. Shapes began to appear from the huts and men stood from the wooden sides where they crouched to take their positions in the ranks. Mick crossed to his correct point in the dust.

As the lines formed around him, Mick noticed gaps, and men also finding the new spaces beside them and shuffling across to fill them.

The Japanese commander commenced to bark words at them, and he and the other prisoners bowed forward, deep through their painful stomachs, as they must. Shapes swaying, out-of-time, ragged and some struggling to right back up. Then unexpectedly the guards began with purpose to stride out, and with gestures of their rifles, move men out from the ranks. They were collecting the few lower ranked commissioned officers not already taken away the autumn before; some of the key men too. One man who looked near bone-thin was discarded at a word from the commander, left to shudder his legs back into line.

The Japanese officer spoke to a soldier nearby, and looked and nodded in Mick's direction. There was a distance across the yellow dirt between them, but the man's eyes seemed to have been looking directly at his - perhaps to the man at either side.

The guard strode out, cutting sharply, angrily through the statues of soldiers. Straight to him. The prisoners parted to a gun pointing and a head superiorly nodding him to step out. He glanced at those around him:

diverted eyes, some meeting his, also lacking understanding. He obeyed the gesturing command of the rifle and stepped from the ranks.

The selected stood in a waiting cluster out in front and to one side of the lined-up prisoners. Orders were shouted and Japanese guards motioned with guns for them to move into the funnel at the gate. Mick glanced around at the watching, silent lines they were leaving, at a few familiar faces, and then to the weary, thin and starved men whom he was in the midst of. Many were trying to walk tall and show resolve on high held jaws of off-colour and stretched skin. They were thinned to single file, and counted. Behind them the gate was shut.

Had he looked too strong still; had his reputation passed through Japanese lines of communication, even across flooded ship's hold and silence? A year and a half in the prison had ended. Now, to be shot, or moved elsewhere?

Mick walked on down the guard-lined gauntlet, keeping single file, toward the palm trees and tropical tree line. There the prison road branched onto a main tyre-rutted track, where lorries waited.

***

Another journey in the metal hold of a ship. More days, of half sitting and standing on interminable repeat. Thuds and straining metal groans travelled down one wall or another of the hold. The box that held them seemed to be twisting by the corners and edges, threatening to snap and contort and hurl them at metal walls. It seemed to be getting colder, unless it was just his own weakness, his strength finally leaving, a chill claiming him. The floor of the ship's hold was always cold, and the air above the prisoners always stinking and hot and barely breathable; but now the air did seem to have lost some of its humidity, and at night the heat was replaced with a growing cool.

One day, with the echoes came the sounds of Asian shouts and urgent calls as heavy lines were tossed and caught and missed, and slapped down on the wet docks. Things quietened down, for perhaps hours, as if they had been forgotten and would die in that hold. At some time, as cracks of daylight were fading, clear sounds of loud vehicle engines churning over and burning fuel, before revving down, reverberated outside.

****

The enclosed world opened, and Mick and the other transferred prisoners were led out blinking, down a metal corridor that made him duck, before stepping into brighter light that made him blink all the more and his vision faze. They were led off the ship under guard, sullen and traipsing, down a gangplank and onto the unwavering ground of the dock, eyes adjusting to the glare. He saw that light was almost gone and the clouded sun would soon be setting.

He stood in line on the dock front. The guards had moved slowly down the rows and bound each mans' hands in front of him. Now they kept a loose watch and ate in small groups, clustered around the bonnets of the two army lorries. The lines waited, hunched copies of each other, shoulders pulled, rounded, heads facing the dirt.

Darkness fell, standing, watching the fishing boats moored further along, bobbing gently, empty. Beside him the transport vessel was far smaller than the boat that had taken him to Formosa; it looked commandeered, like it had once been a merchant ship for some struggling businessman, and had been seized, and they the P.O.W.s thrown in its hold as it had happened to be passing. Now they were somewhere else. The talk on the journey had been of Japan; but uncertain days and nights in a ship could get you a lot of places.

The line moved, so Mick took shuffled steps forward. The men at the front began to clamber onto the open-backed lorries and the clang of metal footsteps patterned the foreign air. Progress stalled as each fresh man at the front altered stride and struggled to pull his weakened frame up. Bit by bit the shortening of steps passed down the line, until it was Mick that came to a full stop. A rifle butt, angled with purpose, struck with a sharp edge, like a spade trodden down onto soil that wouldn't give. He jarred to the side, but didn't look back or round.

Up ahead the dark forms of officers and the clang of each man's steps, layered, until they had sat, and then faded. A Japanese soldier watched over them with rifle in hand, standing on the frame that held them, whilst leaning casually against the back of the truck cabin.

Mick moved slowly forward, in line, behind the open-backed lorry. It was already all so familiar.

CHAPTER 10

Sun-a left the large house. It was two storeys tall, old and built of timber; she felt it towering behind her, over her as she stepped onto the street. She never looked back to it, but could see it there in her mind, the picture, leaning into the road, eaves overhanging, alongside smaller, one storey offices and buildings, all bearing emblems of the army and the empire. She walked into the road, looking briefly each way, and continuing regardless; she stopped when the corner of sight told her too, and waited for the cars and trucks she had seen to pass barely in front and behind. She stopped and started and crossed like an animal. Headlights blazed close past her. Horns honked, but she reached the other side, and life carried on as before: women hurrying along the street and soldiers heading to the old comfort house; some Korean guards, standing, talking in accented Japanese. An officer she recognised strode briskly across the road, not ten paces away, but did not deign to look her way. She understood.

With her head down she walked awkwardly under the gaze of the guard tower, past the prison entrance. Where the road turned around the prison fence ahead, a new line of Japanese buildings flanked it. She crossed to them, to a one storey structure with Japanese wording on its front. She could read little of their language, and it was dulled in the dim electric light, but knew it said 'hospital.'

***

Sun-a sat in a painted white corridor, on one of two chairs beside a closed door. A woman sat next to her – another comfort woman, with whom there had been little chance to speak. Sun-a did not want to talk, anyway. And she doubted the woman beside her did, either. What could be said when you sat in that place?

Sun-a let her hand rest on her pregnant belly. She didn't like to touch it – often avoided doing so – and so it was a conscious decision to stop her hand wavering and lay it down. She swallowed at the sensation. Soon one year old. A second later and she removed the hand, saw it held half to her side, half in front, as if it had gotten lost and didn't know which way to turn, then put it conspicuously beside her on the chair seat.

She noticed the material again. Her kimono was no longer appropriate; the folds of cloth slipped, and the obi was too awkward to tie around and keep still in place; her one-piece dress no longer fit. For one month she had been wearing the Korean dress.

Without turning her head she looked at the stomach-lump of the woman beside her. It was big, a vague mould under her loose-fitting skirt and blouse beneath. Bigger than her own, by some way yet. Sun-a glanced up at the woman's face – slightly older, even though the woman had only arrived at the comfort house the year before. She wondered where she had been before then. At least she herself had been friendly with Gum-Il-ja and Kim-Hye-ran before it had happened. It was a shame, she belatedly thought, that she had not been able to speak to her.

They were the unfortunate ones. Sun-a felt emotion rise that might perhaps have gone some way to tears in another woman, but it stopped where it did. She would not be with her friends for much longer now, before they sent her away. It was what had happened in the past, and it would happen to her. She would likely end up raising the baby in another comfort house – one for cast-offs and less desirables, where she would have to split the worse food for two. Soldiers got transferred – one of them might still be the father. Any face she half recognised. She brought herself back to the painted white corridor.

She allowed herself another cold glance down at that stomach, and hated the curved sight, obscuring her body, and beginning to vanish her legs. She looked away.

She had thought that carrying their child would make them stop. But it hadn't. Perhaps they had thought it would knock the baby out of her. It had often happened – the woman put back to work the same day. But hers had stayed. It wouldn't be long now.

The door outside which they waited, opened, and a young doctor in a white coat stepped partially out. He didn't speak, but looked at the woman first in their line of two, and with open palm showed the way in. The woman stood and went with him, then the door closed.

Sun-a still sat alone in the empty corridor two minutes later when footsteps sounded around the near corner. A tall man in a military uniform strode past, followed by a nurse whose shoes clip-clopped fast, short steps to keep up. The man wore an ornamental sword at his side, signs of rank on his uniform, and looked at Sun-a as he passed. She had seen him before. His cold face gave nothing away as he seemed to study her, then broke his glance and opened the door, followed by hurried apologies from the nurse.

The door closed behind him in the nurse's face. She steadied for a second, then turned and hurried back the way she had come.

Sun-a sat alone and waited.

***

The doctor stood up immediately at Kamakura's entrance, from where he had been on one knee beside the woman. The man bowed, arms respectfully by his side, and Kamakura returned a nod of the head. The woman sat on the bed, looking fearfully at his arrival, but he didn't allow his eyes to settle on her, to establish acknowledgment, only to identify the doctor as their target.

"What are you doing?"

The young doctor spoke nervously: "I was a little early so I carried out a preliminary check. All seems well-"

"You were instructed to wait for my arrival."

"Yes, Sir, but I thought I should attend to medical matters-"

"This hospital serves the Army of the Empire of Greater Japan."

"Yes," said the doctor promptly and bowed his head.

"In future, you shall know that I will attend to these matters, until you have learnt the system we operate here."

"Yes. Captain, I should not have overstepped my position."

Kamakura Hideyoshi nodded, displeased but sufficed, and twisted on the spot, feet turning on the clean tiles as precise hands on a clock face. He faced the patient, hand at leisure on his scabbarded sword. He looked the woman up and down.

He looked back to the doctor. "You're new, and this is not the gynaecology you are used to. You will learn that there are military imperatives that apply in this situation." To the pregnant woman he said, in good Korean, "How long have you been at Jinsen?"

The pale-faced woman took a moment to adjust to her surprise, then replied, "Since last summer."

"Then you are unfortunate to have fallen pregnant so soon. In many women the shock causes delay."

The doctor stood aside, hands kept still behind his back. Kamakura noted his ill-at-ease, but had seen it before and was not unduly troubled. He tilted his head as he was aware was his habit of doing and considered the prostitute's raised stomach with his downward gaze. After mere seconds he looked over to the doctor.

"I estimate she is eight months."

"Yes, I would agree."

Kamakura spent a glance to observe the young doctor. The man's demeanour said nothing, which he read acutely as there indeed being something to be said. Hidden, undisclosed. No doubt the doctor looked down on a military surgeon, on military jurisdiction sullying medical jurisdiction. The fool would learn that the two were truly one and the same.

"Do you speak their language?"

"A little," the doctor replied.

"Good. Then listen, and observe." To the woman, Kamakura said in Korean, "Has it affected your work?"

The pregnant woman raised her head slightly at the sound and her eyes moved from side to side with caution. She appeared to consider her words carefully before her reply. "No. I still worked."

"Good. Indeed, there are many men who enjoy... the feel... the novelty. But we cannot have your blood spilling on the Emperor's men. To touch you is bad enough, but necessary. To touch your bastard, is no comfort of any kind."

The woman tensed. Her breathing rate had increased.

Kamakura drew his sword. The woman began to shake and sob.

"What are you doing?" complained the doctor, with a step forward and an arm half outstretched. "You can't-"

"Abortion of the problem."

Satisfied that the stupid practitioner would step no further, Kamakura pulled his glare back and ran it over the woman. The torso, the belly, the high noose of the skirt under the armpits, the moulded folds of fabric. He thrust his sword into the pregnant woman, below the sternum, ribs winged to either side. His other hand he put to her mouth, to smother the cry.

He heard the new doctor stumble back into a table of metal implements, clattering many to the floor, and flasks and tubes tumble and roll in individual concentric circles on the metal surface.

With his military surgeon's precision he sliced all the way down the woman's abdomen, fighting spasms and resistance with a steady grip. The blade met firmer material but cut through keenly. He stopped before the pubic bone. Satisfied, Kamakura pulled out the metal, hearing the squelch as it left gore behind it and came out with smears of red, but relatively clean, with polished patches still showing.

He wiped the larger mess on the woman's billowing skirt as her body fell back onto the hospital bed sheets. Then he walked to the sink, ran the tap, and cleaned the blade under a stream of cold water. He looked up to the doctor to his side, who still gripped the edge of the table like a terrified school girl.

"Unpleasant, but your stomach will settle. Cover the body. There's another outside waiting, and we don't want a frenzy."

***

Two lorries bumped along an uneven road, the sounds of the coast to the right, low buildings sometimes dropping oil-light on scrub to the left. Mick sat with a dozen other prisoners on the metal floor of the trailing vehicle. Having been almost the last to climb aboard and take his seat he held to his knees at the rear by the closed tailgate, in between the two soldiers who watched over them. They perched on low stools on either side of the lorry, rifles a second away from poised, watching the slumped forms in the darkness.

Night now truly had its grip on the convoy, and had brought with it a quick falling cold. Only a little moonlight made it through sprawled clouds, and illuminated the side of a face, a guard's undisguised look of underestimation, the edge of a ragged British uniform, or gleamed on the thin metal cylinder that ended a rifle.

A few lorries, too few guards. Resources stretched, or lack of wariness for men long imprisoned and weak? Forgotten soldiers. Transport insecure. Guards tired. None in reserve. Through his own great tiredness the thoughts settled, assembled.

The lorry rocked through potholes and dried-mud tyre grooves that had formed competing ditches in the track. He saw the ground through the moves of the lorry. Captured soldiers bumped and clanged down on metal in their enforced lethargy. The sounds of the sea began to fall behind; low banks lifted into blackness beyond the lorry railings; illumination from the roadside vanished. Mick glanced to the guard to his left. To the one on his right.

He acted without thought. He kicked out firmly at the stool, pushing his foot right through its legs until his own leg was stretched, joint locked, and the seat was flying. He saw the Japanese man, tilted forward, airborne, face stretching toward a shout, surprise and fear breaking out in black eyes. Mick hated him, and the other one.

As he instinctively planted his bound hands and swung his lower body beneath him, he knew he had had to act; though it was instinct and rage he felt the certainty that he knew what he was doing. His weight expertly shifted. He struck a kick, up, high, to the other side. His boot met with force, the face of the other soldier, just as the man leaned forward at the shock of his mirror image falling. The crack of sound was solid, and Mick felt it call up the justice that had to be meted out. The horrors, the terrors that these Godless bastards had served out, would be confronted, stood tall against. Then the man too was falling, but the other way, back, his head recoiling on its spring of a neck. It hit hard against the side of the lorry, and bounced back like a punched punch-bag righting itself.

Mick was pushing off all fours like a springing tiger. Though his hands were lashed as one, they strained out, claws flared. He saw the first man off his stool, now sprawled and rebounding from his fall on the metal deck, his eyes blinking, then fixing, still with shock that a prisoner would ever dare. The gun in his hands was turning. Mick's hatred gave clarity. Assurance. He felt righteous. Invincible. A man acting by providence. And he saw the rifle swing his way, and made his leap over the enemy, tied hands grabbing him by his Japanese uniform with strength that a mortal man's weight could not resist.

Then they were up and over the side, and falling from the moving vehicle into the darkness.

The gun was flung, instantly gone – the lorries not a score of feet away, and everything already plunged into black. Mick picked himself up from the fall, staggered, and came to a stop with a kick into the vague head where the darkness plunged even denser yet. The thud, perhaps crack of bone, a skull, stopped the rustle at his feet.

The moon was gone, swallowed behind cloud, to aid his escape or to slow him he did not know. A moment in the darkness, the lorries carrying on into the extinguished terrain, their dimming lights the only specks in a circle of black, whichever way he looked.

Mick took a breath. Felt that his side hurt from the fall. The shock of how he had come to be standing there in the darkness. The gun was gone; he could see nothing; he knelt on an invisible ground and felt it against his knee, holding him up. He reached out in front and found the uniformed chest of the Japanese man; perhaps he breathed, or perhaps a false rise and fall, as he padded where the sides should be, until he found a belt, and the knife he had observed during their transfer.

Shouts sounded, panicked, but more distant than he could have hoped for. He had a chance. Mick saw out of the corner of his eye, the vehicles stopping, and figures silhouetted by yellow headlight standing tall atop them, arms waving, guns pointing at the captives and the discovered scene – as he ran, ducked low toward the blackness at the roadside.

PART 2

CHAPTER 11

A soldier hurried onto the white corridor, knocked briefly on the door, and opened it without waiting for an answer. Displeased Japanese words answered his entrance, and he responded with a flurry of out-of-breath sound, no spaces left to mark the in-between of words. From within the room came a reply – a growl of exclamation at unwanted news. Sun-a found herself leaning out and towards the door, to catch a glimpse of the man inside. Her belly made twisting impossible and her curiosity futile, and she jolted straight-backed against the chair and wall at the first impression of off-green in the doorway.

Sun-a looked up in surprise at the Korean words in the air. She saw the man with the ornamental sword striding past, following the soldier. Without turning to her he had said: "Wait there. I'll be back."

***

The soldier led Kamakura Hideyoshi on the edge of a run, out of the hospital, onto the road, and toward an untidy conglomeration of parked vehicles and soldiers. It was an irritating walk, seeing his destination in a clear line of sight while it discussed without him. He observed the personnel involved and the unusual sight of prisoner trucks: new prisoners were rare now in this part of the ever-expanding empire, and transportation of them an occasional occurrence. Both trucks had stopped mere wheel rolls from the held-open prison gate, in an uncoordinated confluence of orders.

Kamakura arrived as ordered and stood before Lieutenant Colonel Goro. The officer responsible for the prison and its surrounding facilities was a not unusually short man, of unnecessary weight. The flesh between neck and jawbone betrayed him at every meeting.

"Colonel." He made a salute – never a learned response. He did not bow; he rarely bowed, unless deigned rank made it unavoidable. He had been criticised for it often: this terminal posting was likely not unconnected. But to misplace honour and gain a better posting – he looked down to the prison commander for the reason of his summoning.

Goro looked up with only the briefest nod, then waved a man forward into the crossed beams of headlamps, which illuminated their conclave in the darkness.

"A prisoner has escaped. He did this."

The timid guard stepped forward and tilted his head back slightly to reveal dark shades of red beneath a cut on his brow, where blood had been wiped clear by a sleeve. Undoubtedly the flesh would have looked redder, its topography swollen and raised in electric lighting; the man's nose – perhaps twice as wide as normal – filling around his eye sockets deep blue, purple.

Kamakura looked down his nose at him as he surveyed the damage. "One guard?" he asked.

"You can have the other one when he's been disciplined. And don't let him sleep. He has done plenty of that already tonight."

"Yes, Lieutenant Colonel."

As junior officers took receipt from runners and unrolled maps, Kamakura stepped forward and seized the injured soldier's head in both talon-spread hands. "Into the light," he said, stepping back and around and taking the man's head and shuffling feet with him. The hair at the back was matted and bloody, and the parting of a gash could be seen below the occipital protuberance, heading toward the neck. The strike to the face had obviously caused the skull to impact on something sharp to the rear.

"It will need stitches."

He released the head, and the soldier took back possession and looked up fearfully.

"Be at the hospital in fifteen minutes. I have one patient to see first."

The solider nodded, but Kamakura had stopped paying the man any attention. He moved over to the conference around the maps, and looked over them, indignant to be included, though it was not his role.

"He cannot run inland," said the lieutenant colonel with indiscriminate sweeps of his hand over the yellow-lit paper – "or he will die there. This is a peninsula, and his nearest ally is... The Soviets." Carefully permitted laughter sounded from behind tight-lipped mouths. "Does he think he will walk through Keijo? There is nowhere to go. Thin the patrols inland. Redeploy along the coast: search warehouses, factories. But keep it quiet. Railway lines. And have men stationed at the port. A prisoner will invariably try to flee as far from patrols as he can: some thousand miles back to British territory – while it lasts. He will double back, so let us be there ready."

Goro walked from the group to look down the dark road which led from the prison away into the mainland. His officers moved quickly to their vehicles. Engines growled and the iron cars and their soldiers passed to his left and right and into the darkness.

Goro turned to the scene, taken off guard at how black it really was now its illumination was driving into the night behind him. He considered the two trucks with displeasure, loaded with soiled prisoners of war, sitting miserably, hunched to their knees, heads bowed, and his small army of tense guards who ringed them – every man on sheer alert after what had happened.

"Take them through the gates."

The military surgeon had long since faded away into the blackness when Goro walked after the slowly moving trucks, between the tall fence posts, back into his prison camp.

***

Sun-a waited in the painted-white corridor. The door opened in the wall against which she sat, and a doctor looked out. A young man, he appeared to look both ways to the ends of the branching corridor, then said with a repeated wave of his arm, "Come in. Quickly."

He shut the door behind her then backed off into the middle of the room, wiping his hands nervously to either side of his lower back. He looked to her and swallowed, and Sun-a could hear his breathing from where she stood by the door. She had not seen many doctors – only one other when not long after first arriving she had been ill with fever – but she realised that his manner was odd. As with any superior, it was for him to begin. And yet he did not seem to want to.

Her eyes fell across the room: the charts on the walls; the tables and metal tools; two beds. She saw the shape on the furthest bed, covered by a sheet, with the prick of two feet holding it up and letting it fold down over the hidden table; the two horse shoes of blood that had soaked into the sheet – fine lined at the edges, growing blotted and filled in at the middle. Still filling in.

Sun-a felt her stomach grow cold like winter, even compressed as it was behind the heat and bulk on her front. She knew why she had not seen the other woman leave the room. There was blood in a pool beneath the bed, red dyeing the sides of the sheet, right along where it draped the frame. A sound escaped her mouth – a faltering cry that she had not called for. Her hands were shaking, and she looked down at them, and then up to the doctor.

In the same fractured Korean with which he had called her in, he said, "You must leave now. This way." She realised his Korean was not poor; that he could not speak any words. She caught his fear.

It was with hurried steps that she took the direction of his unsteady, open-palmed, doctor's gesture. Through a door at the back of the surgery, he led her, onto a stunted corridor that was dimly lit, walls pallid by damp, or yellow light bulb. The young doctor opened a heavy door at the end of the corridor, and held it, onto grass and dirt and the dark night outside.

Sun-a stepped to the doorway. At close-quarters she looked at the man who held the door, who pressed against the wall to let her through. He looked away, out into the night.

"Thank you," she said, in Japanese, and then Korean.

"Go. Get as far away from here as you can."

Sun-a nodded. She thought of laying her hand on the young doctor's shoulder, but it was not appropriate. She stepped past him into the night and heard the crunch of gravel soil beneath her thin shoes, as if it was a sound and a sensation she had never encountered. She stood on a dirt area hidden behind the hospital buildings, lit in part by a shaft of rectangular yellow light from the doorway, with dark land spreading out before her.

She didn't see the doctor close the door – just heard the final creak of hinges, the bang as it sealed in its frame, and saw the light cut down to nothing from right to left. It made her jump.

There was only a glare of light over complete blackness – light that was not there anymore. Blind for a moment, she stepped forward, trusting the crunch of gritty soil underfoot. When the haze faded, she could still see nothing. She stood, heart pounding, and then gradually her eyes accustomed to the darkness: rough land, small hills, buildings, bushes and trees, tracks cutting across; small squares of window light like large fireflies fixed to the landscape at distance. Roads to pass; houses, should anyone be still at work outside; the outskirts of Incheon before the countryside. She had to get away from it all; where they could find her, where someone would see her.

She began to walk – held the rounded underside of her belly to stop it levering against her. Onto the unsteady soil and stones. The darkness seemed to swell around her as she left the cover of the hospital building. She felt herself disappearing into it.

She looked up, over it all, beyond the criss-cross of paths, a railway line, beyond the factories and houses, to where the blackness truly began. The complete dark, distinct as a silhouette against the sky; the hills and mountains inland.

***

Kamakura Hideyoshi strode into the surgery. The doctor stood exactly where he had left him, unmoved. Waiting. A second's glance confirmed that neither was the second patient in the room – the corridor outside had been empty.

"Yes. Where is the girl?"

The man bowed, slowly, respectfully.

"Gone. She is not in the corridor."

"Gone where?"

"I presume she returned to the comfort house. I do not know where those girls go."

Kamakura looked hard and unflinching at the young doctor. His eyes did not blink.

The doctor looked away.

"The nurse's station would have informed me had the whore run past."

"They must have missed her."

"No," he said at once, furious within at the slight. "This is my hospital and my nurses do not miss things."

"Yes. I have no explanation."

Kamakura's tone did not falter, consistent, accusatory, but to a colleague: "How long was your training?"

The doctor was smaller in height, but Kamakura could see the other man's perceived self visibly shrinking yet. They were both conscious of it, transmitted in their now locked stare. Kamakura did not relish it, but there was strength taken and gained in necessary victory.

"I studied for the same time as any other doctor."

Kamakura nodded faintly, his stare-hold not breaking. "A waste. All thrown away, for this?"

The doctor made himself stand tall in his white coat, his chest pushing out, but nothing hiding the fear in his eyes.

Kamakura concluded. "Five years, spent on one whore."

The doctor did not respond. Kamakura observed faint shaking, an uncontrolled tremble stemming from the man's unmoving legs.

"There is no proof of any error."

"This hospital is my command. You have aided an enemy escape. That is treason."

"A comfort woman cannot be treason."

"Your medical career has ended today."

"No," the man stammered. "Doctor, that is... Captain, you cannot."

One solitary arm seemed to escape its shaking owner, and uncoordinated, stab out, aside, pointing at nothing.

With an effortless lift of his fingers, Kamakura slid folded steel from its scabbard. One sun. The pathetic man jolted a half step back against the table, his eyes wide, staring at the source of near frictionless sound. Kamakura held the sword there, hand guard resting on his thumb. He did not move, just waited.

The doctor's eyes met his own, capillaries strained. Muscles in his cheeks and around his mouth tremored.

"You have gone directly against the orders of a superior officer. You have broken your bond to the Empire. You can preserve some honour at the last."

The man seemed to enter a trance, head moving slowly about the room: dead body under sheet; diagrams on wall; curtain and rail; table and implements, his hands gripping its edge.

Kamakura watched him, measuring. He let the sword fall softly back with a faint click, and moved his hand away from the mould of the sharkskin hilt.

Kenji Haruto looked to the items on the table, and clutched at a pot beside a range of flasks. He brandished, as if he had found a great treasure, an empty syringe. His unhinged elation immediately drained away to less than nothing, and his tearful eyes beheld the weapon of his choosing. His mouth gasped, and his stare drifted out around the hospital room, not seeing. With no warning the here and now claimed him again, his vision returned to near-sight and the object dead centre before his chest.

He couldn't think. He couldn't grasp his predicament, the sudden change in velocity, the impossibility of what was unfolding. He planted his shaking legs apart, well-spaced, and took the syringe in his hands. With the difficulty of a first year medical student, he pulled back the plunger in the cylinder tube and let the air in the room rush in. He fumbled briefly, but turned the long, thick needle to face himself. He looked to the army doctor, but expected no reprieve. He saw none.

He carefully secured his grip with both hands and held the needle poised before his belly like a samurai blade about to plunge in and stomach-cut. Kamakura was watching him, but the man had ceased to be relevant, even as he stood still, executioner in all but name. Kenji Haruto breathed his last long breath – a ragged, shaky, draw of turbulent air – then slowly flexed the artisan, doctor's fingers of his left hand over the hilt. Suddenly, in immensity, he wanted to weep – could feel the weeping taking over him. He couldn't think if it had been the right or wrong thing. Or what it had been for. There was just fear, and grief, and desperate petition inside him.

Kamakura watched with some respect, as the new doctor attempted to steady himself and his wavering surgeon's hands. The man lifted the point of the thick glass needle and readied it over his white coat.

He stabbed the syringe fiercely into the left side of his chest.

He staggered and stared out with red eyes. He began to push the plunger down firmly with straining thumb. His eyes watered as he fought the pressure of the air in the syringe; his shaking thumb moved steadily, until down flat. A slurry of air bubbles now roiled along the man's circulation. The doctor gasped, uselessly, for his lungs would not move.

Kamakura looked on dispassionately as the man convulsed, in excruciating pain; and dropped upon the tiled floor. He stood still and waited over the dumped body. A glass needle not broken on the floor by the curled hands; implements in disarray on the table. A thought – had he stepped across a line? Repercussions. He dismissed it.

He turned and opened the door. He would find a nurse and get the bodies removed. He left the room with the doctor still dying, closed the door behind him and strode along the corridor in the direction of the nurses' station. He had a busy night ahead of him, and that idiot guard's scalp to stitch yet. The incompetent fool would have to wait while he attended to other matters.

He would never see the second girl again. If soldiers found her in the countryside they would use her as she was intended, and kill her when they had raped her. If she was not found she would either die in difficult, lone childbirth, or starve or succumb to disease with her bastard off-spring.

CHAPTER 12

Mick scrambled up a slope of loose soil on all fours. Beneath the low canopy of small trees and spreading bushes the night sky was all but gone: no moon, or stars, just inky darkness, which seemed to hang off him, pulling him back and down with its added gravity. He saw the branches and twigs ahead only in the inches before he hit them, and so darted this way and that, pulling back and around, and then on, then correcting course again, and then again. His legs ached, his fingers dug at stones and smashed at tree roots as they pawed the dirt for grip and traction, and breath wheezed out of his cramped, stretching lungs.

A tree descended like a falling, thrown log - as every rushing obstacle seemed to have been hurled - and he sidestepped, fought losing grip on scree, but dug enough indent with his boot to push on. Past the trunk, he let himself fall back against it, and pant painfully for breath. Stitch raked his sides and his lungs physically ached, just like a calf, or thigh, or any other muscle would.

He'd left a trail to follow. He knew it. Only the night had prevented it being followed so far. He had to go slower. Panic would only leave evidence of flight. And yet he had to outrange their search perimeter. He gasped in air, in, out, in out, and rested his head back, mouth grimacing to the sky he couldn't see. What had he been thinking? He had no idea where he was – not even narrowed down to the country. Yet he felt an odd glimmer of joy deep down to be free. He had had to escape; he could not have arrived in that prison. He was now living the alternative.

Finally his breathing slowed. Then stopped at the sound of shouts far below. How many slopes had he climbed? How far had he gotten from the roads, the last fields and buildings?

Through the darkness he'd felt the gradient swing beneath his feet, at times sheer off to the side, or plunge beneath him so that his stomach had gone green at the drop and for momentary seconds he'd thought he may be airborne, out and over a cliff. Then his feet had crunched down and his unprepared ankles had buckled and jarred and held and he'd raced on.

The Japanese calls were close. A narrow torch beam swept across the mountainside thirty feet below him. Tentatively he peered around the tree and saw two figures fifty feet away, trudging horizontally across the slope, keeping to a contour line. The beam swung back, and he pressed himself flat against the trunk, alarmed at how starkly the forest was lit. There would be no hiding if they began to climb. Then he realised the opportunity, and drank in the details before him. Up above the slope continued steeply, past bushes, tangles of dense undergrowth giving way to patches of plain earth. He absorbed it, mentally fixing the lengths and distances and spaces and the best route through them.

The light pulled away, and without warning blackness resumed. The voices continued, but more distant now. Mick waited, until he could hear nothing but his breathing, then waited minutes more. Carefully he pushed himself from the tree and took slow steps, soon on all fours as the angle of the slope came to meet him. He could see almost nothing again, but in his mind he saw the slope ahead, as when lit. He moved through the scene, past sudden shadows cast by thin, closely driven posts of tree trunks, aside into bare spaces, zigzagged back around trunks that he could not see but swore were there. Soon he was past his map and again into unknown blackness, wondering when the slope would drop down before him, and finding it never did. His hands found a heavy tree trunk in front of his face and he held on and pulled himself around it.

Again he leaned back on it. He listened, but heard nothing - no footfalls in pursuit, no shouts to call troops his way. He would wait a while; listen, and then continue.

***

Mick woke with a start. Panic was his first thought. There was light enough to see - almost dawn light. He had been asleep. Was he about to be caught? Was that what had woken him? He spun his gaze around the sloped forest in search of a circle of troops, closing. He saw none. Only unknown, deserted stretches of woodland fanned out in all directions - and he somehow in the middle of it all.

His heart sank back in his chest and he breathed out a sigh of relief. He smiled. He could almost laugh at the absurdity of it all: stranded in the middle of nowhere, literally thousand upon thousands of miles from home. He calmed himself; composed himself. Hopelessness settled just as quickly. His heart sank further. What was he to do? If he was in the middle of enemy territory, then staying alive would require his every effort - and that probably not enough.

He could be in Japan for all he knew.

The thought stilled him instantly. It was not wild speculation. It was perhaps as likely as any of the slightly less terrible alternatives. Jumping from that lorry had been to serve his own death sentence. Kyoto or Tokyo could be at the foot of the next mountain. He could descend the next slope and well drop onto the Imperial Japanese Army Headquarters.

In Germany a P.O.W. escapee could hope to change his clothes, blend in with the locals and make it to a border with a few muttered words of Deutsche. He was not in Germany; he was somewhere in East Asia: there were no borders, no languages they taught you at school; he was a foot taller than everyone for a third of the world's trek, and visibly not a local from squinting distance. What had he been thinking? Just what had he been thinking?

He stayed where he was, for a minute, or more, letting the time roll past. The forest stayed where it was; the sharp slope did not move. Nothing changed. He looked about him once again, saw no patrol, only his own hopeless options in whatever direction he so chose.

He had to focus. His situation was desperate, there was no changing that. He had to make the best of it. Do his utmost to survive. Make his way to anywhere where the odds were not quite so stacked. And from there, the same again – try and better his lot. He could survive. He was trained as well as any man. Who knew, he could do some damage to the Japanese on his way, if he used his head wisely. There were a hundred reasons why he should certainly fail, why he should likely not make it through the first day, but it was possible.

He looked up the steep slope with recovered conviction. Straight ahead. Through the thin, closely stemmed trees, the early morning light faded obliquely at its furthest reach up the mountain side. Mick squinted. His vision adjusted to the depth and greyed sunshine, and instead saw the bases of trees begin to roll with the ground as it broke from its incline and disappeared from view. He pushed off from his sleeping spot and began to climb to the newly discovered horizon line.

A sharp cry stopped him dead. He froze, waiting for the sound again, not wanting to so much as crinkle a leaf and obscure it: pained, female, adult, straight ahead and to the right. Nothing else.

Mick moved, quickening his pace, up toward the mountainside horizon, a careful distance from the fixed point in his mind. He pulled himself up using one tree trunk after the next as if they were bolts hammered into the slope for a mountaineer. The gradient was steep, and he could feel his heart pounding through his chest when he hauled himself over the hidden line of sight. He found not the next descent that he had been half expecting, but even ground.

The cry came again, louder, pulling his head sharply to its direction. Muffled cries followed it this time, tearful, seeming to beg and plead for relief. Mick moved toward the sound, keeping low, finding himself progressing over a narrow plateau, still wooded, which ran almost flat but for a slight slope.

A soft thud met his ears, and then another pained cry. The crowded forest, which relished its chance to hold to even land, still hid whatever caused the sound. Mick slowed as the trees and undergrowth began to disperse around him, bearing a grimace at the despair he heard. Again the cry meandered between the trees to meet him - something horrible, ethereal, that cut itself apart and did not belong. He crouched and moved stealthily ahead, using the cover as the trees thinned. He stopped ten feet before a final tree line.

Beyond the last posts of trees, he could see from open ground to the sky, bare soil and patches of grass surrounded by a looping oval of forest. At the back of the clearing, stone rose through the dirt into a short mount. Leaning against the rock, facing him, was a young woman, though her face was hidden beneath long, black, swaying hair, down to her chest. She wore a strange foreign dress which hung out to the ground like a tent. In her two hands she held a large rock; held it in front of her rounded belly.

Mick looked about the scene. He saw no one else; heard no other movement.

The woman lifted her head, as her hands lifted and her arms straightened. She was young. A girl or a woman. She was looking right at him, though Mick knew he could not be seen. Rather, she was staring ahead, preparing herself.

Then her face broke with despair and she plunged the heavy stone deep into her belly. She creased over with a cry, and bent double. Her hand still in her folded midriff, her neck strained as she looked out, her mouth open in a gasp. Finally she took in air, then rocked back against the stone peak. Agony held her face in a moment's rictus. Then she half-sobbed and half-groaned, back and forth between the two, neither coming to fruition, and held her arms wrapped around her waist. She tilted aside and rested there against the rock, still gasping against the pain.

Mick felt that he stared, eyes wide, and hurt. How many times had this woman plunged the stone into herself? He looked to ground – he needed to gather his thoughts and quickly. Whoever she was, she was beyond his help. She was not his concern. He drilled through the options, scrutinizing the scenario as he had taught himself to do. She could be a runaway bride; an unmarried girl forced to take care of a mistake: in either case family or involved parties could be searching for her. She could be a whore. He was near the location of a military prison with its provision of soldiers, and all the logistics, supply and demand that such an operation required. Whores could inevitably be found living off such places.

He looked at her. And yet, she was so beautiful. Even with her agony, and the terror he watched on her face, she was... All could succumb to the cruelties of life. He set his mind where it needed to be.

If a whore, then she could equally be being pursued, by whatever arrangement the Japanese used. Either way, he should not be watching. The alarm of the situation struck Mick hard. She had been crying out - perhaps even while he slept; she could have attracted the attention of anyone within a mile or two's radius - though he could not account for the sound-obstruction of terrain and forest. The likelihood of her discovery by Japanese search parties was high. His present location was compromised. Any soldier worth his salt, drawn to her cries, would circle the wider area and discover his tracks. Effectively, his head start on the Japanese had just been cut.

Besides, what was he suggesting? There was nothing to be done for her. He could not help her, and must not help her. She was not his concern. There was no question about it, he must move away and leave the area immediately.

Mick slowly stood, so as not to startle her, and walked out into the open.

He had taken five paces into the clearing when the girl saw him. She raised her head and he saw eyes grow wider still, though wide with pain already. Her eyebrows arched in a look of shock or disbelief, and then her mouth moved hopelessly as terror took over. Mick raised a hand in non-threat, but he watched her look to the side, think of running, glance to her belly, realize she couldn't, and tip back against the rock as her frightened eyes returned to him.

He took a step forward, now well clear of cover, stranded in the centre of the oval clearing. He raised his other hand into the air as well, as he had when face to face with the Japanese rifles in the jungle clearing in Burma.

"It's alright," he said.

She tensed at the sound of his voice. He stepped forward again, closer now to her than to the trees he had emerged from.

She made a noise – something that wanted to be a scream, but wasn't. He took another step forward. Soon he would be within touching distance. What then? What was the plan?

A sound came, like a large, wet sponge being squeezed out. Suddenly the girl wasn't interested in him standing there. The look of terror that held her face was not for him, and her eyes dotted about the grassy and barren ground as if her mind searched for something – a delicate sound it was trying to hear, or a thought she had mislaid. And when her eyes looked back to his, they were just as white, but this time pleading. Terrified, but asking him to save her.

Mick took quick steps across the space between them and was bending to her, moving to one knee, three feet away, when the blood dotted her long dress clearly. It was deep and red, and partly already clotted, and the fabric took it up eagerly. It blotted into the faded pattern on the dirty dress in ballooning concentric circles. Mick leant back, raised hands falling wide, on instinct, as if avoiding an enemy's blow.

The girl-woman whimpered-screamed and placed her hands to either side, against the solid stone for support. Her body straightened out and her stance began to slide. She was flat against the rock, looking at him, lips wavering, eyes begging to cry – almost begging him, begging for an answer.

Then her world went interior again. Preoccupied by what was happening unseen. She cried out softly – a sound of despair that wished it could be any other way. Then her expression changed, and she looked down her front, straight down: her lumped belly; the upside down V of her legs, which she could not truly see. Her mouth and voice trembled, and she grew quietened, gaze fixed. Horrifically waiting.

"Dear God." He knew what must be happening. He inched closer on his bended knee, and looked sorrowfully up into those eyes beneath the straggling, falling, sheer black hair. He wanted to ask 'may I,' and hoped his eyes had been understood.

Slowly he reached his hands forward – trying to hold down his breathing; not to tremble – to the bloody targets which covered her. He touched the outsides of his closed fingers to where the insides of her knees would be. She allowed her legs to part beneath the fabric, seeing him always in her gaze over her belly. The soaked dress made a noise and Mick thought it might rip, but it gave, and fanned out across her until almost taut. There was blood and water on the ground. It had dampened the grass, and bent stalks weak on their side.

Carefully, with pincers of index fingers and thumbs, he picked up the hem of the dress and pushed it up her legs. He rolled it over her knees, looked for consent, saw the same terrified, wide-eyed plea looking back, and pushed the sodden fabric halfway up her thighs.

She groaned, lifted her back off the stone, seemingly pulled up by invisible chains, and leant toward her pregnant belly. She convulsed involuntarily and her top half fell back to the sloping rock. And then she screamed, a quiet, high-pitched, pained, shriek, which Mick oddly sensed had been tempered for his benefit. He looked up to the poor woman, feeling for her, alone on this mountainside, then recalling a flicker of memory of how on earth he had come to be there. It dropped sharply away to the starkness of the present moment. He was suddenly very aware of where he was, of who he was, and of who this stranger might be; and of what was about to happen. A prayer he could not remember passed through him – he'd heard no words, but the patter of their rhythm. Whatever it had said, he meant it.

Sun-a felt her back and stomach and neck and arms unloose, finally. She breathed in and swallowed the spit that had risen. Her eyes refocused and she saw again the man who knelt before her. He had walked out of the forest like an apparition, and she had wanted to run and flee. Now she felt she would have wept if he had left her there alone. His face. She had seen men from foreign lands at the prison camp, but only as distant figures, finger height. Now she saw him, who looked right into her face. Her eyes could not seem to settle on the features she saw. He was impossible. Nothing was real. The pain turned everything into what she had never noticed it to be. It stabbed from her belly, like a spider web of spreading, cracking ice, yet as hot as sticks, black-red, out of the fire. It followed and split into every fork of her veins, freezing and jarring until it pinned her at every corner.

She hated the source of pain she carried beneath her stomach, and she hated herself for what she had done. Guilt was everywhere she looked. It hung between her and the blurring trees, and somehow was the trees. The circle of ground and grass. But it was not him. Not yet. She wondered, that the pain might stop if the guilt went away. And then her.

He looked up to the girl – so beautiful – and saw in the way she looked down at him, and then the surrendering tilt of her head, that she knew the moment was then.

She cried out, and more blood came. This time Mick saw it come. Over cloth underwear, wet and fallen down her legs. Her squat against stone widened; and he knew he would have to catch it. He looked away, but cupped his hands and placed them beneath her.

A stream flowed over his hands and between his fingers. He grimaced, then too late tried to plain his face. A glance. Her eyes were on him, and he looked away from them too. He sensed her clawing at the stone and saw her body struggling. Then she shrieked a terrible cry – and Mick turned his face straight back to her, knowing he was open-mouthed and horribly exposed. He had surely not heard a more pained sound before.

He looked down, and below the blood draped, rolled fabric, saw his bloody, sticky, watery hands, dripping unevenly. He looked again to the unknown woman. As he brought his eyes away from her trembling, fading gaze, he felt something more solid drop. He felt its weight in his hands. Without haste, he looked down, to the dead, small baby, held on a cord, and then to her, it's mother. But she was gone. Out of the three of them he was left alone on the mountain.

CHAPTER 13

Sun-a woke under a roof of branches and leaves. They went from one side of the sky to the other in lines, crossing with centres and points of stars, sprouts and shoots splitting. At their ends, and on buds, the leaves grew as they would on a real tree; but it couldn't be a real tree, because trees did not grow like that, with barely a gap to let the light though. And then she saw it was a flattened shape, with blue beside it, and perhaps some other greens further off.

She lay on her back and her stomach hurt. The sky was above her, above the branches. Her mind moved about the horizontal, giving her a place in the real world. Thoughts coalesced. The terrible pain was still there, but different now. She remembered, what had happened. What she had done, and what had happened.

With a start Sun-a sat up – pushed up on her elbows. The shock of pain made her want to scream, but she contained it, held herself there against it, then let herself collapse back to ground. The pain in her middle ebbed away somewhat, back to what it had been before. Tentatively, she lifted her head only this time. Her neck ached, but she forced herself, and locked the trembling muscles so that she could see over her own body.

She felt her stomach drop at the sight - that it was flat. Almost flat. Her skirt was soaked in blood, deeper red at the centre of her, and watery at the edges. Above it, where the width had filled and lifted out over the curved bulge, it now lay ruffled flat, in folds at cross purposes. She looked beyond it, and aside, through trees, to find herself at the top edge of the clearing - where the man had walked out. Her neck could not take much more; it was beginning to shake. With her last seconds she looked for him, in all directions, but she was alone. Then she let her head fall back, and found herself completely out of breath, drawing in air.

Twigs cracked and someone stepped closer. Sun-a did not have the air in her lungs to feel alarmed. She merely rolled her head to the side and looked, the world at tilted angle, down the length of her body. She saw the foreign man, coming to a stop. He sidestepped into her vision, then knelt on one knee beside her. She could see him clearly now: the same face she did not have the thoughts to describe, no matter how much she stared. But she kept staring, and wondered if he would stop her.

He spoke; a language she had never heard before; a quick blur of sounds, that was instantly gone. He spoke again, perhaps the same words, but again, gone, into the forest behind, before she'd had a chance to hear.

He was looking right at her, simply kneeling. Not rushing yet. His eyebrows raised above his rounded eyes, a strange brown, questioning, kind she thought. But she felt fear, not wanting to disappoint. She kept watching, waiting for his next move, but still he stayed there. His head turned to the trees, and he squinted up to the sky, then back to her. Her eyes had not left him. He was beautiful, she thought; his face was strong though; she had never known there could be such faces to look at. And then the fear dropped over her like a breaking wave from some kind of memory and her heart was thumping. She felt she might die; its beat made her feel sick at the very thought of it in her chest, and the watery blood it failed to move, in squirts and stymied pulses through her head.

She did not want to. Not yet. She could not. And her heart dragged at her chest, until she was sure she would die. Yet, still she looked at him, and still he looked at her, kneeling by her legs, and his impossible eyes mirrored the terror she felt, somehow. He raised a hand to her, but did not touch her - held it above her waist, stuck, frozen. His eyes... His eyes were, not just a mirror. Their fear, was for her? She said, in a voice that seemed too weak even to be hers:

"Where did you come from?"

His expression changed. Just a glimmer.

A surge of pain rose up out of her belly, and she retched. Her back arched in spasm, as far as it would go, and a vile sound escaped her mouth. She had eaten nothing and it was forced from her bruised stomach and sicked up beside her. For a moment she was distant. The feel of the grass and ground against her cheek; the ache in her body; the blood rushing through her head. She had not known she felt sick.

Sun-a let her head roll back to where it would go. She saw the lines of branches over her and the leaves. He had made that for her, she thought.

***

Mick waited for her to fully wake. Her sleep had been still - worryingly so; a young woman lying flat on the ground, not moving. She stilled again, as one who realises they have woken. Her head lifted, not managing an inch, and her eyes looked for him. He stepped closer, and leaned down, resting his hands on his knees. His head level with the shelter, her view would have been of little more.

"Can you understand me?" he said slowly. "Do you speak any English?"

She watched him intently as he spoke, but her expression showed no sign of hearing meaning. And he spoke hardly any Japanese, or whatever language or dialect she did - apart from a few insults and basic military commands.

Her eyes had left his and were flicking about their limited view. Her mouth moved as if she wanted to say something. Panic spread over the features that had not understood. She tried to push herself up, but her arms were weak and the joints would not hold.

Mick dropped to his knees and put an arm beneath and around her back. Carefully, he propped her up to a gentle angle, mindful of her stomach and how the filthy dress creased. He knew he needed to find new clothes for her. Food. Water. Her eyes were back on him, looking closely into his as her head rested by his shoulder. She spoke words. He looked to her, joyful to see her talk, but feeling desperate that it meant nothing to him.

She was moving her hands. Mick leaned back to take in what she was trying to show him. He saw weak hands, that struggled not to hang limp at the wrists. They almost pointed, gestured, and hovered above her belly. Each hand parted to the side as if holding an empty bowl. Mick understood and looked down at her questioning, scared face. He nodded.

Adjusting on to one knee, he locked his arm and began to ease her upward, off the ground. Panic bloomed on her face and her weak neck fought not to lull back like a newborn's. Her hands pawed against his decrepit uniform, in fear, or to hold on. A crisp, discomforting sound made him hesitate, but he did his best not to let it show - even as beneath her it still cracked where it had set. He felt cold wetness at the small of her back where his other hand moved to support her; the thin dress was sodden and plastered to her skin. He thought of wallpaper paste, and another world he was surprised to recall; then of his resolution to find her fresh clothes.

He lifted her slowly upright, encouraging her legs to lock. Behind her he saw patches of earth on which she had lain, the sandy Asian soil dyed soft, uncomfortable pink. Blades of grass glistened, tinged white along their lengths.

He would not see it; he would preserve this girl some dignity. He would need to move the shelter; bury the evidence as best he could without disturbing the ground, more than was unavoidable. He would see to it that she was alright. She would need a bandage of some kind, to stop infection and exposure.

Then they were side by side, his arm around her, holding her up, she unsteady on her feet, wavering nauseously.

"Let me show you," he said.

Step by unsure step he led her through sparse cover, out into the open air of the oval clearing. Her head tilted back to the sky with a kind of relief, then fell down wearily. Sticking close to the tree line's edge, Mick walked with her around to an adjacent side, from six o-clock to three. She would look to him, questioning, then concentrate on the ground in front of her, and moving the legs that within a day had so quickly forgotten how to walk.

Mick slowed their slow pace down. He did not know if she had any clue as to where they had arrived, and supposed that he'd done his job too well. He looked to the young woman beside him, and waited for her to understand.

Before them, in the first few yards of the tree line, before roots grew thick, was a slight lump of loose soil. He had considered a headstone, perhaps just two crossed twigs, but it was already more than could be risked.

Mick looked back to her and saw understanding come.

She stepped from him and immediately dropped to her knees at the foot of the tiny unmarked, hidden grave. It seemed wrong to catch her after what she had done. So Mick took a step back, and let her slump there, creased to the side. It could have been disturbed ground, pawed and kicked up by some digging animal. The baby had been tiny, but he had looked at it in his hands and seen a human being like himself. Surely that potential alone, made it a crime. He had dug as deep as he could allow himself – to hinder any cat or local animal from scavenging it. He had flattened the ground without pressing with his boot, evening the small lump until it was hard to see, and then scattering loose soil, leaves and twigs with no order. But it was still a grave for those who knew.

From where he stood he could see little of the woman's face. He did not think he saw tears. She seemed to be looking forlornly, like one who wasn't really looking. Again, he averted his gaze.

Mick looked about him, finding his soldier's instinct come oddly at that time. Search parties could have walked from the encircling trees at any moment. He could be in the guarded back of a lorry within the day, perhaps standing before a firing squad by midnight. But he had no choice; but to stand and respectfully observe the funeral, and to walk slowly when it was over.

***

Mick crouched down beside the shelter in its new location, further back from the clearing. It prised out against narrowly driven trees that staked up around it like an odd balustrade. It would leave marks and grooves on the tree bark, and there would be stab wounds into the earth which could be covered, but never returned to how the ground had been before. He registered every concern, but out of training and ingrained expertise, which red flagged with alarm any and every lapse. The former site was now covered, but he was under no illusions. They were sitting ducks. And yet, as he knelt beside the young, still-scared woman, and saw her eyes questioning again, he knew with a growing clarity why he was doing it.

"I won't be long. I have to go." He pointed with both arms, away into the forest, where the plateau dropped away under dark canopy, down an unexplored slope. "That way. I will go. But I will be back. Do you understand? I'm coming back."

Her eyes flicked between his mouth and gaze, trying to pick out the meaning, the connection. When her eyes were back on his own, Mick nodded to her. "Stay here." He pointed to the ground. "Wait. I'll be back."

Then he stood. He backed away slowly, eyes not leaving hers. His palms felt the trees that protected her, and he wound around them, then turned and moved quickly into their ranks, disappearing from her sight.

***

He ran beneath a low canopy, trying to keep steady pace, trying to conserve what energy he would find. Brief bursts of sunlight heated his back and flared across his shoulders, showing elongated shadows of branches and patterns of leaves on the ground – a ticking clock as the sun descended west. He wiped the sweat from his brow on the brazed threads of his old uniform. Too long with nowhere to run; too long in the hold of the ship; too weak.

Pines arrowing across slopes, then spreading bows wide; deciduous ground, copses; locked like puzzle pieces across the terrain. And from the trees, a constant screech – an insect, bird-like pitch, high up, hidden; then at shoulder height, and he looked frantically as he darted by, but never saw it. Like the calls from Asian jungle, hidden, on the march, until he lay in wait, or lay down to sleep. Like the Indian cicadas, but one peculiar to this place.

The forest thinned into clear air; the ground dropped, rolled, then fell away. He came to a standstill on the high edge of a ridge, which shed the trees that had tried to cover it; they seemed to have slipped off the mountainside, a dense crowd that would have longed to climb back up. And in the open air, he saw the country he was in.

The steep slope below led to a narrow valley. Tree covered mountainsides faced him, spurs holding the ground in wide waves. He saw the thread of a dirt road; the boundary walls of paddy fields; thatch and tile roofs through branch and foliage. Counting the structures; trying to ascertain their use; already planning his approach. In the distance, wide farmland, settlement, more triangle peaks across the horizon.

He had never seen mountains like these before. They stretched out down the valley, like a series of small volcanoes. Too big to be called hills; each with its tree covered summit; too low in the sky to really be mountains.

He didn't know where he was. He looked again to the valley below; he looked up to the sky. The sun was falling low. He did not have much time. He had to get what he needed and be back before nightfall. Trying to navigate the wooded slopes in darkness could see him missing her by a magnitude of mountains. He might never find her again.

He looked from the beautiful view, his mission clear, and dropped over the edge of the mountain.

***

Light was low. From behind the final cover of the mountainside he waited and observed. Faint voices drifted from the far side of a row of four single storey houses. The speakers were hidden from his current viewpoint, but the sound was stationary, and the voices in conversation, overlapping, good humoured, in their later years. He should have used caution, acquired a new location, and confirmation of the situation he was about to rush into; but there was no time. A quick glance up found the sun gone. It had dropped behind the green peaks. They were not that high.

He moved, out where he could be seen. Keeping low, moving at the pay-off between speed and light footfalls, he crossed the ground, and pressed his back to the first building. Mick watched his angles, but saw no one. He turned around the building's mud brick corner into the scene he had viewed from the mountainside: to his left plants struggled in a vegetable garden, before hoed ground tapered to a point and a low soil-heaped wall marked the boundary with rough land; where the garden met the rough path before him, a row of waist high jars sat, pottery dyed in red splashes around their sides and rims. He had no time to wonder at their contents – only to be reminded that not all details could be seen from a distance. He ducked his plus six-foot height beneath the thatch overhang of the low roof, and entered the now real scene. He moved along the narrow width of the hut, stopped at its final edge, and cautiously looked out at the front of the buildings.

A dirt track ran through rough, foreign ground, which grass could not seem to manage to cover. Onto this street-front the row of huts faced, each with bare earth before it. Past the furthest house was half an aging woman, sat side on, plainly dressed. The corner of the last house cut her in two down the middle, but Mick could see her cheek muscles moving with talking, evidently to unseen people who also sat on the raised wooden platform. In front of two of the houses was spread drying produce: red vegetables and something brown and numerous that covered the earth like a mat. From the nearest of the houses, home-made string ran to a near-dead tree twenty feet away, on which hung drying clothes.

Mick rounded the corner, ducking the softly blowing fabric, keeping close to the wall, feet stepping slowly, eyes on the woman. He knew he was about to leave his most obvious marker yet as to his whereabouts. He didn't falter. He moved aside through the first door, stooping into the dark, unknown interior. There was no one inside.

A second room showed through wooden-post frame, the thin woven reeds which made a mattress on the floor. The main room contained a plain, aged table, a simple dresser against a wall, and a cooking area. He went to it quickly. Fighting the imperative to work at speed, aware that a nick on a lid of an unknown pot could chime like a bell, he searched the assortment before him. In one pot was rice flecked with chaff; in another some kind of khaki paste; in others, nothing; in a tall ceramic jug, water.

He slowly lifted the jug and poured at a close trickle into one of the pots. He gently set the rough ceramic base silently back on the dirt ground, took the cup in both hands and brought it to his parched lips. He poured a small amount of the cool, grainy water into his mouth. His throat stilled at the mercy of it, and he felt strength and alertness return. He gulped down upturned streams over the rim. Levered the jug again; fought to pour slowly, carefully, then gently to set it back on the ground, and still slowly to drink.

He filled the pot, as close to the brim as he could risk this time, seeing a simple pastoral scene engraved into the urn's side, figures, facing each other. A glance to the vacant entrance, greens at distance outside. He took an extra, manageable jar, stacked it atop the lip of the urn, and stepped up to the doorway. He leaned his head slowly out into what seemed bright light: a quiet valley, dominated by sharp mountains.

He had to get the food. He left the doorway and moved beneath the stalks of the roof, along the front of the house - eyes ever on the sliced-figure. He paused, as she rolled back with laughter, but saw her attention far from him as she pointed like a repeating jab at the friends whose laughter and sing-song replies pealed out with her own.

He crossed a narrow alley, jars standing guard, blocked by a resting cart. He moved along the wall of the second hut. The woman continued to face away as he drew nearer, to the second front door. He stilled, noticing his breathing grown too loud, and held it down - then stuck his head into the black silhouette of the doorway. No scream, no flurry of arms and legs at his face. He came back out to the glaring openness of the earth yard - the woman and her conversation still unknowing, fifteen yards away. He eased down slowly, and placed the tower of pottery onto the ground.

Peppers and chillies, familiar from his time in India yet of a different breed, were spread out before him, baked in the day's sun. The mat of brown was made of large, dried insects, - cicadas - many with transparent wings still on their backs. Insects could make-do in the place of meat for a time - he could vouch for it. She would need them.

He reached out slowly, far from the cover of wall and overhang, and picked one of the cicadas from the ground. Despite its hardened shell it was oddly light in his hand, so that for a split-second of fear he thought it had crawled out from his fist, and would buzz into the sky its own warning. Carefully, he placed it in the bottom of the jar, feeling its crisped wings flake at their edges against his calloused fingers. A nervous glance at the still talking woman, and then he took two more of the hardened carapaces into his hand. Hardly daring to breathe he lowered his hand into the pottery again, and let them down. Their hides clacked together as they found the earthenware floor, like the rattle of urgent insect speech, reanimated in a sudden frenzy. Mick froze. The woman exclaimed. His eyes were down on the insects in their tens, and hundreds. The conversation ran on with laughter, light-hearted.

He reached for another cicada and placed it into the jar.

CHAPTER 14

Amongst the trees she could not say when the sun set, or when it was still low. There was simply a deep gloom, that had sunk over the tree tops and slowly pressed down to the ground. She had watched the wound branches and leaves above her, seeing their colours disappear into darker and darker greys, until brown and green were all but the same, except to her vague memory of what they had been. As she lay still on the patch of earth she looked at the stem which had been the brighter green, and the brown of a mottled branch, but the whole world above her had fled. Her mind drifted in the grey-dark.

She heard a footstep crackle on twigs. Terror bloomed in her and she felt it spreading out like blood from a point on her tummy. She turned her head, sharply to look over her shoulder. Her belly stretched, about to tear. No one moved in that glimpse. She looked away. In the fading grey, on her skirt, caught and pulled against the ground, she could not truly see the red spread out. She knew it was there. Then she heard it - another crackle. Had it been a footstep? Could an animal have put that weight on the ground?

Was it him? Or had she been found? She was nothing to them. Yet if they found her, she knew that wouldn't matter.

Then the solitary crunches became a padding, of a human stride. Sun-a swallowed. She twisted painfully and bearing the grimace, peered out behind her. The world she saw was near-upside-down, askew, with trees slatted across her view at an angle. In the dimness with the grey slice upon grey, with the pain stretching through her belly, she held herself there, waiting. Her eyes flared wide and she fought to make them focus.

The foreigner moved through the trees. Sun-a let her twisted body right itself. She collapsed back onto the ground and lay there, her stomach white hot with pain.

****

Mick dropped to his knees beside her and eased the bundle of fabric and pottery carefully down. His arms coursed with overwork and he could only hunch forward on all fours and let the biting pain subside. His lungs finally had their chance to catch up after the climb; slowly the pain which racked across his ribs began to ebb away. Thank God he had found her – unable to see his own track in the dim light, following a recollection of the path in daylight.

When his arms could be used again he loosened the wound fabric and lifted the top jar onto the ground. Carefully, he took hold of the bottom pot; tested his grip on it to be sure. Then he nudged closer to the girl.

"I've brought water."

In the darkness, in the shadows of the trees, he could still see her wide eyes, looking at him, expectant yet not daring to expect far from the worst.

The man shuffled closer on his knees and Sun-a couldn't understand his words. She sensed the pottery was for her, and when he tilted it in her direction she pushed painfully up onto her elbows. She kept her eyes on him as the pot moved toward her mouth. Only at the last moment did she let her eyes glance inside; but she could see only deep blackness. He leaned the pottery further and Sun-a felt cold on her lips and chin. It was a feeling that seemed so unfamiliar, from another time and forgotten part of her life. Her heart leapt at the realisation of wetness, and she had pushed herself higher to meet it as more water filled her mouth. She gulped it down with difficulty that surprised her, like a child who needed to be told when to swallow, and streams of it spilled from her mouth, down the front of her chest.

He tilted the pot upright and took it slowly away. She watched it leave with a pine of regret; noticing, etched lines on its side; something ornate. She hadn't even known she had been thirsty, but she was sure she could have drunk it all. She said nothing, and watched him set it down, feeling the constant fear that she always carried with her, waiting for what he would do next.

Mick placed the urn where a stray, careless foot could not knock it, against the butt of a small sapling, struggling under the canopy. He turned to the jar of food – of insects and peppers, both of which would have heaved the stomachs of most English folk, him included not many years ago. He reached into the dark contents, feeling the unpleasant scuttle of insect feet and the sheen of wrinkled, waxy chillies as his fingers moved past them. Retrieving a small chilli, he held it from the jar, hoping to catch a little moonlight.

"Look. Can you see? Do you like?"

Laying it on the ground, he reached back in and then unfurled his hand before her, to reveal three of the large insects on their backs, wings stiff and frozen as if in mid-flight. He watched her eyes lit with a tentative happiness, flit from the insects to his face and back.

"Take one, please. All three if you can manage."

Mick pushed his open hand fractionally toward her. His free hand he laid beneath the other in the clearest sign of offering from his own culture. She smiled, a flicker, briefly, checked his eyes again, then moved to reach for them.

Sun-a felt herself falling back with surprise. Her head banged on the ground, her weak arm that had failed to hold her weight, uncomfortably trapped behind her back. The foreigner was there suddenly through a quick sound of scrabbling dirt. His arm eased under the arched nape of her neck; his other reached across her to take hold of her side with strong fingers. Then she lifted up.

She rested against his strong arm, sitting upright, hardly daring to breath. He took his hand from her side, brought it back; it passed over her, and she watched it all the way, following it with turn of the head and eyes. He again held out the cicadas in the palm of his hand. She wondered for a second at where he had found them, but then ravenously took one of the dried, broad insects, plucked its wings, let them flutter away into the still air, and split its body to reveal the softer insides. As she pressed the nutty flesh to her mouth and nibbled it free with her front teeth, Sun-a became aware again of the man watching her, intently, with fascination on his face. She tried not to be aware, to look away and eat with no further thought – but she could suddenly think of nothing else: the pressure of his arm against her back, holding her steady, and the closeness of his face, just the turn of her neck away. She munched as quietly as she could on the crisp insect, and swallowed, alarmed at the loudness of her throat and dried saliva. As casually as she could she reached into his palm, which had been waiting for her, and trying not to touch his skin, carefully picked another cicada between delicate finger and thumb.

Mick watched the young woman self-consciously put the insect to her mouth. He leaned back, feeling overly aware of his proximity to a fragile girl. Clearly she had eaten these creatures before, and knew what she was doing, better than he did. A scene came to mind, of British girls feasting on insects in a summer meadow and he smiled at the thought – then planed his face and looked out into the now night-time forest. She had an appetite, that was a good sign. It was the next stage that troubled him, and had been doing for the duration of his trek back up the mountainside.

After another cicada the girl rested her hands by her side, and Mick felt her hair turn on his arm. He glimpsed down to see her eyes, inches away, holding fear and the unknown, waiting. Careful not to rock her, Mick leaned aside and reached for the fabric. Clumsily, he tugged a garment loose and shook it out. In the darkness a dress unfurled. Moonlight caught it as he tried to hold it aloft with one hand: folds and creases, gathered at an edge, glowing ghostly white, before disappearing into black; new lines rippling into apparition before fading quickly.

"It's a dress. For you to change. Clean clothes."

He smiled at the girl, who glanced from him to the hanging cloth. He brought it closer and into her tentatively reaching hands. She said something then.

Mick sought to reassure. She could not understand. Perhaps it was for his own benefit that he spoke. "We need to get you into a fresh change of clothes. Your dress is dirty." He awkwardly pointed to her dark mid-riff while holding a clump of new dress, lest she drop it. "You'll get sick if you stay in this."

"Where did you get it?" she asked again. Sun-a felt the fabric in her hands. It was clean, and she felt surprise at how much her heart lifted within her at that simple sensation. She could feel the threads within it, well washed, and rough, comfortably so. It was someone else's skirt.

The kind man began to stand from kneeling. His arm around her began to take her off the floor. Without her doing she was straightening up, and so she helped, though it hurt.

Mick eased his hold around her back as he sensed her find her balance. With his arm still in place, but barely against her, he gave the dress a gentle shake so that a wave travelled the cloth and drew attention. He mimed, as if taking clothing over his head.

"Yes?" Again he pushed forward the dress. "For you."

She looked at him, and nodded. For a moment Mick felt their world still at a fleeting understanding. Then she had reached and taken the dress; she seemed to measure the weight of it in both hands, and perhaps smile, though the blackness hid it. She gestured with a faint turn of the head, toward the forest on the plateau, and tried to point with a weak and falling arm.

She spoke in her language, a few short words, and Mick spoke in English, 'you want to...?'

He felt her move, though it took his eyes a second to perceive it, as her back turned slightly and the change in pressure threatened to leave his arm. He moved with her, doing his best to give her the freedom to step where she would, but unwilling to let her leave his support for longer than it took each step to catch her, and his arm to bump against her back.

She did not know how far they had moved from the shelter, but her lungs ached, though she tried to hide the gasps. She turned to him, turning in his arm's nook as she did, and realising how much of her strength was really his.

"Okay, here. Here. You can leave me here."

She could barely see him in the darkness that held there, further into the dense cluster of trees. She raised her hands, then hesitated. Cautiously she pushed her fingers against his chest, feeling the strange fabric of his foreign uniform press against him. He stepped back, and away.

"I will stay here. You go back. Please. I need you to go."

The man took another step back. She smiled a part of a smile that she could find, and hoped he glimpsed her gratitude. She could now see barely anything of him, other than a less-black promise of his shape amongst the darkness that was the forest.

Mick watched, unsure. He took another step away, and wondered if he should return all the way to the shelter. The gloom did not take her. She remained lit by slivers of light in the place she had stopped, and so she remained there for him as he did as she had asked. Then he saw her face, where a calm, a trusting, was washed over with fear.

Sun-a felt her legs reveal their lie. She wavered, alone in the dark night air. Her legs could not balance and began to fold at their knees. Suddenly there was nothing holding her up, and she felt herself beginning to collapse. Her eyes were on the figure of the foreigner she realised, where he had been, not asking for help so much as knowing that he was the only place from which it might come.

He caught her before she could fall. The shadowy outline of a woman was real again as he held her at close quarters and again took her weight.

"I've got you. It's okay. I've got you."

A trickle sounded out in the darkness. It splashed down beneath them and pattered the ground. She swayed against him, her arms beating with the force of fluttering moth's wings around his neck. He steadied her, pushed one of her legs wider with his foot, and let her wee onto the ground.

She was still moaning when he sat her down against a tree; her head shaking faintly and her voice ebbing with sobs when he left her and ran back to the shelter to pick up the provisions he needed. He returned, placed the blankets beside them, and on his knees took her hands.

"It's okay. Really, it's okay. But now, we need to get you out of these clothes and into a fresh dress. You'll feel better then, okay? I'm sure of it. A fresh pair of clothes always makes me feel like a new man. Come on, we're going to have to get you up."

Words babbled over her like water, a brook. And Sun-a held on around his neck and pushed up with her feet and legs, and though they held no strength, and couldn't lift to tiptoe, she found herself back, standing. The man leaned her gently against what must have been a tree, and then she felt him disappear for moments.

Mick reached for the pile of stolen, borrowed blankets. The top one felt rough to the touch and he moved it aside. The next of the three was the one he had in mind, less coarse, but not as thin as the last. He picked it up slowly, suddenly very aware of the girl's presence over his shoulder. He pressed the material between thumbs and fingers, though he had already decided on it, masking a different indecision.

He rose and turned, cloth draped in hand, and moved to her.

"I'm sorry," he said. "We have to... I have to. We can't risk infection."

He saw her eyes drift onto his, recovering, so weak, so utterly dependant, picked out by irises which held the elusive light. Mick swallowed, moved closer and took one of her loose hands. He turned it over, palm to the night sky, and pressed the fabric gently upon it. He curled her fingers slowly around, and pushed them into a hard grip. Her eyes awakened at the action.

"Hold this. Okay? I'll do the rest, if you can't."

He was back with her and she heard his deep voice, and felt softness in her hand. She looked down, and saw that she was holding something, and that his palms were holding her, pressed over and below. There was earnestness in his face, looking at her so close. She looked away, hearing his unknown words back, with delay. Shame dwelled, at what had happened, though she was never without it. This was different. One of his hands moved from hers, and she held onto the cloth, taking control of her fingers by recalling a memory. Again he looked to her, and seemed to nod and ask a question with his gaze. Earnest. As if her answer, truly concerned him. Her tired eyes lingered on his own, even on the place his gaze had been, once it was no longer there. She felt her floor-length skirt lifting up her knees. It was cold and sticky and dragged on her skin.

The undergarment had become a wet, wrung-out line of string between legs and in the black he carefully pulled it fully to ground. He guided her hand from behind, whilst raising the stained dress out of the way. He felt her refuse to give way, as the movement asked her stomach to bend. Carefully, he eased back a little, and brought her hand and arm down gently. It was enough. He took the young woman's hand down between her legs, feeling the bloody, wet hem of the dress uncomfortably brush his arm.

He went down to one knee, and reached their hands, his below, hers on top holding the cloth, between her legs. Moving slowly upwards he felt resistance, then carefully took the girl's hand, clasped gently over the knuckles, back and forth, cleaning the wound. She flinched and he glanced up at the acute angle to her eyes. They were wide and unmoving from him, through the darkness, not angry or violated, as part of him, he realised, had feared; but wide and waiting, holding back wells, not for now, but for the fear of what every next moment might bring. They dared not look away. Mick had to; they were all he could see in the shards of moonlight.

She felt his grip move from the back of her hand, but her own hand fell away with it, and he caught her and brought her back. Every move of the fabric hurt her, and she was shocked at how sore the feeling was. But she knew he was helping her, if only for now, and she could feel the sticky pull of gunge and blood and murdered child, that had to come off.

The cloth was set aside in a ragged heap on the soil. Again Mick looked up, this time finding her head lulled back against the tree, her throat swallowing for her drained body. There was water left he could give her, when back at the shelter. He hurried on, wanting the task completed and past. He took up the damp hem once more and lifted it up her thigh, trying to hold it off, from slickly streaking her skin.

Mick tried not to look, even in the darkness that hid most of her from him. Yet he knew that he could, and felt it tugging within him to glance at what he had no right to see. He looked away. With one hand he found an arm at her side, and lifted it high. He reached across to her other side, and took the unresistant arm up to the other, which drifted loosely in the air above, brushing a few low twigs. Her took her thin wrists into his grip and held them there, then with his other hand holding the filthy hem of her dress, lifted it up over her body.

His eyes fixed on the ground that could not be seen, he was all but a blind man, standing close to the woman he was undressing. As the damp dress lifted, the fabric caught on her, and slowed.

"Hanbok..." he heard her say, and murmur further.

He sensed her head faintly shaking, side to side. He looked down, and made out the ravelled dress clasped in his hand; it was bunching against the overlap of a kind of high blouse. He understood. He should have looked at her clothes. It was a skirt, and the one from the clothes line the same; and likely fastened the same.

He leant closer still, feeling himself tower over her small, meek form, and reached around her. His hand searched across the pleats and the band atop the strange skirt, as he turned his face away to the blackness and silver forms of trees. He stopped, his fingers feeling out the shape of a bow. One armed – the other still holding the soiled dress from her – he pulled gently on the thread; firmer, and felt it pull free. The skirt loosed around her chest where it had been held tight, and prised open, falling toward him. He took it in both hands, folding it hurriedly, stepping away.

Sun-a was wide awake. The haze had faded, and her senses returned, one after another piecing together her surroundings. Her skirt pulled from her, as she felt her thighs, and then tummy grow cold with night air. She tensed, but did not resist; she felt nerves, not fear. The blood spilled skirt faded into the blackness and was gone, and she was standing, free of it.

He stepped away for a moment and scooped the third and thinnest of the sheets from the ground. He folded it along its length, into a narrow strip, less than half a foot wide. He dropped to his knees on the dirt and quickly reached between her thighs, then pulled the folded sheet from behind, and back round. It was impossible not to look, and he was thankful the night and her own shadow hid her. He threaded the sheet, making figure eights around either leg, looping it around and around, then once up around her waist, tying it at her hip. The bandage complete, he quickly took the clean skirt from the ground and stood tall in front of the woman. She wore only what he now saw to be the short blouse – fastened to the right of her chest by what had been a wide red ribbon in the day. He looked unwaveringly into her eyes, to be sure he looked no lower.

She looked at him, feeling her breath had been caught in the surprise at what he had done, and that she needed to gasp. There was no time, for he spoke in his language and spread a new skirt around her, correctly taking it under her arms, beneath the overlap of the blouse, stepping so close to wrap around, behind her. She held her arms out, drifting in the air beneath the branches. The skirt pulled tighter over her bosom, and for the first time he hurt her. Then looser, comfortable, as he stepped back, the skirt tied. There was a sudden calm between them, and he was a step further away. He nodded to her, very slightly, his mouth tight, but holding something of warmth, smile, in the darkness. Sun-a didn't know what to do, and nodded in return, in agreement.

Leaving the dirty materials to be recovered and buried later, Mick abruptly moved alongside the girl and put his arm around her to bear her weight. He began to walk, then held a step until she saw his intention and took her own. They stepped and side-stepped slowly back between the trees to the shelter.

CHAPTER 15

The tree was hard against his back, uncomfortable, but wonderfully unmoving. He felt his back and shoulder blades crack at the first hint of relaxation, and was surprised at the feeling of his muscles letting go. Tension ebbed away into the bark and trunk which propped him up.

He had chosen a trunk ten feet away from the girl under the shelter - one with a clear line of sight, with other dark stakes only at intervals to either side. He looked down the gulley, marked eerily by the thin shafts. Below a hovering, brooding black cloud, unrecognisable as the canopy, they seemed to have been driven into the earth from above; and he, and she, were players in some kind of Greek tale. Looking to either side he saw the forest staked out like a maze, grey and less than grey, and deceiving his eyes. He focused back on the barely visible blackness of the shelter, and the shadows beneath where the girl lay, and pulled himself out of the gloomy imaginings.

He never had paid enough attention to those stories in school. Nor to Latin. Nor to much at all if he was honest with himself. The distance descended on him; it had once fallen regularly, but with time was ever less familiar: the contrast between the life that had been, and the life he was now living. The present, on a forested plateau, between mountains, God-knew where. And she knew where. Again he looked into the blackness. Perhaps they could communicate. She could tell him. That was a valuable reason to have helped her so; to have expended so much effort and put himself in a vulnerable position. Yet, he knew that was not the reason that had placed him amongst these stakes, in this Greek drama. From somewhere it came to mind, that were not all Greek tales tragedies?

The nights there, wherever he was, were less humid than on Formosa at start of summer, yet still warm after the quickly heating days. If anything should change, she had her blanket. The trees chirped with an incessant noise; on a branch nearby he saw the outlined shape of the large winged insect from their dinner; it beat its hind body, calling out with a small roar. A kind of cicada; similar yet unknown in its wail, its screech, as from the continent before the boats. A breeze, a brief push of air through the trees, moved by, and then stilled. He eased his head back, and stretched out some more of the unrelenting readiness and tension from his muscles. He breathed out and heard a sigh, the kind made before sleep.

* * *

Mick woke with his back hard against the tree. He did not know how long he had slept. The sky was still black, and still hidden above the low, huddled tree canopy. The moon was still out reflecting slivers of light through the foliage and branches, but he could not see its position in the sky. He looked over to the sleeping form of the girl, under the shelter he had built for her. Staring, he made out her shape, in the darkness, deeper black, against shadow. He squinted, then pushed up from where he sat. His bones and muscles protested and his knees cracked, reluctant to give up their slumber.

He peered down as he stumbled closer to the shelter. He thought he saw her, then felt his stomach lurch as his eyes adjusted to their night fog and he realised she wasn't there. He turned quickly to the left, then right, with a panic that shocked him. Ghostly trees in all directions. Greys and blacks, and every way the same. Moving quickly, he threaded his way between the trees, making for the clearing, pulling himself from one leering trunk to the next, like a man climbing on skis. A memory of icy slopes and hills, and fleeing and shooting. He couldn't place it. And guns firing. Why couldn't he place it? And then clear as looking through frozen mirror-like ice, he knew he was on the mountain, with the woman he had found, and that more than anything he had to find her.

He burst out into the clearing, not seeing the tree line until it was passing to either side of his vision, and behind him. Again, he looked frantically to his left and, saw her there, lit faintly in the moonlight. She was sitting on the ground, back to him, facing out across the open space. Her long black hair lay down her back, gleaming like some carved precious stone, sculpted beyond beautiful. He opened his mouth to call to her, but did not know her name. How had he never asked her her name?

With cautious steps that did not want to startle her, lest she take flight like a deer, or fade like an apparition, he stepped closer. His footsteps were quiet on the sparse grass and ground. She could surely hear him, but she did not turn around. He manoeuvred aside and around, to circle in front of her. As he turned his body and searched for a view of her face, hoping to see calm and the sad, subdued features he so desperately longed to, even missed, she did not move. A sheet of black, obsidian hair, and the night, hid her from him. Even as he stepped round, far into her vision, still he could not see.

Her head turned, and looked ever so slightly up. The hair moved aside to reveal her face, and the moonlight caught her features. She glared at him, with wide English eyes, accusation, and blame, and all on the verge of crying. Her hair was blonde he saw, as the folds of night that hid it parted for a moment from their masquerade.

"How could you leave me?" the woman asked, her head shaking, her blonde curls tussling.

So pretty, so petrifying. Her black-blue eyes stared through him, and her face was pale. Not just by the silver light, but by the whiteness of death. Her eyes were wider than eyes should ever be, and they asked without mercy.

"I loved you, but you never wrote back. I searched for you, but you didn't care. You didn't look for me."

Mick stumbled back, away from Miranda. His hands flung to his head and gripped each side, vice-like. He could not bear to look away. Beneath the long black hair was the girl he had run with across the village green – had led by the hand, and pressed up against the church wall. Had left to die because she had believed his lies. He screamed and pressed so hard against his skull that it should have burst.

****

Mick awoke with a terrified need to breathe, and slid from the thin tree trunk which held him upright. Almost too late, his arm unfolded from sleep and levered between him and the ground, before his face hit and tested the solidity of the pitch blackness. For moments he stayed there, staring into utter darkness, unsure whether dirt was inches from his face, or whether he looked down over a bottomless chasm. The smell of soil and forming dew pulled him from the nightmare, and his surroundings formed in their three dimensions in his mind. With a shaky, aching arm, he pushed himself upright and collapsed back against the tree. My God, what had that been? He exhaled, and let steady breaths find their way to his lungs once again. They seemed strange to him, like something not belonging. Like a man tasting free food when he knows full well he should have been convicted.

His hand went to the pocket for the letter that was always there. He padded it and felt the crumpled paper under the worn fabric.

He looked over to the sleeping form of the girl, beneath the shelter he had built. He could not see her well. Only shadow, and blackness against blackness. He trusted that the shape was hers.

***

The rain gave a few seconds pattered warning, before it drilled down with Japanese intensity. It pounded through the seemingly dense canopy: he heard leaves barged aside in the dark overhead, boughs and shoots blasted; and heavy drops coalesced and splashed down on the forest floor all around. He hurriedly placed their pottery beneath pouring streams and watched joyfully as glimmers of water shone and sounded small fountains on the clay. He relaxed his head back against the trunk and drank in the much needed, cool, clean water. The rain continued, and he waited, setting himself to hold out. The pots filled quickly and he secured them beneath eaves of foliage beside the shelter, then sat back down against the tree in the driest spot he could find. Cool relief in the summer night changed with alarming haste to cold, damp hair and uniform, beginning to numb. The rain went on, unrelenting, as if its mission was to drive him from his trunk under bombardment. He sat, drubbed, and soaked, refusing to move from his watch.

The shelter was feet away. Its entwined foliage shook under the barrage, but held. He delayed, for moments more in the downpour; waited, pointlessly waited it out. He didn't want to do it. He held back, then in reluctant acceptance of the situation, sprang up and ducked quickly to the cover.

There was room to the side of the girl and he huddled his knees there beneath the shelter. He looked down to her, quiet, relatively dry beneath her blanket, occasional drops finding their way through the fronds and leaves and making soft splashes onto the material. Reluctantly, he stretched out his legs, and levered back on his elbows, finally putting his head onto the ground. He knew that if he turned to look, her sleeping face would be somewhere there in the darkness. So he looked up at the quaking shelter and closed his eyes. No search party would be out in this weather; it was the only sensible thing to take shelter.

He had thought the blackness that of eyes closed, but found they were open and that he was seeing the faint outline of branches above. His chest was rising and falling with breaths that would never see him asleep. He tried to concentrate and slow his heart, and ease out the cranks that held his back in a broken, uncomfortable arch, not truly lying on the ground. His heart thumped in his chest and refused to slow. It resonated beneath the rain: the sounds of ten thousand drops trying to fall their way through the canopy, making a storm in the forest. He thought of the girl, and how their paths had crossed in this world, to that plateau in the mountains, of where he did not know, with the crashing forest canopy shuddering above them, and he thought of the clouds above that he could not see, and of how he could not sleep.

There was movement aside and he saw the woman looking at him. Her eyes were open, opaque in the drowned moonlight and rain filled air, like marble pools. He thought he saw sadness there. Then she blinked and the surface was broken; her head turned slightly out of the thin, surviving light. She was uncomfortable, changing her position. He looked down and saw her open her legs, and painfully shift across the muddying ground, closer to him. She pulled the blanket aside.

Mick was at a crouch and back and away, stumbling for balance. His back clattered the edge of the shelter as he stood too quickly and jumped clear. Leaves were pulled free and his drenched army shirt caught, fraying the side. Free of the shelter he stood in the open, soaked air, and looked into the hidden shadows where only the girl's two closed feet could be seen. He gasped for breath, and the relentless rain chased air away from each gulp.

"What are you doing?" he shouted with the drumming all around him.

Streaming with dark water from the sky, he stared, his head shaking, asking. He could see nothing beneath the shelter, not if she was looking back at him, nor the expression on her own face in reply to his.

His shoulders slumped and he back-stepped to the tree that had been his watch. In the steady rain he sat down, and let his arms droop over his knees. He caught his breath, and looked over to the hidden enclave of the shelter, and still could see nothing.

***

The day was crisp in the air above her. Sun-a was wide awake, as if from nowhere, and the details of the veined leaves and wilting ferns of the shelter were sharp in the light. It must have been at least late morning. Not much later. She could tell somehow in an instant, by the newness of the air around her, and the far sounds of birds. She lifted her head, and felt a moment's exultation at the strength in her neck. He wasn't there, in her line of sight, where she seemed to remember him sitting.

An odd sensation dawned on her, and she realised she had expected to see him there. It had been his voice after all that had woken her from her sleep. Wide awake.

Then she recalled like a river bursting a dam and rushing into her mind, what she had done. Her head dropped back to the damp dirt and she almost gasped with horror at the full recollection. The urge to turn over on her side and curl up small, and hide away from it against the ground was almost consuming. But she fought it and lay flat as she deserved, and hated herself. She looked up again, to the place where he had been, and then around about her, with quick turns of the head. He was not there. He was gone.

A sinking feeling, of great heaviness descended on her stomach, even though she was as flat as the ground itself. He had gone.

What had she done? He had held her dead baby in his hands, and buried it in shallow earth. He had seen her disgrace and the worst of her crime. And she had presented it back to him, with open legs. Like an open, seeping wound. Of course he had pulled away in disgust. She was disgusting. She'd seen herself mirrored on his expression. Though it had been dark, the move of his mouth, cheeks, the light in his eyes, through the blackness. Revulsion for her. She was alone. The reprieve that had come from nowhere and that she had never deserved, had left her. She was alone, and he had gone, as was only right.

And yet, his voice had woken her.

Sun-a froze, at the sound of Japanese.

She dared not breathe: no murmur that would pick her out in the quietness like quarry. She must wait and hope that the rain had smudged out her presence.

She saw them a moment after: two men in well-known and hated uniform, peering at her between the trees, one pointing the way to his friend with outstretched hand. Index finger directly on her.

Sun-a thought about clawing from the shelter on hands and knees, and running; but she could never get away. She could not outrun soldiers, not with the pain in her belly and the weakness that occasionally trembled up and down her legs, that would see them fall out from under her. And once they had chased and caught their prey, the rest would be inevitable. Far better to keep still and let them not think of her like that – anymore than she feared and knew they already did.

So she lay as she was, as they had pointed her out. They approached, keeping their eyes on her for an escape, as they ducked branches and carefully trod out unknown ground. There were smiles as they drew close and saw she was not fleeing. Sun-a swallowed and knew her face was slick with fear. She had been used like this a thousand times, but not again. Not here. Not again, not this time, please.

One of them, with mountain-tiger ears beneath his small peaked cap, grinned with young vileness. The other, typically short, but taller, with an angular, cutting face, spoke. Their eyes were on her at all times.

"It is very house..."

No. They'd said, 'easy.' Her Japanese was poor; she rarely spoke it.

"What is she... here?"

She could see the thoughts coalescing in their eyes. The possibilities. The limits, as they sized them up. She read the evil there, far clearer than she could read words on paper. She could see it writing across their yellowed, bloodshot eyes; knew their minds before they did.

"She's.... fucking whore. Must be... close to the prison."

"What are you doing here girl? Where's your husband?"

The tiger laughed beside his friend.

"Did you run...? Didn't get very far, did you? Anyone... think you didn't... want to leave."

The angular one glanced his narrow eyes to his colleague and pulled his belt strap tight to free it from its notch.

Sun-a observed through a kind of detaching, intensifying numbness, their weight begin to shift, boots to lift, as they began their steps toward her. She winced inside at what was to come.

He came from behind them and to her left. His knife was raised. She could see where it was going before it struck. She realised her eyes would give him away, but then saw it would not matter.

He was already moving to the next Japanese before his hand had pulled away. He was over their shoulders, passed the sliver of space between them. As he whipped his hand back it span the choked man a quarter circle. There he began to fall to his knees to die facing empty forest.

Sun-a watched with staring face as her protector moved with frightening speed. The knife stabbed the second man before he had time to look to his colleague. His hand snapped angrily by his side in search of his rifle. But the knife was out of the kidney at his side and pulled savagely across the throat that had been turned. An immediate red line appeared in a blink where it had not been before, and the hateful man made an involuntary gulp, without the chance for a last breath of air.

Sun-a felt no pity, nor shock at her own self. He had not deserved any.

And still Sun-a saw the hand straining for the rifle. The fingers flicked it, strained at each of their horrible bony joints, then stayed strained, locked as they would remain in death. The Japanese man fell to his knees to face her, still wrestling for control of his dead arm and hand. Across the strained skin over his cutting cheek bones, a soul to be reviled looked out, straight at her in her shelter.

The foreign man pushed him over with a knee, and the man toppled, aside, to the dirt.

Those who would have attacked and used her lay dead. Sun-a breathed in a desperate, shaky breath, suddenly unsure if she had breathed in minutes. He had not left her. He had never left her. When she breathed out, tears trembled out with the air, and she found herself clutching at the soil for support, though her body lay flat. He was by her side, and speaking fast words, panicked, and frenzied; and hands on her shoulders, the sounds soothing. He said one thing to her, slowly, with eyes locked upon hers unblinking.

He was over her, arms spread like wings, sheltering, a movement away from cradling her. Instead Mick wrapped his span around her back and under her arms, and lifted her upward, even as she poured out words and tears. He had her on her feet, and still she was lost in sounds of relief, perhaps barely aware that she was standing on his strength.

He put a hand softly to her face, steadied it and brought its eyes to rest on his own. For a second the tenderness of the moment pushed aside even his own urgency at their situation. There was surprise there that he had created such a thing – and then away.

"We have to go now. To go." He pointed the way, jabbed his finger repeatedly. "Look." He gestured to the bodies. "We must go, now." He took a breath, taking in the sight of the young woman on his arm, knowing intimately her condition, and what he asked of her. "Run."

It was as if she knew the implication of the word. Her babbling quieted and she looked at him seriously, the whites of her eyes glistening from just stopped tears.

"Run. Together. Do you understand?"

She did not nod, but Mick saw the agreement between their stares. Quickly he stepped her over to the nearest tree. Each step she took was unsteady, each leg unsure of how its muscles could work together to lock and pivot. He refused to think on it. There were two choices: leave her with the dead to the same fate from which he had just saved her. Or take her with him. There were not two choices. There had only ever been one, from the moment he had glimpsed her from cover, alone in the clearing.

He grabbed the shelter in both hands, picked it up and tore his arms as wide apart as they would go. The lattice of branches ripped and leaves and moss fluttered free. Again he tore at it, angle by angle, destroying the signs of craft, into smaller and smaller pieces and flinging the evidence far and wide. He returned to the enemy soldiers, crouched down and turned one of the rifles over in his hands: useless Arisakas. Ineffective from range and most sure to kill when fired close behind a charge. A gunshot would be like ringing a bell to their location. Nevertheless, it might be needed. He detached the loose bayonet from the muzzle, looked over the sharpened sword blade and then took the scabbard from the side of the dead soldier to secure it. He dragged the rifle strap from trapped shoulder and flapping, falling arm, and the satchel of ammunition after it, which he filled back to the brim from the other soldier's half empty pack. He checked for provisions: only one of the men carried a canteen; no mess tin, no food - prison guards, recommissioned for his emergency. He threw the bottle's strap over his shoulder.

Sudden slowness amidst the pace: he brought the cup of rain water and held it gently to her mouth; as he carefully tilted the angle she took long, deep sips, gasping after each. He took his own rapid gulp, which would be his fuel for the test to come. He wrapped the one remaining blanket securely around their pots and the last handful of vegetables and insects. The gory knife he quickly wiped on grass then stowed back in his belt. He returned to the still standing girl and threaded his arm under hers and across her back. He looked to her and nodded the question with raised eyebrows. She nodded her reply with seriousness. Yes. She was ready.

Mick moved at once, at first taking her with him. A cry of pain, or difficulty, uttered from her, but when he glanced, her mouth was firmly closed and she was looking ahead. Trees passed them by, and still he carried the majority of her, while her legs struggled to find traction. But as the trees ahead began to visibly dip over the oncoming slope, they found pace. He looked at the girl, not expecting to see her dirty shoes hitting the ground at each step, and her grimacing face, determined through the pain she surely felt. Her steps were her own, even if her weight remained his.

They left the mountain plateau, and disappeared over the edge of the slope.

Behind them lay two slain figures in Japanese army uniform, and the telltale signs of a recent camp.

CHAPTER 16

Her belly coursed with pain. Each step twisted her stomach muscles diagonal-left, then diagonal-right, then diagonal-left. Onwards, and downwards, daggering her calf muscles, which hurt like she had never known them to. The foreigner guided them between trees, moving quickly, guessing their path. At times, a sound would escape her and she saw the concern, the care cross his brow, and felt their hurried walk slow. At such times she did her best, forced herself, to pick up the pace as much as her screaming muscles would allow. She would not be left behind. She would not give him a reason, though she knew he carried plenty already. She would not give him one more, in case that was the one which left her alone on the mountain slope, waiting to be recovered by the Japanese pursuers.

They stopped. He stopped, and she looked up from watching her feet, to find they had. Dense bushes scarred the air in front with thick interlocking twigs and thorns. Like an unmanoeuvrable cart from her youth they backed up awkwardly, and he pivoted them around. She couldn't help but cry out. The turn was slight, but her empty belly coursed with fire-like pain. At the horror on his face she stifled the cry – it felt like keeping her mouth shut to a frenzied animal that would prise open her lips with its claws and burst out. The man looked behind them, up the slope, then back to her. He said something, reassuring, though perhaps she had not heard truly in the agony. And then he was taking her onward, and she was making sure to keep step with his.

As her head lulled, and she fought to stay focused, it was like being carried by the wind. She walked, and yet her heaviness was elsewhere, and she was swept through the air. Trees passed by, trunk after trunk, dense all around. She fought to be there. He had rescued her. She had woken and thought herself lost. And now she was running through the forest. On the arm of the same man. Running, and carried by the wind. Escaping the Japanese, and everything in that old life.

***

The ground fell away beneath them. Even knowing that each step would drop deeper into nothing before it hit ground, the jar of impact on loose skidding soil, the slide out of control before the next step and plunge, was a shock and sickening surprise. It felt as though the mountain slope fell away beneath them. Perhaps behind her where her head could not turn, there was no ground, just a chasm of falling soil: upended trees, and trunks flung like haphazard spears skewered the soil-clouded air to the sky, always just one pained stride behind.

Mick carried her, though the fall carried them both. Trees rushed at him with frightening speed, so fast there wasn't a hope of avoiding a collision, until they were somehow past them and rushing onto the next stakes. Gravity had run them faster and faster, and he, with his arm around the girl and the other holding their scant belongings, had accepted its flight

They had to get as far from the dead soldiers, as quickly as possible. Tracks would be tracked regardless. Distance was key before nightfall, and then all the more.

***

The ground had levelled off in a minor valley between two slopes, and they wound with its arc, the young woman breathing with real effort. Every four or five shallow breaths she would gasp - a rhythm that maintained their difficult pace. Mick stopped without knowing he had made the decision.

Her weight rolled off his arm, and around, to face him against a tree. Their eyes met. Her head rocked a little with each shallow inhale. How much more of this could the girl take? He was killing her. The woman he was trying to save. She had only begun to recover from the abortion, and now he was driving her at a pace that would have had any trooper spitting phlegm with hands on knees.

She spoke her language - perhaps not Japanese; he wasn't sure - in-between rocking motion and salivaless swallows. Her eyes pleaded.

"I can still run."

Sun-a looked intently up at the tall foreigner. Perhaps she had not appreciated just how tall he was until standing there now in front of him.

He spoke something back in his language, flatter tones, that flowed easily one to the next, but less like a song than her own. His hands gestured something about staying, and he rested on an adjacent tree.

"We will catch our breath."

She seemed to understand. Her breathing slowed. Her lungs opened. They could wait a short while.

***

Darkness fell around them. He'd watched it, caught it, through rare breaks in the branches when it was just a little less than blue and the glimpse of cloud was unsettlingly off white. He'd needed it to hold off, for day and flight to stretch longer, for just this one time. Every glance at the gaps above, ever harder to spot, had pleaded. The light shone fainter through the canopy as they hurt and struggled to navigate the untrodden ground. Making their own path, aside slope, over rises too dense with thin trees and too sharp to be walked by any past travellers of this land. Their tracks could be followed, so make them lead where they ought not, to put moments of doubt and hesitation in their trackers' minds. It was something. Somewhere in the interior of his mind Mick knew it was pointless, but the need to keep the girl upright, and to fight the aching muscles of his arm – to keep going – was all. He held her steady, from shoulder to curved fingers, sometimes shaking for want of rest, seeing the near-tears of that expression, on that pretty, dirt streaked face, that he carried beside him. He looked away again, and to the forest, dark, darker than before the turn of his head. They had to stop. He looked to her again, and saw that the dim light hid her and the slashed dirt. Yet he knew where the streaks lay; he had seen with memory the lines that were too black to be made out. He looked away. They had to stop.

He guided her up the valley slope, further into the never-trodden dirt, further from where a path would most naturally fall. The ground was steep and the gradient change painful on calves. He dug in to reserves that had not failed yet, and carried her weight almost by himself, up the hill.

With the narrow valley bottom only just in sight, Mick stopped, and almost collapsed the girl to the ground, and he beside her. Sweat ran down his cheeks, and moisture, whether from his skin or the humid air, beaded on his brow.

Sun-a could barely gasp for air, so exhausted as she lay against the steep slope. Summer heat was all around, and yet she felt a cold running the length of her. Unable to hold her head from lulling left and right against the dirt head-rest, she let her eyes roll up and across to await orders. She saw him unfolding the bundle he had somehow carried beneath his other arm, carefully taking out their water jars and peering deep over them. The blanket unfurled and he ran his hand over it to test for spilled water, as he had done once before in daylight. This was their bed for the night. The thought came with such a wave of relief and thankfulness it was as if that soaked blanket had been pulled over to cover her snuggly. She felt its warmth at once.

****

Kamakura Hideyoshi stepped into the prison office. He was breathing too hard, composure a thing he could not secure. He rarely demeaned himself with disguise, but he saluted the higher ranked officer squat at the desk, and bowed through the rigidity of his belly.

Lieutenant Colonel Goro sat behind the desk. The rotund man covered a chair and did not stand upon Kamakura's arrival.

"Yes. Lieutenant Colonel." It galled him.

Goro saluted quickly, off guard. "Yes. You know we found two dead men. Never returned from patrol. Inland."

"I'm aware."

"I can't have him reaching Suwon, or being seen near Seoul."

The lieutenant looked ill. He shifted in his chair.

"I can't spare the guards," he went on. "To cover the inland. So a change of tactics."

Goro hated the attitude of the taller man, and that he, with his rank must be able to sit and command effectively.

"Take another five men. Track the bastard who made a fool of a few young soldiers. Quickly. And bring him back to be shot."

Kamakura felt his stomach settle with unexpected relief, and he sought to steady his face so that a smile would not force through: Goro had delivered him a reprieve. The junior doctor was lying in an unnamed compartment of the tiny hospital morgue. He had told no one – bar the on-duty nurses – of the incident. With distaste he readily accepted the other man's wrong move and made his mouth resume a sneer. "So you want me to mop up your mistakes, Lieutenant Colonel, before your superiors learn of them?"

"Before they learn of your mistakes, Kamakura. This search is under your authority. I'm sure a man of your record will not fail."

Goro paused, and though it might not serve him well, he said with pleasure: "You have a deputy now in your clinic. Take some time off from treating Syphilis. Use the skills of which you have often spoken, and find the foreigner who fell off a truck."

Goro's breath held a moment, as he watched the tone of his words sink into the taller man's unwielding countenance. For a moment he regretted it. He stood up behind his desk and saluted. Orders over; he wanted the man gone.

Kamakura Hideyoshi gave the salute, doing the action with venom and condescension in his eyes. The duty, and the indignation reared snake-like, side by side, cancelling each other out, and his moral core retained its sure footing. He would live with the hissing, temporarily.

He lowered his locked-knife palm, down to his side, not a movement out of place. As honour dictated. As Bushido dictated. And said "Colonel." He turned precisely and exited the lieutenant colonel's prison office. He breathed with a ragged euphoria; he saw his hands shaking – a kind of relief, a desperation that was beneath him. Kamakura stilled in the empty corridor and glared at his hands, turning them over and looking from the backs of veins to palms which caught light in their sweat. The missing doctor would be explained at a later time, perhaps cremated and gone before this mission; questions would be swept aside when he returned, likely never asked.

He would put a samurai blade through the stomach of Goro. First he would deliver the escapee, dead, to the colonel's superiors.

***

Sun-a awoke, with a lighter grey around her than had been there a moment before. Confusion became morning in her mind. The previous day's trek returned to her as a delirious series of half-rememberings, and she felt a startled thankfulness to have woken from that exhaustion at all. Her hands moved to her stomach. Still the pain, but now the tenderness seemed reassuring.

She looked aside suddenly, recalling where he had dropped nearby on the slope. He was there, awake, and turned his head, as if he had waited for her to look first. A slight sorrowful smile crossed his concerned face, and Sun-a felt a gratitude she could not remember feeling before.

She waited for him to speak, knowing from something withheld in his manner, that he had been waiting to talk to her. The man who had saved her, decisive, unstoppable, was defenceless, searching for something. It might perhaps have been in the short space of air between them, or in the forest his eyes darted across; but then his gaze became still upon her, and the restless almost scared search had stopped.

Mick wondered how the days had possibly passed without him broaching this conversation. Here on this mountainside, under low tree canopy that had never sheltered anyone but them before, he would ask her name:

"I'm Mick." He tapped his palm twice against his chest. "Michael Bowler." A moment's wait as the surprise on the woman's face hinted at understanding. "And you?" he asked with a gentle point.

Her expression had hesitated, questioning. Again he said, "Mick" and rested his palm on the rough fabric of his army uniform. The palm opened to her.

"Mik-uh," she said with some timidity.

Mick nodded, excited by what felt a gigantic leap.

The girl brought her own hand to her own chest. "Sun-a," she spoke.

Asking for confirmation with his eyes, Mick moved his hand between them. "Sun-a. Mick. Mick. Sun-a." He nodded for affirmation. She smiled and nodded in reply, a kind of bemused wonder on her brow.

Mick smiled, a wide, honest smile that opened the delight inside him, no barriers imposed.

Sun-a looked at the man, anticipation rising at what he would ask next, smile returned. He stood to his feet with an energetic jump, and pointed with big movements of his strong arms that made her want to laugh. She couldn't understand the sounds that accompanied the waving, but had begun to guess the meaning before he started to draw.

Seeing the stick on the dirt floor, Mick took the idea at once and began to scrape a child's drawing of a house into the ground, with a front door, three windows, and a triangle roof on top. He didn't really know what houses looked like in the girl's Japanese home, but the way her grin had grown as he'd constructed their four walls, windows and door, told him probably so. His knowledge of foreign life was focused on tactics in jungles and on tundra, but a home was a home, they could both see.

"Where?" he asked, pointing to the house in the dirt between them, and then back to his haphazard points of the compass. "This way? This way? This way?"

He smiled at her, seeing that she too bore the weight of his question in her expression.

Sun-a found herself not wanting to answer, not even to attempt, not to point. She had no home. The laughter that had been within her breast seconds before was vanished, and the heaviness of the mountains all around pulled her tired body into the ground.

"Sun-a. Ho-ma? Weh-re?"

There was a strain on his own expression as he read the feeling she had foolishly not hidden from her own. Immediately she determined to answer.

Sun-a struggled to her feet, finding more strength than she had expected from the memory of the previous day. She was upright, by herself. He had made a move toward her, but held back, and watched, ready to jump to her side.

But she looked away, to the gaps in the leaves overhead, to the glimmers of the sun. East. She gained her bearings with ease. And pointed.

"Sun-a, ho-ma." And for herself, "Sun-a, home."

"Sun-a, jeeb."

Mick nodded. Sun-a jeeb, he said within his own mind. That was where they would go. That was where he would take her. And where he would leave her. He nodded to himself, then smiled to her, a sad fraction of the joy from only moments earlier.

He said in prison camp Japanese, "Yes."

Immediately she tensed, looked horrified – as he finished, sounds trailing off: "Jeeb. Understood."

She replied to him after a shake of the head, side to side that kept going. She said words he didn't understand. Was she not Japanese? A dialect? Japan or somewhere else? A local girl who hated the sound of her own land, with good reason. She had clearly understood.

For moments they waited. He let the mountain quiet reassert itself.

"Breakfast," he said, and moved cautiously to her, gesturing with his head and gaze to the bank behind.

Carefully he put an arm around her back and another at her elbow, and lowered her to sit. Then he took their few remaining chilies and plucked insects from the dirt and what little water they had left. They would eat and then be on their way.

Sun-a didn't have the words to tell him what she needed to. It was too far. It was half of the country away. And it was not her home. The thought brought a burning sob to the back of her throat and she swallowed it down and forced her eyes wide and dry against the morning air. She shook her head. Did that mean the same thing in the unknown land of this man?

"Ho-ma. Ho-ma," she repeated.

"Yes," he replied and nodded his head, down, up. "Yes." And again the motion that meant, 'Ye, Nay.'

She copied his nod, "Ye. Ye. Nay. Yes-uh. Nay." Then swept the nod, mid-way, into the horizontal; her face she held serious and his eyes she held in her own stare, as she shook her head and knocked the nod away to either side. "Annio." He was watching, understanding. "Annio."

"No?"

"No," she repeated back to him.

Mik-uh looked concerned. Troubled. He gestured into the distance, then again pointed out into the mountains. "Sun-a, ho-ma," he said.

And he nodded, the language they both understood, and turned it into a question with the lines of his eyebrows. She saw pain there, of a kind, desperate, but constrained, held and kept in his brow.

Instantly she understood, and felt a fool, a selfish fool. What new burden would she heap into his hands? The man must be rid of her. He was kind beyond anything she had known in the second-life which consumed her memory. And she would not. With a nod, "Yes-uh. Nay."

"Ye." Cautiously.

"Ye. Yes-uh."

"Ye. Yes."

Understood.

She made herself smile, and smoothed the creases on his forehead.

Then the smile held deep within her as she saw the transition upon him, and she stilled. Side by side they sat and looked in the direction of the mountains, east-south. She would show him the way to take her to that house. She would say goodbye to him there and let him think he had taken her home. And she would let him leave in peace.

CHAPTER 17

A familiar row of houses looked small, neat, from a painting, with a collection of tall pots, and vegetables grown to the limits of rough, rising ground. Had they only gone this far? A hopelessness blew over Mick in the still air, catching him off guard. He let it blow on past behind him, and looked down at the valley with a steadier gaze, and a deep breath. They had taken the sides of mountains that swept one to another, around the wooded bowl of a valley, heading in the direction of her home. And just now they had descended the steep slope on the other side of the mountain, slipping, and losing footing as the soil lost its own footing and tumbled in grains beneath them. And he had brought her to look down on the opposite side of the very same valley from which he'd secured a little food days before. A knot of worry in his stomach began to tie at their disappearing chances of escape. But he wouldn't listen, and could not let it show on his face.

So he turned to the girl he was trying to save, and smiled. She looked beyond weary. Her left hand was on her stomach, as so often held there.

Mick looked back at the view.

Sitting, waiting below, was the one place in this unknown land where he knew they could find food and water. They had drunk once since morning, some mountain sides ago, and the jars and flask were all but empty. Perhaps finding this hamlet was good fortune.

They hurried on, falling, running and stopping, he helping her down the more giving soil, winding through the thick, low forest. In what seemed only minutes they arrived at the foot of the mountain slope, and keeping low ran out through tall grasses. Exposed, if a head should but look up from a garden to see them. The narrow field ended seconds after it had begun, and then they were out into the open valley floor. They ran across a mud embankment between paddy fields, he leading the girl by the hand, all the way, running at a crouch. Over the track at the bottom of the valley. Scampering up to the row of houses – then pressed against a wall, facing a garden, that Mick seemed to have been in only moments before. The days had blurred; everything looked much the same. Quiet. Still. Plants not moving, without a breeze, tall storage jars, stained red at their lids, standing unmoved.

Sun-a looked to the soldier. Her lungs coursed with running and the desperation to drink and fill with water. She tried not to gasp – knew she must not make a noise; hoped he would not see the worry in her scared eyes. But unusually he didn't turn to her. His back was to the wall, his stance low, on strong legs that looked like they could leap regardless of the mountains she had crossed with him that day. Very slowly, all control, she watched him lean, balance, to the dried-mud-edge of the house, and look out.

Her breath caught, waiting for a shout, that would end it all, and see these amazing days over. Suddenly she realised just how wonderful everything had been, despite the horror: to wake on a mountain slope, free of her life, and to walk in a direction, past trees she had never dreamt of threading through. And she knew dearly how much she didn't want it to end. She stared at Mik-uh's uniformed back, one moment from disappearing around the corner, and willed him to turn back to her and not have been caught.

Mick took a breath and leaned back on the flaky wall. The small vegetable garden lay in its narrow raised point of land before him: green low leaves – something like rhubarb – herbs and small sprouting bushes, rows of green tufts which could have topped fresh orange carrots hidden each in their little soil mound. The air remained still, barely a bird call to ruffle it from all the forested slopes about them. An unusual world this. He saw the pleasure of owning a shard of land in a valley, and for the brief moment he allowed it, could see himself there tending the plants. The girl was beside him, against that wall. He composed himself, took a breath of fresh garden air, the smell of herbs, and of chilli from the row of sentried jars, and set the next moves to mind. He nodded to the girl; she looked scared. She understood.

Sun-a felt her aching legs unsteady with nerves. She did as his beckon asked and stepped after him into the unseen around the corner.

There was no one there, just house fronts with their open doors, and baked dry soil which she recognised from her youth – where her mother had laid out vegetables and fish and corn kernels to dry. Over the empty ground she followed him. She stopped still, watching the soldier move from beneath the thatch eve, out before the blackness of a doorway – step where he could be seen in full daylight, but could not yet see within. Their journey was to be this she realised: a thousand chances taken, that must all go their way. She held her breath for the shout.

Mick squinted into the gloom. Was that a figure huddled in blankets on the bed? It hadn't seen him yet. More give from his arm, gripped on the mud wall; he levered out, blocking more of the daylight, bringing the room more into view. He squinted at the shape, clouded in dazed-mist, lines and texture emerging and merging in and out as his eyes accustomed. He needed it now. Fractions of seconds. To pull back, before being seen?

He waited, hanging, off balance. His eyes went to grey-black, nothing, blind, then suddenly saw the room in full, detail precise: the cupboard to the left, the cooking stove, the crockery, the fallen rice on the dirt floor, the bed through the one other doorway, the folded blanket with no person inside it. Everything almost exactly as he remembered it. The insects and chillies were no longer drying; they had to have been stored somewhere.

Mick-uh leaned back out of the house doorway and motioned for her to follow. She hurried after him, into the darkness. She looked around. Nobody seemed to be at home. It struck her then, made her stomach jump and freeze there. This was her first time in a home, since... Quietly he opened a cupboard door, chest height, in an old wooden cabinet. She knelt and did likewise, glad to be occupied, forcing herself to be. The door creaked at first pull, and she froze it there, horrified to fail at her one task, a task so simple. Slowly she eased open the door, beyond the creak on its rusted hinges, and smiled at the sight inside.

She pulled gently on the man's trouser leg, by his boot, and looked up expectantly. He crouched beside her, and together they beamed at the bowls of cicadas and chillies. As Mick-uh reached inside and carefully lifted the bowls out, Sun-a watched behind him, and realised that he had been here before. This was where he had come for her. All this way. And he was back there again, for her.

Mik-uh lifted a heavy jug from aside and asked with his eyes. In a moment she knew, and quietly, with almost shaking hands she took the cup he passed her from the blanket and set it on the hard dirt floor. He carefully tipped the tall jug and she watched water, dark inside the pottery, well and finally ebb over the spout, suddenly clear, transparent. The sound of pouring water was loud in the silence of the room; she looked anxiously to the bright rectangle of the doorway, seeing only mud and fields and mountain slope. She waited; he righted the jar; then he nodded to her. She cupped the storied urn with both hands, and watching the shining, clear water, brought it to her mouth.

When she had drunk he filled it again, and when she offered it to him he shook his head. She drank again gladly, feeling the water replenishing her life within her. Finally he took his turn and drank and refilled the cup and drank again. She heard her heart beating fearfully, for sudden footsteps, paces from the doorway, and then figures in the light, turning to enter, and see them. He poured from the jar again, tipping it further and further to its side. He told her with his eyes it was for her. She wanted to offer it to him. She glanced at the doorway. Still empty; still view of dirt and growing rice and green slope. Desperately thirsty she lifted the pottery with hands she saw trembling and quickly drank – just a little; the rest to save.

Mik-uh finished filling the Japanese army bottle and set the light jar back in its place by the wall. He then began to hurriedly, near silently, gather food. She leant over against the pain, to help.

Mick came out first into the surprising brightness. Sun-a followed, blinking. Their rolled blanket wrapped hidden supplies. No one was in sight. No conversation on the deserted wooden platform at the end of the settlement.

The sound of a bee drifted from afar, from a place too distant for a bee to be heard. Mick tensed at once. He knew the sound.

They were in front of the row of buildings. The small bee was revving down the road toward them, sound rushing all of a sudden, deceptively held back by the spurs of the mountain. They would see the motorbike in seconds.

The edge of the furthest hut, with the vegetable garden and tall jars just out of sight, was too many steps away. Mick turned to Sun-a and grabbed for her hand. She reached out and took his, the alarm on her face telling him she knew the stakes. Immediately he sought to pull them back, to fade toward the tantalising shadows, and the black of the doorway behind them.

A shape pulled from the dried-mud edge of the furthest hut. Mick glanced up and saw it form into a woman. She turned the corner, out onto the open ground. They had barely begun to move. The woman was late middle aged, with black-grey hair tied back, and she stopped still when she saw them. She stared, puzzled, and then outraged. The buzz of the motorbike was now a roar, uncomfortable for the ears, dragging attention.

Mick looked to the woman, saw her anger, rooted unnaturally to the bare ground. He glanced and saw the motorbike riding into town, the Japanese helmet yet to turn his way. And he saw perhaps one slim chance of escape for them. He fell back into the darkness at once.

Sun-a stood alone before the low house, facing the old woman. She felt panic rise in her with the deepening sound of the motorcycle, a slowing mechanical rumble even as it became louder still. Right behind her. Then it spluttered and cut off. The forested valley became itself once again, seeming utterly quiet, and then she heard a scuffle as boots ground onto dirt, and footfalls, one after the other. To her side. Coming closer. Still her eyes were on the old woman's, which looked angrily right back at her. She thought she ought to turn, and so she did, and knew her face was pale with fear as she saw him.

It was a soldier. Only soldiers rode motorcycles. He was Japanese, with the cold, arrowed smile lines on his face that she had expected. With inquisitive tilt of the head he stepped past her. Into the space between them. He looked over to the old woman, then back to her. Measuring the animosity of their standoff. Calculating the situation he was dealing with.

From behind her came a murmured enquiry and a shuffle of old, or hesitant feet. Sun-a let her eyes follow the soldier's hawk-like peer over her shoulder. She glanced round.

Mick pressed against the dried mud wall beside the dark rectangle that kept human eyes unaccustomed – a portal that had to be stepped through. He had made the call in the instant, as he had made calls before. In the following moments he would listen and find if he had been right. If not, then he would move through the doorway not a foot away, tackle the soldier, kill him, and save the girl. She would not be taken: even if his trail had to become red hot again; missing patrol red hot. But he was counting on the likelihood that the search was for him, not the girl – that she was a nobody whore, to them.

If the girl could think on her feet, there was a chance the soldier would pass on by. Mick pressed closer to the doorway, as close to the shadow's edge as he dared. He would be ready. Then foreign language started.

The shuffling old man called past her to the other side of the standoff.

"Bak-Gyeong-seon?"

Sun-a found herself turning, acting her part; she had to convince. And with her eyes she pleaded.

"Everything's fine." And to the soldier. "Is there something the matter?"

"Bak-Gyeong-seon?" said the shuffling man, past the parked motorcycle, now almost at his house.

The Japanese soldier cast his angled, inquisitive beak toward the woman. In chopped, sliced tones he spoke Korean: "Bring me food woman."

The old woman nodded. She broke the ten pace stand-off and strode past Sun-a, flashing an explosive glare that made Sun-a's neck rock back with the shock.

Mick froze. Someone passed inches from his face, his hands, through the portal. In the blackness, and the change from the outside glare he couldn't see who. He held his breath, and tensed his hands to pounce about its silhouette neck. Then from outside came the foreign words of a man, the age of a young soldier. And he was back against the wall.

The voice moved slightly, verging on the portal. Just the other side. More words. Mick's cheek pushed against the mud. He could feel the texture the ground had dried in. The woman squatted feet from him at the cabinet - opening doors, searching pottery – while unseen, the voice outside continued a brief move away.

One eye pressed close to closed, the other angled as acutely as the wall and the skull could allow, he waited. The line between darkness and light seemed drawn down the centre of his face, the doorframe distorting shadow and day into a disbelieving contrast. In the gloom of the day-dark line, the shape, outline of a flattened-bridge nose, and the shape, gone, then there, of narrow eyes, and cold cheek lines. There then gone, just the other side.

Sun-a waited, standing as she had, not daring to look.

"You have no rice cooked?"

"Sorry, no. Vegetables. Peppers."

She felt the air change somehow, eyes on her. She was not surprised when the topic changed.

"Who is this?"

A cold shiver traversed her back, and she was helpless not to show it.

The man was watching her, waiting, so she played her part and slowly turned to face him, terrified eyes failing the role.

The soldier looked back to the increasingly confused, hunched man.

"Do you know this girl?" he asked, gesturing dismissively to Sun-a.

The old woman stepped from the doorway, dusting her hands on her old skirt. "Of course I do. It's just look at the state of her. Of course I know her. She's my daughter."

Mick breathed in quietly, deeply. He would have to act on tone, on anger, on a guess at meaning. He readied to launch if the woman sold out his element of surprise.

Sun-a looked to the woman. Terror and now shock. She had to convince.

"Your daughter?" the soldier repeated back.

"Yes." And Sun-a nodded to go with it.

"My daughter."

"Then why have I not seen her before?"

"She was in the woods when you last ate our rice. Look at her."

"You're sure." The hawk was not convinced. His cold-lined beak turned from one player to the next.

"Old man, no words? Is this your daughter?"

The old man looked at Sun-a, and stilled, no movement. "Of course it is. She's wearing my wife's skirt isn't she?"

The Motorcycle Soldier looked from the skirt on Sun-a's body, to that on the old woman. He raised his eyebrows in a question.

The old woman considered Sun-a, from ground to shoulders. Her face wore a hateful blankness, a move of the mouth from a despising sneer.

"It looks like my skirt."

The soldier paused, and considered. Apparently satisfied, he turned away without expending eye contact. He mounted his motorcycle, and with his back to them said in Japanese, "Clean her up. She... mistaken for anything."

The growl of the motor, from nowhere taking all sound, fast and high pitched then falling low and deep and discomforting. Over the growl, Korean: "Remember, I like rice."

Then, as he lurched suddenly away, in Japanese Sun-a heard, "country idiots," and he was gone.

The motorcycle sped away down the valley track, out of sight so quickly that the last minutes seemed to have been unreal. Mik-uh stepped from the blackness; the old man half shuffled back and inhaled a wide-eyed gasp.

"I want my blankets back," said the woman.

Sun-a nodded. "There is this," she said, and moved to her foreign protector. She gently took the rolled blanket from under his arm. He let her. Turning back to the woman she presented it, the solitary blanket, and all their provisions.

"Thank you," Sun-a said, and bowed to her elder.

The old man spoke out from behind the scene: "You should have turned her over to him, woman. You'll have us marked down as traitors!" He spat the words, fiercely whispered.

"Traitors to who, fool?" Then with a point of the head toward Mik-uh: "He's already eaten from our bowl."

Mik-uh put a hand on her shoulder, and nodded for them to go.

"Foreigner!" spat-whispered the shuffling man.

She and Mik-uh left the thatched-rice homes by the valley path, which they walked a few paces, before crossing and disappearing into another covered mountain slope.

Mick found himself breathing hard, as at the end of a sprint, or a fierce skirmish in jungle or above ice fjord. The tension began to dissipate from his lungs and the imperative to get away opened them out. Ahead the beckoning silence of the forest, and behind the faint, angry whispering of "Waygookin! Waygookin!"

CHAPTER 18

Kamakura straightened his back, releasing the hunched shoulders which he found had remained long after the climb. He rolled his shoulder blades and leant his neck to one side, then the other, two and a half each way.

The prison guards had already moved the bodies by the time the scout had led them to the site. He had actually arrived to find the two dead men being carried into the open – one minus rifle and ammunition; their carriers' feet kicking a path through evidence as they went. Nevertheless, a survey of the area had revealed much: there had been a shelter, well-constructed with branches entwined in multiple layers and a reasonably watertight canopy of leaves lashed over it; someone had torn it apart, hastily, and the construction was amply clear; there had been a bloody blanket half-buried in the wet surface soil, along with a saturated skirt; there were shells of cicadas, stems of chillies, and the odour of urine at trees a distance from the camp; and there was this.

Kamakura sniffed against, not a smell, but a thought, an imposition. The grave was tiny, the soil recently turned, damp and mottled together on the surface from the soaked-in rain. A nasty fertile brown. At the head of the mound was planted a cruciform of two crossed sticks. The Japanese did not mark the places of the dead with such insignia. The Koreans no longer marked the places of the dead with such insignia. The foreigner had done this.

He considered for a second, exhuming the body. But he did not want to smear his boot, and the predictable find would provide only tangential information.

He looked around with distaste. Had the escapee stumbled on the camp of a whore? Was this a hideaway, a stop-off frequented by fleeing comfort women on their way home? Kamakura smirked an ironic nudge of his lips – but not enough to fully uncurl the revulsion in his sneer. Was this site a whore's den set up by sadistic prison guards, to keep their favourite, imprisoned, but out of the reach of others? Possible. Had the search uncovered the woman in her isolated prison, and the foreigner too? Making use of her? Occupying a deserted camp?

Kamakura exhaled, breathing steady. There were no signs of imprisonment. And what would make anyone choose women's bloody mess for a place to sleep? Discovered food would be carried away. Logically, the man should hardly have set foot there, and yet he had pissed by trees and stuck a Christian symbol in the ground.

And then there was the woman who had fled from his theatre, heavily pregnant; and there was the mound in mud before his feet; and there was the bloody material at the base of the centre stone; and the bloody, smeared peasant's fabric; and a missing enemy soldier. He discounted the elaborate surmises; the evidence incised to a single point like knives.

He would welcome ending the life of this lesser thing he must chase. It would not be a difficult objective.

Kamakura turned at the creak of stretchers as the two bodies were lifted from the open ground of the clearing behind him.

Precise kills.

With another sniff he raised his right boot, trod out and down and onto the cross. It began to splinter, rupturing and splaying soil from the base, then kicking free of the grave. Kamakura crunched down on the flimsy sticks and crushed the cruciform beneath his black boot. He turned and walked away to give his orders.

***

The land was one of small mountains, expertly crafted, forming lines and curves around farmland and small settlements, in great flat valleys; or forming pathways, layered back in thick mountain spines that seemed to veer and part and intersect across the whole country he saw ahead. Triangles after triangles, none high enough for the snow covered peaks he'd seen in photographs of the Alps, Snowden, or Ben Nevis; and none as towering as those he remembered in Scandinavia; but impressive nonetheless, every one covered in green forest or shrub, ancient land folded up and preserved.

The sky changed above them, from clear and blue with wisps of cloud, to blanketed white so that you couldn't make out the individual clouds at all. And then to black-purple, and to night. He led the way often, but fell back as much as he could so she walked beside him. She had pointed the direction based on the midday sun, and that was what he followed. Evidently neither of them had ever crossed this country before, so he guided them over the landscape as best his training could suggest.

Sun-a put a hand to her belly. The pain was always there, coming and going, but always there. She took the hand away. She didn't want him to see - couldn't allow him to see. She thought of her dead baby, but looked at the trees they passed, and the browns and greens and mosses on the yellow ground ahead, and the thought moved back in her mind.

Twigs cracked under her steps. She followed him, just behind and to the side. Walking the side of the mountain, sloping always, always adjusting for the diagonal ground beneath her feet, the trees always pointing the shortest way to the sky. She blinked at a brief pain. For a moment the world was at an angle - the mountain slope and her balance losing which way was straight up. She felt she should lean, to make the ground flat and even beneath her, then felt with alarm gravity tugging her over. She clasped to a tree with both hands, and clung to it. Mick-uh was only moving steps away, but it made her panic, to be left behind. She swallowed, caught her breath, waited for vision to again find the depths between trees and leaves and shadow and bright light.

Again she was on the slope, with the trees pointing straight up. She walked on, hurrying after Mik-uh. He turned to see where she was as she caught up, and he smiled.

***

Sun-a knew this landscape well, though she had never walked this path through it.

It was Korea. The country she had been born into. Though she had long since ceased to think of it as her own. For most of her life, the life of memory, it had been a prison, a nightmare ruled by Japanese demons, made flesh. She had no country. Such a feeling was meaningless in a nightmare. The comfort house, the prison camp and guard huts it waited beside, had been in no country.

Seven years ago she had made this diagonal trek across Korea, in the opposite direction. In the back of an overcrowded truck, with smells of sweat and urine, and no room to put her shoulders back. And now... she looked up from the route of her feet, and caught a glimpse through leaves on branches, of sky, and a mountain she did not know.

Korea seemed different somehow.

***

They crossed a small stream by some large rocks, which looked like they had been cut for a wall long ago. Sun-a noticed the roundness of the square edges, the stones still in place. She knew of pebbles and the sea and what a tide could do; perhaps a stream carved rocks in its own way. Mick was crouched on one of the boulders, as she could not, cupping his hands in the water. She looked longingly, then saw him stand and step over to her rock, and raise his hands to her mouth. She drank, badly, awkwardly, and felt hot with embarrassment as half the water spilled down her front. 'Thank you,' she said. He bent down and lifted more water to her. The second time, she let her head fall back and her eyes look to the boughs and the patches of sky, and felt the cold water soothe her parched throat as it ran inside her.

Mick-uh only then lay down flat on a stone and lowered the Japanese soldier's flask into the stream. Had he noticed her discomfort when she drank from it? She watched in the sunlight, as he submerged the bottle, and bubbles gurgled to the surface. He brought the bottle out in a splash and tipped it upside down so that water splurted out in gush after gush; and then dunked the gourd again, cleaning it in the stream.

She managed to lower her weight, to sit on the rock that supported her. Her feet swayed above the water and she looked out into the woodland ahead. Aside, Mick-uh doused the bottle again underwater, and brought it up full. She reached for it and he passed it up to her to drink.

***

Another valley, another path to skirt, as he took her along the slope. It hurt their feet, their calves. It hurt his, so he could only imagine how it hurt hers. She struggled on, but it was taking its toll. He tried not to look and let her see him notice. But he observed, with ever more worry, day by day. And the way her hand cradled her stomach more and more. When they paused to rest, and her eyes searched the horizon, he saw it move there; when they walked and walked and he looked back to check she was okay, and her eyes met his, she did not even notice that she held herself there. And he would look away so she would not see the concern on his face. And speak some pointless English about their journey, that she would not understand.

***

The trees were lush above their heads, as they rested beneath them. Mick looked to the beautiful girl, where she sat, opposite, at an angle, back against a tree, as he did. She was beautiful, and pale, and it worried him continually. She needed more rest than they could take.

There was no need for her to make this pace. She did it because he was on the run. She did not need to be on the run. He ought to find a quiet town away from their trail and leave her there to recover. He would go on, keep going, away from her. Leave her behind.

But then, what would happen to her? Would anyone take in a... girl such as her, in her condition...? No, and then he would be leaving her to a life on the street with no one to find her food and bring her water. Surely it was better she stayed with him, as punishing as their flight was, as dangerous as it was. Yet, if they were caught the Japanese would view even one of their own, helping him, as a traitor. It was far beyond dangerous. But he could not leave her. It was a risk. He knew these thoughts well; they revolved through his mind, across valley, and through mountain passes, like a gramophone recording upon which he could not stop setting the needle back to the start. Every time he chose, for the both of them; every time he turned and saw her face and her old borrowed skirt, and her hand beneath her stomach.

Surely she knew. She took the risk, as he did.

But for now they could rest.

***

Neither of them spoke, and the sky had become night. How many days had they been together? Two at the camp when he had found her. Another, five, six, seven, a week had it been, since then? He did not know. The days were so alike, marked in his mind only by the brief words they had exchanged for mere moments on a mountain side, a new bridge between them; or how she had looked so tired stepping over the ridge of a spur, that the image had jarred in his mind's eye for every mile after.

She lay some feet to his left, waiting for sleep on the same gentle slope of grass and earth.

He heard her turn onto her side, but he did not look.

She reached out, squinting in the darkness, and felt the cold shell of one of the cicadas in her fingers. As they often did, unless they came across fruit, waiting, hanging for them from its branches, they ate cicadas from the trees. He had left a few and moved them nearer to her.

She turned it over in her fingers, trying to see the detail of its shell, the faint marks from where they had pulled its wings. But on this journey the nights could be truly dark. There had always been light in her former life. Always low and smoking, and left on most of the night because you didn't want to leave the room for the hassle of finding a flame. And you didn't know which rooms were unoccupied in which to find it. At the comfort house she had never really seen true darkness. Perhaps never ever. She thought of it for a moment.

But here on the mountain, when the canopy hid you from the stars, it swallowed you every night. She could have been out of the world, but for his soft breathing while he slept, always a short distance away.

A bounce of moonlight from a rustled leaf brought the carapace glistening into silver, grey and black. Then it was gone and she again relied on the touch of her fingers. Closing her eyes, she moved it, turned it over, and felt a sadness settling.

He lay on his back. She started speaking. Slowly. Quietly. He looked over, but couldn't see her. Perhaps the shape of a girl, her head and the curve of her hair to her neck. The trees murmured above them to announce, a sound like faintly clacking pebbles on a beach; and then a lesser darkness, the patterns between leaves moved over her, as they moved in a breeze. The air barely altered on the wood-slope floor, just a slightest change of temperature around them. He saw then that her eyes went between him, and something held in her hand. That she was talking to him, in kind at least.

"Years of hiding under ground," she said, to no one, and herself, and the space, but mostly to him. She let the cicada roll down her fingers and come to a stop in her open palm. She could feel him watching her now - saw his head turned aside, her way, in the darkness. She told him more:

"Waiting out the sentence, to take to the air for just one week. Do you see many cicadas where you come from?"

Mick heard the question, and then in the silence returned her conversation: "Sun-a, you know, you don't have to come with me." Then, "You may be better by yourself."

"My grandmother used to say, when I was a very little girl, 'a bowl of cicadas gives more health than a whole chicken.' More flight in their wings, she thought, than a chicken can dream of."

Quietness. Only the mountain; still trees.

"But she was wrong. There are a thousand lives between them, I think. A thousand deaths."

Mick found himself nodding gently. "Strange where you end up in life. Isn't it?" He said the question weakly. Foolishly. But went on. "I'd never have pictured myself here. You'd have asked me back in Derby, me and my pals pratting about... where I'd be... I'd never have imagined... this. On a mountainside...here... with you."

"Do you think it's so, Mik-uh?" She paused. They both did. "Years of hiding underground, waiting out the sentence, to take to the air for just one week." She looked to the black shadow, upturned on her palm. "I am sorry for you; but it is better to be plucked and dried in the sun, than get too used to your wings."

There was a silence; it seemed to him it could have lasted on, and there would have been comfort on that dirt slope in the darkness. But he wanted to tell her something:

"You know, before the war, there was a girl."

Sun-a still lay on her side, head angled up against the dirt and grass. She could barely see him, but knew his face well enough.

Mick paused before the words. He didn't know if he'd ever said them out loud. Certainly not to anyone else.

"I killed her. She was waiting for me, and I killed her."

Sun-a heard the change in his voice. Lying, curled on her side, she found her neck straining to him, to hear, to console.

"She waited because I gave her reason to. I don't think I ever had any intention of going to see her. I put her under those bombs."

"I hated it. That's why I did it." Sun-a almost stopped in surprise at having spoken. There had been his pain mirrored in her own voice. She had heard it. "I want to tell you. You of all people, deserve to know. That's why, because I hated it. With every bit of hate in me."

"It wasn't me who pulled the trigger, who opened the hatch, and let the bombs fall. But I played my part."

"I killed it; and I'm glad."

"But there's not a lot you can do when something like that's been done."

"I am the worst mother."

Mick saw her then, sorrow etched on his face; for him, for her, for them both. Though he did not understand the words.

"And I will suffer for it all." She waited, and let her thoughts collect. "If I do nothing but good for every day I have left, it won't make a difference. Maybe I will be born as an insect instead of a worm. But I will slave as an ant, only to become the worst of beetles. And I will live a hundred lives to be born..."

She let her eyes leave his form, and return, to the shape in her palm. Dry and brittle, wings plucked, a pointless former thing in the palm of her hand.

She let it roll and fall, as she turned onto her back, and stared for relief at the blackness above, which she knew was leaves and not really sky. To her side she heard the slight grind of head and ground as he did the same.

Then they stared up from the mountainside and didn't need to speak until morning.

***

For once the ground sloped gently, rolling down under glades of low trees. It formed something like a valley and wound its way, still high above the real floor of that land, in curves between three peaks. The low mountains were pyramid hills at the height they walked, and but for the branches, the sky took up more of the world than it usually did.

Sun-a upturned Mick's palm and covered it with her own for a moment. When she took her hand away, three of their precious dried insects were left behind.

"Thanks." He picked one and was about to eat, as she bit a tiny piece of her own between front teeth. Then he hesitated, thinking of the night before. He held it out to her.

"What's this called?"

She raised her eyebrows.

"This. What is it?" He tried again. "Mick... Sun-ah..." and next gestured to the shell questioningly.

"Meh-me."

"Meh-me," he repeated back. "Mehme."

"Nay. Mik-uh, hago, Sun-a, hago Mehme." And she smiled.

"Mick, Sun-a... hago?"

The girl nodded encouragingly.

"...hago... Mehme," he finished. "Sun-a, hago Mick, hago Mehme."

She grinned this time. "Nay."

"Nay?" A beat. "Yes."

"Nay," she beamed back, nodding.

"Ye?"

She considered, then hand out, stopped before her chest, throat: "Ye." She moved her hand toward him, the slightest point, then brought back: "Nay."

He was watching her carefully. Respectfully, he echoed her moves: a gesture toward her, "Ye," and his hand returning to wait before him, "Nay." She seemed to consider the exchange and with a faint smile, almost treasuring, "Yes-uh."

Their situation disappeared. They were two people taking a stroll through a beautiful mountain pass somewhere.

"Yes."

"Yes," she said with her accent that made him smile.

She went on, "Mik-uh, hago Sun-a, hago Mehme. Yes." And laughed a delighted laugh.

"Sun-a, hago Mick, hago Mehme. Nay." And he laughed too, and he clapped his hands together twice, in applause for them both.

"Sun-a, and Mick, and Mehme. Yes."

He nodded encouragement for her to follow.

"Sun-a, and Mick-uh, and Mehme. Yes. Ye."

And they laughed together.

Then the land dipped for a few steps and rose again, to bend around a small spur in the mountain. As they took the curve they found fruit trees welcoming them on their right. They draped over the path they made, like an orchard magically planted for just this journey.

Sun-a actually ran a few steps, to pluck an apple from an offered bough. She turned and held it above Mick's hand with both of hers - a submissive politeness that was foreign to him, but sweet and instantly understood. It was a glimpse into her character; the woman he was getting to know.

"Thank you" he said, with a gentle bow that he didn't think about making. It met her gesture somehow, and then he lifted his head to meet her eyes as she stepped back.

Mick held the apple out into the space. He lifted his other arm in a comic, questioning shrug.

"Sagwa," the girl replied, pleased.

"Apple," he replied.

"Sagwa. Apple."

"Apple. Sagwa."

They carried on beneath the boughs that seemed divinely planted, so against the grain were they to everything that had come before.

"Sun-a, hago Mick, and Mehme, hago apple. Nay?"

"Yes."

CHAPTER 19

The old woman shuffled back to her dwelling, where her elderly husband looked on. The old man had shaken when questioned: at first taken aback by flawless Korean, and then by the questions which took foreknowledge as their starting point. Ask what you already seemed to know absolutely and answers were more expedient, Kamakura well knew from experience. The man had shaken with nerves beyond his ailments – arthritis, balance linked glaucoma most likely, past scurvy and resulting bowed tibias, and the onset of dementia. He'd babbled of strangers stealing from his wife – who didn't know what she was doing – and apparitions descending from the mountain woods; of mountain spirits and a white man.

They had undoubtedly aided his prey and committed treason against the Empire of the Sun. In different circumstances Kamakura would have drawn his sword and sliced them down right there on the spot. But he was working beyond the jurisdiction of his posting, tracking the escapee where other military divisions would ask questions. It was essential to make smooth progress – to be a blade that sliced through the Korean hinterland until it struck through the skull of the foreigner. The less bodies the blade met on its path, the quicker and cleaner the cut would be. He intended to have this demeaning chore out of the way as soon as possible.

His personal honour withstood the pathetic country babble of these locals. He felt like a mighty statue, carved from rock, towering over broken straw men. What need have stone to worry about the honour of dried grass? Another couple of winters would finish them off, and by then the old man's mind would be a sodden mush, a living nightmare, to drive the woman insane.

Kamakura smiled and looked on down the country path, a trail that fell from higher ground where mountains crossed. Ahead the worn path continued past measly areas of crops, and mountain spurs. That way. He would find the trail where it began again in the fresh ground beyond the farmers' huts.

That was the only item of curiosity on this perfunctory hunt. Two tracks. At first it had been the cause of their delay, for they had found only tracks by the pair, and had logically presumed them all to have their origins in the disorganised search conducted under the watchful gaze of Lieutenant Colonel Goro. Tracks had circled the mountain at various levels, criss-crossing, before heading out every which way to every which other mountain. It had been a testament to the debacle of discordant organisation and purpose, and it had taken days to eliminate the falsehood. He felt his rage boil up, simmer and fill his lower neck. He breathed out hatred through his nose, and felt peace at the thought of killing him with little effort, Goro's eyes deigning to his vast superiority as they panicked and died.

But two tracks. The only bit of interest on this search, which was soon to be concluded.

"We're leaving, now."

He turned to see his men emerge from the row of huts, mouths stuffed, hands bearing their salvage of bread, and poor produce. They ran to his location, none of them delaying even a moment to complete the particular instance of pillaging they had had underway. Kamakura nodded to himself and set off before they reached him.

Behind him the other tenants stood about their houses and land, in exactly the same locations as when he had arrived. He heard the inane mutterings of the old man and woman. Soon to be left behind. The next curve in the path would take him out of earshot.

With sharp hand signals and no words he instructed the prison-guards-turned-man-hunters to relocate the trail. They fanned out to either side of the path, studying the ground, the furthest of them disappearing beneath foliage onto adjacent mountain slopes.

He wanted this over with.

***

Mick was following the sun, as his ancestors once had. As it moved through the sky he caught glimpses of piercing brightness through the canopy, and when in the open, crossing a field of rice, or hurrying across open valley, he was aware of it, in its great arc, looming over him. As it made its way to nightfall he sensed where it was heading and felt its compass instinctively in his senses.

And so they had made their way across the landscape, until the city of Suwon spread out beneath them. That was the name Sun-a repeated. From their mountain view it was shrouded in late morning mist, wide and uncoordinated, houses and buildings and carless narrow streets, and people.

Mick was struck by how far they had come. He had never heard of its name, and had only a rough gauge of the miles covered; but they were still alive, passing a city, unseen. He looked at his companion and felt hope, that they could really do this.

***

Japanese scout cars drove in single file around a bend in the road. Fumes buffeted against shrubs and low, surviving trees on the roadside. Soldiers looked out from their vehicles, weary of the journey and the potholes that shook the convoy.

Mick watched beside Sun-a, only yards into the greener forest, sharp slope rising behind them. She was looking to the ferns and sprouts and the soil beneath, keeping as still as she could; her chest moved in slow, terrified breaths. He held the Japanese rifle in two hands, across his front.

The noise rumbled on; the cars left sight, around the bend. The exhaust cleared, or settled and took the shape of the ruts on the track.

When the sound was all but gone, Mick took small movements forward, opening his angle of sight. He looked back with a quick nod, and then, leading Sun-a by the hand, ran low, into the open. The road was deserted, to the left and the right. Only quietness, left behind by the convoy.

They crossed and ran up the gravelly slope, threading themselves between thorny bushes and hardy, undefeated branches.

***

Sun-a jumped at the whistle and pressed her back closer to the stones of the bank. She had heard it before, a distant noise from her room, through the window. Sun-a breathed; she had, only now so close: the noises, and the smell like army cars and trucks. Mick-uh was looking at her, and she swallowed and forced her shoulders down; they wouldn't go, but she forced them. The sound went on, wailing, dying then screeching out again. It was everywhere in the darkness, in front and around them, and filling the whole evening sky.

The train whistle faded quickly, vanished. It seemed quiet, but then she heard it was a sound, a low, rumbling hum, that caught her breath again.

Japanese shouts came from up above, checks called and answered. Earlier in the daylight they had seen from the trees, the trains and the soldiers on guard.

Sun-a looked up, fearing a helmeted face looking back down at her. Again nothing over the ridge but the dark sky. Mik-uh had his back to the steep bank beside her. She knew that he was listening. She trusted he would take them past this.

She turned to him, wondering when they would move, and watched as he reached both hands to the ridge of the bank, and began to pull up. She saw diffuse yellow light strike across his head, his eyes, as he moved from cover. She couldn't watch. She turned to face the wall, ready, breathing fast, desperately willing him not to crash back down, for no gunshot to sound, no cry of discovery, and end.

He crouched above her, outline aglow in the yellow light. His hand found hers, and they clasped. He lifted her, and she climbed up the steep slope, dropping onto her knees. All-encompassing noise surrounded them, of hissing steam and impossibly heavy motion, metal and weight.

They were over the embankment and running. A metal line passed under her gait; another running step, and then the glint of a second track sped beneath her and behind. They were running for the train. Sun-a looked around her. A guard far to the left walked away from them. Her gaze fixed on him in panic as she ran the other way, but he did not turn.

A presence at the side of her vision brought her back, her head whipping round to see a line of huge heaviness rising at an edge before her. It moved past her. A gap. And then another impossibly heavy carriage moving of its own will. Wheels that resisted turning, turned beneath it, amidst shapes and black, oil and steel.

Mik-uh's hand was clasped in hers, always. His arm lifted her, and she went with him. They were suddenly so close to the train; it towered over her. Fright, and she wanted to pull back, but let him lift her and stepped where he had. And suddenly she was sitting, rocking over with the train's movement, between the bulwarks of carriages. Mik-uh pulled in her feet, swivelling her round. Light left her face and she found darkness concealing her.

They were together, sitting on the link between cars.

Sun-a looked up warily to the sheer metal which rose vertically backing her in, and forward slicing up. A nightmare returned of vast grey cliffs of metal rising from the sea, as if they had grown from the ocean floor. Battleships so far away, but with guns that would slowly turn and fire if they saw her. And they had seen her. And she was splashing in the water she loved. But she could no longer swim. She was going under.

The train churned on at a constant speed. Darkness remained as they needed it to. When they crossed the bridge over the river, they let their legs swing out over the drop. She felt her heart fill, exhilarated. Never had she seen anything close: a river curving below them, the water glistening with hundreds of pieces of moonlight; the whole scene was alight in silver. She realised that the moon was so much brighter than she had ever thought; it had just missed the water to shine upon. Or had she known this, in her former life? A memory nudged somewhere beneath the corners of her mind, of sea and waves to the horizon, and the view of a girl, gazing, half open mouth – half smile. The Korean coast, beside her village.

Past the far bank and into darkness, toward the silhouettes of mountains. As the train slowed uphill, they jumped, and ran hand in hand into the utter blackness.

***

Together they walked an old trail, overgrown with reed-like grasses and low spreading plants, seemingly not used for years. Still just visible, it guided them between crags of rock and loose, tumbled declines. They had walked for weeks. Twenty-five, twenty-six days, Mick thought. They had gone north, when they had needed to go south-east, circled around mountains, and cut across valleys, to try and lose any who might have tracked them; to try and hide their real destination. They were still uncaptured, undiscovered, and he was taking her home.

Sun-a stopped as the shrubs that tried to span from either side broke away to reveal a clear fork in the mountain path. She breathed deeply, glad for a chance to catch her breath. She felt good, compared to before. Her belly ached only from time to time, and the bleeding had stopped. The mountain air; the smell of trees and bark and moss and dew when she woke each morning; the happiness she felt: it had made her well she thought. If tiredness still slowed her legs, and thirst lived ever at the back of her tongue, she could always keep going. She trusted him.

Mick looked at the two possibilities. One to slightly higher ground, one perhaps towards a valley. They needed water. Their canteen contained only drops, and his already thin frame was struggling.

Could he could keep walking; but he had carried her, hadn't he? He breathed in and looked at the land ahead. He was still strong, despite two years in different prisons. The forced work on Formosa; the meagre rice each day – he had seen his weight fall away, far beyond what the jungle treks had stripped clean. But he had survived the waves of disease which in turn swamped the camp. He knew he had been fortunate; he had seen men break – simply drop by the lake they had carved out, and not carry on. In that tropical bowl of a prison he knew that he had spoken to few, but he had recognised the bodies being carried out of the huts, heard the curses and the hatred and the promises against the guards. They had all heard tales from transfers around the island, of much worse conditions – whole camps of soldiers dying, starving.

He considered the rough paths, each a thin, jagged line between overgrown bushes and scrub. Sun-a's eyes were closed, head up, as she breathed deep breaths.

Four, perhaps five days ago they had taken raw pork cut in strips from an isolated cottage. He had felt guilty taking someone's food. The cicadas still sang all day and into the night, but he and Sun-a walked on for much of that time, taking only easy pickings from the bark, not risking the slowed pace or the tracks needed to fan out, climb trees and collect a harvest. He knew they both used more reserves than they ate.

He had to choose correctly. He exhaled and looked to the sky, for its blueness, for its wisps of cloud, for inspiration, ultimately for God. Which way?

He turned to his companion. "Which way?" he said in English, as he often had, and smiled at their private joke.

Sun-a seemed to consider the roads carefully.

"Morugessumneeda," said Mick.

Sun-a turned and grinned at him. She looked back to the two roads, then with a deep breath she again turned to him to deliver her verdict. "I don't know," she said.

They each wore a tired, wide smile as side by side they considered the ways ahead.

Sun-a waited for him to decide, as she always did. He would know.

Mick made the choice. "Go, this way," he said, in her language with a point to the higher path. It was the safer route, with less chance of being discovered. Yet with less chance of finding habitation and food to take. If they were lucky they would find a stream, near its source.

Mick led the way, holding back prickly bushes like English gorse, to let her through.

"Today, cool," Sun-a said.

"Nay, jogum dadut han," he agreed.

It was true. The summer was stifling, the sun boiling when out from the cover of trees, and the air seeming close to jungle humidity; but a strong breeze blew past them on the open hillside. He thought how welcome the change to Autumn would be – but she would be safe by then.

Sun-a craned her neck back and looked up high. "Blue sky," she said with a delightful little laugh.

Mick laughed too. Unhindered, with no worry of being discovered. This was their life. They walked. They talked. They laughed together, through this amazing landscape of unfolding mountains. They slept with the stars just beyond the leaves.

He had taught her that yesterday. "Very good," he honestly congratulated her. "You're doing great." And he craned his neck back to see how blue it was.

She picked up English with eagerness, a natural student. And he was learning her language, or dialect much the same. Perhaps another form of

Japanese; not on the main island. There were sometimes pieces he recognised, from before, and yet so often her voice entirely distinct, original. She had looked without answer on the rare occasions he'd broached the subject, words, 'Nippon.' It was an odd, troubling thought, to be so enjoying the language of his enemy. But he knew it was learning from her. When he woke up on one mountain slope or another it was the first thought he had: to talk with her, and the rush of joy that for another day he surely would.

***

The path wound its way through low shrubs and spreading bushes in competition to claim the mountainside. Together, they squeezed and prized their way between rows of razor-sharp thorns, beneath occasional spindly, determined trees, and climbed tricky, loose stone passes. By late afternoon, with the sun at about four o'clock, a woodland appeared over the hillside, and the tinny notes of fresh water met their ears. Sun-a looked to him with expectation.

Their weary walk neared the edge of a run, and they couldn't help laughing; they hurried round a bend, and then another. The stream was at their feet so suddenly that momentum carried them jumping over it, and then turning back together, a bundle of relief and excitement, his hand on her back ushering her forward.

The stream was clear, beautifully so, making delicate jumps, eddying and elegantly splashing the sides of newly carved rocks. They walked into it, the cold drenching their hot, dusted feet. They knelt and splashed water up on their faces, to wash, to drink, rolled their sleeves up and doused scorched arms.

They sat and drank, and talked about water and mul, and mog marrayo, thirsty, very good and jeongmal johda, and in the moment languages, and words and meanings all seemed to blur together into one, without distinction. They were thankful, the canteen replenished, and they drank from their hands and ate some of the seeds and berries they had found that morning.

Then they sat and said little, and simply rested. The stream played tinkled notes and birds made flutterings in the trees. Mick noticed he didn't even turn, nor flash his eyes open, at the disturbance in the foliage. He rested and felt something like peace.

Sun-a stood, when they had waited a while and looked at each other and nodded it was time to go. She felt warm inside, perhaps from their walk, the constant exercise, the middle of summer. But happy too. Light; a lightness that seemed to lift her a little from the ground with each step. As they set off the strangeness of the thought moved with her. How odd that she should even know it.

She thought of their imagined destination, her long-ago home somewhere past the rocks and jagged mountain sides, beyond them and further still. Distant walks, paths and her young girl's running feet came to her mind, then drifted away. Then more remembrances of brightly coloured, starkly real scenes, all the greens and yellows of leaves and grass, and she panting for breath, and doubled-over, laughing. Things that had really happened. Once. On that soil she remembered under her toes. The place that was real, over there where they would soon be standing again.

She put her hand to her belly and felt the flatness that was returning. She smiled, in a sense of wonder. What she had never contemplated imagining, seemed to be happening.

Mick saw a building through the trees. An edge, blue, and an overhang of roof, striking up in Oriental style. Sun-a had stopped beside him. He placed a gentle hand on her back, and guided her to crouch with him. Keeping low he moved forward, she knowing exactly what to do after weeks evading discovery.

They rounded on the structure through the copse of dense trees which had hidden it from them. He could see the path they had been taking arcing around to a kind of dirt courtyard cleared of trees, before branching off again into the woodland. There didn't appear to be anyone there.

It was the first building of its kind he had seen in this land, though something of its shape reminded him of temples he'd seen in India and Burma. A simple square with doors wide open onto a dark interior, it was built entirely from timber, raised on a stone foundation; vivid colours, greens and golds, and reds; fine craftsmanship, even from a distance, as wood curved and intersected and seemed to fold up in layers, intricately dovetailing somehow.

Still no one moved. The doors had been left open. Perhaps that was normal custom.

Sun-a leaned her head to his ear and whispered slowly, enunciating for him: "Sanshingak." He did not know the word. Mountain... something, perhaps.

Mick stood slowly, and Sun-a rose beside him. He paused, about to motion for her to remain; but she knew of this place. Moving cautiously he began to make his way through the undergrowth, Sun-a treading in his steps. The trees thinned and fell away to open air. The small structure grew ominously as they approached, its overhanging roof seeming to lean out, with its concave black roof tiles sliding out from the wide middle peak, to end overlapping at the edge.

Out into the open. The last time he had stepped into the open of a forest clearing – Mick looked around him in the present. The cleared land was square, far larger than it had seemed from their cover. Undergrowth had encroached somewhat, but not enough to mean the place was unvisited. Behind the elegant roof a stepped outcrop of rock cut into a hillside covered by trees; to the other sides the mountain forest spread and rambled over rough ground. It was a solitary building.

They stood at a corner of the structure, with the tiered roof rising high above them. From this vantage point the eaves beneath the overhang revealed their depth: carved wooden shapes, locking beams and supports, reds and yellows, beautifully intricate. The colours had faded and in places the wood showed through.

Sun-a moved from his side, taking slow steps around the corner, toward the wide, open doors. Mick caught up, but stayed back, letting her take the lead. She mouthed some soft words as she looked up at the building, and then as she read large letters which spread over the double doors. She took the large step up onto the foundation of stones. She stepped inside.

Mick waited a moment. If anyone was inside, he would hear Sun-a greet them, and he could wait in the treeline until she returned. He trusted that she could handle herself.

No one spoke. He walked up to the entrance, a large formidable square of darkness. He lifted his English army boot and placed it through the portal, and down on the other side. Past the sharp contrast of light, it wasn't so much darkness as gloom. Sun-a stood to his left, back to him. There was little space where he stood, but more to either side. He looked right and tensed, on instinct almost throwing his shoulder to swing the rifle on its strap, around and into his ready hands. But the faces were not moving, demonic expressions rigid. Dead statues in front of a wall. There was no one else, he and Sun-a alone.

He looked up finally, to the centre of the room. On a platform which cut into the space, dominating the building, was the Lord of the temple, a golden painted figure, sitting eight feet tall, large head up to the criss-crossing, coloured carpentry. Buddha. Its face was the same he had seen across the Asian continent; the same fixed expression; false when met in real life. Mick looked away from the troubling idol. Sun-a was standing before a mural that filled the left-hand wall. In the gloom, Mick moved respectfully beside her and too studied the picture: a tiger, back curled, fangs concealed; an old man sitting beside it, with the Buddhist expression, long, long white eyebrows and white strands of beard. Mick saw, as he watched her, that Sun-a wrestled with the scene.

She turned and left him for the opposite wall. For a time Mick remained, trying to see what she had seen in the painted characters, in their mountain backdrop.

He at last followed her to the right-hand wall. He saw his instincts had been right, for the three statues were life-size, towering over Sun-a on their pedestals. Each held a sword out to strike about her. They stared past, towards him, with distinct, ghoulish, snarling faces, as he approached. They were cartoonlike in their grotesqueness: ballooned features, wide eyes, bared teeth; headdresses, garnished with feathers, or flames. He moved closer, seeing the peeling paint on old wooden carving and breaking plaster, then took a step away. He half-wished he had shot them. He saw her standing stony faced.

Guardians. The taste of dry blood was in the back of her throat. She had only just quenched her thirst.

When she moved away, past Mik-uh, she caught the question in his expression.

"Yeogi, saram. Ee mweo?" he asked, pointing to the statues, and then across, to the painted ones.

She looked to the painting, then to ground, and considered how to say it.

He watched her. She moved her hands like a child making butterfly wings, one atop the other, climbing higher and higher, but a different flight, more like whispers, like rising smoke. Then she said 'Meh-me.'

She looked again at the unforgiving figures, for that is what they both were, Mick saw – the eyes said it, the smile said it, spirit and cat alike. And she said, low, "shingak," and turned on her heels.

Mick went after her, as far as the doorway, where she had stopped. She pointed.

A pattern of rain drops spread dark grey over the foundation stone at their feet. Mick considered the air outside. Damp. The fresh smell of forest and moisture and air soon to be clear. Glancing up he saw darkening sky and clouds being swept by winds they were yet to feel on the ground. Dusk was not far away.

She looked to him and nodded her consent, then sat down on the stone base, legs dangling.

CHAPTER 20

The wind howled outside the temple. The doors were closed, but still wind whipped inside through the thin crack which separated them, making red paper lanterns sway from the ceiling and red ribbons bluster furiously where they were tied to the rafters, calm suddenly turned insane and lost control.

Beneath their sole blanket, at the side of Buddha, with his sentry guards looking down, Sun-a stared up. Mick-uh was beside her, the space of several people between them, as always. Below the roar of wind and the whoosh of rain being flung, she could just hear his breathing, asleep. But she could not follow. Her eyes kept opening, fearful.

She looked to the demon visions of men who hung over her, leaning from their pedestals, swords high, ready to bring down and strike. In pieces of moonlight, perhaps thrown with the rain, which made it between the doors, she saw flashes of the whites of their eyes. Wider than eyes, rounder than eyes. Even than Mik-uh's. And his eyes were beautiful, like nothing she had ever seen. She looked again, seeing the thin line from the moon dart across the monster's face; his black painted pupil seemed to roll with the motion. Why would they give a demon the only kind of eye in which she had not witnessed hell?

The light swept across once again, but she turned away. It was not them that she truly feared. It was the nagging, in her stomach, that she was not there by chance. That she and all she had done was part of a horrifically bigger picture. The clawing feeling that she could not clean away, of contamination, of curse – of the true monsters painted flat on the other wall, from which she hid. The mountain spirits who it was said ruled these places, in whose domain she had...

She frowned. It broke through, and immediately made her push up on her elbows.

A voice.

In the rain. A sound of the storm. Or coming from it?

She eased the blanket from her legs, stood, and slowly walked through the darkness to the large double doors.

Not wanting to see, she leaned forward, a gap between her and the aged, paint-worn wood, and put one eye to the crack. She could see the clearing, and the soaking rain, and a man running at the edge of the forest, with a gun.

Sun-a stepped back. Mouth at a scream, but wise enough not to make a noise. She turned, floundering through the suddenly pitch darkness, and all but fell onto Mick, hand on his chest, shaking, trembling, shaking him back to her.

"Mik-uk, Mik, Mik, Mik, Mik-uh."

Mick jumped from sleep. He knew he had been a fool; too comfortable; taking too much for granted – before his eyes had even focused on her. He took her hand, and stood them both to their feet.

They were here. Their hunters. He knew it. Could feel it somehow.

He ran to the doors and pressed his eye to the slit. Figures moved around the edge of the clearing, hand-signalling their spread, their perimeter. He watched, taking it all in. Three that he could see.

His heart thudded in his chest. He split apart options in an instant. There was no strategy. He had trapped the two of them in a bunker with one exit. In seconds the Japanese would have secured the surroundings; seconds more and they would move in. He had one gun, weak from distance, and a poor vantage point against theirs. He looked around – scoured the room in one glance: wooden swords, blunt paint layered edges, useless statues, a bunker that could be burnt to ground or snapped into pieces.

Mick looked to Sun-a, deadly serious. Her head was in his hands.

"Dwee-aya dwehyo," he said. "Dweeayo," in a frantic whisper. "Sun-a, dwee-ayo."

She nodded, fervently. Eyes wide and terrified.

He let his hands drop to take hers.

"Dwehyo. Understand? Run. We meet, downhill. Run, around, and down. Run... apart." He held his hands in front of her, then split them apart in opposite directions.

She said, "Understand."

They turned to face the doors. He stopped, and took the rifle strap over his head; he ground the safety with the heel of his palm, left, off. He held out the gun; he put it into her hands, moved them into position, pulled her index finger out over the trigger with his own. She looked at him with wide, intent eyes, hands staying on the gun where he had placed them.

In her language he said: "You run. Run away. Keep, down. Skirt." He pushed the gun down, hidden by the breadth of material. "After, in trees, forest, gun." He pulled the rifle back, clasped it again into her two hands. In English: "They find you, shoot. Fight." And he raised his empty hands to rifle position, and fired.

She nodded, scared, definite nods, and stood ready. The doors. He glanced to her, then didn't want to look away. Finally, he did. He placed his palms on the doors, one on each, his weight ready.

"Run. Meet in the valley. Gol jagee eh-seo manamsheeda," he said.

"Meet in the valley." She adjusted her feet, a sprinter's start.

They had taken too long already. He didn't look through the slit a final time. There was no point.

"Run." And he threw his weight into his arms, locked, rams against the doors.

The ancient double doors powered open, swinging hard on hinges, parting and flying in opposite directions in the night and rain.

They were off, barely looking, one to the left, one right. Shouts sounded. Figures in drenching rain, raised arms, swung rifles, a machine gun. Voices cried. He couldn't understand. He was hurling himself through the rain, pounding his boots into strides across slippy mud. Streaming toward the forest.

He prayed she'd make it.

Tat-tat-tat-tat-tat-tat-tat-tat-tat, on and on the machine roar went. Single punches of rifles joined it.

Exploding wood. Splinters. The sounds of the temple splaying, snapping into little pieces. Peripheral vision saw moments, of timber erupting in tiny bursts, ten, twenty, thirty, random spread, blooming in frantic speed. Timber cracked, and screamed as it snapped. He turned his head a fraction. Saw a pillar, carved, paint flayed, cracked, pieces ready to fall; and partway down, one place the wood torn, severed, all but gone.

The roof cried out, a howling screech. Not human. He wasn't hearing human. Tiles began to run, to jump over each other in their desperation to escape, to fall and tumble through the air as they flung and were pushed from the edge. The crack crack, crack as they exploded and fragmented, raining upon each other, line upon line upon line.

There had been no human scream. Could she have escaped this? Could she really have outrun them? And he was bounds from the tree line. To his far left a soldier stepped into the clearing, took aim, and fired. Mick ducked, and as he did his body turned, and he saw into the open.

He saw a figure walking into centre ground. Steady. Poised. From it, curving toward the ground, the black silhouette of a sword.

He was thrashing into undergrowth. The bullets had missed. Wet leaves, and branches sprung like traps in his face. He raised his hands to fend them off, seeing little, racing into darkness, avoiding trees.

And then he pushed off on damp mossy ground that gave like a gymnast's trampoline, sharp to the side. To see through the plan that he had known with certainty behind the closed double doors. That he knew beyond knowing. It was simply what he would do.

Racing through the forest, around, and behind, hidden by gunfire, and dizzying muzzle flashes. He heard the temple scream again as another limb crunched and stabbed into the muddy ground.

Soaked hair flung about her shoulders, across her face, as she glanced back, and turned and ran. Screams, whimpers half-sounded through her gasping breaths. The rain seemed to have pulled the air to ground with it.

She had fled back down the length of the temple, crouching low beside the foundation, hearing bullets crack and bounce from stone. Then into the night and the forest.

A figure was there, ahead, cutting across, moving slowly, not looking her way. She came to a stop. The soldier turned at the crunch of twigs and motion given up. He smiled; she saw it. Raised his rifle, at her. She darted away, as fast as she could run, risking impact with a ghost trunk, over bullets. She turned back, rifle atop the fallen tree, and fired. Tried to calm herself, and look. A shadowed shape of a man and she struggled to reload, jagged on the metal lever, and she fired again. The figure ducked in panicked shock and bounded into cover. Up and turning, clutching the gun, she ran, between trees; lurching aside as solid black bloomed in front of her, running along a bank of bushes and roping branches, trying to find a way through. Uphill. Awful blackness and the drumming of a thousand points of rain. She skidded and her hands met rock: fallen boulders, or a crumbled hill. She wound her way, escaping. Turning. And then she saw, close, through a break in the trees ahead, the collapsing temple.

Mick didn't stop. He took one huge diagonal bound from the trees. Out into the open. The Japanese soldier was looking the wrong way.

Mick thudded his knife to the hilt, into the man's chest, and struck with his shoulder, catching the shorter Japanese under his helmet and lifting him clear off the ground. Momentum carried the man airborne, while Mick half spun, never letting go of his blade. He took the rifle from the air, and dropped to ground, the knife acting as a brake to bring him crouching down.

A step back towards the forest, and it took him again. Onwards he charged, rain lashing, falling like collected mortars from the canopy that held it back. Great splashes fell at his feet, as he darted past, between trees, leapt over undergrowth. He would not fail her. He would save her yet.

A figure, a shadow, turning, searching every which way. He sensed the enemy almost before he saw him. A vast flying step out of the forest. Feet on open, baked mud turned mire, firm, pushing off. Rifle already ready.

Fire. A single explosion; a lightning flash gone before it had been seen. The soldier fell, arms still spreading from the killing force through the chest. A step away, leaping, gone again, never seen. Zig-zag, zig-zag. The circumference of the pit.

The man was behind her. She could hear breathing through shouts. Japanese. Laughter. There was nowhere else to go. She ran hard, out into the open, wanting to cry. There was nowhere else.

Then she saw him. Coat slick black wet. The cutting angles of the face, the eyes peering through sheets of rain, over the nose, like a guide, a targeter, a sight.

Sun-a came to a slow stop. She was unsure how close to step. The soldier was behind. He, was in front. The temple knelt to her right, the ornate tiered roof brought low, entrance collapsed. The Buddha trapped inside.

She looked to the monster she remembered only too well.

He returned the stare. In one hand he held a Japanese sword; the other stretched out toward her, holding a pistol. His head tilted to the side, like an animal she could not place.

Some kind of grin. Then the doctor spoke:

"I know you," he said with an oily, crawling pace. In her Korean.

Kamakura's face fell. Perhaps his subconscious had heard footfall on mud, an anomaly. He span in an instant. The bullet struck him as his back arched, his arm twisting. The pistol flung from his hand. His shoulder flared with pain and he cried out. Rage.

A shape hurtled through fits of shadow and mirror sheets of rain. He saw a foreign face, dark hair grown long, plastered to scalp, eyes that held clarity to be wary of.

The man leapt, shoulders turned, rifle bayonet like a spear. No bullets.

Kamakura acted on instinct, drilled and honed through countless kata.

He let the direction of the bullet finish, twisting fully round and reaching to his side. He gave up his footing. Hurled all of himself into one decisive, live or die move. As he rotated he drew his samurai sword, smoothly, without friction, even while airborne, turning a pirouette.

And like a snake he lashed out, throwing the impact, all momentum, the growing grab of gravity, through his arms, turning wrists, hands about the handle, blade.

He struck high, and round, a full sweep that cut the air.

Mick saw the Japanese move. Saw him twist and spin, instantly out of reach of the bayonet he was ready to strike down. The man was gone from view, a blur toward the ground, a gap left where the rain had yet to fall. Such speed. He was going to miss. But he was already airborne. And then a glint of silver. Impossibly fast.

Mick knew what was coming. But his body belonged to the rain and the wind; there was no ground to move off. The silver was a line that cut through his vision. Diagonal, horizontal, then diagonal again. Vertical, reaching its peak. So fast, a glint of light, exploding like light-bulbs bursting, blinding. And he strained every muscle in his back, and his arms, and stomach and legs, and threw the rifle around to intercept.

The metal blades scythed.

His flying body ducked, head into knees, legs out behind. His back yelled with the agony of pressure exerted.

The sword pushed the bayonet back the way it had come, and split the night air in front of his head. He felt its breeze.

Then it was gone, and he hit the ground with a fast roll, completing the somersault begun.

He was up and running, never stopped. Sun-a was before him, standing there, aghast.

He ran hard, pounding the mud underfoot, straight at her. Her terrified eyes grew wider still. He raised the rifle, into striking posture.

"Neh ree da!" he screamed.

She didn't move. Her eyes beheld him... not comprehending... heartbroken.

"Down!" he screamed again.

At the very sound of the English, she dropped. Vanished from his vision in an instant, to reveal a Japanese soldier looking pleased with himself.

Mick smashed the rifle butt so hard into his face that nose and skull sunk. Blood sprayed. The man left his feet, and flew back.

The world was racing. Sun-a looked up from the ground. Her hand was in his and he was lifting her to her feet, with poise given to a princess. Then he pulled so suddenly it hurt, and she found her feet flinging mud behind them, the temple groaning in pain as it rushed past them. Mik-uh stooped, dropping a rifle and picking one up from the body as they ran.

The black line of trees was nearly theirs again. Theirs to be hidden from this hell. She willed it closer, for it to reach out its branches and wrap them inside.

A voice boomed out through the rain. She had heard it speak but little before, but she knew it too well.

"And where will you run?"

His language.

Sun-a watched in horror as Mik-uh let his steps slow. She squeezed on the hand that held her own. They were almost there. So close.

Mik-uh raised the rifle and turned to look back into the clearing. She saw the doctor, standing up from hands and knees, where he had scrambled through the mud to his pistol. He aimed it at them with one shaking hand, the sword held in the other.

"Just where do you think you can run?" In Korean.

The man stood in the clearing. Were they not too far away? They were on the very edge of the forest, with mountain slopes and valleys and villages ahead of them that would never end. She wanted to leave it all behind. She looked to Mik-uh.

Then again in the foreign tongue: "Where will you run?" She understood the words.

Mick stared down the Japanese officer. He did not speak.

"You are on a peninsular. So just where will you go? You may as well be on Japan itself!" The man laughed an insane, delighted sound.

Mick frowned – blinked away rain.

"It is a stone's throw away across the sea. I'm right, aren't I, in the use? To the other side is, let us see, China, Shanghai... Singapore, that bastion of British Empire arrogance. I do not know how long it has been since your war ended, but I tell you, many things have changed in the world!" Again that laugh.

Mick pulled gently back on Sun-a's hand. They stepped further into the darkness, the shadows folding over them, deepening, layering with each step.

The swordsman roared in defiance. "You can run nowhere! I will hunt you! I will kill you! You and the whore!"

They were gone from view. Only he, the rain, and the incompetent dead remained in the scene. Kamakura boiled with frenzy inside.

He spread his sword arm wide and bellowed with every sinew that his lungs could command: "I will make you my war! Do you hear me? I will make you my war!"

Mick and Sun-a were running, running through the forest again, as fast as they could move. The scream hung in the soaked air above the trees, and fell to earth with every drop of the plummeting torrent; it wound between the trees with the gusts, coiling, serpentine, this way and that, after them.

And hand in hand they ran deeper into Korea.

CHAPTER 21

Kamakura Hideyoshi walked slow lines across the open ground. The sky was cold, lighting pale white, with blue only at the top of the world. It hung above like a huge window cut into the tree tops. He considered the task he had yet to complete.

He had spent five years in London studying medicine. He had recognised the uniform, the accent in a few fleeting, shouted words while he had been on the ground, pain roaring from his shoulder. He instinctively swiped at the mud, soaked and crusted onto his uniform. The man had even looked English. He knew very well where this man was from.

Yesterday's mire smeared underfoot. Each step sank in. Blood lay in small pools in the disturbed ground, in the grooves of boot prints and the cuts and tears, the record of the night's fight. Bodies faced the early morning sky, eyes still open, or lay crumpled atop the mud.

Kamakura turned sharply and cut back across the clearing. He passed the dead body of the last man to be killed, his face a mess, no longer a face.

He could prise that piece of lose bone and uncover the man's brain, the impacted frontal lobes. The man had stood in front of him and saluted the day before. Kamakura recollected the look in the eyes, wary, fearfully obedient. Now a cadaver, internal workings exposed. A thought came of that first dead body, on a table, in a high-ceilinged room, in St Mary's Hospital, in Paddington, England, white coving when he had looked up; of the streets outside, London buses. He stopped himself walking, and glared at the scene.

The fallen temple sat toward the back of the clearing. It looked like the carcass of a huge cat; some great beast, dead, collapsed forward against its haunches; now useless, barely held together. A monster, dead without leaving its pedestal. Kamakura could see pieces of the Buddha statue beneath struts and bars. Gold paint peeled thinly where it had been cracked. The plaster severed. The hollow inside, exposed like a Russian doll with no other selves.

Kamakura walked on, his gaze moving to the forest fringe, to the churned mud.

Two men remained alive, three dead. The living simply so because they had been scouting further away. He lifted a hand, moved a finger. The beleaguered looking soldiers went to a body and picked it up by underarms and boots.

The man holding the ankles braced his back against the weight that threatened to pull him over onto the mud. He glanced to the only other survivor – the doctor didn't count in the tally, naturally. Their feet shuffled awkwardly, in no particular direction, just back, away to the trees, so they were carrying it somewhere. He saw uncomfortably how his opposite number tried to wriggle aside as the dead head banged against his chest with each ungainly motion. He saw disgust down-turning his mouth, and how he nudged the head with knocks from his side, until it stayed put under his arm, the hanging neck dropping the head from sight. He would have done the same. They shuffled on, with what looked a decapitated corpse from his view by the boots.

He had thought this a fine distraction from the tedium of the prison and watchtowers. But now his friends were dead. He himself was only not dead, he suspected, due to where he had been standing when the orders were given out.

A look back to the doctor saw him pacing slowly, still. The man scared him. The whole thing scared him. What were they doing out here? It felt like an unstoppable, gathering nightmare; like that first journey by train, to Nagasaki, those years ago; and he now knew there was no brake. They would be going on, further and further. They were never going to stop – until they had all crashed into these treelines.

He felt a sob rising unstoppably from the pit of his empty stomach, to throat, where it caught and he had to grit his teeth to stop his eyes from crying. Like a bubble rushing up from a bucket of ice cold water it broke free. He coughed at the crucial time, and shook his head to mask the stinging that made water pool on his eyelids. He couldn't wipe his eyes; his hands held the two boots. So he looked down at the laces, and the blurred mud beneath, and shuffled on with Rago's dead body, to the woods where they would leave him.

As the tears dissipated, he dared look back to the captain. Still walking slowly. He looked away.

The doctor put a hand to his shoulder, grunted a little at the pain. He tried to flex the muscles in his hand, to clench a fist and release it. He felt sinews and tendons screaming protest on the edge of themselves. His hand trembled. Fingers barely moved. He growled in disapproval.

He would need to have the bullet removed, by someone vaguely competent. They would stop briefly at the next town, closest to the trail. A bullet to the shoulder and the whole arm incapacitated. It was intriguing, the difference between diagnosis of injury and experience.

One of the soldiers spoke: "How will we get their bodies back?" It was not a question – there was too much weakness and disbelief in the voice. The man already knew the answer.

"We go on," Kamakura said. "We will commandeer whatever supplies we need from other troops."

"On what orders?"

He was surprised at the reply. He almost turned round.

"On my force of will."

He ignored the sound of squelching mud as it restarted. Annoyance grabbed him, and he crushed both fists. Only one of them closed.

Yes, he was sure, almost certain – as much as the night had allowed. He never mistook a face. That girl – he had seen her before, in the corridor of his hospital. A brief turn of the head. Her. The pieces of the puzzle had somehow put themselves together on that mountain plateau – had aligned for him alone. He felt a rush of providence filling his veins, acknowledgement, the sacred; approval from the myriad Kami. It was his mission. He would catch them.

He was at the end of the clearing, trees rising before him. They felt like enemies.

***

The boat was tied to a tree, nestled between tall reeds on either side. It was what they had been searching for, taking the risk of the riverside. Even at night it was a place that locals might be found, securing cargo to a barge ready for the morning, or drifting downstream to make good time. A lantern shone on strangers walking the riverbank could easily pick out a white face.

Mick untied the tether, then helped Sun-a to set foot on the prow. Gathering the rope, he followed her onto the small rowing boat. The wooden hull rocked tumultuously, side to side, under the sudden change of weight. Instinctively Mick reached for Sun-a, to steady her, to stop her falling, to catch her before she went over. The boat tilted at his movement, one edge suddenly rising, about to crest and crash over them.

He reached out, and saw Sun-a nimbly adjusting her feet, stepping aside, even turning round to face him as she did so. She shifted her weight, put a hand to the side about to tip over, and made a soft noise, as if calming a frightened horse from rearing up. She countered the surge and the sloshing water as if she had done it a thousand times. He watched her, transfixed, slightly stunned; then he was grasping at the air, suddenly alarmed to notice it was his balance that was not there. He found himself landing with a bump, sprawling back on the seat, legs stuck up in the air.

The boat steadied with countermoves from Sun-a's wide stance, as she looked down at him with an amused expression. He was glad it was not daylight; the moonlight was plenty.

Sun-a picked up one of the oars, and made to sit down next to him.

Mick shook his head passionately. "No. Annio, Sun-a." He placed a hand on her hanging skirt, over her stomach. "Bay, Sun-a, No, Sun-a, Nanun hal su itnun. Hal su isseo."

They paused, he sitting there, she about to, slightly above him, looking down. He saw her in the faint light, silvers casting her face from shadow. She nodded, her eyes holding a tenderness, and then she moved to the opposite seat a few steps away. The boat rocked gently.

She took her rifle's strap over her head and put the gun beside her on the seat. He pushed them from the bank with an oar, and their boat brushed through the tall reeds and out onto the open river. He let the oars submerge and gently steer them beneath the blackness. Then, careful of the surface of the water, he slowly rowed them into the midstream current. The only sounds were the tinkle of the river against the hull, and the soft drip from the oars as he brought them in.

"Bay," she said, with a hand to her stomach, and then, "bay," with the same hand placed on the side of the boat.

"Oh," he said with a nod.

The river was perhaps a hundred feet across, though the far bank rarely showed through the darkness. They drifted, on the open, flat water, the furthest from cover they had ever been; he saw almost nothing of the dark water as he glanced over the side; he had to trust that the river would hide them and carry them, past miles of land, sleeping villages, a day's tense trek. Mick knew it was their best chance. The Japanese would regroup and follow their prints over the damp ground, footstep by footstep. They would have access to vehicles as soon as they neared an outpost; they would radio ahead and have a net spread ready for them to walk into. He had needed to do something different, and beat the setting trap. As he sank low at the bottom of the boat, oars held against his chest, he knew they had to have a chance.

He looked at her, sitting on the opposite bench. The girl who had become his responsibility. They had escaped certain capture, which he should have known better than to allow in the first place. They were running south for now, wherever the river took them; but soon they would head east, to her home. They were still together. He would get her there.

To her home, across Korea. He couldn't help but smile. Korea. His opponent had lied about certain things he was sure, but somehow Mick did not doubt that part. The pieces fit together. This was not the Empire of the Sun. This was an occupied land whose inhabitants in their villages hated the Japanese just as he did. Sun-a was...

He looked to her, across the night, in their boat. The reality of it, the pain of it, hit him.

Sun-a was Korean. She came from a place far from the prison camp. She had been brought there. Taken there. Against her will. She had been forced to do what she had done.

She had been raped. Perhaps for a lifetime.

She had killed the baby they had put in her.

Mick wanted to cry for her. Her head was turned aside, so elegant, regal, on the bench of their stolen rowing boat, as she watched the forms of trees and reeds go slowly by.

He wanted to clamber to his feet, and step across the boat, and hold her. He wanted to cry for the girl and the blood and the small grave, in that clearing, on that plateau between mountains. He wanted to get up right then and... make it all go away for her.

He had lived two years as a prisoner; she had lived a life.

She had been born into a country that was a prison. He thought for a moment of what that meant. Of what it really meant. A Britain where German or Japanese troops walked the streets; where young women were seized, to service the bored, occupying army; where his young cousins, Jane, and Emily, and Caroline, would be brought up, loved by their parents, ready to be taken away. And never come home.

He was in the boat again, looking at her, the beautiful young woman sitting not four feet from him. And then he smiled as a lighter thought graced him: it turned out he could speak Korean. Some, anyway. He could have laughed, but didn't want to disturb her, sitting there, watching the world go slowly past.

It occurred to him – how could he not have realised sooner? – that she had likely never seen scenery pass by before. Prisoners, in jails, or brothels, did not leave. This had been her first walk in mountains, and along valleys; her first journey down a river. What had her life been like before? For how long had she been there? Soon she would be home, but he had no idea what that was. There was so much he didn't know about her, and yet he felt he knew her so well. She was clearly better in boats than he was, that was certain; if not on a river, then, the sea? Had she sailed on oceans before it all?

A terrible possibility fell again; it had plagued the prison camps and they had fought it, their war then. For what if the Japanese swordsman had spoken the truth in full? What if the whole world was a prison? Then there was nowhere left to run. There had never been a realistic chance of escaping the Japanese heartland, he had always known that – and being one country further along made little difference. His hopes had depended on Allied victory, and surviving long enough to see friendly tanks come rolling in. But if Singapore had been the beginning of a rout that never ended; if British troops had been pushed all the way out of Asia; then he was truly alone.

She was everything. And he marvelled at her, from the floor of the boat, with the oars held under arm. Had she not been everything for a very long time? When had plans for escape last truly concerned his mind?

Mick had no answers. He let his thoughts settle and his mind become the sound of the lapping water and the gently drifting hull.

"I knew him."

He pushed up from the deck, awkward, not letting either oar slip. Surprise, at her words – to hear her correct English tense; and then to hear who she must have meant.

"Who?" he asked.

She replied with a word he had yet to learn.

Seeing he did not understand, Sun-a reluctantly began her mime. She pretended to hold a sword in both hands, and to sweep the air with it. Then she turned the imaginary handle over, and placed the blade on her belly. She met Mik-uh's eyes sadly, then with a sudden jolt, thrust her hands to her stomach.

By the wide-eyed expression that gripped his face, she saw he understood. She let her hands fall away. But his eyes remained a moment on the sword stabbed through her. Then he looked to her.

"Sun-a," he said, pained.

She nodded. And again she said in Korean, "doctor."

Mik-uh nodded, and repeated it back to her.

***

Sun-a was dreaming, she could sense it, and the tug of water on her feet as she kicked through it, and the sea air, a vast expanse stretching away, which had come from so far to be there. It panged her heart to see, to be there, in that scene again, even in sleep. And the dream continued, and she remembered less that it was.

A young girl paddled in the water, keeping afloat, keeping her neck back a little, her mouth gulping up, to evade the wash of the waves.

There were battleships on the horizon, and she was swimming to them, and crying. Her arms splashed over her head, stroke after stroke, pulling her forward through the water, although she begged to return to the shore.

"No, no, no," she moaned through the water which rose at and over her mouth, between breaths and waves and gasps.

Her head shook, side to side, and her body turned with the shape of the strokes.

"No, no, no," she pleaded, and tears ran down her cheeks. When the edge of the waves met them, they immediately vanished like they had never been.

Suddenly it changed and she made herself stop. Her arms flailed wildly, splashing, cutting into the waves and she screamed as loudly, as raw, as her lungs would force. Breaths panted from her as she trod water, struggling to keep her head above it, fighting against tiredness and hurting muscles. She began to win.

Hands reached up beneath the water and grabbed for her. They stroked her sides, and pulled at her arms and legs, slipping off, and clawing up again. She was twelve, thirteen, fourteen, and they were touching her, sliding down her, then reaching again, and she screamed, and twisted and spun in the water, round and back and around again, to get away. They began to take hold, and to pull. Short sharp tugs, then let go. Then holding on longer. Hands, so many of them, from five, to ten, to twenty, hands all over her, heel, thigh, belly, chest, then cupping the top of her shoulder and dragging her down.

The water rose above her nose, and her eyes shot wide with fear. She kicked up with all of herself, and burst just above the waterline, and immediately they had her down and under. Her forehead felt the cold lapping sea, and she squirmed and she could see nothing in the reddening salt. The waves fell away, and she gasped in the shallow of the crest, just a girl.

And she was a woman, a young woman, as she now remembered she was, and the hands were stroking and evil and gripping on to her limbs, and about her waist, working in twos, in the pairs that they really were. And she cried the tears of the young girl and the woman, and she knew what the poor girl must endure.

The battleships loomed, huge steel buttresses which sank to the sea floor and could not be moved. And she wanted desperately to swim away. She had not swum toward them? She had not. But the hands pulled her head under.

***

Sun-a led the way. At times she appeared confused, and stopped, then agitatedly crossed the path, back and forth, looking about her, pushing up on tiptoe. Mick waited patiently, holding within his own agitation, standing back, watching her run her hand repeatedly through her hair, as she spun around, searching for something in the scenery. She walked flustered on, unsatisfied; other times he had seen the brief break of a smile on her face – a momentary flash of recognition and joy at the way the hills shaped, or perhaps the kind of trees upon them. She would turn to him beaming and beckon him on. He had watched her mood, rise and fall that past week. The closer they got, the more she was absorbed by familiar surroundings, the more nervousness showed on her face, in her restless hands.

They had taken open paths, small tracks, overgrown. Occasionally he had taken her onto higher ground that overlooked the road, or had her wait in cover, while he scouted around hidden bends, or checked constricted sections where the mountains would hem them in. But she was leading the way now, and guiding herself home.

Twice they had had to hide while locals with carts and goods over their backs had trundled past. He thought of the pained look on Sun-a's face.

That morning they had crouched behind rocks on a hillside and observed a junction some distance away in the valley below. Japanese guards had operated a road block, pulling over trucks. She had grown quiet, and simply gazed at the scene, somehow worse than subdued. Numbed.

The path ended abruptly ahead, severed by the road which ran through it. On the opposite side the rough track began again up a steep bank and continued on over low rises. They cautiously approached, and crouching behind cover, looked down along the road. Sun-a nodded to him and climbed down. They quickly crossed, Sun-a scrambling up the opposite bank, not turning to him until amongst the sandy, rough land; her face carried panic, her breaths were quickened. They walked on along the tire-rutted track.

Sun-a's pace began to slow. Gradually. Very gradually. Mick matched her, studying her, seeing no longer confusion or doubt on her face. He felt a knot tie in his stomach. His throat began to burn.

Then she stopped. She turned around slowly to face him. Mick looked away from her eyes. Over her shoulder he saw the path sloping downhill, and where it broke the trees, a faint wisp of smoke rising. Small, controlled – the kind made by a hearth in a home.

"Home," she simply said.

Mick nodded.

"Sun-a jeeb," she said.

Her arms lifted slightly, but hesitated at her waist. Fell back, fidgeted.

Mick swallowed. He hadn't been ready.

"You go now." He had wanted the Korean words, but they hadn't come.

She nodded, agreeing. It hurt him to see it.

"Thank you Mik-uh. Thank you."

Mick nodded, smiled sadly. She nodded, and smiled the same.

Neither said anything. He couldn't believe it was over.

CHAPTER TWENTY-ONE

They stopped facing each other. And they turned away.

Mick walked back up the path she had just led him. He looked back, but she was walking away. Her face did not turn; her hair lay undisturbed over her shoulders, down her back. So he turned away, to the path ahead, and carried on. He wondered if it was just that he had missed her timing, doing the same. But he did not look back again.

The contours of the hillside went between them. He walked slowly, stride without haste. The path took him away.

CHAPTER 22

Mick approached the edge of the bank with a quick glance left and right, as if checking for traffic in Derby. His angles were partially obstructed, he sensed it, yet stepped from the edge with a jump that cleared the sharp drop of the slope. He landed on the road, knees bent, then straightened, and as if crossing from his house to the park on Chester Green, he walked over the dirt road in occupied Korea.

A flicker of panic rose in his gut, and he glanced to the side, where the checkpoint and Japanese guards would be, somewhere beyond the curve and the hillside with its line of trees. Alarm - that he had just done what he had done. Did he really not care?

He climbed the opposite bank where the path continued, taking shape in a crumbling, worn change of soil colour, a darker yellow. He moved quickly, away from the road.

Behind him, the sound of a lorry, a heavy engine and clanking metal. Mick pressed into the boughs of a low bush. Hawthorne twigs and white flowers pushed past his face. There he waited, only half concealed; but the sounds of the lorry rumbled on to slow some way away at the checkpoint. Distant Japanese voices.

He stepped back from the rambling countryside and onto the path that he and Sun-a had taken minutes before. He couldn't grasp it, the lie of the recent. It seemed a different life, or world, perhaps not even his own. And he was walking the opposite way to the way they had come. He wondered whether he would just keep going, all the way, back along the path, and sit down in their clearing, the plateau amidst the mountains, hundreds of miles away.

He was walking on. He glanced up, and saw a Japanese soldier do the same. The man stopped, a mirror of him, as his legs froze. His arm tightened, his hand tensed beside the slung rifle. All was alertness, from out of nowhere. He was back, and the expert soldier who had survived Burma's jungles and capture and everything else that the Japanese had thrown at him. He noted the enemy's own frozen hand ready to take hold of the rifle that hung from its strap about his neck, and still swayed with the gone motion of the march, at his side.

Mick's mind understood and pronounced upon his options almost instantly.

But Sun-a was gone. He had taken her home; he had done what he had set out to do.

And he stood straight from the battle-ready stance that would fire and kill, dead centre of the target in a split second.

His eyes were locked on the enemy's own, but his peripheral vision was focused, unyielding, for the slightest movement. But he did not see the telltale signs of an attack about to be launched, of a warning about to be shouted.

Mick took a step forward. The Japanese had done the same.

Two soldiers walked from opposite ends of the rough, overgrown country path. The man was tall Mick noted, lanky, and his face held fear, terror behind the imposed mask. Mick wondered what his own looked like right then.

Still rifles were at sides. Hands steadied them from banging below rib cages.

One move was all. Whoever moved first would fire first. The other would die, smashed by bullet at close range.

The tall checkpoint guard willed his feet to keep moving. The white man was walking toward him. He wanted to turn and run. He was about to die. He should shoot, but the foreigner would shoot first: his face was like stone, hard, fearless, unfeeling; his eyes like an eagles, so cold. The Guard tried desperately to resist the reflex to swallow. His Adam's apple remained, welded dry, pressurizing in his throat.

In moments they would be at hand to hand combat. The other man would move in a flash and the rifle would be brought about his head. His thoughts danced again past the solid reasoning why shooting first would get him killed, but he knew it was a lie. So much of his life was a lie.

He did not want to. That was all. Why bother?

Fifteen shaku was all it was. Two men who would try to kill each other.

A decade standing at a checkpoint on a road, in a country he did not care about. His eyes never left the round eyes in the other man's face. If he shot now, grabbed his rifle and shot... Angles had narrowed; it was harder to see across the diagonal; he could fire almost before being seen.

But he felt the sadness, the presence of crimes behind his eyes, that as their pressure so often did, made him want to cry. He had raped, when others had done so first and they'd back-slapped and jeered and pointed him on; he had shot some people who had been moving slow, another in a disturbance at the barrier; he had stood by and done nothing when horrors had screamed and clawed at his irises; while they had wailed and moaned and wept in his ears; he had stood by while a young girl was seized, thrown in the truck; while her mother howled beside him. And there had been a little girl who had held the side of the cart like the ground might fall away beneath her and it was all that would remain upright.

He had sat on those seats, in that truck, often, and thought of it.

He would not shoot.

They were past each other. The tension to kill in those last steps. Mick half glanced back, then stopped the turn of his head. He kept walking, slowly on. The Japanese would not shoot him in the back. He was certain of it. He had seen the look in the man's eyes.

The silence was broken by the voice of the Japanese. The words Mick could not understand.

The tall checkpoint guard walked on. He was shaking. He fought against himself, to keep from sobbing. The American might hear him yet. Let his words, spoken at the last before breaking, be the end. 'I see nothing.'

He walked on, a wreck. He had seen nothing.

***

At every step Sun-a saw a building she knew, or a tree placed over the sapling it had once been. Homes, to left and right, baskets and carts, and drying food on mats and bare earth. The smell of fresh fish, and the sea captured with it. The village in pictures within her memory, was there, confirmed, or changed forever in an instant, overlaid and vanished.

She took the Japanese rifle and placed it out of sight in a bush to the side. She walked on, her heart risen, filling her chest, catching in her throat. Her family were here, ahead. And yet she thought of Mik-uh, and the longing was all for him. She wanted to cry – he was gone. They were walking away from each other on the same path. The thought of it seemed so impossible, seemed to run contrary to the world and everything in it, seemed to have been such a terrible break that it could not really be.

But when had the world ever laid a destiny for her? What did she now find herself believing?

Closer she walked. She had not really wanted to come here. She had come because he had asked her, and they could not then speak to say and hear why she must not; because she had needed them to go somewhere.

And now she was there. How could it be? Walking through the village into which she had been born, and from which they had tried to flee.

An old man walked from around his home, to the fishing net spread over kimchi jars. He looked up at the figure in the corner of his eye. He stopped and squinted when he saw it was her. She recognised him. He had been younger, without the bones of shoulder and arm showing under his repaired shirt.

Sun-a kept walking. Her legs resisted, suddenly having doubled in weight. She thought of falling and collapsing. This moment that had been coming, endlessly coming for the weeks of their journey; she had wondered of it, often, but now saw that she had never really expected it. Yet it was now happening. And it mattered so, so much. She thought of Mik-uh, and he mattered, the same; more? But he was gone. This village was everything... and nothing to her; the past and now the present.

Her legs threatened to seize and stop, and with a kind of frantic panic she mentally grabbed each about the thigh and the knee and dragged them on. There was movement ahead. The last building between them had passed aside, and she was looking at the small house she had grown up in.

She saw the chillies laid out in their place before the front door. Fish drying in a row beside them. Someone moved in the doorway. The lightness of clothing breaking the black.

She saw the sparse spread of trees behind their home, their roots holding onto the last of the sand dunes. They folded out behind it, she knew, a short drop, past the grasses that grew as tall as she had once been, and then fell away, down to the beach. Further along rose the cliffs, and the wood atop them with the path she had run along so many times, late, or racing her friend.

She could go there, down by the cliffs, and take off her outer clothes, and swim.

No, she couldn't.

The waves drifting against her toes before they retreated; the mix of sea and sand, the foam, the water sinking, disappearing into the sodden, footprint-sand. A young girl dancing into the waves, waist, shoulder high. Off her feet. Weightless. Carried. Splashing, laughing, turning over onto her front. The sight of the expanse before her, blue, seeming to rise – to slope up to the line of the sky. So beautiful.

She stood, alone in the village square, before her childhood home. She had stopped walking. She waited for her mother to look up.

Gyeong-hui sensed a reason to look out from the clothes she folded and stowed by the doorway. It was bright outside and the figure standing alone in the middle of the village was in a rectangle of colour that seemed more than real.

It was a woman with long hair that fell down the sides of her face, past her shoulders. Straggly in appearance, her skirt hung off her, badly fit, dusty and torn. She knew the woman. She could not breathe. She straightened her bent back and had to step from the low doorway to do so – out into the daylight, and the open space that faced her.

Gyeong-hui put a shaking hand to her mouth to stop her scream. She felt herself shake from side to side, and tears begin to stream her dry cheeks.

The scream escaped her, a whimper of disbelief. It shrieked and seemed to be everywhere in the quietness of the village, hanging there still sounding, refusing to go on.

Sun-a took an unsteady step forward. "Mother. It's me, Sun-a."

Her mother nodded unstoppably. Brimming tears shook free and fell. Her hand moved from her mouth to reveal trembling lips; it moved aside reaching for something or someone. Or holding something back.

Her father stepped from the doorway, consternation his expression at the sight of his wife. He looked out for the cause, and saw her.

"Mother. Father. It's me, your daughter. Sun-a."

A second time, for her dad. So as not to hear either ask who she was.

Her father stared, nothing yet decided upon his face. His hair was greying, and his face was thinner. He looked at her with a dead coldness in his eyes.

His face still betrayed nothing, even when he spoke: "You're not welcome here."

A faint shriek, air expelled, came from her mother beside him. It arched her back like a blow to the spine, but he steadfastly looked on.

Sun-a knew what the words meant, in that order, those sounds. Yet they held in her mind or the air, about her, making the front and top of her head go numb. They didn't settle. Her father's voice; she had not heard it for such a long time.

Her mother was tugging gently on her father's arm, a step taken away from him so that she had to lean to clutch the fabric of his old fisherman's shirt.

"Dad."

Her father shook his head. His mouth moved, pursed, and his expression at last shifted. Between something and something else. Fighting.

"No," he said with a bluntness that cracked out like a breaking board. "You are not my daughter. I had three daughters. Now I have one."

He gasped then, and his mouth dropped open, and his eyes stared aghast at the ground. He rocked as his wife dragged harshly on his arm and cried-pleaded 'Ee-Jin-gyu...' His head shook, perhaps hadn't quite ever stopped.

Sun-a found she could not see. She wiped the blur away from her eyes, looked at the ground of the village square, glanced aside to some who were now not watching. Then back to her parents. She had not gotten close to them; they were half the square away.

Sun-a waited a moment, head down, but looking up at them. Her mother no longer held her father's sleeve, but now stood desolately facing his side. He looked to the ground, but his eyes flicked from place to place upon it, then up to her face. Then away, never to settle, or to focus. They were waiting too, she realised.

Was that it? That was it. Sun-a began to turn from that spot.

There was a rumble of cart wheels, and laughter. She looked over to the path through the wood – the one that led to the cliffs and to the rock pools where the fishing boats could easily moor. The cart, the same cart she remembered, was pulled into view. She saw herself and Hae-ja, one handle each, talking and laughing as they brought the catch home. Except they were slightly older. Taller. Perhaps, fifteen, sixteen... They had never been that old.

Her father and mother looked agitated, watching the cart with her. The girl – her – saw her in the open square. From that distance Sun-a still saw the familiar look, as she remembered it feeling on her own cheeks and lips, as she tried to understand.

The cart slowed, and trundled closer along the grooves of the track.

"Sun-a?"

Sun-a took a sharp breath, taken with surprise by her voice.

"Yes."

Her heart filled at the sight of the girl, the look of wonder and love looking back at her.

"Cho-hee?"

The her by the cart nodded, and smiled.

They had not taken her. Never. She was beautiful, her sister. So much more beautiful than she herself could ever have hoped to be. She had grown to be a young woman – and her friend too. Sun-a tried to recall the young child who had become the friend, and pictured a girl, very small, watching her with the awe and wonder always devoted to a girl just a few years older. Now it was she who looked on with awe, and gratitude. Then the thought came of Hae-ja with a weight of sadness. If only it could have been like this.

Hae-ja's home stood as it always had. But her mother and father were not there, and no cart or nets rested against the house.

Then back to her father and mother, and her little sister.

"Cho-hee," her father instructed quietly.

With a look to her, beginning to pain, sensing the edges of what was happening, Cho-hee moved toward the family house. She twisted round to glance over her shoulder as she went. She stopped a space apart from their mother.

The village watched from where they had dotted themselves. Two fishermen who now walked from the track, trailing behind the cart, their nets over their shoulders, slowed, sensing their intrusion. Cho-hee's friend waited by the handle of the cart, stranded there.

Sun-a asked her last desperate plea, with her eyes, with her expression, please for her father to relent. He met her gaze, steadier now, and said nothing in return.

She turned, a muted noise, not even a sigh. She felt dirty, so dirty. She felt every touch of the filthy misshapen skirt that hung on her, and what was beneath it exposed to the air and the breeze from beneath. She felt so dirty. She felt exactly what she was.

She walked away from their home. People moved, around the edge of their homes; heads craned down the alleys that ran between buildings; eyes peered from doorways; to see the fallen woman leave. A Japanese prostitute.

More muted cries, breaths, notes of despair fluted from her throat with each step. The world was unreal. Her throat shrank tightly, curling in on itself, burning with tears yet to come. Sun-a dragged her wooden feet from the village. Taking the turning of the path, willing it to take her away quicker. Once she felt the trees come between them, she couldn't hold it in anymore, and a cry burst from her. She stumbled forward, to her knees and the ground. Tears spilled, and her hands went to head and chest and beat ever so softly upon the dirt. She wept there, ashamed that they would still hear her there, but unable to stop.

So she half picked herself to her feet and stumbled on; she broke into a run, to get as far away from there as she possibly could. She saw the bush where the rifle was hidden, and left it there. Soon she was racing, away from the village, toward the crossroads. At the last moment she realised where it would take her and veered in panic to the branching path that was too narrow and hilly for a cart to take.

She clambered down the embankment that dropped onto the road, still crying, wiping tears from her face, and scrambled up the other side on hands and knees. She was gasping for breath, and could not run anymore - could not bring herself to. In defeat she collapsed down, skirt billowing and settling, crumpling around her, and she cried where there was no one to see her.

CHAPTER 23

She did not know how long she had sat there, in the middle of the path - only that he was further away now. She picked herself up, stumbling upright on tired, shaken legs. At once she set off, walking as quickly as she could, on the very edge of a run. Her legs burnt from the outset, but she forced them to sustain the pace, hurrying, every movement captured in a kind of unrelenting panic.

Round a curve in the path, a sudden bend, and still he wasn't there. Hurrying, forcing, pushing her aching legs on, along a long, straight section, where she could see to the end that he wasn't there. She had to walk it, tried to stay calm, hearing her breath jump as she hurried fast strides. Seeing further ahead as the path twisted slightly to present a new distant end, and still having to walk it all, knowing he was somewhere else. Fearing, knowing, that when she reached that end and saw the new stretch of trail ahead, she would have to walk it all, fearing again for the next turn.

Hopelessness grew. Panic grew. The trail rose through the low cover of the hills. She saw no one. Her tired, rushed breathing, loud through her head. The panic formed a new set of tears, building in pressure, that she had to contain; it cried out in gasps, escaped with hurried breaths.

Another, winding path. A further hill. The mountains around Daegu looming in the distance. Another bend, and dip, and still he wasn't there. Had he gone a different way?

But which other way could he have gone? It seemed impossible to her that he had taken any route other than their path. Where the path branched aside, she ignored the turnings, rushed on, barely giving them a thought.

Her muscles felt on fire, but she would not listen. Breaking into a run, then back to walk, then to run. Sobs spluttered between gasps for air, and tears broke and ran sideways across her cheeks with the parted air.

Trees grew beside the path. The view ahead was hidden, turn after turn, and each time the path swung back, it was empty.

And then the turn opened into a straight stretch through branches which met above it. In the distance, nearly at the point where the path disappeared from view, a figure walked away from her.

She didn't cry out. She couldn't.

Perhaps it was that her feet had ceased to fall on the dirt, or perhaps there was some other reason – for she watched him slow and stop, and then turn, and look her way.

He seemed to be moving, walking towards her.

Sun-a's heart filled with a joy she could not describe, and she too began to walk, her aching legs somehow light, like they might flutter away.

She saw him begin to run. Suddenly the distance of the path was gone. She stopped at last, and stood, wavering. She could see the look in his eyes.

His run dropped, to a walk, then to stand and face her. He left a gap between them. They were yet to look away.

She was suddenly aware of how she must have appeared: tear strewn, red eyed, the sweat on her brow, dampening her hair. Suddenly aware of what she was doing, of what she, having found him, and now standing on this path, was asking.

"Mik-uh," she said.

Mick took in the sight of her, now close enough to see for how long she had been crying. Her expression held on a brink, in fear and hope; distress contained only just behind her eyes.

"Your family?" he asked in Korean.

He watched her swallow, and her eyes cast to the ground.

He stepped forward. His intent was to walk up to her, and take her hand; but when his foot set down, he didn't follow it. He kept his hand by his side. Turning his body slightly to the open path, he waited for her eyes to look up to him.

Sun-a watched for a moment, the look in his eyes. She took a step, and he took a step. And they began to walk back along the path they had come.

***

Kamakura Hideyoshi strode across the muddy ground with steady even paces. The wide river spanned out beside him. He paused momentarily and glanced across to the far side. Two tiny figures could be seen trudging, haphazardly, heads bowed, then raised, then turning... talking. He stared across the Naktong, waiting. The Bunraku puppets abruptly stopped, and their pale oval faces turned to look his way over the water. Promptly they turned away and began to pace out even strides, heads pivoted down to the river bank. He recommenced his search. Stride after measured stride, observing the ground, sweeping the mud and grass, side to side.

He was certain of his course of action. Rage fumed within him at the demeaning nature of the task forced upon him. It was a strategy close to defeat, and yet could become immediate success in a matter of hours. The English soldier was a competent adversary, but as the western nations always had, until the recent honoured years, he would assume superiority over the Japanese where there was absolutely none. Considering himself free he could be surrounded and killed. A day, even a matter of hours was realistic.

Kamakura sidestepped and passed a tree, peering and scrutinizing the ground around it. He would find the trail wherever it recommenced. His calculation, accounting for the size of the land area considered had been precise. Assuming for the overall compass direction of his quarry's flight and negating erratic and misconstruing deviations, no doubt designed malignly to obscure, he had correctly plotted the most likely disembarkation points. From Jinsen there had been a steady east-south navigation. It was possible that this had been by panicked necessity due to it being the longest stretch of land from the prison into which to run; but the regularity with which every deviation had ultimately, predictably, wound back to that east-southerly heading, had been evident to him. Was there a destination the prisoner or his whore had in mind? Urusan? A port, that faced Japan?

A sigh – a growl, walking on. The route did not make sense. The river traced a virtual perimeter around the east-south corner of Korea, holding in Taikyu, then turning its course to run through Fuzan on the coast. Large cities; Korea's key port. Protected by mountains to the north and the river to the west – natural walls. The one destination, toward which the prisoner ought not to have been headed.

And so he trudged the reeds and marsh on the opposite, west bank of the river, where the Englishman should have remained: the river an arrow to the south, to the wide harbour, Masan-bu, and the seas the British

Empire no longer sailed.

The annoyance of so many weeks, relentlessly tracking, searching a country for scurrying marks on the ground, threatened, began to disrupt his focus - for it did not make sense. Symptoms, pattern recognition, pointed east, where they ought not to have. He kept his eyes trained, one move after the next, even kata steps; his stance lowered, he swept the ground, feet, strides beginning to spread in fighting stance.

"Captain Kamakura!" The shout drifted faintly, screamed at full volume from the far side, the river's eastern bank.

He crossed at the next bridge, and in two hours had returned to their position. The two guards stood awkwardly as he approached, one moving from foot to foot.

"Captain Kamakura."

They saluted, bowed. He saluted in return, and fixed a stare upon them, wanting the information.

"Yes. It's there."

Saito pointed. Kamakura checked the grass for markings and then stepped forward. He leaned over the bank, where it fell away, muddy, grown with tall grasses. Yes, smeared, the side of a boot perhaps.

"And it continues here Captain."

The other guard moved aside several steps and pointed to the grass. Kamakura craned his neck over, then crouched smoothly down and inspected the mould. Light, a partial print in the mud of the sole they were tracking. It had been cushioned and obscured by the grass around, which had now sprung back up, but it was an acceptable match for the large army boot.

"Well done," he said.

He looked out at the river. With a spring he leapt from standing and splashed down two-footed into the shallow water. With wide, ranging steps, lifting out of the silty water, dripping and plunging firmly back down, he waded out. The water rose quickly, soon to his waist. He moved further out, stalking lines, back and forth through the river. It rose below his chest, cold and wanting to push him with it. His leg struck something solid. He put his hands into the water and found the curve of a hull between fingers and thumbs. He strode out of the water, dripping streams onto the bank.

The Englishman and the comfort girl would be caught soon.

****

They walked slowly, back down the trail by which they had come. Mick stepped carefully around a bloom of damp, dark in the centre ground, and supported Sun-a as she followed him – keeping their tracks from the dirt. He looked up, with regular concern, to see the path ahead, empty. An older man and woman had passed them half a mile ago, carrying packs on sticks over both shoulders. He and Sun-a had slowed, but not run, nor left the path; they had worriedly stood aside, as the worried, incredulous couple had done the same, and they had passed by. Others walked this thoroughfare – it was impossible to track on, without hounds.

The stolen and later sunken boat, and the many miles of journey down river had cut their trail. Yet he found himself somehow expecting the Japanese officer, standing there in the rain with that sword, to be approaching still. Could their enemy have been walking straight towards them? Was it half a day's head start that he and Sun-a stepped into, stride by stride, or even an hour's? Was that butcher closing, passing a valley that he could well recall, walking around the far side of the hill on the horizon, or just about to step into their sight on the path, where it turned forty feet away and hid itself?

This was no longer about getting a girl home. It was from this day on about survival.

There was no longer a destination. They were on the run, in a hostile country, being hunted.

In a field to the side he glimpsed a patch of mud, spreading for twenty feet or more, waterlogged, sure to sink in and hold footprints. It led between thorn bushes, and on, to a low copse of trees, then more trees as the hill rolled down. A piece of ruined building, a farm or shack stood slightly back nearby with the remnants of only one wall, and a field of stones scattered from it.

Mick raised a hand to Sun-a, and pointed to the new direction. She nodded. He didn't need to explain; after months of being tracked she knew what to do. If the samurai had recovered their trail then the next few moves would be important.

He took a step back – it was all the path made room for – then pushed forward and leapt. Enough to carry him there, hopefully not too much to carry him off it. He landed one footed on the stone. His other leg wavered, finding balance; inertia tried to reassert itself, again and again, as he fought it off. He put his leg down, breathed, then stepped one leg over to the almost too far, next nearest stone. He beckoned Sun-a on.

"Okay. Jump." And in Korean, "I'll catch you."

Sun-a nodded. Already she knew she slowed his escape. His every look back, the concern she saw; she could not give him reason to regret taking her with him.

She ran and flung herself. She felt her small frame, falling, too soon. The gap was too great. And then she landed against his chest. An arm wrapped her to him, as momentum began to spin her away. His stance trembled, but they held there, her two feet on his, balanced on the stone.

Then he all but picked her up and lifted her out towards the next stone. She reached for it with outstretched foot, and he pushed her through the air. She landed deftly, like a dancer, she had once known at the comfort house. Her balance took too long to return and she reached in panic, clutching a branch above her, which swayed but kept her steady.

Onto the next stone, toward the fallen-down house. This time it was her turn to help, as she reached out, one hand steadied on the wall, the other clasping Mick as he stepped across to her. They clambered over the wall, he helping her to the other side. They were careful as they climbed over the ruins not to disturb the crumbling stonework, not to leave an impression on the moss, or to turn the rotting beams into splintered signs.

Across a denser scattering of stones they placed one foot, slowly, securely after the other. Beneath their steps and careful jumps the wet ground stayed flat as the rain had left it. A toe against an edge of mud; a heel almost slipping. And then they were clear onto the dry ground of an open field.

Mick looked back to the opening to the path, half expecting to see the officer point, and Japanese soldiers come jumping out into the mud. He faced it still – waited. Nothing. Just empty Korean countryside. He turned away, feeling Japanese stares on his back.

***

One day ago, the Americans had created the surface of the sun on the floor of Japan. The Empire of the Sun had been scorched and burnt to nothing. He pictured the solar inferno ripping through the heart of the islands, and the honour of the generals and Emperor melting away like wax. Surrender was in the air, even across the sea on this hated peninsula.

Everything had been delayed. Even he. They had sequestered a day in Taikyu, to confirm the rumours, to settle the shakes of his broken search party. He had dragged them back out after that, clearly against their wishes. But it was not their unwillingness to hunt that had stranded their mission; it was the trail.

It had led them into a coastal village, and nowhere else. The day after the bombings had cost them. His prey had somehow found a way to evade its own trail.

He had crossed half of the country, slicing diagonally, almost to Fuzan at the bottom corner. He now stood at the opposite coast from which the search had begun. The original order was irrelevant – had ceased to have anything passing as jurisdiction, many weeks ago. Even the stink of Goro and his belittling manner had long ceased to concern him. It seemed a world away. A war ago. Kamakura was here, now, on a personal vendetta. And it fermented into a deep rage: that he had not caught the one enemy soldier whom he had faced free from a prison's grounds.

He considered the exits of the crossroads where he stood. One track led in the direction of the village and a dead end on dry dirt. The residents had hidden in their peasant huts at the sight of him and his men, and so he had called them all out. Every hut had been searched. The soldier and whore had not been there; there had been nowhere to hide in those one and two room dwellings.

He turned to the other roads of the dirt crossroads – barely fit to be described as such. It was unlikely that they would have headed south, toward Fuzan – even more so that they would have attempted to double back, right past him. It was probable that his quarry were currently hiding somewhere in the surrounding terrain, having reached the sea and nowhere else to run.

But why here? There was nothing? Why trek across a country, turning every which way, trying to throw pursuers off, in order to come here? A small village, near the main coastal road used by the Japanese. He couldn't understand it.

Frustration tore beneath his skin and facial muscles, and he longed to scream and wrench at his eyes and cheeks, but he remained calm. Though he stood alone he did not move.

He considered the barely competent checkpoint guards stationed there, as they carried their battered roadblock aside to allow through a truck so dusty it could have been painted green or brown underneath. How much longer, he wondered, would they keep up their pointless task?

No, there was still time. He turned and walked from the junction, up the curving road, to where it broke through the track by which he had come. He jumped up the bank, crumbling dirt and old shingle, and strode intently along the worn track, uneven ground, slopes cutting the horizon short, back toward the insignificant village. He stopped.

He moved aside, from the path, stepping around the perimeter of a wildly grown bush. He bent his knees slowly and squatted down.

He reached out and picked up the rifle that had been left standing there, muzzle to the sky.

He had already seen it was a Japanese army weapon, an old Type 38 Arisaka. Checking the magazine he found two waiting cartridges.

Japanese soldiers did not leave Japanese rifles sitting outside Korean settlements.

Kamakura smiled to himself and almost allowed a small laugh to form.

He had been right. They had come here with their thieved weapons. They were still here. He would wait for them.

CHAPTER 24

Rain was falling again, as they hurried down a rounded, sloping hill, letting the gradient carry their stuttered walk into a run.

Mick pointed through the rain to a shape in the blur of water and mist. Sun-a nodded, her face elated through disbelief as if having seen a mirage.

Inside the low stone structure they sheltered, hearing the rain beating down on the old tiles and exposed wooden supports. They huddled together in the middle, knees hugged to their chests, side to side. Even in humidity the rain seemed to have doused the heat from the air, and he could sense a cold night was falling.

Sound came from outside. Immediately Mick tensed, was on one knee with the low roof inches above his head. Ready to fire. Sun-a moved quickly from the line of sight of the doorway, and pressed her back to the wall aside the entrance.

There was a moment's pause, a silence but for the rain. Somehow Sun-a heard it as too quiet, as if she could hear the act of listening, and breath being held, just the other side of the wall.

A figure moved quickly past the stone, low and stocky, stopping in and blocking the doorway. She cried out, in Korean:

"What! Who...? Get out!"

Her arms flailed wildly as if to ward away an attack. Mik-uh quickly turned his gun aside, and reached out to calm her, then back from the striking arms.

Sun-a moved forward into the woman's view.

A Korean lady, late middle age. Her lined eyes paused a second, pupils to Sun-a's side. Her stout head and sun and winter worn expression turned to her, then looked to Mik-uh, and back again. She squatted in the low doorway, a tension taking hold of her.

Sun-a pushed herself from the ground. "No. No!" she called out, hands raising a conciliatory gesture. "No, you misunderstand."

The woman turned to her, stony faced.

"He saved me. He did. It wasn't what you think. I know why you think it, I do." Sun-a quieted, then said clearly. "But he never asked a thing of me. He never has, not once. He's the best man I know."

Mick-uh had not moved. Sun-a saw him warily watching.

The woman addressed her with a considered tone: "What kind of girl speaks like that when her father is still alive?"

Sun-a felt the words hit her. Felt her sadness long to cry. She replied, "I stand by what I say." Then, "Please, we just needed somewhere to shelter. Let it be as if you never saw us. We'll be gone. Just don't say anything."

"And if I mean to run to the town market and shout what I have seen? What will he do to me?" She pivoted on her haunches. "Do you plan to kill me, foreigner?"

When Mick-uh replied in their language the woman had to grab to the stone in the doorway: "We only ask for a little food, and water."

***

The stone hut was low about them. Its walls leant in slightly and from outside could be seen to be much wider at the base. Some mornings when flocks of sheep sheltered and gathered and leant against them, he could see why. Their instinct must have been passed from generation to generation, from former days when a shepherd had slept there. Now, it was he and Sun-a who sat against the old, piled stone walls, to eat, to sleep, to talk, to hide, with the broken roof less than an arm's reach above. In the weeks it had been their shelter, the left side – when they looked at it from further down the hill – was where she slept, and the right side was for him. But the gaps in the tiles above meant that they moved to avoid the frequent end of summer rains.

Mick looked up to the soaked leaves which draped and hung into the skylights at various places, where he had built shelter. It was early morning and the sun would dry them ready for the next downpour. He thought back with a smile to the first shelter he had built for them. This, by comparison, was a palace.

Sun-a stirred beside her wall, opened her eyes quickly, and saw him. It was her habit, most mornings – something he admired, when he was first awake to see it. Her mind would suddenly recall the situation it awoke to and the man who she shared the tiny hut with. At least he judged it thus, and had watched it enough to feel sure. Demure. Bashful. He thought back to the time under the first shelter, and what her life before must have contained, to make her do that. He felt like it had been worth it all that she had the chance to be shy again.

"Good morning."

"Morning," he replied.

"Your breakfast," she said.

"Ama gu yeojaga uri-ehgeh bapul jom julga-ehyo," he said, finding the words.

Sun-a nodded sincerely. "Behgopayo. Achim meoggo shipeoyo."

Mick passed her their bowl of water, with two hands. She took it likewise, in both of hers, and with a gentle bow of the head. She drank, and then passed it back, just the same. Mick couldn't help smile as he accepted the bowl with both palms and bowed his respect. This was their way at all meals, and he did it now as naturally as he did the eating; but from time to time he would see from an old, recovered angle, the wonder of the life he lived, as if half recalling an odd dream, a wispy remembrance, that showed a contrast with the present.

She preferred hot water. He had only been able to learn that since the woman had helped them. She brought the water up to them steaming in their bowl, and Sun-a would follow it with her eyes, delighted, as if it were a bowl of chocolate cake. She'd learnt that he had actually been enjoying cold water all this time, this summer long, and he had learnt, that however hot the day, she always preferred just-boiled. A few times the old lady had brought it flavoured with green tea leaves, and the smell of sheep and soil had been replaced.

Mick offered Sun-a their one plate with the chicken legs. Three. He guessed the third was all or more than the lady could spare. They had shared most of it for dinner the evening before, picking pieces off, and Sun-a dividing it between them – he passing back the extra portions she allotted, until they had reached an impasse, a settlement that they could both rest with. She had been through an ordeal not so long ago, he did not forget that, and she needed it.

From the hillside came the sound of a hurried, scrambled climb, and breathless pants. "Hello!" she called, still some way down the slope.

Mick and Sun-a sat up on edge and looked one to the other. The Korean woman who had been their saviour these past weeks, keeping their presence in the fields above the village a secret, bringing them food and water, had never approached in anything but silence.

"Quickly! Come out! Come out!"

She was close now, he instinctively estimated: thirty feet from their sole entrance and exit. What was she doing? An image flashed through his mind, of the aging woman standing outside the stone hut, surrounded by Japanese soldiers with guns trained, her words ordered.

"Go, now," he spoke to Sun-a, instantly regretting what might have been his goodbye.

He moved quickly to the crouched entrance, one hand taking hold of Sun-a's arm and pulling her after him. They burst out into daylight, and Mick was already moving them aside, ready to round the cover of the hut. Gim-Bong-rye was alone, trudging to a breathless stop, hands on hips, then on knees as she caught her breath. Her face beamed up at them.

"It's happening. It's finally happening." And she laughed out loud, such a delighted chuckle of noise. Mick stopped, forgetting he was still holding Sun-a by the arm.

"This way. Quickly or you'll miss it!" And she was off, hobbling at a skip across the hillside, over the tufts of sparse, grazed-low grass.

Mick and Sun-a stood a moment and watched the woman go. Mick looked to Sun-a, with no answer. He still held her arm. Finally he let go, feeling foolish as she slowly took it back to her side and tried not to favour it at all.

Sun-a took the first step, and they followed the woman across the hillside.

She would have been bounding if her hips had allowed it. Gim-Bong-rye felt a young woman again, not yet married, no path to walk, just an optimistic haze of possibilities of which she was too naive to guess much at. She beckoned back to the foreigner and the poor girl to hurry; her heart filled up at the sight of them, and what she had done. Had she ever done much better? And she carried on across the slope, almost tripping over some raised dirt, and powering on to where the hill overlooked the valley.

The woman had stopped ahead on a high point of the hill. Mick's legs felt weak as he climbed after her with Sun-a. Their trek across a country seemed distant after weeks hiding in a tiny shepherd's shelter. In fact, the whole experience seemed unsettling: being out in the open, with space all around – views to see, and be seen from – to distant hills, and the outline of mountains at the horizon; sky up above, in its full circle, in day, not hiding them at night.

They arrived beside Bong-rye, and Mick heard a sound that he knew to be familiar. Then he saw down to the right, to the wide valley below, where a road ran.

It was an impossible canvas. He could not see it, though he gaped, and tried: the troops, on foot, their guns fanning over the terrain, a joy and triumph in their casual walk; the camouflaged cars and lorries assorted throughout the column; and the rumbling tanks that fed into the painted panorama. He had beheld it all, but in glimpses he seemed to half recall even as he now looked, while the only thing his eyes could focus on were the blazing colours that burst from the greens and browns in little Technicolor squares about the picture. The striped blue and white, and smattering of glowing gold on flag.

"You're saved!" singsonged Gim-bong-rye in that way that Sun-a, and perhaps all Korean women could speak.

They were not Japanese; that was all she knew; they were like her own soldier. Sun-a simply stared. She wanted to take Mik-uh's hand, and... congratulate... celebrate... She did not know what. She did not know what it meant. They were standing in the open, watching the foreigners stride through her country, which had always been Japanese. Her whole life had been Japanese. Was it not now? A laugh, a sound escaped her, and she looked to Mik-uh, who had always known what to do. And she felt a relief that he looked helpless, like a child.

***

Kamakura struggled to breathe. His lungs had seized at themselves, and he rasped them to inhale. He thumped a fist into his stomach, shocking his diaphragm. He gasped.

He stood on a hillside alone, his remaining guards having abandoned him weeks ago. He watched, sickly pale, where a road ran, down to his left, in the wide valley below. They would see him. He had to run. Panic swept a cold sweat over him in an instant. Under the still-hot autumn sun, he resisted the reflex to shiver. Sought control. A sound escaped his throat, like something made by a chicken or a type of fowl. He staggered a step backward.

The convoy snaked into the Korean heartland, and he knew that this was just one head of the American Yamata no Orochi stemming from Fuzan, warping its way between mountains, poisoning the colours on the map. Men, by the hundred, and tanks, and... planes swept overhead. The doctor found himself hunched over, forward and to the side, cowering slightly.

The noise was different to the Japanese engines. There were two of them. Then a further three rushed over the southerly mountains and tore through the sky above him. For a horrible second he feared that they had come for him, and he glanced upwards to check for the falling bomb, before he knew any better.

With rage, and a ferocious scream he drew his sword in one lightning fast motion and slashed through the air at them. But the planes had gone, already disappearing to the north.

****

Kamakura hurried down the hill, on the far side, away from the troops. Gravity kept breaking his panicked walk into a falling run, and he kept arresting it, and looking about him in case anyone had seen him.

He needed to get out of this death sentence he wore. If captured they would put him in a prison, and process him. Many would get out of such a place, but never he. There were those still alive who would give testimony – those of his own supposed side who would bear their grudges until he was hung. He had done things, so many things that westerners would harpoon him with. He was walking-running too fast again. He slowed, looked around, and hurried down the hillside. His feet slipped from under him and he careered down onto his bottom, ridiculous, sliding over the dirt and grass, rustling up a cloud of dust about him. He flapped his hands aside to stop himself, then jumped up on embarrassed instinct, and hurried away from the moment.

Panic frayed everything. Thoughts and hazed memories of the weeks, or longer, before, flared over taken and then forgotten images of the hillside, so that he saw neither truly: trees and grass and running, sliding feet, and tumbling dirt and rumours of imminent surrender, of treachery, encroaching enemies; of he, killing, of troops idling, fretting when he had demanded supplies and provisions for the search; refusals and scuffles, and suddenly he had found himself forgotten and alone, determinedly rushing into the countryside; tracking a trail, that had been false, and another, and being unsure which had even begun where; hunger and looking down at his uniform and realising the time since his last full meal, eaten from a table, sat cross-legged on a tatami mat.

The house was empty at the edge of the village when he snuck up beside its wall. A small garden to his side, he leaned out from the mud-baked brick and peered across the front yard. He saw movement distant at the second of the two house settlement, far enough away. It felt pathetic, beneath him, as he crept out and then darted through the open doorway. He stopped himself inside, heart in his mouth, utterly relieved that no one was there. He felt appalled, disgraced. He hadn't even glanced to check; he'd just dived inside fearfully. The sword smacked awkwardly against the side of his leg as he turned this way and that.

In the sole bedroom with its sleeping mat that made the room smell like a barn, he found the clothes he had so desperately needed. He picked them up and held them in two clenching hands, and whimpered with relief and thankfulness.

Finally, he stood, with his samurai sword lain across his palms before him. He looked at it, unable to comprehend this act, head then faintly shaking.

The man who had been the doctor, who had butchered women when it was necessary, and killed prisoners or let their wounds kill them when they should, and who had healed, and served the Empire of Japan, walked from the hut a peasant.

He hurried to the cover of the opposite hillside and threaded between the trees until he felt himself hidden. Peering between the trunks he looked from one hut to the next, waiting for a figure to break the integrity of the deep, black rectangle of the doorway, or a shout to call out from the valley.

CHAPTER TWENTY-FOUR

Nothing.

Quickly he placed his army boots onto the ground beside a tree. There was little other option, so he kicked some leaves and twigs from the ground to partially cover them. Then he put on the homemade shoes he had taken, his toes curling underneath and the fabric stretching to fit. Panic seized him. Had he been seen while his eyes had faced the ground? Again he stared down the narrow sightline cut between thirty trees to the sheer blackness of the doorway.

Kamakura hurried away. Wrapped inside two blankets, he carried his sword. He had faced the thought of leaving it, and the prospect of being discovered with it in his possession. The blade had lain across his hands, cold metal against the panic under whose jurisdiction he now breathed, and he had felt the lightness of the craftsmanship, the beguiling strength that would slice, and would not break. And the horror of what he was contemplating had struck, double handed, overhead, cutting him open. He uttered a strangled rasp at the wind gone from his lungs. The horror, of the stranger who found it, carrying it away, whilst he wandered, vacant, leached grey and ash white, lost through this cursed foreign land. And he had flung open cupboard doors and knocked aside bowls and jars until he had stopped at the blankets he sought. For the sword was the last vestige of Kamakura Hideyoshi, who had somehow been replaced. To walk from it, would be to commit a seppuku that cut out and left behind his own soul.

He looked about the forested hillside. Still no sign of movement in the settlement below. Just a faint chatter drifting into the forest from the unseen locals. He tried to steady himself, to find composure; but everything was lost, everything. He secured the sword, wrapped in its bundle, under arm.

Kamakura began to make his escape over the mountains of Korea.

CHAPTER 25

14ᵗʰ September 1945

They walked through the sprawling port city of Busan, down sloping, intersecting streets.

The war was over.

How long had it been over? He heard passing phrases from passing locals, only some understood, and Sun-a helped him with quiet words: Incheon and signings; and flashes in the sky – had they seen them, or had they been too far away? Japan burning. Smiles, lightness of step, and relief, greeted, and planed expressions, furrowed brows. Walks tested the beginnings of freedom; so too, confidence, and rage. And he and Sun-a walked down ever more cluttered streets, amazed, deeper into Busan.

Suddenly the past years seemed to sweep into focus, as he had never seen them before. They told a narrative from one place to another, and made sense because the story had an ending – now. The realness of reality around him seemed an epiphany. He could but stare at the vivid colours. And Sun-a was part of it, in the picture as she walked beside him.

Vistas went through his mind: terraced houses; a bombed-out England he had never really seen; the metal wall of a partially flooded container hold; Jhansi in India, and the white-painted Division Headquarters, the lawn and palm trees. With sadness he thought of Gulliver, who would lie forever part of the floor of the Burmese jungle. He thought of the tired marching faces, tracing a circle around the prison ground; of the ones that had died in the corner by the barbed wire; of the fellow soldiers from the prison hut whom he had spoken little to.

What now?

Mick looked to Sun-a. He smiled. Her face tilted up as she walked, to take in the blue, which cut a river above them against the lines of Korean roof tiles. She looked so alive, so beautiful, so unburdened.

***

Sun-a had never walked freely through a city before. She had been herded onto a truck through one, but that was not the same. This was... She didn't know what it was. There was movement all about, coming from all sides, and shops and writing over the doors and open fronts with rows of fruits and pottery and jewellery displayed. She had learnt to read a little as a child, but the stores went past too fast to see what most of the signs said.

Mik-uh seemed to know where he was going, though he could not have. He led them down a street and then turned onto another, which led them onto another street full of people. They joined the noise and commotion, walking downhill. Perhaps it was the general direction that he sought as they weaved from path to path and cut through the city.

People looked at them – looked up from their stalls and from where they squatted in their doorways and by their produce arranged at the side of the road. She saw eyes flick from her to him, or him to her, and then check what they had seen. Often wary. And she avoided them and pretended to be only interested in the way ahead, around trucks and carts and passing people. Yet many others smiled and waved, and even called out.

"American!"

"We love America."

A man jeered and threw his arms up in the air. "Kill the Japanese!" And he whooped in triumph.

People laughed, and others joined in with a shout: "Yeah!"

People went about their daily business. But all around she sensed a bounce to people's steps, like they might just break into dancing.

Mik-uh veered down another alleyway, past people utterly stunned to see him there. Then they were out into bright light and a row of soldiers before them. Sun-a could but stare as they passed them by, ten or twelve, maybe fifteen, streaming quickly in front of her so that she had barely time to try and take in the bigger noses, and round eyes and focus on each one before it was hidden by its helmet and the next face swept close. She stared, but they did not stare long at her; their eyes switched to Mick-uh and registered surprise as they looked him up and down.

Sun-a saw the Americans in their neat uniforms, a dark green, straight lines, uncrumpled, untorn, and she realised that Mik-uh was shabby. His uniform seemed to have little colour left at all, to have lost its tone to the dirt – a browny yellow, baked in the sun, become brittle. Their faces were clean, shaved, whereas Mik-uh had his short beard. And their arms filled their sleeves; whereas Mik-uh's ripped shirt with its worn-through patches, where the remaining threads stretched crossed patterns, hung from his thin shoulders.

Finally one soldier, second from the last in the group, slowed as his eyes did the same as the others, and crinkled up, pulling his cheeks into concern, or dismay she thought. He stepped out as his friends went on, and he saluted to Mik-uh. Like the Japanese. She had not thought of Mik-uh being saluted. He slowly saluted back.

The soldier spoke. His voice was different to Mik-uh's. She couldn't understand.

Mik-uh nodded, replied, something about 'thanks, and 'glad to see you boys,' and the man in the helmet talked again. Then he pointed down the sloping street, patted Mik-uh on the shoulder, and went off to the others who had waited a little further up the road.

The street fell away quickly before them. Her legs had become strong these past months, but she felt her tired calves straining, holding off the freefall. Around a corner, around a bend. Then came sounds in a wave of noise that hadn't been there before, as if it only existed beyond that last ring of houses. The noise was of bells and mingled shouts and transported things being carried and moved; and of fishing. She knew it instantly through years of distance: ropes and nets had a sound of their own, and it filled the background of the air around them. She felt her heart rise in anticipation, as if she were coming home.

Around a corner, and they walked into the place where the noise came from. For a moment it was surrounding her, with the hundred separate sights and movements and goings on of it, and then instantly it was at the very edges. A huge wall of grey tore through everything, leering, leaning out and past the side of the dock, bursting up into her view as if seeing her. It forced her neck to crane back. From the edge of the dock it rose like a demonic cliff face, sheer, impossible to climb. It was beyond the power of mountain spirits; it was a kind of mountain of itself. High at its top it overhung the tiny figures below in shadow. It threatened to keep spreading out, to keep pushing inland. It should have fallen already, and crushing down, flattened those who disbelievingly walked right beneath it. Any moment. She had seen it before, in reality and nightmare, but never so close. It was terrible, and her feet took parts of steps backwards, to get away. He was turning to check, to see the past, all over her, but she couldn't shake it off. She wanted to turn and run, and sprint back up the streets they had descended to get there. Still she knew it sunk deep, deep down, below the dock, through the shallow sea floor, deep, deep down. It had ground its way there, grating through the ocean floor far away. She was struggling for breath. She glanced down to him, wanting to check that he had seen it too, but he was calm and concerned and she let him reach for her hand.

He guided her forward. "It's alright Sun-a. It's a Destroyer. American." He spoke in English, and kept talking, thinking the words would do her good. She looked like she'd seen a ghost, and as he looked at the huge ship he realised what a giant, unknowable, fairytale creation it might seem to someone who had lived as she must have. With a fleeting moment's recognition, he realised the gap between their past lives. He pulled her gently forwards from where her feet shuffled back, breaking the spell of that piece of ground. She had to look away from the ship to adjust her feet and step with him, and he did not let her stop, but took them on into the dock, becoming part of the scene, past soldiers with heavy bags, and supplies hauled over shoulders, and metal poles, and crates and cranes, and vehicles, and Korean fishermen in disarray with repetitive glances to the war machines that filled their moorings.

***

She was standing back from them. It was not so much that he had stepped away, or that the sergeant had excluded her from a private word, yet there was a gap between them as he looked over to her and she diverted her gaze

276

to the floor.

"You're all set," said the American with a thump on the shoulder and a smile that said it wasn't the time for rank and formality. "My God, have you done good! How'd you survive out there, months on the run?"

"I..." Mick wasn't sure what to answer. "I just kept going – we kept going."

He glanced back to Sun-a again. The sergeant followed suit and his congratulatory mood grew a hint sympathetic.

"Your timing's pretty good. The transport from Incheon is due here the day after tomorrow. We'll house you up until then, put some food in your belly. Slowly mind you – you have to take that side of things easy. And then you'll be homeward bound."

Mick nodded, smiled. "It all seems so easy. Nothing's been easy like that for, quite a while." He looked again to Sun-a, pain not concealed from his expression.

"And the girl...?" The American left the question with space to fill in. "She's... ? Look buddy, we've all been in this war, and you're not the first to fall for a local." Mick glanced immediately back to the American. "But you know, you realise, that the boat to England is for P.O.W.s, their wives and families. Those are the rules, cause there's a country of people who'd like to get out of it. You understand?"

Mick was again looking at Sun-a, and she to the ground, hands behind her back, then in front, fidgeting.

"Thanks Sergeant." Mick nodded.

"Shall I get your berth allocated?"

Mick did not respond at first. He considered the clipboard in the American's hands, aware it had the power to change everything. "Thank you."

The sergeant nodded and patted Mick's weary shoulder as he walked off.

Mick felt it heavy, straight on the bones. He walked back to Sun-a.

She looked up.

"There's a boat. Back to my home. To England." She nodded faintly. "I can go on it." Her eyes were on the ground.

It hurt to say the words. His throat rung with heartache, so that it was a conscious struggle to keep his voice steady. He felt a coldness, a numbness deep inside – a gaping space where the hurt would be, where he somehow knew it would land and devastate him later.

"The war is over now. I should go."

"Yes. I am happy, you go to your home."

He switched to Korean: "And you? What – where will you go?"

She appeared to think it over, head tilted, eyes lifting to the sky as they did when truly in thought.

"The war is over. Korea free. I can go anywhere."

Mick nodded, through the lie she had told. She had spoken correctly, but they must both have heard it; it seemed to linger tangibly on the dock between them. Sun-a had no home. She had no possessions, a blouse, only one stolen skirt. She could go anywhere. She could go nowhere at all. He had rescued her from that life, for what?

They stood in silence, facing each other. The gap between them had not closed. Why had he not moved to close it?

"I can stay on the ship." He gestured to the vast hulk looming beside them. "Until the boat arrives from the prison."

She nodded.

They looked at each other.

Was that really it?

That was the end?

"I'm sorry," he said.

But she shook her head softly, and managed to smile. "You saved me," she said. "Never sorry."

And still they waited, and looked at each other across the space he had chosen not to close. Pain seized from his gut in a great fan of hurt, through his chest, his shoulders, constricting his throat. His whole body seemed filled so as to break.

He loved her.

"Goodbye Mik-uh" she said in Korean. "Thank you, much."

She waited only a moment this time, long enough for their eyes to meet, and see, and hold. Then as they must, to break. She turned and began to walk away.

That moment that had seemed so rare a possibility – one, the unlikely, from out of thousands. The possibility that they would part. He had known what he must do, what his heart would have to do. Yet now it had come and gone.

Ahead of her in a panorama of the docks, crates lifted skyward, locals carried fish from their boats, army lorries were loaded to depart, and people bustled in and out of the street entrances, which would take her away.

She was truly walking away, and he was standing there watching her go. Letting it happen. He couldn't let it happen. He couldn't let her walk away.

"Sun-a."

She stopped and turned.

"Will you marry me?"

She stared at him, face humble, eyes wide and waiting on him, asking if he had truly meant it. He spoke the words again, in English:

"Sun-a, will you marry me?"

He crossed the space between them. He took her hands.

Her eyes were wide, black-brown circles that looked deep into him, searching. "Yes," she said, and again, "Nay."

The tears she had known she would cry in private, alone, when she stepped aside from a bustling street and rested against a stranger's wall, rushed to her eyes. Happiness had overtaken everything, in a whirl, a sudden change of what would be, into some kind of unimagined joy. Even the great battleship whose shadow threatened to cut between them if the sun should move, made little impression upon her.

"We will travel to England. We can live there."

She nodded eagerly, unable to establish to herself that it was all happening.

Had she said the right answer? Guilt diluted the brightness.

She would have lived with him forever in their sheep hut on the hillside. She loved him. She wanted nothing else. And he wanted her too; after everything; he wanted her too.

He moved closer to her still, and put his arms around her back. He seemed cautious, uncertain. He held her. It was everything she had wanted those months together. Everything, and yet the colour slipped from rose, yellowing, and she fought it to stay away. Did he truly want her? Why had he asked? Because it was cruel to leave her? Such a life was a burden.

But no, and she pressed herself closer, and held on too. He had already begun to part, and the embrace ended.

Still close. He looked down into her tear strewn face, and she looked up. Slowly, slight move followed by slight move, he brought his head to hers. He moved his lips slowly to hers, and kissed her. Her eyes were wide open, staring, and then he stepped back and put his hands on her arms.

He smiled, and she smiled back, there on the dock, with the wall of the battleship leaning out toward them.

***

In one of the bustling narrow streets of the city which they had earlier passed by, they stood before a stall. The owner picked up items and presented them, but Mik-uh politely shook his head and sifted through the collection at the front of the table.

Sun-a stood next to him, not entirely sure what he was looking for, but enjoying the thrill of it – of a shop, and considering, and the array of colours and shining items and precious things they might choose from. Beside her, he stilled, and touched her to attract her attention. He pointed amongst the cluttered jewellery and waited for her to see it. Then he picked it up, a small silver ring, and held it between finger and thumb. Sun-a's hand hesitated. She wasn't sure whether she was meant to take it from him or not.

It was beautiful, she thought. Subtle, and slight, and feminine, belonging to a slender, most beautiful woman. She imagined it on the hand of an elegant Korean girl, walking in a large courtyard house, long ago, before the Japanese had come. It filled her with wonder to hold it. The gem set into the ring was white and silver like the metal, but glowed light somehow. So small, and she loved it.

He took her left hand and held it oddly, flat, and tilted it a little to one side. Gently he lifted her fingers on his palm, and slowly put the ring onto the finger near the side, next to the smallest one.

"How does it fit?" he asked, and waited on her answer.

She sensed the people around her, mingling and passing by and going on their way, all with the same joy that filled her. It was everywhere; they all shared it. She nodded and smiled so happily. The instant he saw her face, Mik-uh beamed at her and clasped the hand with the ring in both of his. She smiled up at him, full of joy and wonder, and he tenderly folded her small hand closed in the two of his.

"How much for this ring?" he asked the lady whose stall it was.

Sun-a almost gasped at the price. But Mik-uh nodded and brought the coins from his uniform pocket that the soldier at the dock had pressed into his hands.

He didn't barter the price, simply handed the coins over. She watched as Mik-uh took his hand back, smiling, and bowed to the content lady behind the stall, who nodded in return. And with that smile he turned to her, and placed a hand on her arm, near the shoulder. She glanced at it, as it moved tenderly against blouse and skin, and she beamed up into his face, knowing that she hid nothing.

Mik-uh took the hand again, and ever so carefully, removed the ring from her finger. Sun-a looked to him in surprise.

She had never received a gift before. The most beautiful ring was the first; had she been presumptuous to assume it so? A sadness threatened to wash through her, to tell her that everything had been a misunderstanding. He must have seen it in her:

He said, "This is yours. Always. I need to give it back to you, this afternoon."

"Alright," she said, not completely understanding, but completely trusting.

*****

They stood in a ground floor room of a building on the dock front, that until two days before had been a deserted shipping office of Japanese owners. Now it was a temporary headquarters for the United States Navy in Busan.

Mick stood beside Sun-a. She had been given a clean dress, light blue, which seemed to float on her rather than hang, like a summer dress should in the movies. She looked beautiful. And free. It looked like it had always been her dress. He wore a pressed shirt, and dark trousers, and a belt, and polished shoes. It felt strange, the first time in years out of his beleaguered battledress, and whenever he looked down his front he had a disorientating sense of reality telling him of where he was again, and what had happened in the between.

He looked to the woman by his side, who in moments would be his wife. Beyond her by the wall stood the sergeant with the clipboard, and a lieutenant who had just been introduced; in front stood a U.S. Navy chaplain, with the power to legally perform the marriage ceremony. Behind and slightly to the side of him stood a Korean woman looking out of her depth. They had found her on the street outside not fifteen minutes before. She had looked nice and pleasant and so they had gone up to her together and Sun-a had politely asked her to come inside and say the vows in Korean. She had declined and made excuses and backed away, pointing in the direction of the things she had to do, but she had eventually agreed.

Mick had suggested it to Sun-a, and she had immediately nodded at the idea. They would say the vows in both English and Korean. The woman could speak no English, and neither she nor Sun-a were much literate in the Korean script, so they had planned together some simple vows to remember. It made Sun-a so happy to have her there; she had glanced back to him from the corner where they planned, delighted, all excitement. He could see Ju-Kang now, one foot then the other, next to the steady chaplain, nervously repeating and re-repeating her words, her mouth flexing just enough to give her away.

Mick looked to Sun-a, so beautiful in her pale blue summer's dress. Long black hair, stunning, gently curved, angled eyes, so, so pretty that he couldn't take in quite how. So Korean. And he was amazed and stunned that she was about to be his wife.

The door had been pushed back, open, to let the heat out. Now, one of the American soldiers pushed it to. Outside on the dock, work carried on, people walked from left and right, and life bustled past. The door closed.

Inside, the room was quiet.

Busan past the building. People went about their business.

Behind the door, Mick and Sun-a spoke their promises to each other.

***

Mick lay on his side in the ship's sleeping bunk, looking at her. She was on the other side of the narrow cabin in her own top bunk, a trench between them in the dark. It was their wedding night.

Mick felt a gnawing pain somewhere in his core that it was this way. But he knew it was the right thing to have done. How could he have led her by the hand to sit beside him on the bunk below, and then moved her back onto the bed? He could not have seen the look in her eyes as she saw what he expected of her. He would not do it to her. Not after everything. No, he had done the right thing. To wait for her and be sure.

He looked at her, across the night time chasm between bunks, narrow enough to reach across to the rail that kept her in. Her back had been to him, but she had turned since and now she faced him, her eyes closed. Though he was certain she wasn't yet asleep. He knew her breathing completely, from their months on the run: when she was sleeping, when she was nearing sleep, and when her eyes were simply closed, only for his benefit, not for sleep's. Now she was breathing, too aware of it, perhaps waiting for sleep, or perhaps waiting to hear his own breaths slow down.

He had never had to truly consider it before. It had all come upon him on the dock so suddenly – the fact that he would never see her again. They had woken up in their hillside shelter, and now were married, their home an American warship. Until today he had always known the next day would be theirs together. He had been taking her home. He had been seeing them survive. And then suddenly it had ended. Over mountain sides, along covered mountain slopes, racing across valleys, running from villages and cities; resting close together under sparse foliage, without enough cover to conceal them both; it had been their journey together. He saw that it hadn't truly mattered which direction they had been going. It had ceased to affect his reasoning, perhaps even before their first fleeing steps from that mountain plateau. His mind stilled and settled as he truly recognised it. He had surely known it all along, but it had not been rightfully his to consider.

He loved her. He had across the mountains, and he did there in their dark cabin. He would not make her feel something was expected from her. He would never do that to her.

They were married now, yet in the narrow space, it seemed they were sleeping further apart than they had at almost any time since they had met. He found himself missing the damp mud slopes and forest about them, and their stone, hillside shepherd's hut.

He looked at her, facing him in the darkness, and thought he must sleep and let her sleep.

Around them, in their cabin the walls shook and hummed with the vibration of the ship's moored engines.

***

Sun-a stood on the deck. The sea was to every side, stretching on and on. She was not supposed to be there, but two sailors had passed by and seen her, and said nothing. So she remained, looking out, as the great ship plunged through the waves, charging onward to somewhere she didn't know.

The rest of the soldiers were back in their rooms, or on the deck where they walked and got strength back into their thin legs. Mik-uh was there somewhere. She would go there later and walk about until she saw him, and perhaps they would sit on the bench where they sometimes sat, facing each other, and talk.

She stepped closer to the railing and let herself put a hand upon it. Spray rose and freshened her face and dampened her hair as the sea was hurled back from the great walls below, like waves crashing into the cliff face.

She looked left to right, and then ahead. The sea was all around. And she through it. She could barely believe she was riding this steel thing through the waves.

A grey shape that haunted her nightmares. She stood there, and looked out at the rushing sea.

PART 3

CHAPTER 26

19th October 1945

St Pancras clock tower carved its way into the clouded sky above. It was imposing in the elegance of simple brickwork and clear design which said its makers could likely do anything. Mick stared up at it. Britain had just about proved St Pancras clock tower to be a true statement; he had proved it, running around in the jungles of Burma. It was a stunning sight, so unlike anything from his recent memory that he had to search for a moment to understand it as something familiar. He looked to Sun-a.

She stared up at it, unashamedly agape at the structure. She had been wide-eyed, near to scared on the bus ride from Waterloo, on the bridge over the Thames. He had glanced at her almost constantly. He had taken her hand sometimes. She had gazed through the rain-marked windows, her head turning back and forth to see the buildings which went past and were followed by more great, immovable, majestic buildings. She had looked down, as had he, at the surprising craters where just such buildings once had been before the war.

Sun-a gazed up at the red, orange bricks, and rows of doors or windows, strange windows that repeated and unfolded along like the diamond shapes of a perfect net flung out.

She had stopped walking some time ago she sensed, but Mik-uh was there. She couldn't take it in, and she glanced to him to check that he was the same. He was watching her, angled to face her, while her neck was back and her head still gazing up. She returned her gaze to him, levelling her head. People were walking past them, quickly, all in one direction or the other, clothes straight, a little like soldiers' uniforms, but blacks, greys, browns, and she found herself marvelling at the crossed patterns on cloth and the shapes of jackets.

The walking people were all staring, at her, she noticed, beneath their black hats, so wonderfully rounded and tall and straight, and so different to Japanese or Korean. Mik-uh took her hand. Nervously she thought. Flustered, as the crowds thronged around them. In Busan, striding for the dock, and navigating the streets for the ring – she moved her palm out flat, to see it on her hand – nothing could have worried him.

They moved along the busy street, and she had to look up every step she could, between lines of people, crowds and hats. The tower and the great building pulled taut and slowly turned, like a sail blown, incredible against the sky. They were carried with it, and high above she saw the white clock face, the hands pointing almost to the lamb hour, bright blue all around.

They stopped with a bump as a surge of hats floated past her. She looked to the side, and saw again with the noise that went with it, another great red truck. It stopped and people jumped on and off, with sure one-footed leaps, like they were certain it would catch them. It moved again, like a house and she could but stare. Looking from it, pulling back from her astonishment to the wider street, she saw the other ones, spaced far apart into the distance until she could have pinched them between finger and thumb. They seemed to patrol the great, long streets, like Japanese sentries in a slow marching procession. Mik-uh was tugging her hand gently away and she moved with it, while looking over her shoulder at the great red truck, with two stories like a comfort house, as it moved between the flawless rows of tall buildings which were amazingly without a gap between them.

***

They stood on the pavement, across from Chester Green, two houses from the home of his parents. He had asked the driver to drop them off there. Everything looked much the same: the bright grass in English Autumn air, which began on the other side of the road, beneath the trees turning brown and red, as he seemed to have forgotten they did; the streets running parallel, the church and its empty graveyard. The road leading to Derby, back the way they had just driven from the train station. There were too many emotions, and memories, pain, and wonder, and more, to be felt.

He held up a still wave as the taxi drove away, to signal his thanks as English men did and he once had, he thought. He took his wife's hand; in the other he carried their single suitcase, which held all their possessions, and much more trapped air.

It was all vivid and in colour, perfectly real as it had been. For long stretches he had supposed he would never go there again. There were great tire tracks wedged into the front of the Green by the road, and now grown over.

The grass ran like a sea, but flatter than any land she thought she had ever seen. She had watched through the windows of the train as they had passed fields and fields of grass, and cows and sheep, and towns and high buildings. The country had been like elegant lifting waves, which rolled underneath, whereas this lay like a great pond, perfectly still. Tall trees lined its sides in rows, like guards.

"Come on, it's this way," he said kindly and led her toward his home. The terraced house loomed.

The building stretched like the cliffs from her childhood, no break, just a wall, and sheer, up to a great long sloping roof of black tiles. It reminded her of ribbons of scree that they had seen across the sides of whole mountains, the way it glistened black under the sun. Beneath the cliff top, the people had built rows of high windows that stretched on and on and on.

Mik-uh looked up at her, a deeply scared vulnerability in his eyes that she had not seen before. Like that of a boy. And she thought of the girl, who had been her, and another life ago, looking out at the world like that.

He walked her to the building to stand her in front of a large stone step. There was a bright blue rectangle before her, set into brick. He lifted a small metal handle and banged it quickly against it, and she heard the sound of wood. She saw the other stones spaced upon the ground to either side, each before its own wooden, door, and then the windows between each – one large, and higher two others – and understood then that it was just one house; that this was where his family was. Nervousness took her suddenly; they had arrived. She looked to Mik-uh anxiously, and he gave her a small smile.

She said for the need of it being said: "This is your home."

"Yes," he said and looked to the blue door, nodding.

He had told her many times that she would meet his mother and father. She thought of her return to her own home after many years and did not dwell on the pain that rushed from deep inside. If she had brought Mik-uh to meet her family, her mother, her father, what would they have done?

She glanced down the long line of houses, one unnervingly straight and sharp cliff face, right before her. She felt sure her face had flattened to white, just as she had seen Mik-uh's threaten to do on the boat, and trains, and in the car. She moved slightly back behind his shoulder as they waited for the sounds to draw nearer behind the blue door.

The door opened. It seemed to catch on a door mat, and snagged ajar for a moment. Then it pulled back, and swung open, and Mick's mother pushed it to the wall as she stepped forward. Her face asked who had called, and then she saw.

Pam found her gaze meeting that of her son, over the front step. Everything was a flurry. Her eyes were weighing the years that had passed and the changes in his face, even as she was stepping forward and holding her two arms wide and out.

"Hi Mam."

"Harold. Harold! Come quick!"

Mick was surprised at how joy and emotion replaced nerves in an instant. His mum. "Hey Mam," and he moved forward so his toes hit the step, and hugged his mother. He didn't step up – she was so small, it caught him off guard; he was still taller than her even as she stood in the doorway above.

Shuffling sounded in the hall behind, and Mick looked over his mam's flower patterned shoulder where his chin rested, to see his dad stop in the hall as he caught sight of the visitor.

"Hi Dad," he said, and stood tall next to his mother.

Pam felt a wonder that left her dizzy. She couldn't take in the sight of her big son before her, and her eyes flicked from him to the girl beside him, who she'd seen.

Harold walked down the hall in his slippers, newspaper in his hand. He stopped a short distance behind Pam so as not to crowd the porch.

"Michael." And he smiled, and nodded, and then his head shook a little from side to side.

He wanted to throw his arms around his son, so he stepped into the gap beside his wife, reached out and took his boy's hand in both of his. He shook it firmly, and said proudly: "Well done Mick. Well done out there, and good to have you back."

"Thanks, Dad."

Harold leaned out to put a hand on his son's shoulder, and with a pat on the back meant to welcome him inside. He saw the girl in the yard, and continued to pat his boy's back, slowing.

Pam's eyes flitted to the girl, but didn't know that they should stay on her, and so were back to her son, widening slightly and waiting, not to ask. She looked again: saw a girl in her front yard who was beautiful, and had never been there before, black hair that framed a face, slight, and not belonging. The image had been added to the front yard she always saw, and street past the wall, and made her hold her breath. She saw the nerves return to Michael's face, and him begin to turn to introduce. She had seen she was foreign. And what was she doing there? And could the obvious reason that sprang to mind possibly be the real reason? Her hair was black as coal, and fell so straight past her shoulders. She looked Chinese, she thought. And an unusual beautiful with it. She didn't want to think of it. Her heart had stopped.

Mick swallowed. "Mum, Dad, I'd like to introduce, Sun-a." He paused a moment. "My wife."

"Hello," the girl said. "I'm very pleased to meet you." She had an accent that Pam hadn't heard before. She'd looked timidly between Harold and herself, and Pam felt her heart go out to the little thing. And then consternation to be so accepting of a girl she didn't even know.

"Come in, then, and let's sit down."

Sun-a followed inside, into a kind of tall, narrow corridor. At one side a staircase ran up, with a rail of dark polished wood that shone, and was held on its way by a balustrade, like the one they had had at the balcony in the house in Daegu. Her head tilted with it as it folded up above, and she saw a high ceiling and ornate decoration. Her feet clopped beneath her, and she looked down to see beautiful tiles, each with a pattern, each so clean, like the wood. She passed into the thinness of the corridor and felt it closing in on her and the height stretching up. There were paintings on the wall, above a colour of lines and flowers, a fabric that ran beside her – pictures of land she had never seen but that she already recognised to be familiar: with the rise and fall, and long lines of dark green, which cut across each other in patterns across the landscape; and buildings whose shapes and roofs and windows she had seen and collected inside her on their journey.

Behind her Mik-uh's father had already closed the door. She had heard it. The light had changed. And they were leaving the hallway, and she was looking around to see through the doorway that Mik-uh's mother was leading them through.

Harold paused a moment by the front door and watched as the homecoming moved into the living room. The tall form of his son, with broad shoulders he had not had when he'd left. His son. He felt a pride to see such a man, and with it a sadness that it had not been he and his trade who had made him into this man. And then the petite form following him, behind, consumed by his uniformed shadow. Beyond beautiful that girl. His son come home, from the nearly vanished and gone. And with a wife from that life. He nodded at his son done well, and at sadness too.

He thought he had delayed with enough time for himself, so moved down the hall, just with the group. As they filed through the doorway, he waited behind the young visitor – his daughter in-law. What had been her name? He couldn't remember even a consonant. He'd never seen hair so black. She moved through the doorframe, keeping close to the back of his son. He smiled and nodded at that. He felt a pride that he then realised he had always thought a father ought to feel.

CHAPTER 27

Sun-a moved around a low table, following Mik-uh, and then stopped as he did. He smiled reassuringly, and nodded to her. She glanced over her shoulder and saw huge cushions that might have belonged to a queen, red and patterned with intricate lines. Mik-uh began to bend his legs, and she glanced back again, shuffled sidesteps to position herself and then did the same. She rocked back suddenly, into the cushions, as Mik-uh's father moved into the room, and his mother looked to them from across the low table and said:

"I'll just go and put the kettle on."

Sun-a tried to steady herself, looked up attentively and nodded. She hadn't understood the sentence. She smiled, and struggled not to tip back on the seat.

Mik-uh's mother bustled out, and Sun-a caught an odd look at her before she turned. Mik-uh's father was sitting down, across on the other side of the room, next to a fire inside the wall. Her seat was softer than a bed, like sitting on a thick pile of just washed and dried clothes; it moved beneath her, and creaked, and she felt that the pile would topple and send her sprawling across the long chair, and into the curved cushions at the side. So she planted her feet apart on the ground – then looked down curiously to see the tiles were no longer there; instead there was a covering, like many tatami mats, but furry as an animal's coat. Beneath her new shoes, firmly spaced, which they had bought near Busan dock, the patterns and spirals of flowers and colour repeated and fanned out beneath the table, and continued around its edges, and further. She looked quickly up, not wanting to be noticed.

Mik-uh had sat back into his side of the great chair, and his arm was along its high edge. He smiled at her, and his face was asking if she was alright. She smiled delicately back, and looked about her, everything fine.

There was a wide window in one wall, and a thin curtain hung over it. It seemed to have a pattern she thought, like one she had seen on the hem of a girl's skirt. She could see through it a piece of the green grass across the road, and the dark green of one of the tall, heavy trees.

Sun-a was perched on the edge of the settee. She appeared rigid, a statue, her movement an impossible thing needed to change from one carved-in-marble pose to the next. They had crossed a country, often running for their lives, only sitting on the dirt banks of mountains, until the floor of their shepherd's hut. The decking chairs on the transport at sea had been the first time they had sat beside each other on a seat. Now this was England.

He let his gaze fill out to the dimensions of the living room. The straight corner line and the cupboard dresser with the two vases; the perpendicular lines of the skirting boards, perfect as you were taught to draw with a pencil and sketch pad, and the flattened V above of the coving along the ceiling. Sun-a sat on the settee, like a bird, in the midst of it all. She was astonishing to him. That she should be there.

The living room. His parent's living room. He counted the dates: he had not been in that room for, five years. The number left him unsure what to make of it. Time had flown, as they said. But he was someone different. He couldn't remember exactly the Mick Bowler who had used to live there.

"Where did your ship dock, Mick?"

He looked to his dad. "Portsmouth. We took the train straight to London. And then from St Pancras."

"This morning, you arrived?"

His dad seemed to have half asked the question to Sun-a, but finished looking at Mick.

"Yes, six a.m."

"So, you didn't see much of London, then?"

He'd asked it in the same way.

"No. We'll go for a trip another time. See all the sights."

Sun-a met his gaze with a little shock. "Yes," she said. "I liked London."

His dad looked pleasantly very surprised. "Oh, can you speak much English?"

"Some. Mik-uh taught me."

"And Sun-a taught me Korean."

Pam heard the sounds of chatter from the kitchen as she waited for the kettle to boil. She quickly put the teapot and cups onto the tray, ready, and put the cosy on the worktop. The milk. She took the jug from the cupboard, and then went to the pantry to get the milk bottle, which she brought back and quickly but carefully poured. Putting the bottle back on its pantry shelf, she then hurried to the living room.

"Won't be a minute," she announced, and took her seat. Some silence followed her arrival and she filled it:

"It's lovely to have you back, Michael."

"It's great to be back," her son said.

"We only heard you were coming back a fortnight ago," Harold informed.

"I ran outside with that bit of paper. You should have seen me Michael. Told Elizabeth, next door. Your dad had to bring me back else I think I might have told the whole street. Then we had to think what to get ready."

"Your room's much as you left it," Harold said to Michael and the girl.

"Where have you been?" Pam asked. She heard it blunter than she'd intended.

Her son seemed to have to think for a moment. "Well, after Norway-"

"What a farce that was."

He nodded in agreement.

"It all worked out alright in the end, but as I've often said, pity the poor Norwegians."

He nodded. "So, you know I was posted to India. Burma. I was on the front there. Fought there a while, then got captured and put in a POW camp."

"Must have been tough," said Harold.

"Well, it's all done with now," Pam said. "Awful thing. We all knew we'd win, but it didn't half take longer than anyone thought."

"Yes."

"It's a shame you didn't get to France to fight Hitler there. Mabel Robinson's son was near Ypres. You'd have done well there."

A shrill whine was coming from behind her.

"Oo, I expect you're thirsty after your trip." She hurried to the kitchen, where the kettle was steaming busily. She shouted over the noise so they could hear, "I don't expect you got much tea at war."

"No," she just heard Michael shout back.

Smartly, she filled the teapot, placed the cosy on and picked up the tray. Michael and his father were in conversation when she returned, slid the tray onto the table, and resumed her seat.

"It was a good trip. We enjoyed it, didn't we?"

The girl nodded.

"Watching the scenery pass by. I'd forgotten what a sight English countryside was."

"Very different from where you've been, I imagine."

"Yes, very."

"A journey on the LMS Locomotive. Don't suppose you saw many engines when you were out there."

"I did see some. We sent them right around the world."

Sun-a sat, straight-backed, feeling the seat threaten to give way beneath her. She looked at Michael and his father, and glanced to his mother on the other side of the table. She tried to keep still, to keep her neck high, head up, to have poise, and be as pristine as she could.

She watched as Mik-uh's mother leaned to the tray and lifted a rounded, thick woven cover, to reveal... a teapot. Sun-a looked on, disturbed by the familiar. She waited intently for what would happen, her stomach beginning to wring like a cloth. The teapot curved so beautifully, and was lit with colour, rounded orange and yellow flowers, so different from the scenes she had held. Then to her horror, Mik-uh's mother poured it like the Japanese, as she had been trained to do. But she moved quickly, one cup, then another, a deep brown liquid still swirling up the sides.

Pam moved on to the last cup. She looked up from her bent over angle to the girl. The image took her by surprise, much closer, and at a diagonal, her face right there. The girl's expression seemed all amiss, and Pam watched her look to Michael, as she'd noted several times already.

"Does she like a cup of tea?"

"Tea's different over there. She'll try one though."

"Do you take milk?" she asked her, looking at her. And for Michael, "Sugar's still hard to come by you know."

"Take milk?"

Pam wasn't sure how to respond. "Yes, milk in your tea."

"You can try it. I'm sure you'll like it," Michael reassured.

Looking back from her son, the girl said, "Thank-you."

Pam poured milk from the jug. She wasn't sure how much she should pour, and then poured too much. She lifted up a bit and looked away to Harold. She knew he wanted milk already, for twenty-eight years had done, and so looked down and poured his milk. Then her own. She hadn't thought – she'd poured Michael's without asking.

"Do you still take milk?" she asked, feeling off kilter, and suddenly burdened.

"Yes, same as always," he replied heartily.

Pam stood from pouring, and then handed the cups and saucers out one by one. Her head felt flustered, probably leaning too much. Everyone had been watching her as she had poured. She wasn't used to this feeling. It felt like pressure, and things amiss.

"It's not often we've had the good crockery out, what with rationing. Your dad's had to cut right back on his tea drinking, haven't you Harold? You're no sooner sitting down with your cuppa than thinking it'll be your last until tomorrow."

Pam sat down, and found she needed to catch her breath. She lifted her saucer to hide her face, and only then lifted the cup to take a sip. She tried to breathe in, but her chest barely moved. She brought the cup back to her lap where it ought to be. She then said something about cups of tea, and something similar again. She wasn't listening to her voice she found. Her eyes were flicking from her son to the Chinese girl.

"But we got used to it soon enough. We all did," her husband said.

Her gut puzzled how it was possible for the sight to be in her living room. Trying to grasp at it, to understand what it meant. Michael was alive, thank God. They'd only learnt it two weeks ago. And now... his wife. But he was alive, good Lord, and he was sitting in the living room again, not in the seat he usually sat in, but next to it. He looked thin, and older, and different. She spoke again:

"I baked some biscuits – they're in the pantry. Haven't had them for a while. I wasn't sure when you were coming home though, so they won't still be warm, but they should still have a good crunch to them."

"Oh I haven't had a good biscuit for an age, Mam. But we had a baked potato each at the station. So I'm good for now, thanks."

Pam sat back in her seat. "Baked potato, eh?"

"It was Sun-a's first. She liked it though, she said."

"Oh, did you?"

"Yes, and, cottage cheese." The girl looked around the room, seeming unsure.

"What's her name again, Michael?"

Her son sat up in his chair, and looked at the girl warmly as he spoke: "It's Sun-a."

"Suun-a," repeated Harold.

And overlapping him, Pam said, "Soon-ah."

She nodded, and looked at them all eagerly.

"Sun-a."

Harold pushed himself up in his chair. "Well, it's very nice to meet you, love. We hope you'll feel very welcome here."

"Thank-you."

"Suun... Ah?" Pam asked Michael.

"Yeah, you've got it Mam."

"Well, I don't know that I have. Sun like the sun?" She pointed to the ceiling. "The sun in the sky?"

"Like that."

"Sun," Pam said, well I don't know, it's a bit strange. Sun." She nodded to herself, affirming. "I think I'll have to call you Dawn, dear. That'd be more like the English." Pam considered the sound of it in her head. "Dawn."

The girl smiled at her. She seemed nice, Pam decided.

"And how did you and Mick meet then?" Mik-uh's father asked.

Sun-a checked with Mik-uh to her side, that she should answer. There was a trace of worry on his face as he waited for her.

Carefully, she answered, "In the mountains. Mik-uh helped me-"

She stopped herself. She knew he was called Mick. And she had known how to say it for some time. But Mik-uh had always been his name in her head, and it felt wrong to change it.

"Mick helped me. He cared for me, until I was well." She couldn't help herself but look to him. He was watching her, waiting on her next words. She wasn't sure what they ought to be.

"Now that doesn't sound like our Mick." His dad broke the hesitation, and laughed, and patted the arm of his chair. "Are you sure you've got the right fella?"

Sun-a grinned, though she couldn't understand the English.

"And when it came time for leaving, there was no way I was going to be leaving Sun-a behind. So we married right there on the dock. Asked a navy chaplain to do the vows."

"Ah, young love," said his dad. Mick felt a huge wave of relief that it was over.

"What were you doing in China?" his mam asked.

"Oh, Korea, Mam. Yes, Sun-a's from Korea." His mum and dad both nodded. "It had me confused for a while too."

"What your mam means, is what were you doing out there? We'd heard on the radio, a long time ago, that Singapore fell, that the Japs pushed you boys right back. Korea's... I'm thinking of the right place aren't I?"

"Where've you been, Michael?"

"Between China and, next to Japan. Yes, you've got the place." He saw both his parents pull back a fraction, more upright in their chairs. "I knew some from Singapore. A few of them. I was in P.O.W. camps. But I escaped. That's how me and Sun-a met. On the run from the Japanese."

"Dear God," his mother said.

Pam felt traumatized. It had hit her, where her son had been. She considered the girl perched, straight backed in a plain, smart dress on her settee.

Pam said to her son, a little cautiously, "Did you... shoot at many people?"

"Pam," said Harold sternly, leaning her way over the arm of his chair.

She looked away from him, still determined to ask her son. "How long were you in prison?"

"The boy doesn't need to tell us, Pam."

Harold nodded, father to son. A connection that took her by surprise. She did not think she had ever seen that before the war.

Mick had wondered about the questions. He would rather have them in the open, done and said, not waiting for him. He had a mother who asked what she wanted to.

"I shot at people," he said with little emotion. "I was in the jungle –

where India and Burma meet. Then one day my troop had a bad time and some of us were captured. One prison, then another. I was held on an island called Formosa, for two years. They transferred me, and then I got free. And I met Sun-a."

Pam stared at her son. She realized that the boy who had leaned into the living room, then rushed away with barely a word, was gone. She doubted whether he would ever come home late again. He seemed to carry punctuality in him; she could see it there somehow.

CHAPTER 28

They sat at a large table on tall chairs, which were carved with sweeping, tall shapes, all the way behind her back, up to shoulders. Sun-a tried to look discreetly around as she slowly leant back until her shoulder blades touched the wood. It held, strong, as she cautiously eased more weight onto it. She quickly looked to the table again. Mik-uh had seen her and smiled a little, and nodded to ask if she was fine. She gave the slightest nod in reply, not wanting his parents to see. She just couldn't help it. There seemed to be nothing in this tall house that wasn't amazing and incredible to her. Every time she allowed her gaze to wander about the room, as she continually had to restrain from doing, she saw wonders and items and shapes and colours and shades of colour that made her need to stare and try to understand exactly what she was seeing.

Mik-uh's mother brought in another large plate, of triangle shaped food – each piece made of three layers. The outer layers seemed a little like rice cake, whereas the middle one was different. She looked at each triangle one by one to confirm her suspicions; yes, the middle layer was always the same on a plate, and each plate was different. On one it was a yellow colour and thin and solid; on the next it was green, a vegetable thinly sliced. And on the next it was bright red, and gooey, and lumpy, little round lumps, perhaps berries. Sun-a realized she was peering, neck outstretched, and brought it back in. She sat politely, and waited.

Mick looked to his empty plate and smiled. She was wonderful. He could only imagine what it must be like for her. For him it was all new, everything a reminder of a memory that had almost been forgotten, every sight refreshing a faded picture in his mind. But to see Sun-a's reaction to the simplest thing put everything in perspective. He had been to war and come home; she had... He considered it for a moment. He had brought her to a new world.

He let himself look up and see her face. She sat straight-backed, clearly trying to do as he'd told her to. He thought warmly of them sitting in their cabin on the boat, and he trying to explain what she would encounter in England: how they ate their food; how they didn't dry food in their front yards; how there were no cicadas; how people had back gardens, with lawns. On the edges of the lower bunks, facing each other, practicing how to sit and hold imaginary knives and forks. They had laughed a lot, then gone up for a walk around the huge boat.

At meal times in the ship's galley, with sailors and survivors looking on abashed, was where Sun-a had had to try out her cutlery skills. For several days she had struggled, painfully slow to get the food to her mouth while those around her gobbled theirs down. But as the benches had emptied, they had both relaxed, and it had been nice. They could take their time.

She was looking slowly across the table, unable to disguise the mesmerized look on her face. Mick decided to share her view, and took in the plate of cheese sandwiches. Cheddar, he guessed. How long since he had eaten good cheddar, not the government stuff in tins? Then the next plate, cucumber. He glanced aside and waited for her eyes to move steadily across to the jam sandwiches, then had his do the same. He felt so happy, he could have laughed.

It was marvellous to be home. Sandwiches.

And Sun-a. Most of all, Sun-a, he knew.

Pam put the last of the plates on the table, sat and pulled her chair in.

"Help yourself to cold meats and boiled eggs. There's a glass of milk too if anyone wants it to help wash it down."

"Oh, goes well with jam and cheese," Mick said.

"Since you were five years old you've known that."

Mick got up and went to the pantry for the milk, and then to the kitchen to collect the mugs. He couldn't remember which cupboard they were in and had to try two cupboard doors before he swung open the right one and saw the same mugs where they had always been. He heard his dad say from the dining room:

"It's a fine spread, Pam, a fine spread."

"If I'd known when you were coming back I could have prepared something nice."

Mick hurried back before he dropped his arm full of mugs and milk. His mam took them from him and put them on the table. She half-filled each mug.

"We'll need it for our cuppas later. Harold, you'll have to tell the milkman to double our order, I think."

Mick sat down. His dad said to him with a fairly important tone: "Will you be planning on staying long?"

"That's a daft thing to say. Sometimes, Harold..."

"I was going to ask you about that. I was thinking, for a short time, until I can get some work again."

"Of course you can stay here, Michael."

"But he's got responsibility now, Pam."

Pam obviously knew her boy was married. Obviously she must have known he wouldn't live in their home for long. But she felt off-kilter all of a sudden again. "There's only your room, Michael, of course you know. Will you be alright there? Will you fit?" She looked between the two of them as she spoke. She had to. The girl was her daughter-in-law, but it felt odd to do it.

Her son seemed awkward, embarrassed.

"My room's fine, thanks, Mam." He reached for a sandwich.

The girl was sipping her milk. Harold helped himself to a slice of beef.

Harold said, "You can start again at the Works, when you're ready. There's never not been a shortage, for years now. They're only too glad to have you."

"Yes, thanks Dad. That's what I thought I'd do. Monday I'll probably go and talk to Mr Renwick."

"It's a Mr Calvin now; came down from Matlock. Jim had a heart attack last year. He retired."

"Oh. I'm sorry to hear that."

"Decent fella. He'll sort you out. I'll have a word. You'll be back where you would have been if this war had never happened. Before you know it."

Michael nodded, and bit into his sandwich.

Pam saw that the girl wasn't eating. She lifted the plate of cheese sandwiches.

"Sandwich, Dawn?"

Michael looked up.

The girl raised her hand; it hovered over the plate of identical cheese sandwiches, until she picked one. Pam put the plate back.

"Thank you."

Pam gave her a little smile. "You're welcome, dear."

For a few moments, hands reached, knives and forks held still and cut together, and mouths munched.

"You didn't have your wedding in a church, then?'

Mick answered his mother: "No there wasn't time to find one."

His mam nodded as she chewed.

"Your dad's gone all religious, you know, since you've been gone."

Mick looked to his father, who exchanged looks with his mother.

"That's right. War gets you thinking."

"Yes."

"I go to St Paul's most Sundays. You should both come with."

"Alright thanks, we will."

"How's your beef?" Harold addressed Sun-a across the table.

Sun-a looked up from her plate where she had been concentrating on cutting well with her knife and fork. She had felt that all would notice if she had slipped. She'd eaten one piece of the thinly sliced meat.

"Very nice, thank you."

"What did your family say about you coming to England with Michael, Dawn?"

Pam saw the girl look startled.

"They are fine," Sun-a answered, feeling her face flushed with fear. She waited, desperate inside, sitting poised on the tall-backed chair.

"It's delicious Mam," Mick said.

His mother smiled at him. "Good."

"How about a toast?" his father said, already standing, his chair moving back.

"Raise your cups if you will." Harold held his mug high. "Welcome home."

"Cheers," said Mick, closely followed by Pam. The girl chinked mugs as they did, just a step behind.

"To the end of the war," Harold continued, "and a good life to follow."

***

The sun had set outside some time ago, but he had not seen it. His mum had drawn the curtains and put the lamp on when the light began to fall. They had sat in the living room with the radio on, but he had only listened in pieces to the announcer and the occasional statement of things he had missed in past years; he'd had an eye to the curtains that hid the failing light, oddly discomforted that he couldn't see it happen. He had gotten up and looked behind the curtains, stretching his legs and pretending to be occupied in the view left and right of the street. Completely dark, save for street lamps which blotted out the clear sky or clouds above.

The familiar clock on the mantelpiece was at a quarter past ten as his parents trundled off, his dad turning off the radio, and his mam with cups for the kitchen sink. Clocks seemed a curiosity now. He thought of the sun setting and he sitting in light, waiting for the moon above the trees.

He found Sun-a standing by her settee, in front of the place where he had always sat. He swallowed.

"Are you tired yet? We had a long day."

"Yes, little," she said.

He switched back to Korean. "I'll show you where the bedroom is."

She nodded quickly.

He found he didn't know the word for 'the second floor.' Back to English he said, "Before we go upstairs we use the toilet."

She glanced up to the ceiling with his point and nodded her understanding. She followed him through the hall and the kitchen, where his mam was at the sink with the tap running. He opened the back door, letting the cold night air in, and walked Sun-a out in the darkness.

"Keep the door open a little–" he moved the slatted wooden door ajar to show her – "to let some light in."

"Alright," in Korean.

"I'll wait inside for you."

He heard the lavatory door creak a familiar nighttime sound in the cold dark air. He stepped back into the kitchen to wait; his mam finished swilling cups at the sink and upturned the last on the draining board.

"I made your bed ready, last time a week ago in case your boat docked."

"Thank you."

"You'll be alright in your old room will you? It's only a single, but we weren't expecting... well it's all you can fit in that room anyhow."

"It'll be fine thanks, Mam." He paused for something else to say. "Night then."

"Yes, goodnight."

Then his mother moved up to him and put her hands on his shoulders. Mick bent his knees and she stood on tiptoe and gave him a kiss on the top of the head.

"I often didn't think you were ever coming back you know."

Mick nodded and found tears about to well up. "I know, Mum."

She turned and bustled emotionally away.

"I'm just glad I could come back."

She looked around and gave several quick nods, clearly holding in the lump in her throat. Then she went down the hall, and Mick heard her slippered feet climb up the stairs.

The back door creaked gently and Sun-a moved it open enough to slip back through. She looked nervous he thought.

"You can brush your teeth upstairs."

He hadn't shown her upstairs yet.

Mick walked through the narrow kitchen and down the hall, looking back every now and then.

Sun-a felt her heart rising in her chest. Apprehension, and hope, together. She whispered, though she found she was little able to voice the words:

"Your family are very kind."

He glanced back as he walked. "I'm glad you think so. They take a bit of getting used to, but they mean well."

Mik-uh pressed off the hall light as they went. They turned facing the front door, where the foot of the stairs began and doubled back above the hall. She walked up with a hand on the banister above the carved posts.

Each step creaked. Mick felt somehow out of his body as they climbed in the dark, immersed in a sense of the extraordinary, that he was there, and that his wife followed him. At the periphery of his mind, but overshadowing everything he saw and said, were decisions he knew he had to make. He looked back, to Sun-a, and saw her outline, her shape, impossible somehow, but there, the girl he had loved under forest canopies on mountain slopes. His throat was dry, too dry to swallow.

Sun-a ran her hand along the wonderfully smooth, polished wood, so dark now with only a faint light coming from up above. She looked up, and saw Mik-uh glance away from her. They neared the top of the steps, and Sun-a found herself stepping onto a landing. It felt familiar; she had been on such landings before, but longer, with many more doors opening off them; she had stepped out of the door, tired, exhausted, and sick, and leaned on the chipped balustrade.

Mik-uh pushed open a door, and said quietly: "This is the bathroom. You can wash up in here. Brush your teeth."

He didn't know the Korean for 'bathroom.'

She loved to brush her teeth. Mik-uh had showed her what a toothbrush was, and how to do it, over the little sink in their cabin.

"And this is my bedroom."

She followed him quickly back out onto the landing, and the few steps to one of the only other two doors. He seemed uneasy as he opened it, found it stick, and then bumped it lightly with his shoulder as he turned the handle. It opened and she watched him hesitate for a moment. He seemed to pause, in recognition, or surprise. Then he held the door open wide for her to see, and lifted the light switch.

The room was small, with a bed beneath the window, and their suitcase put beside it. She ducked under his high, outstretched arm and stepped into the room. There was a small desk and a bookshelf with plenty of books. She noticed pages that were frayed, fondly read. A wardrobe completed the room to the other side.

He crouched down and pulled a round, patterned basin from under the bed.

"If you need to, in the night, you can use this."

She nodded, and looked around the room again as they stood.

"You grew up in here?" she half asked.

"Yes." He considered the space around him, then: "the bed's comfy. I always remembered it was."

She looked back to him, her face warm, understanding. She felt privileged. She waited for him to look to her, for just that moment between them, then his gaze carried on, past, taking in the room. He said he'd go back down for a drink of water. He pulled the door softly to, then with a jolt closed it into its frame.

Down in the kitchen, Mick rested his head in his hands. It was dark in there. He didn't turn the light on.

The stairs creaked as before, when he began to climb them again. His head felt on the edge of dizziness, and he breathed deeply to steady his weak legs. He was out of breath when he reached the top and the landing, and stood, and swallowed. It was pointless.

He looked with a sadness at his bedroom door. A thin backward C of light shone out onto the landing where the door poorly met its frame. She would have heard him on those creaking stairs.

He thought about placing his hand on the door handle, but he knew he would feel compelled to take it right off.

Back downstairs he stretched his legs over the edge of the settee, where she had been sitting earlier. It had gotten cold. There were blankets, but they were in the tops of the cupboards in the bedrooms upstairs. Mick sighed, and resigned himself to a restless sleep.

His head was at an angle on the hard, cushioned arm. He managed a sad, ironic smile at his own foolishness. Years on wooden bunks in prison camps; years before that on jungle floors, crawled over by gigantic bugs, hearing snakes slither past at a distance, and animals scuttle, and deciding whether or not he was close enough to sleep to bother clearing them away; months later, – at the end of it all it had turned out - happy months, on the run, with the most beautiful girl, sleeping and more often not sleeping to be sure he could keep her safe. And weeks in a bunk bed and he was right back to expecting blankets and pillows.

He stilled and stared at the ceiling he could not really see. The mantelpiece clock ticked across the dark space to his left. Almost silent in the day with others sitting and breathing, it seemed to dominate the blacked-out room. He thought of the town outside and around the house's walls. Lives out there he had not crossed paths with for so long. Chester Green. A fear gnawed deep down where he barely could put a name to it. And he thought of the room upstairs, above his head, through the ceiling, where Sun-a lay. He hoped she slept. The thought of her lying on his bed, staring at her ceiling. Even with the light still on. He breathed and filled his lungs, and tried to exhale.

She was his wife. This was insane.

They had talked little of it in the Korean countryside. He knew they had taken her when a young girl. Maybe too young to have conceived a child.

The thought of so many men; on top of her; she was his wife; what they had done to her. Touching her. Inside her. Left themselves there. She had been a prisoner of the Japanese. As had he. What they had done to her. A fury. Horrible disgust. His wife.

He turned onto his side, head uncomfortable against the arm rest. Such awfulness; he knew it, he didn't think of it.

Their, baby. With a Japanese.

He alone had held it. She had killed it. He knew its sex; he had never told her. And he had had to bury it. He turned back onto his back, staring at the black ceiling. And now she was his wife. He calmed, breathed, tried to purify his mind of it all.

They were in his childhood home in England. They were married. He truly loved her. Beyond the plaster above, she was there; was she asleep; hoping, waiting for him; staring at her ceiling, as he was his?

He had not rescued her from that place, taken her across oceans halfway around the world, for her to feel what she still must do. That he and the oceans away meant little, to nothing. He would not do that to her.

And yet she was his wife, sleeping in his bedroom upstairs.

Why had she married him? He hoped, always hoped that she loved him, that it had been real, true love when she had stood facing him on that dock and answered.

But he didn't know. Did she see herself as his wife? She cared for him, he was certain of that he felt, staring up at the dark ceiling. But how much had her desire to marry him, been her desire to flee from that place, from the certainty that lurked in the warren of streets leading from the dock?

Would she ever have gone back to that, of her own free will? He breathed out harshly. He should never think that of her. But hunger and desperation, and what else could such a-. No. An unvoiced growl sounded in his throat, and he contained it, and remained still across the settee, and breathed deeply again.

He would respect the woman he had promised to love and spend his life with. There would come a time when he would know that she did it not out of an expectation, part necessity, but because she wanted him, without any thought for the protection he gave.

CHAPTER 29

Harold walked into the living room as he did every morning, first to draw the curtains, then to sit down in his chair next to the wireless with the paper. He felt good. His son was home, his wife would soon have breakfast on the table, and the air felt cold in that Autumn way of the full day ahead.

Mick woke from a half-sleep. Shuffling, and soft padded footsteps. At times on the ship, with almost absolute darkness, and the hum of the engines to drown out other noise, he had been able to sleep, and dream. Deep sleep, as he had always found easily before the war; but more often he had slept on the edge of sleep. As he woke and blearily opened his eyes he was not surprised by the settee, or his surroundings, which he had drifted awake to several times in the night. But the daylight took him off guard, already bright around the curtains.

He looked hurriedly over his shoulder, past the settee armrest that was his pillow. His dad was there, paused in the act of walking. Mick felt a knot of horror seize his stomach. Of it being too late to prevent it. As he'd known in the first moments of waking, on mountain sides far away, when fear had struck just as he'd regained where he was, and who was with him, and he didn't yet know what his eyes would see when they opened: a platoon of guards waiting for him, rifles pointing. This was nothing; he had slept in the living room; yet he felt sick.

"Morning, Mick."

Mick grunted a sound just out of sleep.

His dad brandished the paper in one hand. "Don't mind me. I always read before breakfast."

"Yes," Mick said in a croaked voice, and swung his legs off the settee.

Harold veered from his usual route and went through the opening into the adjoined dining room. He pulled out a chair, took a seat, and pulled the paper taut so it bent at the fold and held shape for him to read.

Mick put his head in his hands, to wake himself up, and perhaps in grief – when the time came he didn't want to lift his head and stand.

***

Sun-a sat awake in Mick's old room. She had been sitting on the bed listening, unsure when she should exit. She looked about the room, as if to remind herself that Mick had not come up the night before. They always slept in the same room. She had listened to faint sounds of movement beyond the door, perhaps from down the stairs. Then everything had gone quiet. Completely quiet. She had waited, feeling a panic grow that she was the last person still awake, and had then moved the light switch on the wall.

Now she sat, dressed, on the bed. She had been awake since just after dawn, not hearing anything, until a short time ago there had been footsteps and splashes of water in a basin, and then the fading creak of someone descending stairs. And then more footsteps, but briefly, and perhaps again the sound of the stairs. She sat, waiting, nervously, her feet gently kicking off the side of the bed. She didn't know what to do. This was a foreign land, and a foreign house, and room. She looked around her. In daylight it seemed a different room to the one they had walked into the night before, and she had woken to find herself in the middle of it, stranded. Around her was nothing she recognised. There was the bed she had slept on, the cupboard, the chest of drawers beside the bed, all things she knew, yet changed, different. The shapes, and the colour of the wood, the handles, the grooves, the patterns that lined and turned the corners of the doors and drawers: it all felt unnecessarily done, confusing somehow, at all directions, at all corners of her gaze; and she confined in the midst of it. She didn't know if she should stay, or go. Should she sit and wait for someone to come for her? For how long? There were sounds downstairs, and she felt a constant panic rising that she had been left alone and forgotten up there.

***

His new family sat around the table. Sun-a looked sad, almost like she had been crying, or very nearly had some time ago. His mam put a rack of toast onto the table, beside the jams and the plate of small rectangles of butter.

"The war might be over, but butter's still a treat."

Mick nodded, reached for some toast and lifted a cut of butter on the face of his knife.

"This is toast," he said to Sun-a.

"Yes, I know," she replied, and smiled weakly.

She'd had it often on the boat. He'd forgotten.

Across the table his dad had his eyes down on the toast and jams. He

321

reached for a jar of marmalade and undid the lid. Mick glanced up, then back to his plate, and began to spread the butter as it started to melt on the surface of the toast. He hated the private part of his marriage being public, even if only known by his father. Of course, it always would have been, under the same roof, his parents' roof; they had both probably heard the single set of footprints down the stairs the night before, and discussed it by polite whispers before they turned their lamp out. He sensed, or was he imagining, his father's attempt to act normally as he picked up his toast, and it kept the tension on the knot in his stomach. He felt a failure – back one day and a failure – and shame that his dad of all people should know.

"I thought, Michael," his mam ventured, "seeing as you didn't have a proper wedding, you and Dawn should have a service at the church. You can invite people then."

"But we're already married, Mam."

His mam looked down to her toast. "Michael, I've got one son, and for two years I thought he was dead. But knowing he's alive, it would have been nice to go to my only son's wedding." There was anger in her voice by the time she exhaled and picked up the pot of raspberry jam.

Mick looked about the table for a moment as his parents bit and chewed their toast, and Sun-a didn't seem to move next to him.

"I'm sorry Mam, and to you Dad. Of course I would have wanted you both there, but it was the war, and we had to marry over there."

"Why did you? Why couldn't you have waited until you got back here?"

"Because Sun-a couldn't have left Korea unless we were married."

He felt Sun-a turn to look at him. And his mam, and his dad raised his head.

"Of course, it's only right that Dawn's family got to go, but you could have brought them all here for a holiday you know."

Mick half nodded.

Out of the corner of his eye he saw Sun-a look briefly to his mam, and then down to her toast on the plate.

"It would simply have been nice to go."

His mam looked genuinely emotional, hurt.

"I know." He paused. "War meant a lot of things weren't as they should have been. But you'll be around for all the future things."

She nodded her confirmation. "Aye, I will."

Then her hand began to journey towards Sun-a. It stopped part way and rested on the table cloth.

"We're glad to have you here, love."

Sun-a's eyes were on the hand and then rose, where they met his mum's.

"Thank-you."

"Yes, we hope you'll feel very welcome," said his dad.

Sun-a smiled at them both.

They all bit into their slices of toast, and spread fresh jam.

"Are you going to pay a visit to your old friends today?"

"Oh, sooner or later. Maybe not today."

"They'll be glad to see you," his dad chipped in.

"Yeah; there's no rush."

"Edward's popped round asking about you. Several times, to see if there was any news."

Mick sat up straighter, and paused in bringing the toast to his mouth.

"He survived the war alright then?"

"Yes, fine. Saw action in Europe, but came back alright."

Mick felt surprise for some reason. And a muffled kind of confusion and guilt, that he hadn't been more concerned for his old friend. "Yes, of course I'll catch up with him soon."

They ate a couple of slices of toast each. Sun-a tried English honey, and also marmalade at his dad's recommendation. The sadness left her eyes somewhat, Mick was very relieved to see. And he forgot some of the awkwardness he'd worried about with his father, though not completely as they sat down in the living room with their morning teas.

***

They were all together in the living room, listening to the afternoon wireless. She had baked a shepherd's pie for dinner as a treat to celebrate, and they'd been resting since then. Harold was reading his paper. Pam thought about page twelve by the look of it. She was crocheting, having to return her focus to it again and again, rather than looking over her glasses around the room. She wasn't much good at it, even after all the years since her mother had first shown her how, but she kept at it. Dawn was sitting rather on the edge of the cushion, keeping very proper posture. She was listening to the Light Programme with a studious look on her face. Pam turned her ear to the wireless box: it was some kind of ballroom dancing, a fast tune with the trumpets and cymbals, rat-a-tat, perhaps a foxtrot. The girl was almost frowning with concentration, as if she would pin the music in place. It was disconcerting; the music filled the room; it seemed to have flooded from mantelpiece to wall and left no space for anything else. It was making her feel on edge; the stillness of the living room pressing out, stark, so real-

Michael spoke up: "I'm going for a walk."

"Oh, you going to visit your old friends?"

"No, just stretch my legs, see the Green again. Maybe walk into the city."

Then why don't you take Dawn with you?"

Sun-a broke the spell of the radio. It was astonishing, the sound that still filled everything, even as she tried to listen to what was said.

"Oh no, you can enjoy the music. I'm only going for a quick stroll." And to his mother: "I'll give her a proper tour another time."

Sun-a saw Mik-uh's mother nod, less than convinced. Mik-uh stood and brushed down his shirt from having sat so long. Sun-a looked up at him, longing, not wanting him to go and leave her there.

"We haven't time anyway," Pam informed her son on a spur of the moment that she'd been mulling about for a while. "We'll all go to the Coach before long, for a drink before supper."

***

They walked down the street in the direction of the pub. He'd been a couple of times with his dad, but it had always been a place for the older train and Silk Mill workers. He'd certainly never walked in there with his mam.

He looked back, where tall oak trees reached high, and saw the church, and its turret behind them. And beyond went the road to Derby, to the city, and away to Nottingham Road. He brought his gaze back round, down the street.

They fell out four across where the pavement was wide enough, and into twos where it narrowed. A post box came up on their left-hand side and it made Mick stare, his head turning as they passed: bright red, cast from solid, immovable iron, round, with a Burmese hat. Built like a tank, for the post. Sun-a was now walking with his mother. He glanced back to check on them. They weren't talking, but no one had yet on their trip.

The Coach and Horses was built as if by the Tudors, with black beams and white walls. It sat as it had, at the crossroads with a few picnic tables on sparse grass, alongside gravel for cars. An older man crossed toward the pub as they did, from the opposite direction. His head down, shoulders hunched, he was heading for his beer, then he glanced up, and the short pedal of his legs snagged. He stared across, as they cut onto the drive toward the paned double doors. Mick looked away, seeing the man was gawping at Sun-a. He didn't want to draw her attention to it. But out of the corner of his eye he sensed her notice.

His dad held open one of the doors, and they went in one by one. Even from the falling light of late autumn afternoon, eyes still had to adjust to the dim interior. Windows let in daylight through thick panes, but with the low ceiling and the size of the room around the bar there was a gloom that electric lights did little to change. It was as he remembered from the few visits of his youth. Smoke hung thick, and the way it curled was visible around the lampshades.

Heads had all turned slowly to see who had come in, and would then return to pint glasses, only they now held their angles on shoulders, and some eyes were squinting.

Mick felt himself holding his breath. They had stopped part way in, by the snooker table. Some men throwing darts had paused mid-game. The one with arm bent ready to throw, glanced round to see, and then straightened up as he turned.

"Where shall we sit?" Mick said.

Sun-a looked rigid beside him.

"Alright lads? You're early today Pete."

Harold walked toward an empty table, in the middle, away from the door and the darts.

"Harry, how's doing?"

His mam followed, stout and head held high. Mick put a hand on Sun-a's back to take her with him. It took a moment's force and then she moved, glancing to either side as she went.

They pulled out chairs at the empty table, his dad shuffling onto the bench along the wall. Someone stood up at a table further back, a shape on the edge of his field of vision.

"It is isn't it?"

Mick turned round, about to sit.

"Michael Bowler. Well I never."

Stepping from around his table, passing a chair with a face Mick also knew, side-stepped Eddie. His school friend patted the fellow's shoulders as the man shunted his chair forward. Eddie's small round face seemed to have been grown out from within, by a structure, of hard angles and lines. It was topped by short spiky stubble on his scalp – hairline gone back a bit – which stretched unbroken to the sharp line of his jaw and then wrapped tightly back around to his scalp. Eddie stepped out from the chair, facing him, short, wiry, and yet broader, square across his shoulders as the packs they had all carried had made them. They shook hands, and Mick put a warm hand on his old mate's shoulder. He had not been wanting to meet him he realised.

"Good to see you, Eddie."

"Ah, Teddy now. Haven't been called Eddie in a while. So how've you been? It's good to see you made it."

"And you, pal."

They were still shaking.

"We didn't think you had, you know. Thought you were still out there, not going to be coming back."

His eyes kept flicking past him.

"You took your time, mate," said another old acquaintance, leaning from his seat.

Mick reached over and shook his hand.

"Radcliffe, how's it going?"

"Not bad, not bad. We're the alive ones like they say, so can't complain."

"Yes, true, true. Ah, it's good to see you all." He looked through the murk at the other face at the table. "Gaunt. Good to see you." He held up a hand in a stationary wave.

Heads were peering round him, toward Sun-a, whom he blocked off. He didn't move aside.

"Sad to tell you, Thompson didn't make it," Eddie said.

"I'm sorry."

"Nor, Dawson, Freddie Gibbs, Alan, you know Bob's friend."

"Yes, I remember."

"I was sorry to hear about Mizzie."

"Yeah, sorry Mick," said Gaunt.

"We all were."

Mick's chest had suddenly gotten hot. He felt the need to loosen his collar, but kept his hands down by his sides.

"Thanks." He was nodding. "Yeah, it was really sad. Thought it was us who were in danger, out at war, but..." He kept himself still.

"Where did you end up anyway? We lost you after Norway. Foresters went both sides."

"India."

"Right, that's what I'd heard."

"You missed out in France, Mickey."

"You in a camp over there? Heard bad things about them. That what took you so long after the war ended?"

CHAPTER TWENTY-NINE

"He's right. We've had our feet up back here, for ages it seems like."

"Ah, I'll fill you fellas in, in a bit." To his mam he said, "We ordered our drinks yet?"

He sensed the table trying the more to peer around his turned back.

"We're waiting for you."

Mick moved to sit down.

"Alright, Ed- Ted, I'll come over in a bit. Just have a sit down first with the folks."

"Alright then. Hello Mrs Bowler, Mr Bowler."

Eddie tipped an imaginary hat towards Sun-a and gave a slight tight-mouthed nod.

"Eddie."

"And this is Sun-a, my wife."

Mick stepped aside and gestured with one arm outstretched.

"He-hey, Mick, old boy! Congratulations!"

Eddie patted him hard on the back and looked over Sun-a, then gave her a nod.

"How do. Good to meet you."

"Hello. Good to meet you," she replied politely.

Sunn-aaa," Eddie pronounced, and thumped Mick's back again. "Well I never." He wore a big grin, and slowly shook his head.

"It's nice to see you, Edward. Good for you lads to catch up again," said his mam. "Michael'll be over in a minute."

"Right Mrs B, we won't keep him. You folks get yourselves some drinks."

Eddie waved off a casual salute from his brow. Mick half raised his hand in reply, and it fell awkwardly, unformed around chest height.

CHAPTER 30

Mick moved to his chair, its back to his old friends. He began to take his seat with his family.

"Well, well, Mick..." he heard murmured over his shoulder.

He shunted in the chair as he sat – again where it snagged on the old carpet. His dad was standing up:

"Be a pint of mild for me. What'll it be Mick?"

"Same."

His mind was flustered, only half registering the conversation. Background noise and pieces of over his shoulder.

"Glass of wine for me please, Harold."

His mam and dad looked to him and to Sun-a.

"There are different drinks you can have. You like wine – you had it once on the ship."

Sun-a's stare brought his attention to something, telling him of it. His mam and dad were gawping at him.

"What was that?" his mam asked.

Then he heard back his words and realised. He hadn't noticed. He needed to pull himself together.

"You learnt the language?"

"Yes," Mick said, finally sitting, pulling his chair under the table.

"What language? Chinese?"

"It's Korean. Yeah, I learnt from Sun-a."

"Oh, very good."

"Sorry, it just came out. We often talk between the two, you know?"

"And how did you learn English, Dawn?"

She looked to him first, before answering. "From Mick," she said.

His mam's face pulled back and she said, quieter: "How does that work? How did you speak to each other?"

"You learnt at the same time?" his dad put together.

"That's right."

"Oh."

His mam's chin remained back – a look that said something still didn't make sense.

When the wine began to pour and sweep the sides of the glasses he remembered himself, got to his feet and went to help his dad. He looked over; his mam and Sun-a seemed to be making occasional small talk.

At their table, his back to the pub; time felt like pressure, as in war. They talked about the weather in England, and how it had varied over the war years; they discussed changes to Derby, a couple of pubs that had been renamed, and shops that had opened and closed; and Winston Churchill and what a good job he'd done. Mick felt distant throughout, trying to have something to say, but mostly adding the odd comment here or there. Sun-a listened like an eager student he thought, silent in her chair, looking from his mam to his dad as she tried to hear.

A hand slapped down on his shoulder.

"I'll get you another pint. Come over and have a sit with the lads, if that's alright, Mr and Mrs B, Bs – there's two now, hey."

"Certainly is Eddie. You boys need to catch up. We'll be fine right here."

"Can I get you anything?"

"No thanks, we're alright," his dad said with a nod that signalled the younger generation could go.

Mick turned to Sun-a, unsure what to suggest.

"She'll be fine with us. You go and say 'hello.'"

His mam's raised eyebrows confirmed it, and he went to collect his pint at the bar, then returned, past Sun-a and his parents to his old friends' table, further along toward the corner. As he took the empty chair pulled out for him, he replied to the 'hullo's, and shook the outstretched hand from across the table.

"How are you doing, Gaunt?" he said, and then shook hands with Radcliffe too, and all the time wanted to look to Sun-a.

Each face seemed to hover a fraction over the school-boy image in his mind, unsteady at the edges, until the changed shapes and ingrained lines settled down, and the old picture was gone. He looked across, Sun-a's long black hair falling down her back, hidden by the chair, and his parents in the smoke-hazed background. He felt painfully distant, either for his sake or hers. He shouldn't be seen looking for any longer – and pulled back to his company. Then he raised his large dull-golden pint glass to the toast that Radcliffe called, and saw the bubbles rise wonderfully in the glow of the light bulb above. For a second he felt the amazement it was to be in England, but it didn't soar, just fell away. Eddie said:

"Welcome back Mick old boy. Here's to being back with the boys and the war won! Welcome back Mick!"

"Hip-hip hooray! Hip-hip hooray!" Heads turned around the Coach and

Horses. People smiled, to see what was happening, the great victory extended still further. "Hip-hip hooray!" A few extra glasses raised into the air at other tables and at the bar. Sun-a had glanced around to see him and smiled.

They drank, then put their pints down together with the satisfied sound you made after a drink. Mick glanced from one old friend to the next. He hadn't seen them here since the night of the dance, the last one. They'd been in the Foresters together, in the same battalion for a while, but that seemed unconnected somehow.

"Where did Thompson, fall?" It sounded blunt once asked.

Radcliffe nodded a kind of confirmation as he spoke: "In Africa; in Tunisia. Teddy saw it."

Eddie nodded, but didn't say anything. He looked through his beer.

"Ah, I'm sorry to hear that."

They all nodded. Some drank their ale. Mick left his glass on the table.

"Gibbs was in Italy, at Anzio. We were all in the Italian campaign mostly, after France.

Mick nodded. "I heard about the campaigns, on my way back here."

Eddie looked over to him with a humorous, inquisitive squint. His voice set a different tone:

"So congratulations Mick. Question we all want to ask, is how did you meet the Misses?"

"Right," said Gaunt, leaning forward and gladly joining the new mood. "Word was you'd been captured all this time. Your mam, you should have seen her, vaulting..." He lowered his voice and looked over in his mum's direction with a sheepish grin. Then he continued, "-vaulting the yard walls down the street, waving that army letter in her hand."

Radcliffe and Eddie chuckled.

"Over the moon she was, and rightly so," said Eddie.

"Went to our house, happy as... anything," Radcliffe told cheerily. "Her and my mam were nattering over a cuppa for ages, and I got called in. You don't know how down she'd been."

Mick nodded, looking from face to face as each chipped in.

"What is she, Chinese... Japanese?"

"No."

"So," said Eddie, raising both hands definitively, "you're in prison, sneaky Japs got the better of you just that once, though how they could get our Mick... But you're in prison camp, so what we want to know Mick, is..." He paused for dramatic effect.

Mick's stomach churned. He waited.

"How exactly did you marry a Chinese girl when you were in a POW camp?"

Sly glances were exchanged.

"You were courting through the fence when the Japs were asleep?" Radcliffe laughed.

The questions hadn't yet been asked. They were leaning forward around the table, finishing it.

"We're all thinking it," rounded off Eddie. "I'll say it then." He coughed, then looking serious, with a smirk showing just behind it, said quietly, "there's only one kind of woman to be found around prison camps."

At once he leaned back in his chair, hands up, palms showing.

"The commandant's daughter!" Eddie whispered his punchline with a soft clap of the hands.

Mick made himself smile, though his guts clawed at his insides for it.

"Well, firstly," he said, pausing with his sickening grin, playing his part, "she's not Chinese."

They laughed at his command of the drama, and he felt a traitor.

"Then what is she?" asked Gaunt, keeping his voice down, glancing past Mick.

"Korean."

"Korean? We thought you was in Burma or China."

"And I didn't meet her through a prison fence. They didn't get me that far."

He watched the boys on tenterhooks for the revelation. He felt sick for doing it so well.

"Hey? What do you mean? Then where've you been?"

"I was in a couple of prison camps. But they moved me in the early summer; I escaped during transport."

"Escaped? To where?"

Their faces mostly stunned, eagerly craning forward for the answers.

"In Korea. That's where we met, me and, my wife."

"Early summer, you say?" puzzled Eddie.

"Um."

"We met on the run from the Japanese."

He regretted saying it as soon as the words were out. He waited, held his breath, but they didn't seem to pick up on it.

"You were on the run in Japanese territory, for months?"

Mick nodded to Gaunt, playing it humbly.

"Why was your Misses on the run?"

Mick felt his face redden. He turned to his old friend Eddie. "Who wasn't on the run from the Japanese?" And he shrugged, a little too big a gesture.

He watched their faces. They seemed to buy it, to leave it at that, concerned with other questions of the story.

"It was a shame you got put with the Thirteenth, the Asian lot, after the Eighth. Shame we couldn't have all seen the war out together in Europe. Not for you and your wife, mind you. But..."

"Yeah, war's war."

"It was said you'd asked for the transfer."

Mick didn't respond. He gladly let the sentence fade and paid his attention to the next eager question in line.

"Were you in Burma?"

"Yeah."

"I've heard some bad tales about that place."

"Yes. I've been hearing things."

"So what were you doing out there?" Radcliffe asked.

Mick noted that Eddie had gone quiet; he hadn't asked a question for a while, letting the other two take over. In fact, he had leaned back in his chair.

"I was in India. Fighting in Burma."

There was a pause, raised eyebrows, and minds recalling information. But Eddie leaned forward again, a slightly incredulous look on his face.

"Jungle fighting," said Radcliffe.

"That's tough work, not knowing who's ten feet in front of you."

Eddie said, "Can't have been easy. The Japanese's home turf almost."

Mick felt uncomfortable at the way his old friend's manner had turned.

"It was difficult to get the resources in. Communication and terrain was tough."

"So, how long were you on the front there?"

Mick paused. "I was in the Chindits. We did campaigns into Burma, over the front."

"Shit, Mick!" Radcliffe looked around, realising he'd spoken too loudly,

"You were one of them?"

Gaunt jumped sagely on the end of his friend's sentence: "-Every Tommy knows the Chindits."

"Don't get me wrong," spoke Eddie slowly, "but people say they cost a lot of men. Marching into the middle of nowhere. Not doing a lot."

Eddie sort of shrugged, and leaned back again, as if leaving his words authoritative in the middle of the group.

Mick would go back to his table soon, he told himself.

"A lot of good soldiers died, it's true. But we made the Japs think again. They couldn't push on while we were cutting through behind enemy lines.

Radcliffe looked in awe, Gaunt less so. Radcliffe's mouth hung open, his head gently shaking side to side.

"Well I'm glad you made it home, old pal," Eddie said, and raised his glass to him. Mick picked his pint off the table and they clinked, and drank.

"Ah, think if we had all been slugging it out with Hitler on the mainland here. No jungle for you Mick, but you'd have given him something to think about with the rest of us."

Mick raised his glass into the middle of the table. "Lads."

The four of them knocked glasses, and said "Cheers!"

***

He had excused himself during the next pint, and sat back with Sun-a and his parents for a while, but he'd known the time wouldn't last. Past his dad's shoulder he had kept glimpsing the clock on the wall, and when it drew near to half past seven saw his mother increasingly glancing that way too. She had suggested they go and get fish and chips to take back home. Mick had thought it a fantastic idea, yet known that he would not be able to make a retreat. The thought of missing out was galling: missing Sun-a's expression as she tried them for the first time; watching her face as she unwrapped the newspaper to see the battered cod and greasy chips. He would have loved to share that moment with her, and explain for her.

"You'll be alright," he spoke quietly in Korean, "I'll see you tomorrow, I expect."

She looked stunned.

"My mam and dad will take you for some famous British food," he said in English, just loud enough to include his parents. "I'm sure you'll like it. It's fish."

Sun-a nodded, and looked nervously to his parents, who stood waiting expectantly for her.

He hoped she would be alright. His mother had said, as he supposed she had had to, that he ought to stay with his friends, and that it was good for him. And again they called him over to join the gang.

"Come on Mick. Your pint's waiting!"

"Goodnight Mr and Mrs Bowler." Eddie saluted them warmly from his chair, and then half saluted Sun-a, with a pause as he found himself without her name.

"This way Dawny," said his mam.

Sun-a nodded quickly, and walked with them toward the exit.

"And nice to meet you!" Eddie called as they went.

Thankfully Sun-a didn't turn, perhaps not hearing, perhaps not recognizing.

Mick found he hated his old friends as he walked over to rejoin them. He pulled out his vacant chair and sat and reached straight for his drink.

They joked about old times, passed comment about General this and that and troop movements, like they were generals themselves, but no one went into any specifics about the feet-on-the-ground experience, which was all that any of them had.

Later, Radcliffe stayed on at the bar, head stooped over his glass. Mick stepped outside into the cold, refreshing air, and walked across the gravel to the pavement, with Eddie and Gaunt. They headed back toward the Green. Before long Gaunt turned off onto his road, and the two of them carried on.

"Might as well see if there's any chippies left open. One in the city'll be open still."

Mick wanted to go home, and to be rid of Eddie. But he gave his approval to the idea and they carried on and walked the short road into Derby. The thought of fresh fish and chips – his first taste for years – should have been worth the trip, he knew, yet he wanted nothing more than to leave and go back to his couch in his parents' home.

***

Each with their bundle warming under an arm they began the walk back in the direction of the Green. Mick took the delightfully hot package into his hands and began to unfold the creases, happily hearing the crinkle as the paper straightened out. Then Eddie veered aside from the pavement and Mick saw the paving beneath his feet change to a new pattern of larger stone slabs. It widened out, and he realized the line of buildings had ended. With surprise he looked up to see a breadth of space opened out, black with the shapes of trees in the distance over the river. Sadly he knew right where he was. He'd had his eyes down and hadn't seen.

"No point rushing our food standing up."

Eddie went halfway down the steps that led toward the Derwent and took his seat. Mick looked down at the river, a dark mass tumbling slowly by and sat a short distance from Eddie on the steps, where he had sat countless times before. He looked across at his friend and wondered coldly whether he was doing it on purpose.

"Good fish n chips, huh?"

"Um," Mick said and picked up a chip with the small wooden fork.

"Remember the last time you and me was here?"

Mick nodded in the darkness. "Yeh."

There was silence. The river looked like an oil slick, sliding past, like the blue-black spills from punctured barrels and exploded encampments he'd seen on many different rivers. Those small leaks drifting, dragging atop the current seemed to have prepared him.

He stood. "Come on. A slow walk's better than sitting for fish and chips. Helps them go down."

"Alright."

They left the riverside and began the walk back to home.

"She's a looker your Misses, if you don't mind me saying so."

"Thanks."

The chips were great, but he needed a drink for all the salt and vinegar: a cup of tea, even though it was late to have one, or simply a glass of water from the kitchen tap when he got back.

"I'm betting she can't cook a roast to save her life, mind you."

Eddie chuckled around his mouthful. Mick grinned harmlessly, warily, seeing a direction of where Eddie had long wanted the evening's talk to go. He said nothing.

"Never had an Asian girl myself, never having been there. The way the war works out for us, hey."

Mick felt his temper rising. He stabbed at his fish and prised out some white flesh and batter. It glowed yellow from black and white as they passed beneath a street lamp. The world became its real two tones as they walked on into a dark stretch of street, an older industrial part of town, with an old wall hiding factories and forgotten lots and yards running down one side of the pavement.

"So, what's she like in the sack?"

"That's private Eddie."

"Teddy. I mean, is there much difference? With a white girl, say? Like the French?"

Mick walked a little quicker. He didn't feel like eating anymore.

"Eddie, shut-up."

"I'm only asking? Can't blame a mate for being curious."

No reply.

"A mark out of ten is all I'm asking."

Was it the alcohol, or intent guiding his former friend? No, there was never any difference. He'd seen enough during the war to know that.

"Come on pal, how long have we been friends?"

"You heard me."

Mick walked on. The street seemed to stretch, the end never in sight. What a fool he'd been to let the night go on like this. With annoyed regret he thought that he could have, ought to have, been at his parents' long ago. He'd known what his friends were like; he'd seen what those lads had inevitably become.

"You are taking full advantage of those rights of married life, aren't you?"

"Drop it."

"What? You're not?"

Eddie laughed his horrible laugh, head back.

"Bloody hell! You haven't even poked your own wife?"

Eddie laughed again, more serious this time, and stepped away, walking half off the curb to make a show of getting a good look at him.

"Unless you've got nothing to compare her against. Look, it was the war, we all did it. Whores by the dozen. You should have seen what Italy had to offer. Right?"

Eddie was in front of him now, walking backwards, making Mick's stride slow.

"What happened to you? Did you get your balls blown off or something?"

"Me and my wife are just fine."

"Well something's not right, is it pal, if you won't touch your own bleeding wife."

Eddie looked up, a sordid realisation striking his brain.

"Or is that it? It's her who doesn't work right down below."

Mick felt his eyes flare, and his nostrils widen like a bull's. His breath became slow in an instant and he stared from under his brows at the smaller man.

"Where did you find her again? Hey?" Eddie laughed. "Damaged? Or diseased? Is that it? You married a whore didn't you?"

A roar sounded into the night, the only noise on that deserted street. Anger powered out of him, anger he did not know he had even had. His hands were seized on Eddie's collar and the inferior man was off the ground, heaved aside, and slammed into the wall.

Mick roared like a beast. "How dare you talk like that about my wife!"

"Let go of-"

And Mick saw himself and knew what he could do. He could tear that scrawny man, that war victor over Germany, into pieces. He knew his power; he was an unstoppable force. He had taken on Japan and won, he had crossed nations; he knew in that moment that no one was a match for him, not a soldier compared to him. The anger roiled up in him, the source uncapped, now from unrelenting reserves.

He roared out his rage and his might, and let Eddie drop down to his feet against the wall.

"You fucking bastard!"

Eddie brushed down his shirt for one second, took a step on his regained feet, and then went for him. He flung a ferocious right, round at his head. Mick blocked it with his left. Eddie went off balance; he came back hurling himself into Mick's chest like a rugby charge. Mick spread his feet, slid back paces and heaved back. He found Eddie's stocky frame overpowering him, lower gravity tipping over his height. Mick scuffled steps back, to hold his balance, toward the curb. He threw his arms up, lifting Eddie's shoulders from the tackle and hurling himself clear.

"You think you're some great war hero, Robinson Crusoe?"

Mick stepped forward, controlled and powerful rage. Eddie threw a punch, hard and fast, as one who'd been in enough fights. Mick turned, arm up to meet it. Beside his head, on the edge of his vision in the dark night and streetlight glare, their arms ground, locked, fighting against the other. With his free arm he pushed, before Eddie could attack from the other flank, a bar against his chest. They parted across the pavement.

"You're nothing. Less than nothing. You married a whore you dumb shit!"

"You respect her. You never talk about my wife that way!"

Eddie moved forward quickly, but Mick saw it and stepped quicker, again shoving him backward. His anger was complete, all powerful. He crossed the ground seamless from the push that had his opponent vulnerable, and struck out with no backswing that could be predicted and countered. It came from his chest and he didn't see the strike until he felt his fist compact against Eddie's skull. Mick's front foot went down, his hand outstretched where Eddie had been, and Eddie spluttered back, off his feet, sprawled onto his back on the pavement.

"Never."

His former friend gathered his location, and spat blood with revulsion.

"Where did you find her? I'm just wondering. You were hiding from the Japanese you told us. Where did you find a girl willing to marry an escaped POW on the run? Even that kind of girl?"

Eddie managed to chuckle a breathless kind of sound. Then as Mick stood, and anger simmered, Eddie picked himself off the ground, stood straight slowly, then walked straight past, back the way they had come, almost close enough to brush clothes. After a few paces he stopped to pick up a package of fish and chips. Some chips spilled from the edges of the newspaper as he lifted it.

"Think I'll go and eat my fish and chips back on the steps. Well, you've come a long way since those days, haven't you Mick?"

Eddie walked away, then turned and walking backwards called out.

"You remember her Mick! Miranda! You murdered that poor girl, you bastard."

Mick looked at the ground. Saw his fish and chips upturned, surprised to note that it had fallen. For a few seconds he stayed where he was, trying to let something settle, or dawn so that he could grasp it. But his mind was in a stupor, a concussion though he'd not been hit. He turned and walked away, alone down the long dark street.

CHAPTER 31

Sun-a lay on her bed, with the lamp above her on. She turned onto her side, her face against the pillow. It was the most comfortable bed she had ever lain on. The pillow was plump and folded around her mouth and nose a little, so that she had to angle her head slightly to breath. Mick had not slept on the bed for many years, but still it seemed to have a scent, that was his. She didn't know that she'd been aware of it before, but it reminded her of him somehow.

She lay and waited, and wanted to sob. But she couldn't be seen to have cried, and she held the tears down and outlasted them, until they were an ongoing burn at the top of her chest. She hadn't cried. And she listened.

The sound of the front door, a kind of click, and short creak; the sound of footsteps on the stairs, which she had already memorized so well that she could hear it in her mind, and it replayed there. The expectation, growing more and more desperate of what she would hear. She stopped breathing lest the air cover the faintest sound beneath the door, and listened. There was only silence; no one walked up the stairs. Her mouth gasped involuntarily, in what sounded to her like the beginning of a sob, of weeping. So she sat up straight at once. The pain in her chest moved and hurt; she swallowed down the sign of tears, and waited for it to pass. Looking about her, she settled on the bookcase on the opposite wall, swung her legs out from under the quilt and went over to it.

She ran her finger, hopping along the top of book to book and leant her head to see the letters down the spines. She wasn't sure which way to look at them. A green book took her attention: it seemed older than the others, the top of the binding more pressed. She withdrew it from the row and thought it a marvellous, wondrous thing that people could make such fine things, as she moved its angle in her hands. She sat with it on the bed, and looked at the picture on the front green, sewn material. It was a man in trees, that were larger around him, and faded away to the sides. Perhaps enough trees to have been a forest. He was slightly stooped in order to hold a large bow and arrow that he was poised to raise and shoot at any moment. On his head he wore a strange shaped hat with a feather in its brow. She found herself smiling at him.

Opening the book she saw pages and pages of words, which she turned one to the next. She couldn't read, only speak, so she was about to close it. Then on a slightly open leaf she saw the edge of another picture. This one was a drawing, a sketch, as she had once seen a man on a street do of passers-by. The man had drawn a forest, the same one again she presumed, through which a river ran. The scene was beautiful; she could feel its tranquillity. And it was undisturbed; seemed fitting for the two men who duelled with great staffs amid rocks in the water. One was taller, a mighty warrior, and the other was the man she recognised from the cover. She turned the page and couldn't read the English, so she closed it.

Placing the book on the chest of drawers at the end of the bed she lay down once more and put the quilt over her.

Then she cried. The sadness was too much and she couldn't and didn't want to stop it. So the tears dampened the pillow about her face, and she lay there and quietly wept – as quietly as she could.

She had been a fool. Such a fool. He had done more than enough for her. Who was she to have ever hoped for more than what he had given her? She would be happy with what he had given her.

And she kept crying, and knew it didn't matter because he would not come into her room and see.

The door downstairs clicked and creaked open, and it wasn't in her mind, but a real sound. She snuffled back the tears, and propped herself up, ready to sit straight if needed. Then the sound of footsteps ascending the stairs. Her chest rose and fell, and the tears kept there still hurt her. He'd see her anxiety if he walked in. Sun-a tried to calm her fright. She wiped the wetness from her eyes, smearing it to dry in lines to the sides of her face and on the edges of her hands.

The footfalls stopped. Before long the sound of water from the bathroom tap. Then water splashing from and tinkling back into the basin. She was holding her breath. He would see her tears, but she just wanted to see him, she would think what to say.

The faint sound of a door, and then two footsteps moved onto the landing.

Then the sound of the stairs, which she did not want to hear. She waited, propped up on her arms on the bed, the duvet dropped halfway to her waist. The sounds quieted and became nothing more than shuffles on the tiles downstairs, and she lay her head back down on the pillow, facing the door. She would have to get up and turn out the light, she thought.

***

Breakfast was early, because it was a Monday, Mik-uh's mother had said, and his father had to go to work. Pam and Harold were their names, but she didn't know if she should use them, or what a woman called her new family in this land. Perhaps he would tell her.

She sat with him and his mother at the table, while his father sat in a chair off in the living room, reading a large newspaper which he repeatedly snapped taut. The crinkle and collapse of paper, while nobody spoke.

"I'll have that quick word with Mr Calvin first thing." He had made her start.

"Thanks," said Mik-uh.

"Not enough lads came back, that's the sad thing, so there won't be any delay."

"There's no rush."

"They might even call you in for the afternoon shift. I'll come back at my lunch break if he needs you today."

"Alright."

Sun-a had caught most of it, and tried to puzzle where they might be going. She considered if she'd missed something, or already knew and ought to have followed.

"Right, I'm off."

Harold stood up and carried his cup of tea and the paper out of the room and into the kitchen. Sun-a watched to see what he would do next. He returned with the paper folded under his arm and a square box in his hands. He gave Pam a kiss on the top of the head, then looked to Mik-uh and said:

"See you later son." And with a kind smile to her: "Have a pleasant day."

She nodded, feeling very glad to have been included, and watched Harold then pick up a long bag by two handles, from the stool where it had sat in the hall. Soon after the front door opened and shut.

"Bye," called Pam when the front door had already pulled to.

"Anything you'd like to do today, dear?"

Sun-a looked to Pam after a moment, realising the question had been for her, and trying to hear it back, part the sound into words.

She understood, and nodded.

Pam seemed to consider her expression up and down, then said, "I'm going to Marjory Dawkins's later, for elevenses. You can come if you'd like."

Sun-a nodded, keen to be seen accepting, though she did not know what had been suggested.

Mik-uh stood with his plate and without saying anything went to the kitchen. Sun-a watched his every move until he disappeared around the hall corner. She realized how anxious her face must look, should anyone see, and tried to plain it. The sound of the tap and the plate clinking, and then the water was turned off and the plate slotted into the rack of thick wire that held them.

And then he did the thing she feared, and walked straight past the open doorway, without glancing aside. He just strode past.

Her heart was in her mouth, and she knew her face held every sign of the shock and sudden hurt inside.

"I'm just going out for a bit. Be back in a while."

"Where to?" called Pam with a slight delay, but the door had slammed shut.

"Come on love, you can help me with the dishes."

Pam stood up, and Sun-a did the same and passed the plates from her side of the table. Then she followed Pam to the kitchen.

***

They sat, listening to the radio. Mik-uh hadn't started work yet. Tomorrow he would. The man on the radio was talking about growing food she thought, but there were too many words she didn't understand. And the voice was a different kind of English.

"The perennial variety, to be planted in March-" she knew the month. The voice from the radio continued and she could only catch passing words, which she had to focus on in the moments after – and miss the next words, already tumbled past and gone, impossible to reach back for; and try and jump back in and clutch at the next before it washed through her clasp. There were too many words to ask anyone.

Mik-uh rose from his chair with a sigh. She watched him as he filed past the small table, stepping over her legs, and left the room. Only she seemed to have noticed: Pam kept doing her strange sewing; Harold's paper stayed as it was, blocking his face. With anxiety trapped in the top of her chest again, she looked toward the dining room, seeing the cabinet with the plates propped up so they faced out into the room, and the many vases, and looked at the space before it, where Mik-uh would reappear from the empty doorway.

"Just going out."

The pressure stayed below the bone in the middle of her chest.

The front door clicked open, and then shut.

Harold's glasses looked up over the line of the paper. Sun-a saw a glance and eyebrows move in meaning, to Mik-uh's mother.

"He never changes, that lad."

Pam glanced immediately at her, and quickly away when she found their eyes met.

"Yes," said Pam and kept sewing with the huge, heavy needles. Their pace wavered for some moments.

Sun-a sat as she was. A little time passed. Her heart beat, thud and thud, and did not relent; anxiety and a demand had her, and she did it, and stood, and kept her eyes on the floor as she crossed to the door.

She didn't call out that she was going, as seemed to be the way. Her shoes struck dull notes down the hall tiles – already on her feet, even indoors. Mik-uh's mother would make her some slippers, she had said; Sun-a glanced back to the light parting the shade of the hall. She placed her hand on the front door handle and face aghast against it creaking or clunking, eased it slowly down. The click sounded and she carefully pushed the handle through it, all the way. She looked over her shoulder, down the hall, certain, in fear, that she had been discovered, was being watched even as she had moved secretly the whole time. The corridor with its high ceiling and pictures hung on the wall, was empty.

She swung open the door, caution thrown aside by the action, swapped for panic and haste, and jumped through the doorway onto the top step. Sun-a shut the door. It closed with a bang, too loudly, and she looked to the large front window, waiting to see a face peer out and see her. But she was outside now. She had never been anywhere by herself.

There was Mik-uh, far away to the left, a small figure down the road. She hurried uneven steps, glanced over her shoulder back to the house – already it was difficult to see which house was the one from the row of doors and windows.

She tried to be calm, looked ahead to Mik-uh, far away, where the road left the square of grass and trees. One glance back and he'd see her; if she was closer, one stop and listen and he might hear her steps, and turn. But she couldn't lose him, or what would happen? So she walked ever quicker, risking the scuffle of her shoes, wanting it to be over, keeping to the side of the houses, hoping in vain that they would hide her.

Another road, rows of houses along both sides, some buildings alone, with plants, trees and grass around them. A bus pulled by, its engine loud like a truck's. A shiny car followed. Mik-uh hurried across the road, shoulders hunched, hands in his pockets. Her urge was to reach out a hand, to call him. But she stopped, frozen at the sight and stood on the other side of the large pole on the street that held up wires. She waited until he had gone far enough away, becoming small and distant, so he might struggle to even recognise her if he turned; a car drove past and she ran across in its wake. She walked on, following him. A wall ran beside them, the length of them, taller than her, with trees lined behind it. A lady on the other side of the street turned her head as she walked by; everyone she had passed had looked at her. Sun-a set her gaze on Mik-uh; she glanced back and the lady was still watching, her head turning to her shoulders. She wore a hat and had her hair tied back. Her long coat was neat and smooth and she carried a bag. Sun-a looked at the paving directly ahead; she looked down her own dress and felt cold.

Mik-uh was gone. In the distance, where his tiny figure had been, there was no one. Sun-a stared ahead, walking quickly, but he didn't reappear. She broke into a run, desperate, and knowing that people shouldn't see her like that, but running regardless. At the place she thought he had been standing she saw the wall stop, and she slowed as she walked into the open. Set back from the road was a large stone structure. There were windows and doors and a clock high above below the roof, but she looked down the view that faced her: a large, deep archway, which led straight through the building.

Sun-a walked forward, looking to either side of the wide yard – fearful that she would have to try and explain herself to a stranger, or that Mik-uh would be standing right there. But no one appeared. She walked on to the great arch and saw it fall back above her as she hurried through.

To either side of the wide path an enormous field stretched. She kept walking on, toward shapes which spanned the horizon. The land was covered, changed, so that it wasn't a field any longer. She recognised the shape of some of the carvings; she had once seen Mik-uh from afar, carrying two branches, crossed, through the wood.

Mick stood and looked down sadly. Birds were tweeting in the tall trees, far enough overhead for it to seem distant, elsewhere. To his left he saw someone move into view, and before he turned, knew it was Sun-a. She glanced nervously up and their gazes met; there was genuine fear in her eyes.

He was watching her approach. What would she say?

"How did you get here?"

"I walked."

"Did you come with my mother and father?"

"No."

Sun-a came to stand beside him and faced the grave as she must have seen him facing it. He faced it too.

At the edge of his vision he sensed her leaning forward, and reading.

Sun-a saw letters, lines and cuts in the stone, but didn't understand.

"Who?" she asked.

"She was a girl I knew when I was younger. She died in the war."

She was quiet for a while. The graveyard seemed still, stiller than he had noticed. And he thought what he should say. There were nerves. Waiting. And yet he didn't resent her arrival. He welcomed it.

He felt Sun-a angle her head to look up at him, and then for a time she looked to the grave.

The gravestone with its rounded top, cut and carved, and its engraved words. Other markers stood in the grass behind it, and aside, amongst the trees. Monuments, heavy, tall things, out of the earth, amidst the others, hundreds, lined in rows. She glanced about her, feeling a kind of panic, a confusion and unease about the spreading ranks. The only grave she had known had been her grandfather's, on a clearing on a hillside, a mound of raised earth, before his own ancestors. There had been space there for her own father and mother. And the grave of her baby, whom she had killed.

The graves around her held on to their space, grabbing into the green blades and soil beneath with their stone sides. Such a huge field to hold so many.

Death; she didn't understand death.

She thought of the great Kings' burial mounds in Gyeongji when they had taken the cart there to trade for cloth from an aunt. Trees grew tall on those markers; and they were an effort for a young girl to scramble up. She had been shouted down, by a man she hadn't known, and her mother had slapped the back of her head. But she had been young. She didn't know how young.

The shade shifted from up above, the sun, or a high wind on the branches. She looked to the grave and stone marker before her now. Mik-uh had come there.

"You cared for her."

"No." He shook his head. "Not enough, I didn't."

Sun-a nodded faintly, gladly. But she said nothing.

"I didn't care. But I think she loved me."

She waited.

"Worse than that, I let her think I did." He paused. "She died for it."

Sun-a glanced up to him, briefly, enough to see the pain on his face. Then she looked away, not really seeing the graves, or the shadows, the imprints of shade. A cold knowing settled upon her. It hurt. She knew it, yet she willed it to not be true. It would confirm her hopes as ruins.

Sun-a waited. The pain welled from her breast bone. She barely breathed as they stood there together and looked down at the earth.

He didn't say anything else. It felt worse than she had sensed it would.

He stared down at the damp, shaded grass, and the grave. The headstone didn't belong there. The dates carved into it didn't fit.

They should go. He should take her back. He turned aside, and they slowly began to walk along the row.

***

He felt like he was walking into a thunder cloud, only it was down at ground level: grey and black and roiling off and around him. Shouts and smoke buffeted the air in front of him. The fizz of sparks from pouring steel and the hammers, and grating chain-links of the works. It was a dense cloud about him, and separated from it he couldn't place the echoes, where they originated from.

He did his job, just as he had before, the same number on the team. Lifting, turning the moulds on their axis, airborne, shoving them, as the metal above rattled and swung and they steadied their path across the factory.

There'd been back-pats and 'good-to-see-you's, and 'good-to-have-you-back's, and he'd smiled and nodded at it all, where he should. There'd been a weight upon him when he'd gotten up that morning, that had been there the day before as he'd sat in his living room seat and the others hadn't known it, as he'd bedded down on the too-small settee. It had been there for days, a depression, like they talked of in weather, slowly building until it was clear it was there.

He nodded, turned on his heel, in its steel toe-capped shoe, and walked back down the aisle with the chain rigging clunking high overhead. A high whistle pierced the cacophony of noise; the constant roar almost instantly dulled and changed into calls and shouts and bits of laughter. Mick walked with the growing stream of men that filed out from the crevices and alleys.

Harold saw his boy at the end of tea break as he left the canteen. From a distance – Mick was standing near a corner of the factory, set against the sooted, smart bricks. His son, in his blue boiler suit, cleaner than the men who passed by around him – just the odd smudge of black and grease so far.

Harold raised a hand. "Michael."

As he walked over he gathered that the boy looked adrift: his feet had been scuffing; his eyes were on the ground, then up in surprise at his name.

"Hi, Dad."

"Mr. Calvin wants to see you. He'll be in his office now. You can just catch him before shift-"

"Yeah, I've just seen him."

Harold reached his son. "Alright then." He put a hand on Mick's much taller shoulder. "Let's get back then."

Michael was shaking his head. He looked worried, burdened. Harold turned to face him, some space between them.

"What's the matter?"

"I've told Mr Calvin, I've quit."

Harold took a moment, trying to think.

"What are you going to do?"

"I'm sorry Dad, I can't do this anymore."

"It's a good job, Michael."

CHAPTER THIRTY-ONE

"I know it is."

"So what's the problem? It's got to be difficult coming back and getting back to normal things-"

"I've made my decision."

Harold put a hand on his son's arm and guided him to the shelter of the brick building and its high overhanging roof. Bodies and blue overalls passed by in either direction. The whistle shrieked.

"What about those years of your apprenticeship?"

"I'm young enough there's time for me to find something else to do."

Harold considered it a moment and felt there was nothing to reply. He looked his son firmly in the eyes.

"If you leave now, there's no telling if you'll be able to come back."

"I know."

Harold gave a nod.

"I'll see you back at the house, Dad."

His boy walked briskly toward the main gate, with its small one-person door in the large wooden arch that you had to step up and duck through to get outside. A foreman shouted something after his son, but his tall figure was through the gap, and then couldn't be seen in the rectangle of Derby road outside.

Harold turned and headed for his place on the production line. He felt a great loss. As he walked slowly back he sought the pieces which made sense of it. His thoughts went to the first war against the Germans, and the scene of his older brother going to France – where his body still was. He had just a name of the place. War kept a lot of things hidden.

***

They sat at the table for tea. There was a gloom about the room, under the yellow electric light-bulb in its shade above them. In her posture, the way she lifted her cup, his mam was about to tell him what she thought he ought to do.

"I'm sorry. I don't want to disappoint you."

They looked up at him, quietly continuing to eat their sandwiches. Sun-a glanced up. She probably didn't know.

"It wasn't for nothing, my apprenticeship. Against the Japanese I knew exactly where to place... how to stop their trains. I'm grateful. But I controlled troops, and... I just need a change."

There was quiet a moment.

"Alright then," said his dad.

That evening, as he waited, as he had come to do, for everyone to leave before he sat on the settee, his parents lingered in the kitchen. Sun-a had gone upstairs. He had said goodnight, quietly to her, that was all. Sadness swamped him, alone, and he decided he would just turn off the one remaining light and be done with it. He hated it that they knew he slept downstairs, but of course they did.

"You need to decide what you're going to do, Michael."

It was his mam. He hadn't heard her approach or step from the kitchen – and he always heard everything.

"I know, and I will."

He looked up over the arm of the settee where he had just lain and spread the blanket over himself, but he could see no one in the darkness.

"Night night."

"Night."

CHAPTER 32

Mick stepped from the pavement. There was no traffic on the new street; he stood in the road and looked across at the odd houses, with their unusual colour and low aspect. They sat there, each with brown earth and patchy grass around it, separating it from the rest: they would be gardens in the spring. There wasn't much to them: simple walls, a low roof; three windows facing, a door, a path. He felt elated and his chest risen with hope.

A man in a smart, slightly short, grey suit bustled down the path from one of the identical bungalows along the street. He hurried over, hand outstretched well before it needed to be. Mick shook it.

"Mr Bowler?"

"Yes, nice to meet you."

"What do you think?"

"Great."

"Good," Mr Edmunds said – the voice he took to be the same as from their phone conversation. "This whole estate is new; some have already been taken; but how about number nineteen just over here?"

Mick carefully followed the line of Mr Edmund's arm. He saw a house, two or three along, lovely, set at a slightly different plane as the road moved. He could see the gable end and the sloping lawn that would grow green in the spring. It looked settled there. It would be wonderful; the place they could build their life together.

"That one?" he asked, not wanting to get it wrong.

"Yes," and Mr Edmunds motioned him to cross.

Mick followed, looking about him: the winter street with its recently planted young trees at intervals in squares of dirt along the pavement; the artfully positioned houses, and other rows further behind them.

"Can you pay for one?"

"I've got my soldier's pay, and I'm looking for work."

"Where did you say you served?"

"Asia. Burma."

Mr. Edmunds looked matter-of-fact and nodded.

"Prefab is the way forward. A veteran like you is exactly the kind of man we're keen to have living here. These homes were built for you."

They stopped before the house on its slight rise of land. It was perfect for them – more than he had hoped for. He had to find a way for he and Sun-a to live there.

"Sir, I could help sell these."

"I'm sure you could young man, but we're full up in that department."

Mr. Edmunds stepped back and sized up Mick.

"You look like you've come out of the war alright."

"Yes, Sir."

"Any injuries?"

"None."

"Good for you, lad. Can you lift and carry?"

"Yes, Sir."

"Because they don't need help selling. You understand. We're better than our competitors; got new suburbs springing up all around the country, and we're aiming for more. Emergency Factory Made brought a lot of opportunities, and we've got more government contracts."

"Congratulations, Sir."

"So you see son, what I do need is help building them."

Mick nodded promptly. "I can do that." He tried to look serious, dependable, and held Mr Edmund's eye.

"Excellent. We'll train you up how to build these beauties from the ground up."

"Thank-you, Sir. I really appreciate it."

Mick stretched out his hand. Mr. Edmunds considered it just briefly, nodded, and shook, and it had been agreed.

"And now you'll be able to pay the rent on one of these."

Mick couldn't help himself smiling broadly. Mr. Edmunds clasped him heartily on the shoulder and moved beside him to face the prefabricated home.

"Thank-you. It'll be great, Sir."

"That it will, Mr. Bowler. It's a new world after the war."

***

18th December 1945

Mick stopped with the house spread before them in its full profile, gable end onto the long stretch of the front, land running right around from the hidden back garden to where they stood, and on across the front. He extended a hand toward it in a grand gesture, a big smile across his face.

Sun-a looked to him, to the house, to him, her face wanting to know the answer to her question, just holding back on excitement.

"What is it?"

"It's our house, Sun-a."

The smile just below the surface broke through. She beamed out, up to him, out to the house, such happiness on her face. Her eyebrows were lifted high as she looked up to him, still waiting for the answer to her question.

"It's really our house. We can look for some furniture of our own. We'll go together and find a table, and chairs, and maybe a dresser, and it will be great. We could move in after Christmas I think, as soon as we're ready. That's when I'll start working. They gave me a job; I'll be helping to make these houses up and down the country."

"Oh, it's wonderful, Mik-uh," she said in Korean, the first he'd heard her use it for some time.

"You like it then?" he replied, in the same.

She nodded. She reached out her hand toward his, and he reached for hers. For a moment their fingers touched as they gazed at their house.

***

The man opened the door. It was stiff, perhaps in the cold, as she was; she huddled into her warm English coat and bounced a little on the spot.

"Here we are," the man who had had the keys said, and the door budged open.

She all but hopped in, like a little bird she thought, and eagerly looked around her new home. Mik-uh stood tall, taking in the ceiling and nodding with a pleased smile. She looked at all the walls and how they joined and went one to another, so exactly. The house had a nice, unusual smell; she wasn't sure what. The room was empty, but she couldn't take it all in. Too much. Mik-uh put his hand softly on her back and let it stay there, and she smiled up at him, and looked again at the clean room. She felt comfortable, like she had when the sun had fallen on her and warmed her, with the gentle air-giving breeze, her feet dangling, kicking in the open air off the drop of the cliff face.

An image arose and stayed parallel alongside, of the home of her childhood. Her parents' home. A small hut, the doorway, the ground in front. Her happiness darkened, a chill wind off the sea with the fishermen. She saw the white walls, and Mik-uh was tall and close beside her. His hand was still on her back. How long would he keep it there? She made herself smile out at the room again, and the way the walls joined together where they met.

"The kitchen's this way, the master bedroom over there, with the guest room–baby's room facing."

Mik-uh nodded as the man spoke. Sun-a peered to the little corridor where he had pointed, replaying his words, trying to understand and take them in before they vanished. She swivelled her head to look the other way as he moved quickly, hand outstretched.

"If you'll follow me to the kitchen, folks. All the mod.... A cooker, with... Ref... and a fr..."

She followed after Mik-uh, catching bits and pieces from the busy English man.

∗∗∗

So petite. That delicate frame. Now that she had gotten used to the jet black hair, Pam thought her daughter-in-law was just about the prettiest girl she'd ever seen. She could see why her boy had fallen in love with her – although she didn't understand their marriage. They'd settle into it, as all newlyweds did. Everything was difficult after the war.

"And this is where you put the clean dishes."

Dawn's face was all attention, eyes following everywhere that Pam's hands went, and head quickly nodding after each sentence, taking it in. Pam wondered how a girl could grow up and not know how to wash the dishes; she wondered what life must be like over China way. So different to England.

"This is your draining board."

"Draining board," Dawn softly repeated.

"You'll need a crockery cupboard. You can choose one. Perhaps this one."

Dawn nodded to the one Pam's outstretched hand suggested.

"One for the things that you don't mind getting broken. Well, you always mind, and you should always let the men see that you mind an awful lot."

Dawn nodded, her gathering-it-all-in face staring, mouth a little open, like a child's Pam thought. A doubt arose, that perhaps it was all washing over her.

"And one for your best crockery. Maybe when Michael gets you a dresser in the living room."

She looked at the girl in her flowery dress that they'd got her at Mabel's the week before. Nothing to her. Pam wondered how that slight frame was going to produce her grandchildren. But then, the Chinese had been having babies for centuries just like everyone else, so she supposed it would all be fine.

"Now, the stove," Pam continued. "Did you have these in your home?"

Dawn shook her head.

CHAPTER THIRTY-TWO

"Did your mother teach you to cook? What meals did she teach you to make?"

Pam watched as Dawn struggled and couldn't answer.

"Well, this is your oven."

She bent over and pulled on the nice new oven door, not a trace of grease on it. It clicked open with a crisp ping.

***

She gazed up into the coloured light which came through above her. Everyone else looked straight ahead, and she probably should have done the same, yet she kept her head turned, to the right, into the beams that shot through the air and anchored to the ground in people and at their feet. She turned to see across Pam and Harold to the other side. The sun was to her right and so over there she could not see the air in colour. Yet the whole side of the building was alight, and every window glowed brightly as if drawing in all the light from around and blazing it out in glorious pictures. It lifted her heart; it was an incredible sight; those windows... She sensed Harold lean a little and look her way along the shared seat. She faced ahead, but then glanced back to the high windows and marvelled again – then told herself to listen, her heart still holding the lightness and wonder. It was like a secret that no one else could see, and she wondered suddenly if it might be true, that only she could see the coloured sunlight – before the thought quickly passed into reality.

Sun-a turned to the right again. People in the seat across the aisle glanced her way; they had not stared at her for a while. She smiled to them quickly, and turned her eyes high above them to the large arched windows in the mighty stones. She saw a bright, rich red, as if someone had dyed the colour from fresh petals and put it into light. Blues, many of them, light, and bright, then deep and powerful, each holding together in its own beam through the air. Diagonal, down to the people below who looked ahead, eagerly listening, somehow not noticing the colours that shone on their faces. What pictures - the man, strong like Mik-uh sat beside her; up there he fought, arms locked with the arms of a man with great feathered wings of a bird. And through them the light, white, and yellow, gold, blues and reds and greens and browns of the land. She could feel their struggle - the strength in their arms - though it was a picture, a moment held still there. And she wondered who those great men were. They seemed alive, in some way beyond her - brought into life in the many beams that held steady, held still in the air, like pillars from another world. Her eyes cast deep red, and yellow, and green and gold, and glorious colours as she moved through them.

When they sung, she looked around the huge, tall building and saw all the pictures. The singing soared as she had never heard voices do. It made her look about at the individual faces, to see how that great sound was made, while high around them the pictures towered and glowed. It was as if they heard, and she was with them.

CHAPTER 33

6ᵗʰ March 1946

The table in front of her was made of a nice, light wood. She ran her finger along the grain, which ran the length of the table, a bit like a river, high up in the mountains, mostly straight, just moving slightly. It was one of many little rivers in the grain, all fitted next to the other, right across the table, which sat against the wall in the kitchen.

She looked around her kitchen. It was neat and clean. She had wiped up the crumbs left by the grill and toast rack earlier in the morning. Sun-a looked at the clock. The hands said – she peered, to be sure:

"Half past ten."

She looked around her kitchen. In a cupboard, behind that door was the bag of flour, and the sugar was in its bowl next to the cooker, beside the pot with the wooden spoons for stirring the batter.

Her ration books behind the biscuit barrel, for coupons, and points.

She sat on one of the hard seats next to the small kitchen table.

It was still one and a half weeks before Mik-uh came back.

She wondered what he was seeing right that moment. Maybe a hammer he was swinging down, making a new foundation; perhaps it was a wall, one of these new walls of special material that he was seeing. She tried to remember the name of the town he had told her he would be in now, supervising building. First Bradford, and then now... She couldn't bring the sound of it to her mind.

***

25th April 1947

"I'll see you on Sunday, Dawny. Have a lovely time."

Sun-a nodded and watched Pam turn and walk off the grassy hillside. As always the grass was everywhere, like the new lino that had just been laid in the prefab. The 'Fab,' Mik-uh's mother now called it, and had explained to her it was short for 'fabulous.'

Where she had come from grass had grown in tufts, grouping together but always isolated, never managing to cover the dirt. And it was different somehow. But here, and on the hillside, in between the copses of trees that grew to either side, it was perfect green. Barely any of the dark brown soil could be seen. She looked to her feet to see some, and moved her head to see the deep ground beneath pass in the gaps between the hundreds of shoots.

"This way then, dear."

Sun-a spun and followed the short, wide lady, Mar-jory.

She ran the name through her mind, both pieces of it, trying to make sure she remembered.

Up ahead were two rows of tents with a big space down the middle. They were a blue colour, different to the sand and green ones at the Japanese prison. They were shorter, squatter, and looked fun. They even made her smile.

She had never seen so many children at one time. Little girls ran out of their tents, then quickly slowed to a straight-backed walk, too like soldiers – but with wide grins and gaps in teeth not yet grown that made her smile still more. Others ran freely, where the tents ended, running in circles, reaching out to touch other wheeling girls, squealing with delight, flapping at dresses, trying to evade away with a twist and hands thrown back and up. Laughter sounded from different girls, and screams and shouts. Sun-a felt her heart elated, so light, and part of her longed to go and join them and play.

"Hokey doke, Dawn, this is your six. The Elv-s." Mar-jory lifted a big blue flap of a tent entrance. "You can put your nap-sack in there."

"Thank you."

Sun-a bent over and shuffled in. Little girls looked up at her, wide-eyed where they sat.

"Hello," she said.

They stared at her. "Hello," one voice said meekly.

They had beautiful big round eyes, and hair so neat, and smooth, tied back. A few of them had taken off their hats, while a few still wore theirs: round, soft hats, which sat on a head, a little like a cap, but with no rim over the eyes. Sun-a smiled at the girls and backed out.

More girls ran past, then slowed as they saw Mar-jory and gulped back their words.

"Good morning, Brown Owl."

They wore smart, pressed blue shirts, and skirts with lovely folds all around, like a fan. Just the same as the one that she was wearing. Sun-a looked down at her clothes – the blue of her top and the way her skirt swayed at the hem. She felt pride, and she looked up at the passing girls with an eager smile.

"Good morning young ladies. I'd like to introduce our newest leader, Dawn, to you."

The girls had already stopped. Arms linked together, they had come to a halt like a linked rope at the sight of her. Two of them had their mouths dropped open; a taller one was leaning slightly, her neck long, eyes staring like she couldn't believe it.

Sun-a felt herself back inside her own head, no longer out in the sunny field, on the grass. She tried to keep smiling.

"My name's S-Dawn," she said. She heard her accent and dearly wished it wasn't there.

The girls, in their line, awkwardly bent at the knee in a fashion that made Sun-a observe to see what they would do next. Their lovely skirts spread on the folds, and the girls' sweet heads, bowed to her. Some had hair tied in two tails, some in one. Another girl had hers shorter around her face; waves from beneath her soft hat.

"Walk sensibly around camp, girls."

"Yes, Brown Owl."

"We will Brown Owl. Sorry."

And they hurried along, eyes angled onto Sun-a as they walked by – and she sensed, with heads turned and turning round still as they passed her, though she kept her eyes looking straight ahead.

"Ah, there she is, by the flagpole." Mar-jory pointed a thick, strong arm. "I'll introduce you to Barn Owl."

Sun-a followed her across the space between tents. She saw fires, ringed by stones, and tables laid out, and great big metal bowls with handles.

"And we'll need to choose a name for you."

Sun-a glanced over in surprise. The lady talked quickly, but she thought she had understood.

"We've no Snowy Owl." Mar-jory glanced back as they walked, with a considering expression and slight nodding.

"We've no Snowy Owl, but I don't think that will do, what with your lovely long black hair, and skin colour. I shall have a think. Perhaps one of the sixers or seconds can talk you through the bird book. That's an idea."

They walked on to a group of little girls and a woman around a pole, like the one at the prison camp, only not as tall. Sun-a looked up, but there was no flag. A few of the girls huddled together, each trying to solve a problem, reaching to material in the middle of them.

When the flag was fastened to the rope they all stood back and all the other girls were called over to gather round. It was a kind of ceremony. Sun-a stood amongst them, unsure where to go, as they all watched the flag hoisted.

***

She lay on her rolled out mat, under her long blanket. It easily covered her and she had tucked its bottom under stockinged feet. It was a little cold on her face above the blanket, and she could feel the warmth, so wonderful held around her, that made her in awe of how it did that and where she was. It was black above; she could see almost nothing. But as she waited and looked up her eyes adjusted again and she could see where the tent was, sheltering them in the darkness. Turning her head, with a smile, she rested her cheek on her pillow and looked where the little girls were under their blankets.

She smiled broader and her eyes felt tears beginning. She felt like a mother. There were six beautiful girls, little girls, their mothers' slides which had been clipped in now unfastened and neatly placed beside them.

At first they had been scared, she thought, but then they had gotten used to her. One of the girls called Re-Bek-a had asked her if she was English, and then where she was from. The little faces had looked at her in their torchlight, and beams had swung and felt out the features of her Korean face. The beams had danced like stars and bursts of light around the sloped walls of the tent, on and off her. And then the six had chatted in excited voices, each under her own blanket, with her bag behind her pillow, and they had laughed, and Sun-a had caught words and phrases and smiled, and looked excitedly from one to the other, trying to catch up.

Pam had said it would be good for her to get active, and get out of the house. She liked the Brownies. She felt so happy to be there. She wondered what Mik-uh was doing, and if he was sleeping in a tent, or in a house he had built.

***

She ran with the girls, just behind them, laughing as they did, watching them wheel and cut across each other, feeling little bursts of concern that they would bump and fall. The air felt alive; it always seemed fresh in England; the morning sun was never too hot. They ran down the slope toward the river, where they all slowed, breathing fast, still smiling. Some of the girls dropped to sit cross-legged amongst the abundant grass, or knelt down, adjusting their folding skirts, and like the girls already there began to pick little white flowers.

Sun-a watched, fascinated, as they used a fingernail to split part of the stem and then threaded another stem through it. They then reached about them for one of the flowers which grew all around and linked it with the others. A girl laid the lined stems on her wrist and looked at them with tilts of her head. It was jewellery made of small white flowers, and it was more beautiful than anything she had seen on a wrist made of metal or stone.

Another of the six unfastened the toggle on the pouch at her side and brought out her knives. They were all kept folded within the small metal container, as the girl had shown her when opening the tin of beans on breakfast duty. Her brother had given it to her, and she 'treasured it,' she had said. Sun-a looked again in some amazement as a short knife snapped out straight. Delicately, the girl used it to cut a flower stem as she held it tall with her other hand.

"What are the flowers?" Sun-a asked.

"They're daisies," Ser-uh said.

"Oh."

"Don't they have daisies in your country, Dawn?"

Sun-a shook her head. "I don't think so."

And Jen-nee nodded and looked back to her work.

"You could make one too."

Sun-a sat by the river bank with the green grass shoots pushing past and around her crossed legs. There were daisies all around her; they never seemed to run out. So she reached to one side, or saw one to the other and gently picked them to make her jewellery. There were cows across the river, eating grass, and more birds chirping and swooping from the large trees than she thought she had ever heard before. Her heart rose within her. It was a remarkable life she was living.

Later they gathered by the river, and edged closer on their tummies to look into the sparkling water; clear, bright under the nearly noon sun. Fish darted about fresh, green weeds and muddy rocks at the bottom, and vanished from their peering row of shadows.

"Look, fish!"

"What kind?"

"I saw them too."

Sun-a thought about their dinner time; in moments Brown Owl might call them back to stir the big pots or set out the plates and bowls. It would be good for her to help.

She reached down into the water with two cupped hands. The river was cold and refreshing and she felt at peace as she left her hands, a short distance apart, the water halfway up her forearms. She nudged up across the ground until the top of her torso overhung the water, and kept her head aside against her arm, to take the shadow away and leave her hands where the sun warmed across the surface of the water.

"Dawn, what are you doing?"

"Catch a fish."

One of the girls inhaled a wondering breath.

The fish swam with two others, out from some stone and weeds, which rocked in the gentle current. It didn't see what was ahead as it swam forward, turning a little left, then a little right. It made its path straight for Sun-a's waiting hands, and once between her separated palms she closed them on it in an instant. In a slight splash and whoosh of water breaking and filling the gap left behind, she swung her arms back over the bank and placed the fish onto the grass.

Girls stepped back. Sun-a smiled and reached out a hand to ask for the knife. Ser-uh put it into her palm, then moved back a little from her.

Sun-a considered the metal lines, cold in the sun on her wet hand. She pulled out one and happily saw a knife.

It was a kind of fish she hadn't seen before. Turning the fish over, right way to face her, she cut a line through its head, diagonally beside its eye. It stopped squirming and its tail stopped weakly beating the tufts of grass. Its gills dropped flat. Pressing the fish to the ground with one hand, she cut into its belly near the tail. A muted sound came from the girls. Surprised to find the blade was not sharp, she had to saw the knife in. As she had done a thousand times she sliced a line from tail to head – but the blunt knife dragged on the fish flesh and tore at times when it should have cut, making the line ragged and jagged edged. Sun-a dug her thumbs into the serrated cut, rotated them out and pressed the belly open; the flesh pulled apart down the line, uneven, stubbornly at times. She was disappointed. A quick cut under its head, and she reached in, thumb and a finger, and pulled out its insides – a long line. Out through the made slack-jawed mouth. She held the spine and guts out over the river and let them drop.

A girl screamed to her left.

Sun-a looked up. One girl had tears leaving her eyes and suddenly leaving trails right down her small cheeks. Sun-a sat back off her knees to squat and starred from one horrified, traumatised girl's face to the next.

"I'm sorry," she said, and she knew she had made a terrible mistake.

Re-Bek-a cried a brief sound, then dropped herself forward to ground. Before her hands had planted themselves, some vomit purged from her mouth, mid-fall.

"Re-Bek-a!"

A girl shrieked. Then another.

"Brown Owl!" a girl's voice called.

More girls had begun to gather, to be drawn in to their point on the river bank, like fish on lines. Dawn felt the tranquil scene wheeling around her as she turned her head to see.

"I'm sorry," she said.

She looked to the gutted fish, not yet cleaned, and thought if she should throw it away into the river. But it would be a waste. They could still eat it for their meal.

"I wasn't scared," said another of the girls, to one of the six.

A girl whimpered, not yet crying.

She couldn't remember their names; they had gone from her head.

*****

Sun-a climbed the step before the front door. In the doorway beside Mik-uh's mother she turned as the room allowed.

"Thank you."

"Not at all, Dawn. You have a good sit down."

She walked back into the house, down the thin tiled corridor with pictures on the wall. Her cheeks felt moist with tears, though she'd wiped them away.

Pam turned with pursed lips back to her old school-girl friend.

"Marjory, really. Couldn't she have stayed till the end of camp, at least?"

"I'm sorry Pam, we can't take her. She cut a fish open right in front of the girls."

"Why?"

"She said, 'for dinner.'"

Pam nodded, trying to keep her face plain.

Marje considered what more to say; it was unpleasant to be forced to have such a conversation. Pam was making the best of it, and so she had sympathy for her – the son returning out of the blue with a foreign wife. It had been a great joy and a great shock for her.

"Pam, you understand, there's no telling what she might do. She must have had such a different upbringing."

"Of course, Marjory, I understand, but she's such a sweet girl. She likely thought it a good deed. I'll tell her she mustn't do that in England."

"I am sorry, Pam. But it's the girls' welfare I've got to think of.

Marje paused and sought a way ahead.

"Perhaps when she's adjusted to civilized life she'll be better. We could try again later, when the girls' parents have calmed down, or the girls have moved to the Guide pack. Although many do have sisters."

Pam nodded. She'd had enough of the conversation.

"Well, thanks for bringing her back, Marjory. I am sorry. She's a good girl you know? A very good girl."

"I'm certain of it, Pam." A pause for softly nodding. "I'll see you at Joyce's on Thursday morning?"

"Most likely, yes."

"Afternoon. I must get back."

"Goodbye."

Pam waited politely as Marje in her Brownie's uniform and beret turned and walked away. She gave a short smile when Marje looked back, and then shut the front door.

CHAPTER 34

Pam stood with her daughter-in-law in the queue at the butchers. She shuffled forward a place as an elderly lady from Marcus Street, whose name she perhaps had never known, hobbled away from the counter. Dawn moved forward beside her.

Everyone in the line stared at her from time to time. A teenage boy who was there with his mother carrying a woven basket, glanced around again and leaned out a little to see her. When she met his eyes the boy spun back and into the line. A cross-eyed woman who was much taller than her and Mik-uh's mum, looked around and gave a little smile. Sun-a smiled back politely.

She and Pam took a few tiny steps forward and stopped. She glanced to the older woman with her hair of curls; their heads were the same level; Pam wore smart sturdy shoes with strong heels. Her own were similar, but flatter – a younger style, Pam had said in the shop.

Some more people opened the shop door and the little bell rang again, as the square shapes of glass in wood, swung open. The grown-up daughter, who was with her mother, closed the door behind her, and the bell dinged slightly before the door made the pleasing closing sound in its frame. They joined the line, the mother looking in her handbag, and the daughter looking briefly around the shop. When the daughter's eyes fell on her, they stopped passing immediately, and widened and stared, and then glanced away, still wide and round and white, to the tiles, when they saw her looking back. It was the same every time. Sun-a wondered about her own narrow black eyes. She wondered what it was like to have round eyes, and what it would be like to look at her own.

Pam gave Carol Bedford's daughter a mildly disapproving look, though the girl wouldn't see, and looked briskly ahead again, to be unperturbed. She notched her head aside and looked into the glass counter, tutting inwardly that they hadn't come five minutes earlier, willing the ladies in front to ask for the mince or the black pudding.

The shape of someone passing moved through Bulliment's paned door and onto the long window in front of the rib of beef and pork chops. It was Edward, her son's friend. His head was turned casually to look in as he strolled past with another lad. Belatedly, through the reflection he seemed to see her. Pam saw the boy's eyes move off her, looking aside, and find Dawn.

He stopped in the butcher's window, and his eyes didn't move from Dawn.

Pam felt a tight worry suddenly seize her gut; a surprise, a not understood instinct to have about her son's old friend. It was the boy's stare. Edward's face wore a snarl, a bit like an animal – no, a sneer more like. A move in the lad's balance seemed to be toward the door. Pam looked ahead to the brass door handle, with a fear that she would see it press down, and a customer who she knew was not there to buy anything, walk inside. But the shape of Edward in the glare and lines of shade in the glass window, rocked back. She watched him and saw him then, as he was. His eyes relented their stare and fell again briefly on her. She felt a relief for Dawn, and met that gaze, blurred through the glass, that showed no sign of shying. Then Edward swivelled, and hunched back into his shoulders, left the window.

Sun-a thought she recognised the man, Mik-uh's friend from the pub, though she had only met him once and it had been years ago. Pam breathed a little uneasily beside her, and she saw the lady's chest rise and judder slightly as it fell. Sun-a also felt unsettled, but by a sense of not knowing from what she had escaped. A restlessness grew in her, that she should have run; it was what she had learnt to do – the only way. He had been staring straight at her, almost pushing her back – Pam spoke suddenly beside her, as she shuffled forward a place in the line. Sun-a moved with her-

"What cut would you like to get today, Dawn?"

She turned her head to the older lady, who in spite of their heights she always felt she needed to look up to.

"You know how a butchers works in Britain now, don't you? I'll leave it to you to ask. I'll get the sausages and some of the bacon."

"Bacon or ham."

"Or you could try something different: what do you think of liver? He's got some in. You could have it with your bacon."

Dawn tried to look around the queue to the counter.

"Do you like liver?"

"I'm not sure."

Pam puzzled. "How would your mam have cooked it?"

The girl didn't answer right away, and Pam sensed immediately there wouldn't be an answer. Standing there, looking blankly through the shop window, past the glare and reflection of light to the glazed world outside, she found the horrible sensation that she knew what she hadn't known before. A passerby with a pram strolled past; across the road a car pulled over. Her son's friend had gone, but the seared memory of his eyes preying on the girl, combined with all that she knew of her. Images and remembrances of conversations and places passed: the first time she had seen Dawn, on her doorstep; what her son had said at the table; the things he hadn't said; the girl's acts, a thousand ticks that had passed her by.

Pam forgot to move forward into the space. She found Dawn looking at her, prompting her to take her step with asking eyebrows. Pam feigned a collected expression and took one step forward into the vacated space. Her sensible, smart shoe clopped down on the mopped tile. She looked at the back of the pale blue hat on the head of the lady in front.

Sun-a felt her world slip away. A sinking feeling emptied the air from her lungs and descended on her gut. The older woman beside her, knew. Below the anxiety, the fear and sickening realisation, from that place in her belly a familiar pain began. It took over. She had to stifle a cry, and only just did so, so far away had she suddenly become. Sun-a refused to think of it, refused to acknowledge it, but as she found herself in the queue in the butchers then, she wanted to sob. She glanced aside above the straight arm of his mother's warm jacket; it went from the smart cuff, without a fold or a crease up to the plump sewn line at the shoulder. Pam's face was turned away, looking determinedly straight ahead. She was stood differently, taller, her thick neck always strong, now fixed, unable to turn easily to her side.

The pain in her belly flared out – an emptiness, an ache, that needed her to curl over. She bled little; sometimes not at all; there were months without; this though was a hurt from long ago. Yet she stood as tall as she could on her smart shoes with their gentle heels, and was aware of her coat about her, with its folded-back collar down the front and its large buttons.

She looked ahead too. They each took two half steps forward as the person at the front of the line picked up her packed paper bag and book, and walked to the door. The bell above knocked and rang and a small gust came into the shop when the door opened. And she hurt, and simply wanted to leave and go back to her empty house.

Pam sought to put away unreasonable notions. She tried to look without sign of it to Dawn as they stepped forward to take their turn at the counter. She asked for their orders. The liver was cut and the orders weighed. Dawn handed over her open ration book, and the butcher stamped the coupons; Pam passed over her own and Harold's books. The orders were string wrapped, and soon she was saying goodbye and turning to leave.

Her hand touched briefly on the girl's, to guide her out. At the touch of Dawn's flesh, she thought of it as she had never done before.

***

A Korean woman swam off the coast. She turned against the water to face back to low cliffs. Her feet gently kicked and coaxed at the water to move her, and her hands fanned and cut through the salt, opening and closing, slicing through, then palms pulling back - but it wasn't enough. She saw the cliffs, and the trees atop them and bushes and grasses up to the edge. She looked down and saw through the distortion of the water, an English dress about her legs. One moment it flapped open in the waves and current, and the next drew tight and wrapped itself around her like a wrung cloth. Sun-a kicked against it, but it was a knot about her. She could feel the thick material against her skin, coarse and heavy and soaked in sea water. It began to pull her down, as if hung with weights from the hem. She kicked, but her ankles were caught, and the tiny moves were the thrashes of a fish.

She panicked. She knew the danger she was in, and her hands pushed against the water, quicker and quicker, fingers gaping open in desperation. She could feel the water pouring down her throat – though it still lapped her chin. Her head span from one side to the other, staring, not comprehending, clear of water, and her legs and midriff twisted, trapped and bound, and she didn't think she could breath, with the silent water rushing into her lungs.

Sun-a threw her head back, so the base of her skull lay in the sea, and panted up into the sky above. From the nape of her neck her submerged hair spread out as she sought to stay afloat, making black shapes in the water, opening and closing, a sunken fan.

She pulled her head back desperately, but it only made the angle steeper, and she felt the horror of the drowning plunging straight down inside of her.

Desperation, turning to tears. Hopelessness that made her want to scream and cry out.

Then the current turned her, a perfect half circle, and stopped her dead. Like hands steering beneath the surface. She faced the battleships, grey, a wall in long, high, deep pieces, pulling slowly together, closing by some great mechanism that slid far beneath the surface, along the sea floor. All was enclosing her: the world was a grey-metal machine thing, a sentience to trap her and pull her under, or make her paddle, forever there, about to be. Forever. But never to drown. She wanted to scream.

Sun-a made toast for breakfast. The dream still hung on her, as she carefully lifted the toast from the grill, put it on a plate and took it across to the table where she had put the butter. It was just for herself, but she'd been taught how, so she did it and sat down.

***

She saw him still, somehow more of him, stopping, though he sat unmoved in the chair. He looked too tired, too many of his prefabs built.

She dared to say it one more time: "You never asked me, about what I did?"

She intently saw him, nod slowly. "Which?"

"Any."

Mick-uh nodded again, his head moving with left-over effort.

At first she didn't continue. The house she thought of as only hers seemed to hang there, held from falling, dropping away, only by the pinning of the two of them.

"When I killed it."

"I was there," he said. "What's to ask?"

She nodded. He didn't turn, kept his eyes down. The words were in her head, as so often; to make them real, with all the awful possibility.

Sun-a spoke: "Can I... forgiven? Can you, forgive me?"

He looked to her then, head turned, pained, fully now. And he waited a moment.

"I think... Yes."

Her throat caught.

"How?"

His gaze turned back to look out of the front window. A moment, where it seemed he would not answer the question. And she had to break it apart.

"Was it terrible, Mick-uh?"

A moment, and he nodded to her, eyes sad. "Yes."

She looked away, out of the window. The net curtains.

"And all the other?"

CHAPTER THIRTY-FOUR

"Yes. But done to you."

Finally she said: "I know."

She kept staring out, through the glaze of the sunlight, and reflected street on the window.

"I once told you of a cicada," she spoke in a daze. Half Korean. "Can you remember?"

He looked across to her, a frown, trying to recall.

"It was on a mountain, near the beginning."

She looked to the window again, to let him leave, to watch the world beyond the glass panes.

"When I was-" He coughed, cleared a dry throat. "In - near India - Burma. In the last months before the Japanese, got me. We were living in the jungle. There'd be ambushes - we killed lots of them; and sometimes they would spring from nowhere, when we thought the jungle was green and peaceful, and it seemed so still.

"And in those days a lot of men died. They were shot. Sometimes many times. Legs, lost. Stomachs..." His hands gestured, words halted. Then arms fell too. "And I'd have to make a choice. Leave him for the Japanese to get, maybe to torture, to do God-only-knew, what; and I, or others, had to make that choice. End their life and have it over with, or leave them, or try and haul them on our backs and take them with us."

Sun-a didn't take the gap he left to interrupt. She remained, straight-backed in her chair, eyes moist, teared. Horrible to see.

"The way we decided who lived or died, was always the future. Did this man have a good chance? If he might live long enough to recover; be strong enough to survive, a long enough while, in a Japanese camp - should I let him live and risk the Japanese making it so much worse for him than it already was? If it was inevitable - if he was going to die soon, in the day;

should I... kill him now?

"And I did. I put bullets into those, I thought, were dead already. But a man who would live, even if he's passed out on the vines and leaves, blood, body opened-up - those I let... I left there. That was for God to decide.

"It seems to me that's how we decide - even when we don't know we are. It's not the question, is this person alive now; in this instant; not, conscious, or awake, or looking around, or even is his chest rising and falling high and low? But, could it be? Will he awake, one day? That's how we people have always decided. The future - the what will be."

"Yes, I know," she finally said.

He nodded, regretfully; and she had eyes brimmed with tears.

"But I also know it was, terrible, done to you."

He stood immediately, like an action at war, and crossed to her. He put his hand on her arm.

"Many..."

Her lips were pressed closed, so as not to let it all out. Eyes, narrow, still slightly teared, beautiful, but seeming as he looked, to have enough water behind to keep flowing over and wash drenched lines down her patterned dress.

"Um." She made the noise, acknowledging.

"I'm sorry."

"I'm sorry." Her mouth split open, and her voice cracked out. She shuddered slightly, the whole of her. Mick pressed his two hands in as he leant over, holding her up by the arms, in her chair.

CHAPTER 35

S un-a had cleared the table and washed the plates. Two pans were soaking. Mik-uh had dried as she had put them on the board. They had said little. Then she had wiped the worktop and put the knives and spoons and forks in their drawer. After that there was nothing else to do, so she had gone to the living room and sat by the radio. Mik-uh was in his chair that he sat in often when he was there.

The news on the radio was troubling her. She leaned closer to the wooden box, though she could hear fine back in her armchair.

"Dinner was very nice, Sun-a. Thank you."

"You're welcome," she said.

"You're a good cook."

She smiled momentarily and then quickly returned her concentration to the posh voice.

"You know, you don't always have to cook English. You could try Korean food sometimes, if you like."

"They don't sell the vegetables."

"No, I suppose not. But do you still cook English food when I'm away?"

"Yes, always."

"Oh."

Mick watched her, leaning out of her chair, one elbow resting on the arm. She wasn't concerned.

For a moment his mind pulled back, and he felt himself there in the room with a wider perspective opening around to either side, and Sun-a the centre, and he felt amazement to see the girl from the plateau in the room before him. How had the two of them gone from there to where they now sat? And then it was gone, and he was unsettled, in his chair with the paper on the arm that he didn't feel much like reading.

He looked up, across to her again.

She was stunning, even as she sat awkwardly, neck craning to the radio on the sideboard. So beautiful. She held everything about that country, in her. Her long black hair. Her eyes that curved, that glided to a point. The softness of her nose. Her neck, now letting go of its strain, as she eased back from the edge of the cushion. Her body. Her face, she looked troubled.

He wanted her so much. It raced, and occupied his whole mind, his whole being, so much of the time. He was never without it. Her.

He thought the same arguments every evening he was home. The same arguments all day long, re-said in his mind, that he thought for all the other days. Why do it to himself? He tried to clear his mind, to be free of it.

In the stillness of the room, the truth lit from above; as always, if he would see. He struggled for calm; against pain.

They would go through the kitchen, down the short hall, quietly to their bedroom. For months - so far away they now seemed - they had slept two arms' reach apart. In their stone hut, with the animals outside. The sounds of the lambs at night; the feeling of safety coaxing him to sleep, from his always-poised nightmare of being discovered.

On the mountainsides.

Yet, they would sleep either side of their double bed, and it was different.

She would be on her back, looking at the ceiling, where the stars would have been.

Or they would sleep on the ground. He had come back late one evening to find her on blankets on the floor by her side of the bed. She said the mattress rolled a little like the sea.

She had pulled back; back to Korea, to Japan, it at times seemed. He thought of the dream of their home, and then the reality of it. What was her life in it when he wasn't there; how far down did the past pull her? Things that had been submerged when survival was all, that now tormented them. On her back, thinking, remembering, little to say, looking through the gaps in the stone and thatch.

Her head was back, against the cushion. She was listening to the quiet voice of the radio. He turned to it - something about Korea, he thought he had heard.

The voice was too quiet, and his concern went back to her. Had it been too long? Panic grabbed around his heart. Please not. Months on the road. Building houses for strangers. They never met anymore.

Were they closer, or further apart?

He again looked across their small living room, to the woman in the chair at the opposite side, turned away.

If she had been going to love him, she would have. He had been doing the right thing, he was sure of it. But perhaps that dream had never been going to become reality. And it was meant that he would live with it.

The hurt ballooned in his chest. A munition detonating, time slowed down.

"I'm tired," Sun-a said.

She rose, turned off the radio, and crossed the diagonal to the door.

"I want to talk to you," he said.

Sun-a stopped, close by him. Mick was frozen for a second in his chair. He had just said it. He did not know what he would say next.

Sun-a waited, looking down at him. Her shoulders were leaning over; her eyes, no bags, but wide from a tiredness.

"What is it?"

Mick wondered if he should stand. Felt he should, that it was needed. He looked up at her. Though she waited, he saw she simply wanted to go. It was tiredness with him, with it all.

His chest was tight, constricting tighter, as he said, "I don't want us to be like this."

The relief at having said the words almost rushed over him, but stopped, bound – only tightness that couldn't bear to breathe, until she had answered.

And Sun-a stood there, and she seemed to almost make a laugh though her cheeks lifted so faintly in upset. And she gave up, and shaking her head left the room.

Mick scrambled out of the chair and after her, into the hall. He reached out and took hold of her trailing hand. The change in force spun her round. She seemed for a second about to whip her free arm up, and perhaps lash out like a cord. Her face was exasperated, suddenly brinking on fury, and anger, and helpless rage, or hopelessness, and he had never seen that on her. Then she screamed a noise, a growling, rising note, becoming a sentence: "How can you say that to me?"

Sun-a exploded, flinging her held arm out, throwing off his already loosened grip.

"Mik-uh, how can you? You brought me here! Always! Always like this!"

Korean, to English, back and forth. And she was crying, dropping to the floor. He moved quickly, and just caught her arms before her legs folded shut beneath her, and he pulled her back up, half in his arms, half rag-doll in front of him. At such close range he looked into her beautiful eyes; he hadn't been so close to her for such a long time – maybe since the last time she had been collapsing before him.

She then seemed to realise that he held her and her arms beat against and pushed from his chest.

"Sun-a please... it's alright. Don't cry. Talk to me. Tell me..."

A sad smile, and she said, "You've forgotten your Korean."

She was right. He barely spoke it anymore; he'd been struggling for the words, getting them wrong.

He moved back respectfully, as she stood, she watching him, curiously, as if she hadn't observed him before. Tears were down her cheeks, by her lips.

He spoke in English only, carefully: "This is not the way I dreamt it would be, Sun-a. Between us. It's not. I don't know..."

"You won't even touch me."

Her face broke and countless tears teetered as she fought to hold them back. Her chest pounded and convulsed with all the sobs inside. Through the hallway become a watery haze she saw Mik-uh's image lurch toward her, arm outreached. She stepped back and put her own palm out to stop him. "No," she muffled.

"Sun-a... Sun-a..."

"No. No, Mick."

He withdrew his arm in shock. She had called him as everyone else did. At that word, his own name, he saw it all slipping away.

Sun-a knew what she'd done, and felt it a horrid slight, some kind of disavowal of their past. Then she heard him say, though she saw only the floor, blurred and dazzling, and did not look up nor wipe her eyes:

"I didn't want you to feel like you had to. Not at all. Never like you had before."

She looked up to see him through the watery mists, which wavered the outline of the man and the room around him. Even in that mist she could tell he stood distraught.

"Why marry me?" she asked resolutely.

He had to tell her everything he had so long wanted to tell her; he could not get it wrong. He should have known – had it planned. There had been two years to plan an answer. Yet he had nothing.

"I watched you walking away from me, toward Busan and its streets and all of Korea above it. I couldn't let it happen. I..."

He saw her looking at him, still then, with an unemotional clarity, despite her tear streaked face and reddened eyes. She said with the tears held back from her voice:

"You thought I would go back to that life."

"No..." And then he spoke truthfully, "You had nowhere to go."

It hit her fiercely, like a point, a blade, and stopped her breathless. The worst fear. She swallowed down a breath and said:

"Do you still think I am, a whore?"

"No." He answered firmly. "No, Sun-a, I'm sorry. No. I know you would never have gone back, to that."

They faced each other, a mist of tears between them in the space in the hallway.

"And you are no whore, Sun-a. You never were."

And still they faced each other, arms by their sides, watching the other as they caught breath and their chests rose and fell.

"Mik-uh." She said his name, and nothing else followed.

CHAPTER THIRTY-FIVE

"Sun-a, I loved you."

An intake of breath, as at hearing something impossible.

"I married you because I loved you. Because I couldn't bear to leave you there; to watch you walk across that dock."

"Which one?"

"Which one?" he asked back.

"Yes," she entreated him, "Which one?"

She watched him flounder there where he stood, seeing exactly what she so dearly hoped not to.

"How can they be any different?" he said.

She was still. She looked at him, weighing it as he spoke:

"I couldn't let you go back to that life you had lived. But you must know this... If you had been walking across that dock to live in a country house for the rest of your days, I would still have called to you. I was always going to ask you to be my wife. I love you, Sun-a."

Mick lowered his head; it seemed a bow; asking with his eyes if he could take a step toward her.

"I'm sorry," he said. "So sorry."

When he looked up her teeth were on her lip, biting softly, and tears were streaming down her face, her neck, dampening the collar of her dress.

Then she crossed to him, and lifted her arms to put about his neck, and he stepped toward her and lifted her close, off the ground and spinning. Then feet to ground, and his hands went gently to her face. He nodded softly to ask her, and she nodded her reply. He kissed her lightly on the lips, and her hands up about his neck, holding on, she kissed him back.

***

Before the doorway of their bedroom, with hands held, they quietly faced and stood. She gazed up at him, tear steaked, hair strands damp. A seriousness swept her expression; she blinked, looked away, then back to his eyes.

"Mik-uh, did you do this with many girls?"

He shook his head. "You're the first."

She looked at him, eyes wide, searching.

"This is the first time?" she asked.

"Yes," he said.

Sun-a smiled the gentlest, most beautiful smile he had ever seen. Mick hesitated, reluctant to take it away, then slowly began to bring his lips to hers; but Sun-a lifted her neck, reached and kissed him.

Their kiss parted and they looked at each other, so close.

***

The past months had been the best of her life. It seemed a tragedy that years had been wasted, alone, and yet perhaps so very necessary. Perhaps it had been the only way.

She was so deeply grateful, as she had told Mik-uh; to be waited for.

They were in love and now knew it of the other, and it was wonderful. Sun-a felt the smile that was always on her face as something so different, for it had never been carried there before. She sometimes wanted to look down her cheeks to see it there, what it was like.

The impossible could happen; she saw that there might be escape from that cicada life. And when she sat and listened in the bright light in the church, there were moments when she knew and her heart began to understand and lift all the more.

And yet, she also carried a nagging thing, a gnawing that was obscured and disappeared, then gradually rising up and up to the surface of her world.

On a Wednesday she stood with Mik-uh's mother in the line at the butchers, as they usually did. Pam had spoken about how well she looked and colours in her cheeks. She had smiled and thanked her, and known it must be true; she could feel the colours there herself.

A young woman walked into the shop, ringing the little bell above the door, and Sun-a glanced to see, as she always did each time. The woman had two children with her – a small hand held in each of her own. She moved them to the back of the line and whispered to them to stop and stand still. One was a little girl, up to the side of the woman's hip, with brown-blonde hair, thick and curvy, which pushed at the hair slides that tried to hold it in place. The other was a boy, swinging against her hand, resisting his mother's control, swivelling on one heel, but managing to stop himself from breaking free into a run. Sun-a didn't know how old they were; she couldn't guess children's ages well. And then it hit her, deep, deep into her belly: the ache from a mountain clearing a long distance away.

The pain seized her, made her gasp – mute in the shop full of waiting customers. Pam's head didn't cast aside, still looking ahead, waiting their turn. It was her soul, an agony. She saw herself cruel, terrible. How could she? So completely and heartbreakingly selfish. What had she been doing – thinking? Biding her time, to destroy.

Pam took half steps, shuffled slowly forward. Sun-a saw and did likewise, moments after. Her happiness gone.

***

Mick arrived home that day in the mid-afternoon. He had been to the Rail Works in shirt and tie to a meeting he had arranged with Mr Calvin. Sitting in his small, factory office he had apologized for leaving him and the works in the lurch. He wanted nothing more than to get back to work on the tracks. It was what he was good at; what he knew. Mr Calvin was only too glad to have him; they needed men like him back after the war. They had shaken hands and Mick had headed quickly home, running and skipping some of the way.

The house was empty, and there was a piece of paper on their clean kitchen table. Sun-a's writing. He was seized with a horrible premonition when he saw it. He nervously crossed to the table, picked it up, then began to read: her poor letters, the words full of spelling mistakes, but still tying their meanings in his mind.

She addressed him as Mick. She told him that she was sorry. She told him that she loved him, and that he was good. She wrote, 'I cannot give you children,' and he stopped then and held the paper lower and looked straight ahead at the kitchen wall and cupboards.

'I am so sorry,' she said.

'I should not have said yes in Busan.'

'I am bad.'

'Some war in Korea. I will go near to my family. Don't come after me. I am sorry. I have the money you gave me.'

'Pray me,' she had written, and he wondered if she had meant 'pray,' or 'forgive.'

She had written 'Sun-a.'

She had gone.

PART 4

CHAPTER 36

Mick stood on the dock at Southampton and looked out to sea. He ran a hand through his hair, exasperated, without answers, in an ever-present panic that had been part of him for two days. It shouldn't have been hard to trace Sun-a through England, but he had reached the coast and hadn't found her.

The Station Manager at Derby had easily remembered her, on the platform. She would have taken the one forty-five to St Pancras, while he – not five hundred yards from her, further back along the tracks – had sat in a chair in the secretary's office, waiting to meet Mr Calvin. From there she could have changed for another line, or stayed in the capital, alone. London first; then Portsmouth; or Dover, or Falmouth, or a dozen more? Portsmouth, the one route she had taken before: he had spent the late evening rushing from hotel to hotel in the town, enquiring about his wife. He had spent the rest of the night frantically fighting cabs and cars to make his way across the coast. By then it had been a wild terror – not knowing in certainty if she was hidden in Portsmouth – but having to leave and chance he had chosen the wrong port.

No ships sailed to Korea; she would have to make her way ship by ship; but which destination first: Spain, the Mediterranean and Italy, Egypt, through the Suez, India, Hong Kong?

The woman in St Pancras ticket office had remembered 'a Chinese girl,' hurrying. To the platforms, with one bag, a dark green coat – but Mick had seen the way she had looked at the fire in his eyes and the fright it had brought in her own. The poor woman had grown desperate, to offer assurances with the doubts in her own voice: 'probably; most likely; must have been.' So he stood at Southampton, feeling the sun go down behind the clouds of the English Channel. Feeling the panic screaming inside him, knowing it was dying, defeated.

***

In the snake of steaming air and drifts of smoke which wound about the rigs and sets and chains, Mick smashed the hammer into the rivets.

Sun-a, a prostitute; she had been a prostitute. She was not! Perhaps it was for the best. She was his wife. How could it be? She was the woman he loved and would always love. He swung the hammer over his shoulder, and crashed it against the still red, glowing metal. Around the edges it burned almost see-through. Arghhh! Again, he beat the rivet through into the sleeper. Sun-a was his wife!

Sparks roared and fizzed nearby; pouring molten metal. A great noise amongst the din, and Mick roared out frustration, a warrior's cry. He shouted the scream past the furnaces. A head turned down the line, perhaps thinking it had heard something – then went back to its work. Mick bent over, hands on either side of the supports by the burning steel. He drew in breath, gathered his rage back in. Clouds of steam-smoke blurred and

400

passed through the air in front of his eyes. She was his wife.

He had stormed gun turrets; fought tanks and jeeps from jungle and foot, and won; trekked across a continent; and Sun-a was lost, and he couldn't find her. Truly lost. What could he do? Search every route, every road, every town along the way to Korea? What was he supposed to have done? Should he have been in Korea, waiting by her home town for this past year? What should he have done?

***

5th *April 1950*

Mick sat in his parents' living room. They had eaten tea off plates on their laps, listening to the wireless. Sun-a's space on the settee was empty.

Could he have sailed that day? After her? Somehow found her? He'd thought it ten-thousand times. He had barely had enough money to give workers doing a favour to a fellow railway man, to see him standing on the postal service back north. Sun-a had travelled with the little money he'd been able to send home. Could she have got to Korea? For him it would have been a challenge. For her? How many countries would she have needed to dock at, to travel through? Was it possible she had made it that far? Or was she dead in an Asian ditch that he would never find? Where was she? Ten-thousand times. Sitting at her parent's home, reconciled, him forgotten, living the life of a Korean woman?

As it had done for months past, the voice on the radio talked of China and the Soviet Union, and Korea. It was like a personal message, each day for him, and the way his parents looked quickly at him, then avoided his gaze, they knew it too.

Then he felt it crack, finished, suddenly about to end – the air itself, the way that reality hung about them.

"What are you doing, Michael?" It was disappointed, exasperated.

He looked to his mam.

"How many of the enemy did you kill?"

In the past years she had never asked him anything else about the war, certainly not about combat.

"I killed a lot."

His mam nodded, seeming to take it in and weigh it for a future need.

His dad was looking at the two of them, his paper dropping, creasing over at halfway and folding as it lost torsion.

His mam went on. "And then you met Dawn. And she's a lovely girl, Michael. You... You're lucky to have her."

He kept looking at his mam, a little stunned.

"I know."

"Son," said his dad, and Mick turned to him, hearing the difference in his voice from anything he had previously said.

The paper was dropped over the side of the chair; his dad's eyes never left him.

"I don't know too much about Christianity, son – a lot of it goes over my head frankly. But one thing I've learnt." His dad looked at him seriously, firm in the eyes, unwavering. "If you really love someone, distance doesn't stop you." Their stare like never before. "You go from Heaven to the grave and back again, if that's what it takes."

The room was still.

His mam spoke then, with a tip of the head to his father: "I'd expect your dad to come and find me. War or not."

His father met her gaze, assuredly and nodded once. Then his mam looked away, satisfied, having got the due answer.

"Whatever's happened, you know she's waiting for you," she finished, and reached for her knitting.

"I know."

***

Mick opened the back door and went out onto the yard. He lifted the lid from the dustbin, considered the letter in his hand: brittle, hard paper, fired orange from jungle soil in places, dampened by rains, her blue ink more often a blur. He dropped it into the bin. That letter had travelled with him for a whole war; it had been upstairs in a bedroom drawer for the past few years.

He placed the metal lid back down, then thought once more if it was at all disrespectful. But no, Miranda was long gone and so were the words on the paper.

Two gardens along the row, Mrs Grogan was beginning to peg out her washing on the line. Mick held up a hand in greeting over the fences, and then left the yard.

Less than an hour later he stood with his bag at his feet in the tall hallway. His mam was tearful, dabbing her eyes with her handkerchief, and shaking her head from time to time. Mick knew he may well never see them again.

"You be careful."

"I will, Mam."

"And you listen here. You kill as many of those bad men as you have to."

"Yes, Mam."

Mick gave her a big hug, squeezing tight.

"Well done, lad."

"Thanks, Dad."

His father held out his hand and Mick shook it firmly. They were two men. Still holding the grip, Mick gave his dad half a hug with the other shoulder.

"We're proud of you, Mick. Very proud."

He picked up his heavy bag and slung it over his shoulder.

"Goodbye."

And he left the front door and the step. 'Goodbye' they called from the doorway as he headed onto the street. He looked back with a last wave, then faced forward and walked on, heading for the train station, and the coast.

***

The sun was low over Kamakura Hideyoshi's shoulder, falling. It cast a half light, which picked out the dust and poverty hanging above the ground. Everything seemed Korean soil-yellow, a too bright hepatitis tinge. He watched from the cover of a small rise of ground, obscured by shrubs and low bushes. She was down there.

Japan was over. As the Japanese nation had crumpled, so its men had become nothing. Incinerated; the strength burnt out of their veins. Too many of them had been nothing in the first place. In their uniforms, at their posts, across their lands, their honour had smoked into the clouded sky. Not he.

For weeks he had been watching, being sure as to be stationed there. When the general had told him to reposition his troop he had disagreed, and he had stayed where he was. When the units had been replaced he had disappeared, then re-emerged weeks later, taking a command. The hierarchy stepped aside at his will.

After the destruction of Japan he had walked north, a dust covered man, coated head to foot in grey. Just his sword and he, trudging through valleys. All his memories of that time seemed grey, duller than the blacks and whites of motion pictures. He had wandered and stolen what little he ate. Locals had peered at him and whispered and seen his samurai sword; he had walked on, past them. At town after town, vengeful, weak men had followed him on the country tracks to confront him and notch one enemy kill. Some of them he had cut apart. He had walked on.

Wandering north. It had felt the length of a country – further – that China would never appear on the distant horizon – could never appear. A nightmare of endless, expanding Korea in which he was trapped. A wandering ghost; a vanished, soulless man.

And then for no reason he had stopped. He remembered looking up and around, awake, and then suddenly raw and alive with hatred, and a destiny to cut down and break, utterly snap in his hands those who had done the savage dishonour to him. He would break them all. He would make them weep, dropped on their knees, heads and shoulders tilting, about to topple, souls wracked with the breaking and utter victory which he would stand tall on the field of battle and be. He was that supreme victory; he had always been, and always would be that victory, that last warrior on a battlefield.

So he had become the man that would take him there. Horang-ee, the villagers had called him – 'Tiger.' At first, for weeks, they had been wary, suspicious – but he had been resolute, unflinching as the man they thought him, and convinced them. He had found the sword on a dead Japanese. He spoke fluent Korean, never dropping his guard, and if there should be a frown, narrowed eyes at a whisper of dialect, he had overwhelmed it. He had played a lost and desolate man from the south, whose family had been brutally slain by the occupiers. Freed from prison by the Americans he had travelled north, searching for a home. He was a doctor - a highly skilled doctor, cruelly deprived of his living. A man had been dying, lying filthy in his straw, stricken on his side and moaning. 'Come and look at him' they had said. He had stepped inside the hovel, performed his exhibition, methodically diagnosing what he knew outright - the death within the cattle-thin stomach. He had called for kitchen knives, which he had submerged in a large bowl of boiled brown water; he had ground down poppy seed-pods from local produce and fed them to the patient. Then he had operated, to their horror and amazement - their wild, pathetic, stupid eyes, unable to decide whether to beat him with their brooms. He had cut out the festering tumour.

With dirty boiled thread he had stitched the man, and two days letter the gift had walked onto his baked-ground terrace amongst his scrabbling dogs, healed. The man had lived the extra year necessary for his reputation.

They had given him an empty house in the village, and pleaded with him to live amongst them. He had obliged, biding his time, taking a young wife, the daughter of a grateful local for his pleasure. And he had waited there.

The tide had been slowly turning, slowly moving about its axis like the moon on a heavy arc around the black sky. Rotating and rotating until the waters drove south. It had been in the air: one could stand in the open air at that time and feel it - the great turning about the horizon, like the pivot of a typhoon-sized machine above them all, slowly turning against the weight of its vast anchor. A vast and unreasoning anger, building. He had been watching, eagerly, for the torrent to unleash, driving south.

As he had travelled from town to town, attending his patients, he put himself where he would become known, indispensable. The doctor from the South. He attended meetings; he ordered meetings; he bellowed for war, for justice, for the lie.

One of the soldiers under his command approached. Kamakura heard the salute; he didn't turn from the view of the village.

"No more enemy movements, Comrade. They stay at their line."

"Yes. Thank you, Comrade. Dismissed." He turned briefly to nod the man away - a small North Korean, in the same green uniform and cap that he himself wore.

With their gross flaws, their grovelling, scrabbling nature, he knew them all as the same at their core. All men were about honour.

Their shouts and demands and vilifications claimed to be about giving honour to all men, but they were not. Their ideology; their calls for a new world - that he often led when they flagged - was the dishonoured, in greed, hacking at the legs of the honoured. Land owners and merchants had fallen around his own village. Yet they always needed a doctor - more so in war. He would have out-manoeuvred and out-thought them and altered tactics, if it had been needed, but they had worshipped his ability to cut men open and sever limbs. Easily he had ruled.

The glory of the nation, the people who would rise up, united as one - of course it was a façade, for every poor man knew that there were some more glorious than others. Those were the men they followed; bowed before; who told them where to march, where to put their stupid feet, the idealism to follow.

The glory of the nation! Simply the glory of a man who stood above them all, whose unsurpassable honour shone over them all.

Time was needed. Patience. To regain the one cut of honour that had been taken from him, and to magnify it tenfold.

And so he watched yet again through the yellow haze, the very girl whom he had tracked across that land, walk from her village hut about her day's chores.

CHAPTER 37

The summer sun was baking down on Hong Kong. He was exhausted and soaked in sweat, his memory feeling the heat and calling up sudden impressions of Burmese jungle, ferns and creepers and trees rising up like walls on all sides, or of one Korean summer, mountain slopes, steep low forests, the stifling, unrelenting midday heat. Yet he would look up and see all the signs of Britain: familiar cars, shop signs and buildings, then see their odd setting of palm trees and tropical backdrop. There was at least a breeze off the harbour, picking up now and then, lifting seagulls in their spiralling circles. He stood still, weighed back by his heavy bag, and took a precious moment to plan the right attack.

A few hundred metres to his left sat the two huge ships of the British navy. Behind them a train moving the last few feet to its standstill, heaving clouds of steam into the already sweltering air. At a shrill whistle, which carried across the dock, soldiers began to detrain: the first few stepped from their carriages simultaneously, then more, then long lines spilled out. All wore berets, carried heavy packs, with helmets strapped on the back of those, and walked with their guns in hand. Mick hurried into motion, sweat instantly springing from his skin and replenishing the slowed streams. He had arrived in Hong Kong only just in time.

The British paving of the seafront glared sharply white as he strode across it. He had to get on one of those boats. Sun-a was out there, not far from him now. It had been only a small achievement to make it this far; if he didn't succeed in this final leg he would be desperately bartering with a fishing boat to take him to a warzone.

The ships loomed large, one cruiser and an aircraft carrier further on. Men were already taking their places on the various decks, getting the best spots along the railings. The ships would be sailing by noon.

He needed to speak to the right officer and plead his case, but he was a war veteran out of war. Or – as he studied the oncoming gangways, the last few loading cranes – he needed to smuggle himself onboard, unnoticed, stay hidden and reveal himself when it was too late and too costly to get him off the ship – all the way to Korea.

"Quiet Man?"

He knew the voice, and when he turned around there was a man he had last seen in the dust of a parade ground.

"Alistair MacCallum," he said.

The man was fatter in the face, and the neck – of course less gaunt, years since starving. His eyes were without the deep black bags and the sunken cheeks beneath, but the face was still recognisable. The man who had held their hut together.

In his strong Scottish accent, MacCallum said, "Quiet man, it is you as well. It's good to see you. Alive, and all."

"And you."

They shook hands firmly, grinning. Mick marvelled, to see the past, a man, revived: victorious. His friend's expression seemed to suggest he saw the same.

"You off for another war? I didn't know any Forrester's were here."

"I'm not in the army anymore."

MacCallum considered the large bag over his shoulder and turned his eyes on him with suspicion. "No?" his highland accent drew out.

"I need to get on one of those ships."

Mick watched the man's eyebrows raise.

"Right."

"My wife is in Korea."

MacCallum seemed to be considering things. "Right. And you're going to go over there and find her and bring her back?"

Mick shrugged and nodded at the same time.

"What's she doing there?"

"It's her home."

"What's your name again, Quiet Man?"

"Michael. Bowler."

"Think I heard it before. How did you get here?"

"From Singapore - just arrived."

"And you think you're going to be let on one of these, just like that?"

"I'm getting there one way or another."

"Not if you're detained in a brig you're not."

"Please. MacCallum. Help me. Just help me."

The man he had known sighed and viewed him like the last thing he needed.

"Listen Quiet Man, it's good to see you, truly it is. We talked about you back at the prison - wondered what had happened to you: executed, building some railway somewhere. You know, Collin the English fellow, he didn't make it."

"I remember him. I'm sorry to hear it."

"Neither did Breck; the Indian, Jihar, might have done. I don't know. They pulled me out of there when the war ended, not many of us left, not many at all."

The sun still blazed above them, but its heat didn't have the same affect. Both men gave slow, sombre nods.

"You're a good man, I remember that much, though you didn't say a lot. If I could help I would, you understand."

"I know."

Mick looked hard at the bright pattern lit on MacCallum's army uniform shoulder. He had always respected the man; and he could not afford to let it rest.

"Captain MacCallum, I need your help. My wife needs it." He nodded to the insignia.

"Took a while to get back on my feet, but I stayed with the Argyll and Sutherland." He rubbed his army-cut head, then shook it. "It would be a powder keg to let a grieving man go to war. And you're a civi now aren't you – I can't just let you go walking around Korea."

"I've walked it before, and I speak Korean."

Captain MacCallum looked stunned. He waited.

"That's where I went – where they took me. Incheon prison camp; only they never got me there. I escaped during transport. That's where I met my wife, on the run."

Alistair MacCallum was frowning, squinting at him, mouth open.

"Are you having me on?"

"No, Sir!"

"If I put you in front of one of our interpreter lads, you won't fall flat on your face."

"No, Sir. Be good to have a chat." Mick stood back straight, army posture. "I can help; I can be of assistance to the war effort, Sir."

Soldiers filed around them, a few glancing at what was going on.

Captain MacCallum took a moment. "Go on."

"I walked across Korea, Sir. From Incheon to Busan. I know the terrain and what we'll be up against. I have experience with the locals and culture – although to be fair we were on the run and in hiding most of the time."

"You out-ran Japanese search squads?"

"Yes, Sir."

"What rank were you?"

"Sergeant."

"What's your experience, Sergeant?"

"Campaigns in Norway, Burma, Sir."

MacCallum looked serious, then nodding. "Aye, I recall something like that."

Mick knew it was his chance. He stood straighter still, looked straight ahead, not in his superior's eye.

"What can you do?"

"I have expertise in explosives, jungle warfare, tracking, survival skills, warfare tactics, hand-to-hand combat. I was in the Chindits, fighting behind enemy lines, Sir."

Mick glanced at his old roommate. The man was staring him fiercely in the eye, sizing him up as he spoke.

He went on. "I believe I can be invaluable to the campaign in Korea, Sir. I request to be enlisted immediately, Sir."

He held his breath at his last sentence.

There was a pause where they stood on the dock front, the battalion fanning around them. "At ease, soldier," said the captain.

Mick relaxed his shoulders only slightly, still facing a superior and best hope to find Sun-a, rather than an old friend.

"Quiet Man, you understand what you're asking? Desertion is desertion. You see your wife across the way, you don't go running off and leave us in a firefight. If all goes well and by some chance you find her, you have a quiet word in my ear and if we're at a lull, I might give you leave. Then if we need you, you come back to your regiment and fight to the bitter end if needs be. Understood?"

"Yes, Sir."

A hand clapped him on the arm, the pat of an old friend.

"We all lived tedious, hellish years in that hut. And you tell me about the Chindits now? We could have had some interesting conversations."

"I had a lot on my mind at that time, Sir."

MacCallum nodded. "It's a good job you left the army, or I think it might have been me saluting you."

Mick grinned. "I really appreciate this. I can't tell you how-"

"I know the lengths I'd go to if my Sue was in trouble. I understand. Yes, Bowler, I'll find a way to help you out."

They shook hands again. Then Mick stepped back and saluted, soldier once more.

***

29th *August 1950*

The stretching ocean and the towering sky filled the view, yet the two did not meet, for the line of Korea ran thin across the horizon, holding them apart with immeasurable strength. He looked over the Scottish army berets of his fellow soldiers at the land which seemed still, to be waiting for them. They would be there in less than an hour.

Mick felt aware of the green army uniform he wore, the gun strapped over his shoulder, the ammunition at his belt, the heavy pack resting by his feet with his steel helmet fastened to it. He looked to his boots planted on the solid deck of the H.M.S. Ceylon, feeling it rise and fall, like some small mountain set to sea. Aside of their cruiser was the silver bulk of the Unicorn, light aircraft carrier, not seeming to bounce at all, just ploughing on, a juggernaut, churning great waves from its hull.

The men of the battalion stood and waited, all watching the Korean line. The huge engine hummed its low growl like a mighty animal baring its teeth, ready to pounce. Water roared and crashed down around them.

Sun-a was out there, he was sure of it. She had to be. He would search for years if he had to - comb every inch of that land. He thought of what had happened there in years past: meeting her; the image of the girl in the clearing. He felt his mood darken as if the sky had just turned - though it still glared above. The thoughts of her before he had known her: what had been done to her; how many men had she lain with? Them touching her; over her. Had she enjoyed it? She must have, sometimes. The same dam pain: as if an old, rusted Japanese bullet from a decade before had flung out over the waves and struck him, drawing blood. It was a burden he had often refused to acknowledge, a burden he knew would always be carried. How he hated those who had done that to her.

Yet, if the pain came, love would carry it. Sun-a was his wife. She had always been his wife. There had been no chance or luck in finding her at that moment on that mountain side. She had been his wife then, and he would gladly go to the ends of the earth to find her.

Mick felt the strength in his chest soar. He stood proud, facing forward, rifle resting in his hands.

Ahead lay Korea. The coast was becoming more distinct, less of a haze. Shapes, rises and falls of terrain could be seen. He felt then that he was returning home, perhaps even more so than he had when disembarking back in England after the war. This was his land. He knew it better than anywhere, the way it went under your feet, the direction it took.

He felt a sorrow for it then, for all it had endured and still would. Above that brave line at sea stretched the vastness of China, and above that the hulk of Russia still, their weight of men pressing down. Korea was a stepping stone, between the continent and Japan; a stepping stone between China and the ocean and island chains beneath; a land for battles to be staged upon.

And Sun-a was there, in the midst of it. She had to be.

CHAPTER 38

Korean hills ran in front of their position, over the river valley. Mick breathed slowly, observing one slope, then the falling next, then another rising, low peak after low peak. Birds were scarce, even in the countryside, so different to England; the calls were of cicadas, blaring when in a tree passed by, then distant warning sirens. The air was humid, still, and he heard his own breaths and the rustle of uniform, the grind of a boot on dirt, or the chink of a moving strap and gun. No sign of the enemy, though the North Korean line was a short distance away.

He was west of Daegu. Sun-a's village was far on the opposite side, east of the city, right at the coast.

27th Brigade – the Argyll and Sutherland, the Middlesex and a few others – had been given a stretch of the perimeter on the left side. Their brigade was the contribution of a tired Britain, with the job of representing everything the army had long fought for. They all felt that, he suspected, as they looked out at the quiet hills. Only he also had his mind elsewhere.

The Busan Perimeter was what it was called – the two sides of a box, left and top, which protected the city of Busan in the bottom corner of Korea.

The North Koreans had flooded down, surprising and overwhelming the South. American reinforcements had been in short supply, struggling to hold positions, falling back in a terrifying rush. But they had held at the last moment they could not afford to lose, around Busan.

The towering ship, slowly turning in the harbour, casting its shadow over the dock front; he had remembered the city well. The merchant sailor's office in which they had had their ceremony; the narrow streets and low buildings taking the shape of rising hills. Korea beyond. U.S. and Allied troops had been arriving at the port for weeks, bolstering the line. The fight back had begun.

Mick walked south along the road with the rest of his company, a track that moved closer to the river and the perimeter in the mile ahead. They would not patrol it much further.

A whistle sounded off to his right. He began to glance over and heard the distinct shriek of metal through the air. The disarming soft thud of a clod of soil leaping up. He saw it twenty feet away, in the air, grass tufted, splitting apart slightly, then falling back to earth, raining a cloud of soil. He was already hunching, shaping his form away from the threat – his instincts immediately war-ready after years away.

As more rounds fizzed at them, the lieutenant's voice shouted, "Down, down, get down!"

They were spinning off, for mounds and trees and drops away from the road, all while dirt leapt and the air made howls of impossibly fast metal.

The shots were flying wide, one thirty feet away, the next thirty-five, then forty, only split seconds apart: it meant a gunner at distance. They were being strafed. Somewhere in the mountains, across the river. Then the sounds stopped and the quiet resumed. Mick concentrated. After the sudden attack everything seemed surreal, as if it couldn't have just happened. There was only the sound of the slow summer river in the near distance, and the far screeches of cicadas which never stopped.

"Anyone hurt?" came the shout.

No one answered. Then they were all in one piece.

"Fall back. Get away from the road. Keep in cover."

Mick crawled back, eyes on the distant hills, seeing no glint of give-away reflection, no movement. Only the green of the trees and sandy spaces of unoccupied scrub. All so familiar.

Bullets pulled up dirt not ten feet away. He stopped, eyes fixed on the bare soil. Backwards he pushed himself, like a crab struggling to reverse. Patters, impacts, scattering debris, swung across the path. A bullet pumped into the soil close by with a distinct shriek and the sound of air into a bicycle tire. He scrambled up, over vegetation, reaching strides, sliding down; pressing his back along shallow cover. His heart was hammering and he felt scared in a way he didn't remember from the last war.

He didn't want to die; he couldn't get hit – to bleed out on that slope of dirt, so close to Sun-a, and she never know he came.

***

The patrol dismounted from the vehicles and moved to the dingy ready to lift it. He saw Captain Penman look out at the river.

"Hold on lads." The captain considered the water, swirling visibly, small eddies between fast moving streams. "The boat isn't going to be any good. We're going to have to wade it."

Penman walked over to them and patted his batman on the shoulder. "Can you swim, Mitchell?"

"Yes, Sir,"

"Bowler, you up for it?"

"Yes, Sir."

They moved to the bank, the rest of the patrol spreading out watchfully around the vehicles, looking across to the mountains on the far side. Heat baked down, even early in the morning and cicadas chirped endlessly from every tree.

"Have you been at this stretch of the river before?" asked Captain Penman.

"On the other bank. I took a boat down river and crossed in the night."

"Evading the Japanese," said Mitchell.

Mick nodded. "I was taking someone home."

"Aye, and we all hope you find her."

Penman and Mitchell smiled. He hadn't spoken much of how he had come to join the regiment. It seemed they knew.

The Argyll and Sutherland lads had welcomed him with no fuss. His first bout of Korean quick-fire talk had left him stunned and doing his best to hide it, but it had earned some respect. Of course they always let him know he was still a southerner.

"We should have a mile until we're in range." Penman slowly moved his binoculars across the terrain. Mick took in the vista before them, identifying strategic points and checking with his own glasses. It seemed unoccupied hillside so far.

The captain unfolded his map, contours of green and added details and notes in pencil. "See this clump of trees; four hundred yards beyond the last spur? We'll meet there. Move slow and keep low. This is reconnaissance, ready for the push out. Get an angle on their position, and get back."

"Sir."

"Cap."

Penman turned to the rest of the patrol. Mick stood on the bank, looking out at the Naktong River, the plain and the mountains on the far side. He wondered if he and Sun-a had passed by there years before in darkness, keeping low in the bottom of the small boat, heading south.

They splashed down into the water with more speed than they would have planned. Icy cold water sank their legs, freezing after the boiling heat of the day. Mick trudged through it, feeling it drag at him - feeling ever a target for an awake and watchful gunner. They didn't speak, just exchanged looks; he saw the cold and the tension on the two men's faces that he felt in the grimace of his own.

The summer - he had heard widely said - was too dry. He thought of sheltering under the canopy from the rains, he and Sun-a backs against trees. Then at halfway they dropped into the deep river channel. Heavy booted feet weighed down instantly; he pushed off the river bed, feeling silt slip and squirm out underfoot - his titled head gasping just above the surface. He jumped in awkward weighted bounds, spitting water, then doggy paddling as the ground disappeared beneath him, his boots kicking, bricks in the fast current. Water lapped around his throat, over his closed mouth and under his nose as he struggled through the river.

A whispered shout sounded from the right, downstream, barely audible above the crash of the water and the cicadas loud on either bank. He saw Penman, twenty feet away, and Mitchell further still, fighting against the rushing surface - suddenly caught, his heavy weapon become an anchor dropping into the water, its strap tight around his neck. He was going down.

Penman swam quick strokes, flung by the current, tried to brake with spread arms, and grabbed hold of Mitchell's uniform. For a moment both men dropped - most of their heads plunging below the water line - and then they reemerged, Mitchell blustering water, heaving the heavy weapon with one hand and front crawling with the other. Penman swam with his free arm, and they stayed afloat.

The river took them all down stream, alarmingly quickly. Mick swam hard, fast strokes, only cutting a steep diagonal across the wide river. And then the currents were behind him, a weaker hold around his torso and legs, and at a stretch his feet touched down. The opposite bank rapidly approached.

Dripping water, breath heaving, the three of them stepped onto the flood plain on the other side. Mick moved at a continuous crouch through the tall growth on the river bank. The mountains loomed, the details, rocks, rubble, trees, dotted bushes, small ravines from run-off and arching spurs picked out with sudden and disconcerting clarity. The background, become tangible, real and imminent.

They dropped to their knees in the small copse – much smaller now they were in it – across from where they had been attacked on their previous patrol: just a few trees and low, crisp, dry bushes. It provided a shelter from the massive, low mountains, which rose imposing, without warning from the flat plain.

"Now we wait."

Flat on the ground, still, behind cover and in shade, Mick studied the facing mountain sides with his binoculars. The two men beside him did likewise. They waited. Watching, resisting frustration. Waiting, just as the machine gunner was watching, somewhere up there.

"Eleven o'clock," Penman said at a whisper. "Where the ridge falls down – another fifteen feet below."

He saw it, high up, toward the edge of a barren dirt-yellow, dead grass stretch of slope: where it seemed too open to hide, the snout of a black machine gun and a short stack of concrete blocks. In the shadow of a slight overhang there was no face visible. Sparse branches crossed from the left side, over the wall. In the odd summer darkness, perhaps the shape of a helmet, a blacked out green.

"We'll need this for when the advance begins," whispered Penman. He pulled the crinkled map from waterproof jacket and noted the position with a small pencil.

The machine gun remained looking away as they crouched and watched the hillside. After scouring the slopes for any other hint of movement, reflection on a lens, colour or shape that didn't belong, they backed out of the copse, turned, and keeping low, headed slowly back along the river bank.

Crouching through grasses, pushing through reeds, the back of his head to the enemy gun on the mountainside. A waiting tightness held behind the breastbone, the whole crouched half mile, the crawl back into the river, the low stalk up the bank to the cover of the jeep and the watching troop.

CHAPTER 39

23ʳᵈ September 1950

Mick stood with his section and others nearby, looking out at the hill in front. Numbered 282, it rose up right before them, a low ridge on the left leading to a long flattened arch of a hilltop. It stood out against the volcanic-like background of layering peaks which he was used to. He sat back down on the bank of the dirt road and carried on waiting and watching.

Up at the top of the hill the tiny figures of Argylls could be seen and the constant crack of rifle fire rang out and echoed around the terrain. At adjacent and further hills, North Korean soldiers moved like ants. Flashes lit up around them, mortars and machine guns, always out of time with the rolling cracks like thunder. Mick watched on the edge of war, disconnected, yet seeing it all around.

Red and gold, glinted and flashed in the sunlight as the men on Hill 282 held up their cards yet again. Mick looked to the adjacent hill and as they had seen all morning, saw the white recognition panels that the North

Koreans had, lifting and blinding signals at the passing planes. The bombers roar approached from behind and he looked up over the trench wall to see if they'd drop this time.

Rows of hills, falling back. And he was facing the wrong way – Sun-a's village was to the east. Always he thought of her. Was she there? Had she been able to reconcile with her family after all? Yet he saw her, five years before, crying, running after him, turned away, on a path not far from there, near a crossroads and a checkpoint. If not there, where? She had to be nearby.

The roar grew. The sound of propellers and engines, and soon the rush of wind behind them.

Over those hills, soldiers spread across the country; higher still, more soldiers, in other uniforms, massing, and waiting, and funnelling supplies. They had beaten the Japanese, sent them back; they'd beaten the Germans and sent them back; and now the Russians had stepped up from their place in the line to have their turn to try and rule and oppress.

The shadows swept over them, and Mick looked up, as did every other waiting soldier. Three American bombers flew in the centre of the scene; ahead of them on the hills flashed the yellow bursts of identification panels, and the aggravating white of the desperate Koreans.

The planes headed for hill 282. Mick looked on, his stomach beginning to rise, seeing the planes not turning, dead ahead. Others around him were standing, sensing it too. But the planes kept going straight, roaring on, the sound past the trenches now, the Korean soldiers on the opposite hill still dazzling their signs at the bright sky.

'No," he said quietly.

"What are they doing?" someone asked further down the trench.

"The bastards haven't tricked them...?"

"Ahh..." Someone made a noise.

He watched as parcels tumbled from the bellies of the planes and began to fall, spinning and toppling through the air.

"No."

"Fuck no!"

"Run! Run!" Private Shearer shouted.

The bombs hit. Every man was on his feet to see it, staring, gawping in disbelief.

The top of the Argylls' hill erupted in sudden, shocking flame. Like a crown the devil might wear, it reared up, great warping tongues of orange, burning red and yellow, stomach churning-bright to look at. All around the flat hilltop it sat, napalm roaring its noise across the scene. It was a scream made into fire, wrenching, howling. And then a change in the wind, or just his eyes' perception: it was a vile set of teeth biting down, incising, impaling into the hillside and refusing to let go. An awful sight.

"Dear God."

Men were running toward the hill, waving their arms at the aircraft which were circling around. Though no one could see the bullets the sound washed back over the terrain, as they strafed the wrong hill.

Finally the planes roared away from the site of battle and the horrible mistake.

Mick stood and looked at the hill on fire, black smoke billowing up in a huge, growing, top-heavy tower and the vast vista of mountains and ridges and valleys becoming indistinct into the distance. He did not feel the inferno was due to those tumbling packages, but to minds, far to the north, looking south over that terrain.

On the opposite hill, the sight of dozens of miniscule figures running down their slope, heading for 282.

Mick bounded onto the dirt road. Orders were being shouted. Men were readying, checking the gun on their side they had been sure of seconds before.

And he was running with his adopted company, Scottish voices shouting out vengeance and fury and encouragement as they charged. The hill was steep, suddenly there, a tough gradient underfoot; they powered up it, thigh muscles straining, heaving their way up, boots on the dry ground.

He could feel the adrenalin rushing through him, bravely charging on. Yet he was afraid – not of dying, but of dying and not seeing Sun-a. He shouted his war cry and held his rifle high in one hand, leaping onto the spur of the hill, going up, up and round, to cut off the onrushing Koreans. From the hilltop, perhaps in a break in the inferno came the boom of a mortar round being fired, and screams – shouts and the roar of burning ground.

Mick aimed and fired. A running Korean soldier stopped in his chest, mid-air, and his legs and arms flung forward with inertia. More steps, another shot, another to the right. Guns fired all over the hillsides. A soldier was hit beside him and spun around with the impact. He leapt on, fired, saw the enemy falling back before they could jump from their downward spur to where it locked with the Argylls'.

He moved with his squad, running up to higher ground. The heat came in sudden waves as if wafted by a great heavy sheet right into their running faces. Men cursed around him at the near-pain on flesh. To have been at the top of the mountain when the fire had exploded.

The climb was difficult, the ground flaking out in dust as they pushed off. The flames reared high above them as they drew closer; Mick had to shield his face; the fire screeched in their ears. Such a noise.

He skidded to his knees amongst the escaped survivors a short way from the flat crest of the hill. The soil was too hot against his knees, through his tough army trousers. The man before him was dead, covered in burns, now thankfully motionless. He moved on, shots and war ringing around him. He watched his flank – fired at a distant Korean shape in the pluming smoke. Below, he saw sections holding ground, ordered, the whole regiment it seemed doing their jobs together.

He moved with other soldiers. The major was there, uniform sooted and burnt but insignia just distinguishable. The mortar that had kept firing was beside him and the other survivors. The man gritted his teeth and another round boomed out at the advancing enemy.

"Major Muir," someone said.

The major leant back, breathing hard.

"Are you hit?"

Muir nodded, wearily, looking faint, struggling to keep stable on his elbows.

Shouts from the right.

Mick dropped to a marksman's position and scoured the smoke. He fired. Readied. Fired. An enemy soldier dropped. A fellow soldier positioned beside him. The Argyll fired. Mick fired. Two men on the hillside, plumes of black oil-filled smoke drifting across them. Coughing.

"Identify yourself!"

The shape of a North Korean uniform. To wait the fraction of a second to be sure. A rifle raised. And Mick fired, the man beside him too, and another beside him too. More Communists ran through the smoke. The third man yelled and fell back. Shots flew past them. Mick fired. Sun-a. She was out there, across Korea. He aimed. And fired. Reloaded, quickly, too quickly. The bullets were in. Aimed. Fired, and another Korean fell. Boom. Boom. All around. The cracks of explosions everywhere. And the roar of the fire, leaping overhead – no time to look up and see if it was ever about to fall upon him.

Behind him he heard Major Muir say, slowly, voice at its edge, but clearly still:

"The gooks will never drive the Argylls off this hill!"

They had fought on, in choking napalm smoke. The major had died and men had died of their burns and of the battle. With ammunition running scarce they had picked scattered bullets off the ground to reload their rifles and taken them from the dead who no longer needed them.

Mick sat stunned in the evening, feeling flutterings of the day's sights and shouts and roars and flashes about his mind, unable and not wanting yet to piece together what had happened. He said a prayer of thanks and knew he had made good decisions and been spared enough. It was war, and Sun-a was still out there, waiting he was sure of it. And he would find her yet.

***

Captain Alistair MacCallum handed him the folded piece of paper. Mick took it from him, knowing what it meant.

"Thank you, Sir."

"This letter should get you across Korea alright. Says you're on a mission to locate a missing Korean National."

"I appreciate this, thank you."

"You've done well Quiet Man. Still haven't heard you say a lot, but you fight well. I know I, and the other lads have appreciated you fighting with us."

"An honour, Sir."

MacCallum dropped formality and slapped a hand on his shoulder. "You go and find her, alright Bowler. Then get back to us soon as you can."

"I will."

They shook hands.

"Word is that we'll be out of here in a couple of days. Pushing north, and quickly, driving them back. Not sure where we'll be, but you try and find us."

"Will do."

The captain stepped back and saluted. Mick drew himself up tall and returned it.

***

He sat in an American jeep, bumping over Korean roads, the sound of the engine and the wheels on the uneven track loud in the open air. He looked out at passing fields and houses. It seemed odd to travel through the valleys and the flat and wide open land.

The jeep slowed at a junction to allow another vehicle to pass, and for a moment Mick heard the cicadas, their noise suddenly rising from nowhere, though they had surely been there all along. They seemed to be a part of the country, or perhaps they just accompanied the war – he had never been in Korea without them. He wondered when in the year they began to sing; if they stopped at all.

They dropped him off in Daegu, a stiflingly hot city in a bowl between far mountains. The buildings were low, one storey houses, with black tiles and sweeping eaves curved elegantly. He walked through a small square where roads intersected and the buildings were taller. A three storey town house leaned slightly, ramshackle on its jostling street, old wooden frame and lanterns lit in the windows even in day. Other buildings looked older, a few with recent timber, all struggling and weary.

He boarded a supply truck heading to the line to the north. It was some distance from where he thought Sun-a's village might be on the map; he'd need to go on foot from there. He sat at the edge of the truck bed, beside two American marines, with wooden crates stacked high and rumbling precariously over them as they bounced over the ruts and tire tracks of the road. Mick watched the dirt path lay out behind them, glad for the moving air which met the dense heat beneath the tarpaulin. How to find her he had no real idea, just a set of memories and views of landscapes from years before. He tried not to think about it too much – he just needed to wait until he was walking through a field he knew. If he never recognised where he was – wasn't being considered. There was nowhere to retreat, just the need to find her.

***

The train track was a few hundred yards from where the American front line had been; they should have moved north by now. He walked on the low ground beside it, in the bushes and undergrowth which leaned out toward the open space of the bank. The tracks headed roughly east between hills, the small triangle mountains which seemed so natural to him.

He stepped up to the tracks: the lines were bent and twisted from their sleepers, serrated by heat and explosive and severed, frozen up into the air. He walked on, his army pack on his back, seeing no one, just countryside he didn't know.

He slept by a ditch, as he had the night before. Looking up at the night sky, he saw the stars so clearly and the familiar patterns, though he knew few of their names. The moon was there, near to full, unchanged he thought from when he had seen it from their seat on the side of a Japanese train. He lay there looking up and felt he would cry, unable to stop himself. He heard the cicadas, calling out. Quietly he sobbed and his shoulders shook, on the ground beside the ditch.

***

Then suddenly he was there. A crossroads that he remembered clearly. Once it had been guarded and blocked by barriers. It was deserted, with a large crater to one corner of the middle, mortar sized, cutting through the thin layers of gravel and road and revealing all the light brown soil beneath.

Cracks of gunshot echoed out from the road ahead, separating and apart by the time they reached him.

No.

He began to run, breaking into a sprint, hurtling down the road onto the dirt track it really was. His gun in one hand slowed him down as he held it high to stop it banging against his side. Dodging dangerous ruts dried in the mud, old cart wheels and imprints.

No. He couldn't be too late. The shots were more frequent.

And he burst into Sun-a's village, a collection of spaced huts, carts resting, and the advancing American line not twenty feet ahead of him. He looked beyond them and saw North Korean figures amongst grass and vegetation, stepping back, returning fire. Mick aimed his rifle and stepped to the line. An American turned on him in shock - took a moment squinting at his face.

"I'm with you! British!"

The man nodded, still confused, but without time to question it. Mick moved with their formation, advancing, firing at the enemy.

Crack! Crack! Stepping forward. Crack!

Korean soldiers darted and pulled out from the cover of bushes and wooden sheds. The American line began to arc round at either side.

In the middle of the ground an enemy soldier pulled back from tall grass, firing, a snarl visible from distance on his contorting face. The man to Mick's side stumbled, ducking low as shots disappeared overhead. Mick stepped forward, centre ground, growling back, firing, taking aim, firing.

The Korean soldier moved back belatedly, still steps ahead of the rest of his unit. Mick stopped in disbelief. Shock held him. Impossible. That snarling face – he knew it. The man had a sword strapped at his hip, curving just slightly, a simple handle, too thin – samurai.

The man then glared back at him, something like a horror of recognition spreading across his ghastly bared-teeth face. He actually took a step forward, as bullets whizzed about him, and Mick saw a hand reach slowly for the hilt of the sword. And then the man finally backed away, quickly, running and disappearing.

Sun-a!

A sickening feeling crunched around Mick's guts. No! Sun-a. Where was she? It couldn't have been! What had he done to her? No! He ran to the nearest hut, past an American hand, which sought to ask him questions. He ducked his head into the dark interior. It was empty, just a chair, a straw mattress, pots, worn bags of rice. He threw himself out from the doorway, flying to the next hut. Again, the same. No one there.

He ran at a panic, ignoring the placating Americans, across the empty ground in the middle of the village, to a hut with a cart upturned to lean on the mud wall, and dried chillies and cicadas spread out on the land in front. He looked at them doubly as he strode over and gripped the sides of the doorway.

"Hello! Is anyone here?" he shouted in Korean.

It was empty.

Mick turned to the village. "Hello! Sun-a! Is anyone here?"

American troops looked at him where they stood spread about the re-captured ground.

"Soldier! Hey. Who are you looking for?" asked an officer as Mick strode across.

"My wife," he answered, then ran on to a hut across the way.

"Who is this guy?" he heard a soldier ask.

Empty. No. He ran on. Running out of huts.

At the end of the village a wood began. Mick ran to it, past American troops.

"Hey, English, it's not secure!" a voice yelled.

CHAPTER 40

Mick followed a narrow path through the woodland, moving too quickly, scanning both sides, possibly running through North Korean lines. If the villagers had fled from the perimeter; if they had been taken. The path split in two and in a split-second he dove right, leaving the left path unknown, rushing on. Too fast, too fast.

"Sun-a, he screamed." Too loud.

He would not have been surprised when enemy soldiers stepped from either side of the track, yet it remained deserted. No one, just him, careering on, eyes wildly scouring the vegetation and rows of trunks rushing past, blurring into bars along each side. He sensed the trees begin to thin – the trunks narrowing, shrinking, and he dropped his speed a step.

The wood was over: a brief border of grass opened out, then immediately died away into an abyss, leaving only sea and sky.

His boots scraped for traction on the dry soil. He held his breath, reached back for stakes of trees. Dust and specks of soil fanned out, and he ground to a stop a yard from the tumbling edge.

He stood atop the cliff and looked out in amazement at the Korean coast. A sea of deep blue reflected the sunlight as waves moved, the East Sea before Japan. The sound of waves breaking on rocks – and he saw a pebbly beach. It was a short span to the water, a run of narrow land with no time to fall away before the high line of the sea. Then he leaned forward, and peered over the cliff edge to the beach directly below.

There were people there. Clustered together at the foot of the cliff, wary faces turned up to him with scared eyes, waiting. Then a woman stepped away from the crowd, long black hair, turning to look up and see him better. In her arms she held a small child.

Mick moved in a daze along the cliff top, following the land down beside the wood until the height of the rock fell away enough. He climbed and slid down the steep slope, onto the pebble strewn beach.

Sun-a was hurrying across to him, quick walk then a burst of stumbling steps on the uneven ground, clutching the child tight to her chest. She wore a long Korean skirt, the traditional blouse. Behind her, the villagers moved out, curious.

They stopped a short distance apart. He removed his helmet and let it drop onto the beach. He didn't know what to say. His eyes moved from Sun-a, to the child, Sun-a to the child. His wife was as beautiful as ever. She was where she had to have been. He had found her. The child had its back to him in her arms; it turned its tiny face to look toward the coast, or him.

"I'm sorry, I'm so sorry. By the time I knew, it was too late."

"It's okay."

"I wanted to come back. But I couldn't. I'm so sorry."

Mick crossed over the rocks and pebbles to her and put his arms around her. The child's head was close to his face and it was a stunning truth.

"This is your son," she said.

Mick nodded and looked at the baby who sat between them in his mother's arms, looking about.

"What did you name him?" Mick asked.

"Jeong-tae. You can change it if you like."

"No, I like his name. Hello Jeong-tae."

He leaned his head to Sun-a's and looked at his son. The child considered him for a moment and a chubby hand waved up and down through the air.

"I'm your father," he made sure to say in Korean.

He wanted to burst out in laughter and joy. His forehead resting on Sun-a's, their eyes smiling, so close at last, he said:

"I found you. I'm so glad I found you."

"I always hoped you'd come, but I didn't know. I didn't- I'm so sorry Mik-uh. I'm so sorry I left."

"It's alright. We're here now."

He kissed her on the lips, and for a moment they rested there, heads together, their child held safe between their bodies.

He sensed the villagers watching then, and with a look to Sun-a, turned to face them. With an arm around her, Sun-a then guided him to the small crowd.

"This is my husband," she said. "Mik-uh. The English man."

Sounds of understanding and surprise cooed from the villagers.

"Mother-"

Sun-a moved the child across to her other arm and reached out a hand. She took the hand of a hesitant looking lady, a strong middle-aged woman with long black hair and only a few grey streaks.

"I introduce my mother. Mother this is Mik-uh, my husband."

Mick bowed his head, and offered a handshake. His mother-in-law looked puzzled then touched her hand to his. Mick shook it politely, he doing all the shaking.

Gyeong-hui looked up at the tall, broad man, happiness beginning to warm inside her that her daughter's life might be alright after all. And confounded amazement. She couldn't quite take in what she was seeing. The man was huge, so powerful, like he could have swept them all into the sea with one arm. Yet he looked so moved, so open and innocent, as she had rarely seen any man. Her Sun-a, so recently returned, so thin next to the foreigner. She sensed questions in the back of her mind changing how she saw her own daughter: she had met this man? How had she met him and married him and loved him? The knowledge, the tale her daughter had told of travel to a far away land, all became shockingly real.

They were standing there, looking and not speaking. She felt the pressure of the villagers she had known all her life, behind her. She took back her hand and held it in her other, feeling it, never having touched a foreigner before.

"I feel honour to meet you," the foreign man said.

She returned a slight bow. "I am happy to meet my daughter's husband." And she smiled at Sun-a, and up at the huge man.

All so unexpected; she wasn't quite there. She had needed time to prepare for it. And the man spoke her language, and his accent was bizarre, quite terrible.

Sun-a beamed from her mother to her husband, an out of control smile, completely unable to stop it.

Mick couldn't stop glancing to his son and then the face beside him of his wife. She looked glorious. The sound of the waves crashing slowly in the background; the gentle tapping of rounded pebbles; the sigh of water and shingle, drawn and rolling back to the sea; the sunlight glowing on her face; all seemed incredible.

A young woman stepped from the crowd, arms held in front, seeming bashful, but wanting to be noticed.

"And Mik-uh, this is my youngest sister, Cho-hee."

Gyeong-hui looked at her daughter, bemused, having discovered a new person there altogether, in just a few moments. The girl had spoken some other language entirely.

Mick reached out to a sister-in-law he had barely known of. She was beautiful like her older sister, perhaps still just a teenager. She had Sun-a's smile and a similar light in her eyes. Her arm wobbled as she shook his hand, but she grinned widely, clearly more than pleased with it.

"I look forward to getting to know you all. You can help me with my speaking Korean, I hope."

The young Sun-a nodded eagerly. Villagers laughed behind her, now talking to each other, nudging, pointing, taking up a celebratory mood.

"I want to learn English. Then we can talk that way too," Cho-hee told Sun-a.

His son was looking about, trying to turn and see the excitement from his mother's arms. Incredible. He had had a son for... He was more than one year old. All that time, on the other side of the world, on ships, across foreign waters, fighting, the burning, the never knowing – his son had been here, playing or gurgling, seeing his beautiful mother every day. His chest panged to have missed so much of it. But he was there now, and it was like standing on a beach that was truly a stretch of heaven.

Everything had changed for his whole future; it was dumbfounding, yet somehow it just carried him with it, swept on.

"Hold him for a while," Sun-a said, and passed their son to him.

"This is your Ba-ba," she said quietly by the boy's ear.

CHAPTER 41

They walked across the beach to where the cliff came down to the same level, and they could join a path over sand dunes. It wound over reed covered land, rock and sand becoming familiar Korean soil, with the village visible over the rushes.

"I would have liked to meet him too."

"My mother told me, when I arrived, that my father had died two years before. She hasn't talked about it much. She goes pale when I try to, so now I don't."

"I'm sorry, Sun-a"

"I think he had a lot of grief."

She was quiet for a while then.

"You had two sisters you told me. You were the eldest of three."

She looked ahead. "She never came home. No one knows where she is."

He nodded slowly, and said nothing as they walked together in the trail of villagers from the incoming waves.

"She was called Yun-jeong."

Mick put an arm around her. She turned, her head down to her chest, and he held her to him. They stood on the outskirts of the village and dunes, low houses dotting around the open ground. He watched his son, Jeong-tae, with his grandmother, arrive at a house facing the middle of the square. The boy's grandmother sat, squatted in the shade by the house wall, and his aunt crouched down, talking and playing with him.

"I had a best friend here too, when I was young. She never returned either. Her family used to live in that house there."

Sun-a pointed gently as they walked on, and nodded to a quiet building. Mick saw the village about him, women standing, looking and checking the wood line, then becoming busy with food and small gardens in the dirt, and some men carrying a small upturned boat together, with net and lines over their shoulders. Another life.

Two American soldiers strolled through the village square and another stood on the path to the crossroads. They had fought the North Koreans there not a couple of hours earlier. A thought occurred, unpleasant, but pressing. An uncertain image of an enemy soldier, stopping and staring at the sight of him.

"Sun-a, has the war here been fierce?"

"It has been awful. For so long we thought we were safe, but the Americans and Koreans were rushing back down the road here, huge numbers of them. And then the Communists seemed to draw a line right through our village. The fighting has been here. We have lived on the beach more than in the houses."

He wasn't sure how to say it. "Did you see anyone; recognise any of their soldiers?"

Her face was puzzled. That was a good sign.

A whistle, a shriek of a bullet at their side – and then he heard the bang, loud, seeming to cover the whole landscape.

The ground shook violently with the deep rumble of munitions. The aftershock held them all looking to the dirt at their feet.

He saw then the army clothes he wore, the rifle slung around and the weaponry, and was a soldier. His threw his helmet back on his head.

The horrible rattle of machine gun fire strobed through the air. He was moving, arms outstretched, penning Sun-a over to the house, her mother and sister, to the wall of the house. He saw his son, tiny at his feet, looking up at the noise, so far below his protecting arms.

A gap in the shooting.

"Run. Run south, to the sea!" he shouted.

Sun-a's mother was fallen back against the mud wall – a look of fear gripping the rest of her rigid – like some toppled garden statue. He pulled her up, feeling the tension in her legs break, and her taking her own weight. To his sister-in-law he said, "Go south, hurry," and placed her mother's hand in her own. Sun-a was scooping their son from the ground.

So soon. Another attack, just hours later.

Mick looked to the tree line: countless figures were emerging and writhing their way through the trees. Gunfire, continuous now. Light machine guns – three, perhaps four. Dust shot up into the air throughout the village square.

The American soldiers darted back at diagonals, heading for any cover. Returned fire. Mick levelled his rifle, chose his target, fired. A running man in the wood fell flat on his face. Moved along a horizontal plane, picked a target, fired. The man kept running. Fired. He spun on one side, arm dead and flailing, and went down, knees giving up the sprint, taking it into the ground.

He moved to his wife, the child held pressed to her, one hand beneath him, one hand holding the back of his head as a shield.

"Sun-a, take Jeong-tae. Run south."

She looked at him, stood there, then gave her reluctant consent.

"Find us," she said.

Her mother and sister ran past, ducking low; her sister reached out a hand.

"Big sister, come!"

Mick moved forward from the hut. He needed to provide them cover until they could get away. He took aim, fired; glanced over rifle, shoulder – Sun-a watching, horror at what he was doing; he heard her mother and sister calling for her. He stepped forward, fired, casing spinning; he secured the next round; fired.

He saw shapes looping overhead, leaping out of the wood like some horrific monsters from legend. Mortars. Glanced up; they were flying wide. A machine gun opened up like a raging animal, snarling, close up. Mick dove-lurched for the next building, scrambling, falling to his hands, and pushing off.

"Sun-a!" He screamed it, glancing back around as he fell into cover.

The mud wall exploded in small pieces above his head. He fired over the building, dropped quickly down. Looking back he couldn't see Sun-a – just the side of her home, the cart against the wall, plants in the garden between them. The cart cracked and moved as he watched, trying to escape. Bullets pounded small craters and bursts of dust in its wake, wood splintering and snapping.

He tried to look around, but bullets screamed past, in ghoulish sounds, one after another. He had to give her more time. Mick chose a moment, gritted teeth against it being the wrong second, and fired, aimed and fired, ducked down. Running figures from all directions. He tore a grenade from his belt, snapped the pin out and hurled it, screaming into the emerging North Koreans. A second. Two. It exploded and he saw bodies flung to either side – firing, one shot, another, then back down.

Two American soldiers gave fire across the square with hurried back-steps, facing the enemy. They took cover behind an old house, shedding flakes of mud. They saw him, he reloading the rifle.

"English, come on!" one yelled across, beckoning back with a great sweep of his hand.

A machine gun ripped into life yet again, and the dirt leapt high in a rushing line across the square.

"Comfort whore!"

The insult boomed through the warfare.

Sun-a brought her head up from her chest, pressed close against her baby's. She looked out from where she sheltered against the wall of her home, hemmed in by a never-ending stream of bullets and explosions.

"Incheon whore!"

It boomed like the blast of a gun or a bomb, louder somehow, and lasting the way the ground had trembled. She couldn't hear the bullets.

Despite herself, she rose to her feet in the maelstrom and searched the scene of smoke and darting shapes of soldiers. And there in the middle, striding, calm and with intent. Walking dead toward her it seemed. It couldn't be. Yet it was.

"Mik-uh!" she screamed.

Mick saw him too. And then he glanced round in horror at the sound of Sun-a so close.

"Sun-a, go!" he screamed to her as loud as his lungs could.

And he opened fire at the doctor who they had faced a war before. The stakes burned in him, a fury, a will not to be defeated, not to let a sickening sense of inescapable fate claim them. To tear the ghoul from that reality, who was without right to be there, and throw him back from where he came.

In his peripheral vision he saw American soldiers moving back; calling him on with great circles of the arm like bowlers at full tilt.

"Fall back! Fall back!"

Mick glanced back to Sun-a, still there, her shape clutching the child, as he charged into the open. Forwards.

"No!"

There could be no retreat. He fired, rifle gripped at his side, recoil pulling back. Diagonally, cutting across the open ground, hurling himself across the square. Bullets whipped past him: fizzed high; at head height; where he had been. Reloading, even while he ran, leapt.

Returning fire in support – the Americans rallying. The cover of a village home – paces away.

The samurai figure, a glimpse, rifle tracking him, aim slowly turning, hand on a clock. Mick spun to meet it, flying. Rifle out in one hand.

Sound evaporated, as when napalm dropped on water. Vanished. Such a sound: a bass note that shook flesh and ear drum the same. A sky-tall wall of one single sound. The mortar fell short, digging an instant hole into the baked dry ground – in the space he had crossed, to his right.

His only thought was Sun-a holding their child; he had no time to look for them. A wave rolled into him and past him, an irresistible force; though he wanted to put his feet down, he couldn't. It heaved him up effortlessly and he was moving back with it, standing but in the air.

****

He awoke. The sounds of battle were around him in the darkness. Hurried footfalls, past him and grinding steps in dirt, toward him.

It crashed into his mind, his predicament: North Koreans, Japanese, crossing from the trees that moment, to drag him to his feet. And Sun-a. His eyes flashed open and he was heaving himself up, demanding it happen, yet feeling the spirit level rise and tilt unbeknownst to him. He had been on his side on the ground, amongst a scattered, detonated, mud rubble, which he now saw sway and shrink below him. Groggy as he stood, he staggered against lurching balance and lifted his head and clutched for the rifle still strapped around his shoulder.

Mick looked determinedly to where the Communists would be running from, and saw arms and turned faces disappearing into the stacked tree line.

No sign of her outside the house – and no big and small bodies lain out across the dirt. The blast had been far enough away from them. She must have already run.

Americans moved past him as he got his bearings, and in number from the left flank, the landward side, pouring in from the road, from the direction of the crossroads. A hand clapped him on the shoulder.

"Good, English?"

"Um. Yes."

And the soldier moved with the rest of his squad staking out the village land. Gunfire rattled in from the distance.

Mick was running, charging, feeling his legs still strong, his limbs all attached, his whole body aching from the survived mortar blast – his helmet lost in the rubble. He moved to the steadily progressing formation of U.S. troops, and kept going, into the woodland, jumping a fallen tree, feeling his muscles protest but clear it. Landing. Everything was yet to be real. Coming back to him. He knew his purpose: the Japanese doctor could not escape.

He was tracking him.

CHAPTER 42

Kamakura back-stepped, slow breaths fuming out of his nostrils, moving with his troops, behind as they hurried out. The trees thinned around him, and his guts clenched like a fist. He glanced around – Koreans flocking away toward farmland and hills their comrades had already deserted.

He stopped his forced, reluctant steps, and stood facing the woodland. He began to walk forward, steadily, then quickening. Trees passed by him again. From far back he heard a Korean shout, "Sir?" But it was gone, left behind in the world outside the enclosed wood. He cut through the trees.

There was fury behind his eyes as he scoured the lines of trees which fell endlessly back. They encircled him anew every few steps as he passed one for the next. Surrounded him; but he outstepped them, moving between trunks, his stride not altering. The fury turning his head, searching his aim, running him.

He swept a branch aside. Stepped through. With his other arm blocked tree limbs and swept them. He moved on, feeling the kata he had trained in as a boy being called on as it had long ago been laid down - stepping low between the trees. He would destroy the English soldier. He had been right to wait there outside the village - to watch the woman and her white skinned son. He had known the man would come. He had known he would be able to get his vengeance; he had just had to wait, to wait and watch and wait. He missed no detail, seeing everything of the forest in stark, glaring lines and discordant colours. At the edge of the wood were the Americans; he was walking right to them. It didn't matter. He could not be stopped.

Everything was rage. He wanted to bellow out in the fury that would rip his enemy apart. Silence. His mute scream tearing through his skull; his epiglottis ever howling, shaking with the hatred. Ventricular folds would shred themselves apart; gaping long tears would make sliced gullies of his thyroid cartilage. He roared out his scream, face unmoving, still, eyes searching, wide. He stalked without a sound: none from his footfalls, gliding the steps of a kata along the twigs and leaves and detritus.

He was deep into the woodland, past its middle. One hand rested on his samurai weapon, the other an iron grip on the rifle.

He saw the soldier through the trees.

Mick stopped still. Fifty yards away, the Japanese doctor stood small amongst the posts of trees. A woodland was staked out between them.

All was suddenly movement. He burst into a sprint, seeing his opponent do the same, before he disappeared. Mick ran with rifle locked into his shoulder. Line of sight flashed into being and vanished; the trunks slotted together and overlapped and seemed to sidestep each other, shuffling position like alive things, as his charge powered past them. He jumped left as he flew, past a tree; he saw the Japanese; he fired. Boom. The man was gone. Mick hadn't stopped. His heart thumping in his head. Boom. A shot fired against him. Running on, always forward, side stepping - flying diagonals. He feinted. Right, left. Went right. Bark exploded into soft shrapnel and dust in the air, but he was away from it, aim desperately searching, then glimpsing him. Instantly firing. The bullet lost somewhere into the maze of tree trunks.

They were close now, frighteningly near. A glimpse between rushing trees of the face – clear, fleshed-out features. The man was darting like he was, zigzagging between the trees and smashing through low branches: the sound of predators careering at prey. Twenty feet.

The last shots. Firing. Yellow flashes – painfully sharp. Trees thudded and burst in bark smoke. He feinted, dove aside, past trunks, weaving. Bang. He felt it rush near him. Firing again. The face already gone. They leapt from the last trees, into the open, rifles exploding, yellow fire without aim.

Even through it all he saw white light catch on the samurai sword. It drew with the grating sound of a blade being sharpened on stone. They pounced.

He flew through the air, rifle become sword, bayonet raised high to cut down. The Japanese man, flying at him, teeth barred, roaring, as he too roared. Momentum and inertia that could now not be changed. They would clash in the air, between the trees in that Korean woodland.

And then the butcher-doctor cut down, double handed, with impossible speed. Mick arched his body in mid-air, in desperation, bringing his rifle around. To stop its slice, a foot into his side, kidney and guts.

The razor-sharp blade blunted against the metal of his Enfield's magazine: it deflected and notched deep into the wood near the trigger. He clung to the gun as they passed each other, smashing shoulders and arms, feeling the Japanese sword tug at the rifle from his hands. He landed, stumbling, still holding the gun. Spun round, reached, in an instant reloaded, and fired – but the Japanese sword had lashed up, catching the bayonet, throwing the dead centre aim into the sky toward the low canopy. Leaves shot and tumbled.

From there the doctor hacked down, below his rifle; Mick saw the move would come and jumped back. The blade sliced through the air, so close beneath him he couldn't see its end. His stomach was not spilling, he thought – had probably not been torn – as he reloaded in a breath, bolt back, forward, locked, and dropped the rifle in front of him. He fired. He was fast; he couldn't believe the man had moved in time. The flare bloomed against snarling face, seeming to set ablaze his hair for a moment. Then Mick saw the doctor bring the Russian rifle, secured and fixed between side and arm, around. Mick met the Communist muzzle with the edge of his palm. Desperately, he braced the Enfield, one handed, as the samurai sword cut at it. The thin blade seemed to cut right through, scything down the side of the attached bayonet and chopping into the metal where it curved and fastened to the muzzle.

With his gun hand the doctor fought back, turning his body and rifle with it; Mick battled against the clocklike turning of the arm. Surprised at the man's strength. Pushing back; the side of his palm blocking, the bayonet stabbing past. One hand against one hand, the other arm against the other. Mick's grip on the Enfield's wooden stock began to slip, to bend and twist; the Japanese sword dug at the metal near the muzzle, sawing there as they struggled. In horror, Mick saw a groove, slicing through, more each second. He pulled the trigger on instinct. A hollow click. Neither man could free the second hand needed to chamber the waiting bullet.

He was screaming with the total exertion of the fight, every muscle battling for supremacy. The sword ground and metal shrieked from the bayonet. The rifle creaked and yawned, the sound like a ship capsizing. The doctor changed the angle of his own bayonet attack; the barrel slipped

Mick's hand – he grabbed for a hold of the enemy rifle; felt the searing pain of the bayonet blade split his palm, before he grabbed on atop the barrel. He cried out as he refused to let go, blood slicking the wood and burning metal, and heaved his weight onto the rifle as the doctor dragged it back to his elbow.

They were stumbling back, around, with the force of the struggle. The doctor sent a knee crashing nimbly, up, high, into his ribs – barely caught as Mick jumped back. He drove his boot at the doctor's knee, shin, needing to snap the joint back.

They spun and smashed though branches. A great weight thudded whole against his back and deadened the wind from him. The sword twisted in its lock, sharpened edge to him, pressing in. His fingers and thumb were on fire, trying to hold the Enfield still – not let it turn. His other hand was an agony, flesh pulling apart over rifle stock.

Mick heaved off the tree, all but lifting the Japanese man off the ground with the force of his rage and the shout that went with it. The doctor lunged his whole form forward, dashing his head down and his scalp like a stone into Mick's nose. He heard the crack reverberate around the bones of his skull to his ears, and was all dizziness, staggering, not seeing, everything devoted to keeping his arms outstretched, locked where they were. He kicked wildly. Made contact. Kicked out again, savagely and felt leg tremble at breaking point beneath his boot.

Spinning, a hurricane of sword and rifle and shouts and pain through the woodland. Bouncing off trees. Branches snapped and broke with the sound of falling timber; twigs cut and lashed at his face – countless attacks it seemed.

The Japanese kicked out at him – somehow, in that short, chaotic battleground. Sharp from the knee and before he could move fully back it planted in his stomach. He refused to let go, either rifle, stomach concaved, unable to breathe; enemy unsteady, snapping the kick back, stumbling; crashing through low branches, undergrowth.

Their shouts, a roar of noise – suddenly vast, filling a great space.

Then the trees were no more. The woodland floor was tall grass beneath his out of control feet. He saw a flash of blue sky. The tree line, which he had passed from. He saw the vile doctor's face look wide-eyed in terror.

Side by side, they toppled clear of the cliff face.

Mick saw sky above him; the bayonet and sword scrape apart, glimpsed aside; the doctor swing wildly, weakly, too far away; the hurricane pulled apart in the air. The sky was piercing blue. His own legs lifting above him – his army trousers ballooning in the rush of air against their seams. He was plummeting on his back. He saw the cliff shoot up into the blue and he thought of Jack and the Beanstalk – that grew impossibly fast. The cliff reached up to take so much of the sky. And he realized fully in the pit of his rising, falling stomach that he might well die. He thought of Sun-a and his new son, Jeong-tae, and in the second he had the pain was terrible.

His back impacted without warning: a mighty thud which slammed and spread instantly to shoulder blade, pelvis, rib. He felt his head hurled back to split and dent upon stone. There was a rush of bursting sound and then a force throwing his head back up the other way. He opened his eyes – found they had closed shut, tight – and saw steaming bubbles, all sizes, frothing madly. He was still plunging, dropping from them. A dull thump of a great weight settling.

He saw the sea above him, and felt blinding salt against his open eyes.

All was impetus. He was alive, in the sea; the Japanese doctor too – next to him. He thrashed his arms for movement and kicked down and behind, trying to lever himself from the sea floor, and up, to his feet. He burst out of water suddenly, gasping, and with surprise placed his feet down, standing, the water at chest height. Funnels of water dripped from his hair and obscured his vision, as he turned and gasped loud lungfuls of air. The tide had come in. He was still alive. He spun - where was the Japanese? Saw him. The man was looking down, through the water. Mick looked too, and saw a rifle, drowned on the rock floor. He saw his own: its strap went around his shoulder and the rifle was still held in his locked hand.

They charged. He felt himself from some legend of old, doing battle on the foundation of things. He was there in the reality: cold water; the air and sun roasting hot. He lifted himself through the heavy water, dragging through it with ratcheting, storing force.

They clashed, rifle meeting samurai sword, fighting over head height. Mick reached a free, damaged hand and smashed it into the Japanese's face, as the man swam his head aside, and punched back with speed. Mick rocked back, steadied himself, feet trying to shuffle, dragging against the water. A pulse of light, warning high in the air above him. The long sword snaked a path down and he sought to parry it, but it sliced into water where it could not be seen for the leaping, frothing salt waves. In panic, he knew he had to stop the circle; he turned his flank exposed and crashed both hands through the water, his rifle dropping loose on its strap.

He met the grip and guard of the sword somewhere underwater, as its angle began to turn inwards. His muscles shouted out as they wavered and fought back against the direction and momentum of the underwater blade. He saw the face of the Japanese man, teeth gritted, nostrils flared, eyes monstrous, bloodshot beside him as they wrestled. He felt the skin on his fingers buckle and rend, simply opened and cut into. He roared and in a fountain of water, as a detonated torpedo sent, he heaved the samurai sword and the Japanese arm from the water.

The Japanese man lurched with the shock of it, and as he teetered for balance Mick brought one hand down, and seized the rifle and bayonet blade. He struck his arm out with all the speed and force he could find. The blade cut down aside the man's neck, into the coarse uniform, and collar bone.

The enemy howled and jolted back, taking the rifle with him a moment, dragging it from Mick's grasp: it tugged on the strap about him and rebounded, sliding free of the wound.

Mick had lost hold of the lethal samurai sword. The doctor snarled a battle enraged war cry and wielded the sword high above him, now gripped in two hands.

The water held him back, but he was under the blade before it fell. His own two hands clasped around the hilt. The blade teetered, pointing to the sky above them. It caught the sunlight and gleamed, sending dazzling reflections down to the water and their eyes. A wave rolled into them, lifting the sea over their heads, then falling, leaving them gasping, coughing, still fighting.

Mick shouted a furied cry. He heaved the Japanese man off his feet, lifting trains of the salt water with him. He turned as he did and screaming still, smashed the doctor against the side of the cliff.

The shorter man hung there and Mick crashed his hands into the cliff face. The doctor snarled in pain, and still held the samurai sword. Again Mick smashed his hands into the rock. Again and again. The Japanese man dangling against the brutal rock face, refusing to let go, knees and boots kicking out, smashing into Mick's legs, chest, stomach.

Mick roared as the sea crashed around him, and with all his strength brought the sword and grip again away from the cliff and hurling back into it. Through the booming sound of a sea behind him, he thought he heard the sound of bones breaking. The doctor cried out, and for a moment the sword was loose. Mick grasped his fingers for the wound, bound leather of the hilt. The doctor screamed words close by his face, desperate as they fought for the grip. With a shout, the sword tore free. It hurled away, high over the sea. He saw the Japanese man watch it go, his hateful face, mournful.

Mick brought back his arm, elbow high, out of the rolling water almost level with his head, and crashed his fist into the doctor's head. The monster's face, staring in a trance along the cliff, rebounded against the weathered, solid rock.

Mick fumbled for his rifle, followed the strap and quickly found the Enfield floating beneath the surface. He took hold of the gun in both hands. The sea seemed grown around him.

To finish it.

The doctor screamed suddenly, salt water and spittle flying, the sea swilling about his mouth. Seeing his intent his enemy plunged his bloody hands around and through the surf and grappled for the English rifle and its knife.

To end it. Mick would not be beaten; this evil man would never win.

He was the stronger, and the blade circled up, away from him. With an iron grip he felt the resistance of kneecap – as the doctor howled and his head craned back and his neck stretched sinews to the sky – and then the cut into thigh muscle. Through the water he saw an image of the doctor's blurred hands scrabbling, desperately pushing on the blade itself.

A jolt. Something had snapped.

The Japanese man reared back, and the Enfield exploded from the water like a leaping shark. The bayonet had broken near the muzzle, edge partially serrated, then snapped clean. The doctor fell away, back to the cliff, hands clutching at the blade in his leg, then bloody, fingers throwing it up high, bloody lined to their bones.

The sea was tall around him. And then a sound of thundering waves, though he saw no more waves breaking against the high cliff he faced. A deep rumble, from the outer sea itself.

Suddenly a force like nothing he had experienced, more terrible than the mortar on the land, picked him off his feet. He was utterly helpless.

He saw it hurtle past far to either side: immense walls, rising higher and higher, perhaps hundreds of miles thick, ramming battlements into the cliff face. He saw the Japanese man's face, looking the other way, terrified, and knew his own expression was much the same.

And then it hurled him like a pebble. He yelled out, and hit the cliff face.

Kamakura Hideyoshi could go nowhere. The Sea of Japan ploughed him back against the cliff face, drilling into his pinned arms, ulna and scapulae, though his chest, his lung cavity, his immovable legs, riveting him permanently against the rock of the Korean coast. His held skull shook against the bombardment. And then it was over and it dropped him back to shallow water.

He knew what he must do. As more waves - the sea become a storm - broke about him, he dragged himself across the cliff face, clutching at the rock, losing hold. Walking like a spider, horizontal across the rock and the lifting water. He knew what he needed to do.

He glimpsed the English soldier, further out in the sea, hands flapping, occasionally head above the water.

No, he knew what he must do. He pulled himself on, fingers struggling to grip. Slowly snaking across the cliff face; waiting, absorbing the punishment as waves returned to attack again, then clawing on; coughing up water, heaving in painful air. It had to be there. A sword would sink. The sea wouldn't have taken it out. It would still be there, where he had seen it land.

CHAPTER 43

Mick pulled himself onto the sand dune coast. He was beyond exhausted - consciousness seemed a puzzling sense. He thought he had seen the doctor, clambering by the cliff; he didn't feel sure. The last minutes of memory did not seem real.

The wind was strong, whipping up the sand, then quietening, then gusting cold again. He turned heavily over and looked out at the sea. Waves were breaking, but it did not seem unduly fierce. Just a blustery day. He looked left, and right, then allowed himself to collapse back to the beach.

Thank God he had survived. Thank God.

He trudged toward the sand dunes, trying to put momentum into his movements, shaking the cold and sea water from his head. He checked the rifle, flecked in shingle which he brushed from the wood, then knocked the barrel against the side of one leg and then the other. Drops of water flung away from the muzzle. The beach lifted into land beneath him. He took a charger clip from the pouch at his belt and fed the bullets into the magazine, struggling against the lack of movement and pain from his hands.

And what of the doctor? He had badly injured him. It was unlikely he had ever made it out of the water.

In minutes he arrived at the southern edge of the village. There were craters and dents in the wide track. Barely any troops. He could see the wood to the north and a few American soldiers spread in a thin line across it. The U.S. troops must have pushed the Communists back through the woodland, turning the Korean's surprise attack into a rout. Was that it then? Was it over? Sun-a and her family had surely, hopefully escaped the mortars far to the south; he would see them again soon – a new family to suddenly get to know.

He smiled to himself at the thought. It hadn't gone as he'd expected crossing the seas on those many boats with all that time standing on decks, holding the railings, looking at the deep, vast water go slowly by. To have a son. He had only known of him for part of a day, mere hours, yet already it seemed like it had always been; he tried to recall what it had been like to not have a son, but he couldn't. Was his journey finished? He had succeeded? Found his wife, his son.

He would check with the Americans, then go and find Sun-a and Jeong-tae. When the new advanced line was established, well clear of the village, he would bring them all back to their home.

He passed houses. Damaged carts were upturned and broken; he saw large kimchi pots with smashed holes, leaking bright red juice from the compacted vegetables inside. A man was turning over scattered wood and thatch which had been knocked from the gap on his house roof. Mick glanced into the dark interiors as he walked by, but no one else had yet returned. It was as he had found it earlier that day when he had first arrived, only more beaten, with bullet scars all around.

He heard a noise, which didn't belong to the recovering calm of the ruins and surviving buildings. A scuffling. Muted voices. He looked where the sound seemed to come from, away at Sun-a's home. He began to move towards the small one-storey hut, its dried yard drawing closer. Disturbed chillies and fish had been thrown from where they had dried in the sun.

The sounds had not stopped. There was someone inside. His rifle slowly lifted, past his chest, now held in both hands.

The doorway was a black rectangle as he stepped toward it, dark against the afternoon light. It was Sun-a's family home; there was no reason to be cautious. The darkness gave way for a moment to shades from the afternoon: a glimpse in layers of blackness of figures, more than one, movement, something tense, stilled.

Immediately he fell to the cover of the building's wall.

"Sun-a?"

There was fear in his voice – he had heard it.

By the black obtuse shape of the doorway, on the ground, there was a red smear – thick and red.

"Sun-a!"

A horrible fear dropped, bomb-like, down into his stomach. What had he seen? He had not seen her leave, had he? Only presumed.

He was moving into the open black of the doorway. He did not recall deciding; he was observing himself do it. And the black flickered and suddenly gave way to the dimness of indoors.

He saw Sun-a on her tip toes, arching back, their son suspended in the gloom beside her. A thin, glinting blade ran across her throat, pulled tight and high, forcing her neck to stretch; the samurai sword continued on, to its sharp cut end beneath the turning head of his little son. The doctor's face was between the shoulders of mother and child, low and smirking. He held the baby with one bent elbow trapping the small chest, so that the infant hung as a shield. His other elbow cut high, aside into the dark interior, from where it drilled the sword down, across the two captives.

"Look who I found waiting here for me."

The rifle was locked at shoulder level, the aim to his eye.

"Let them go."

The Japanese man kept his head ducked low, weaving through the gap between mother and child, hiding behind the two prisoners.

"Nothing changes," the doctor coldly declared.

She had run into the house to shelter from the shelling, with her family already fleeing south from the village. She had never left. The monster had somehow found a way to scale the cliffs – had found the sword beneath the waves. He felt sick to his stomach that it should have come to this. Across Korea, across years, it had still come to this. A fate that could not be avoided. That would not be avoided. He steadied himself. Swallowed. Willed his legs to strengthen against the lack of feeling and the beginning of trembling that seemed beyond his control.

Sun-a was shaking, tears and the sound of crying slipping from her as she contorted back from the blade against the Japanese doctor.

"Do you know, I studied in your country? London was where I learnt my discipline."

The man was speaking English – he had barely noticed. He had to gather himself; he needed to think clearly.

"So, what do you suggest, English man? If you put the gun down, will I let them go free?"

"I will kill you."

"I will shortly bleed to death without surgery. But I will grow faint before that. You wouldn't want the blade to slip."

Mick stared at the fleeting eyes in the darkness.

"I am a man of my word. You heard me."

"Oh, we are both men of honour." The Japanese man appeared to think as he writhed behind his prisoners. "Perhaps that is why only you presented a challenge."

Jeong-tae began to cry, the slow jolt of a child deserted. Mick saw Sun-a's eyes move as far aside as they could, pleading for a glance. Yet her face stayed as it must, arched back and up to the roof, for to turn it would be to slit her own throat. Mick glared down the rifle sight, fighting the quake that murmured his two hands, that resonated even from his shoulder. The Japanese man was favouring his wounded leg, leaning as his sword began to wave unsteady.

He needed to sight him. But the doctor kept low, covered by the woman and child Mick loved, his body hidden behind theirs. The man was a coward.

Jeong-tae reached for Sun-a, desperately sobbing. His short arms grasped above the metal line. Then through the cries the voice of the doctor:

"Your mother swam out to meet the battleships."

The sword began to lose stability. Blood ran down the long silver blade from the cut-clenched fingers on the hilt; it ran and hung on drops from the steel that gleamed, taking all the light from outside.

He needed to kill. To wound would be to watch the blade slit Sun-a's stretched throat and sever across Jeong-tae's. In one move. He had to kill.

He glimpsed a grimace on the doctor's face, then gone. He tried to breathe. But he was fury. Calm. If he went for the head, for a fraction, for the edge of the skull that drifted out and behind, out and back, if he went for the head, and missed. If he missed. He couldn't risk that shot. He was good. Very good. But if he missed. Calm. He told his hands and arms not to shake, to be steady. To breathe.

The time since he or the doctor had spoken was glaring. They both were readying. This was the time when one of them would act. He needed the shot. He stared down the sight, burning his vision along it so that the man must show himself.

"You are a man without honour."

The very edge of the doctor's scalp. An eye, movement, sideways. Half an eye. A glare. The very edge. Around Sun-a's head.

Then he knew what he had to do. Years of warfare, in snow and ice and jungle and heat; war and kills and tactics and victory and defeat. The samurai sword began to shake, to lurch.

This was the moment.

He swung his aim. Aside. Lower.

Please God.

He fired.

The boom filled the tiny hut, compressed and deafening.

He moved again, before he had seen, in the noise, reloaded. His aim, had to be quick. Perfect. No time to see. He fired. He saw the red explode. His breath held. He saw Sun-a's eyes wide, at the vanished sound, at the unknown.

He saw the face of the doctor, leer back, an eye frenzied in shock.

The doctor's hand bloomed red; fingers twisted, splayed out at angles. The blade was high, high beneath Sun-a's throat. No.

Mick stepped forward, reloading in an instant – keeping the rifle trained, needing to kill; needing to reach for her. The blade still high; Sun-a was arching back, even further, neck straining above it. Held in the doctor's embrace. The blade moved. But the fingers he had shattered beneath the hilt, couldn't hold.

The enemy screamed, a roar, from the cover of his captives; a convulsed horrible wave along his sword arm. The first shot had struck true, the elbow, material frayed red. Yet the sword lurched.

Mick dove forward, aiming rifle out with one arm, reaching with the other. He saw Sun-a, throat exposed, teeter back; the samurai sword, a dark silver line, lifting; her head desperately above, stretching, higher.

"No!"

He saw the lethal blade stab out toward his son, held by the enemy's other arm. Time seemed to have slowed; his stomach frozen; his eyes only a stare. No.

Sun-a's arm squirmed up inside the cut of the blade, cloth catching, skin slicing, to beat out at the pivoted, trapping arm.

The rifle was out before him. He saw the doctor, his face a bared ferocious roar, moved into the open. Mick pulled the trigger; and shot him in his temple.

He let the rifle drop. His arms flung wide. Not too late. Had he saved them?

He saw the samurai blade, waver, and move away from his wife's throat. The blade fell free, from the falling bloody hand. Sun-a turned with the razor sharpness a breath away, desperately reaching with an outstretched hand.

The boy was trapped beneath the doctor's arm as the man began to collapse back. Mick stretched for his son. Sun-a's fingers clutched at Jeong-tae's clothing and Mick's large hand wrapped around his small back. They seized the boy from the doctor's weak, failing grasp.

He heard the sword clatter dully on the dry house floor. His rifle swung by his side.

Sun-a clutched her child against her, and to Mick as he wrapped her within the fold of his arm and brought his other arm around. The boy cried out, in pain and fright, now safe in the hold of his mother and father.

The doctor floundered back, a dark circle of red against his forehead.

Relief flooded him as he held his family close and he and Sun-a searched and ran their hands over their small son's body. Sun-a gasped; Mick placed the back of his hand on his boy's chest, and wrapped his fingers around the wound on his tiny arm.

"It's alright Sun-a, Jeong-tae; it's alright."

He had done it. Together they had done it. It was over.

He held Sun-a and their child, turned and sheltered against his chest, and looked over them, down to the Japanese doctor.

*****

Kamakura Hideyoshi lay on the ground in no particular way, just broken there and fallen. He felt a great shock, a disbelief, at where he now was.

He was dying. He had been shot, hadn't he? But he couldn't feel it.

How had the man done it to him? He felt a horrid surprise, an awful, sickening disconcertion. To have been defeated. To die and have his honour incomplete. The terrible creature was towering up there somewhere. He couldn't see – only the roof, dark struts and reeds – but the man was there, looking down, out of sight, in possession of the honour and he couldn't reach for it. He couldn't reach, sit up, and reach, and slice his sword through and take it back. He couldn't reach for it.

He couldn't move his head to see. He couldn't move his eyes. They wouldn't move. He could only look ahead. Fear. Claustrophobia. A terrible panic. He tried to reach out, to feel for where his sword might be. He thought he still lay unmoved, where he had fallen. Crumpled, in no particular way.

The panic worsened – as something changed in his body. It was horrified butterflies, or birds, flapping about his stomach; no, it was a writhing, a worming; it was a pit of snakes, hollow inside him.

He tried to open his mouth, and scream. One of his last breaths.

The panic became a frenzy. He couldn't die. He didn't want to die. Yet his arms wouldn't move and beat out. He screamed inside himself. He howled out.

Darkness rose from the hollow pit of snakes within him, and sunk in from the corners of his vision. Blackness. Everything was black.

***

They hurried outside to the bright sunlight, she cradling their child.

"Medic!" Mik-uh cried.

American soldiers were already running across the village square to them.

"We need a medic!" he shouted again.

The sunlight flared all around, dizzying with its white glare on the dirt ground, brown roofs, green tree tops; whatever the colour all seemed also white. She breathed, eyes to her son, seeing him weak in her arms, crying stopped. Mik-uh's hand clasped Jeong-tae and little new blood seeped under it.

They were standing close, their son between them, and their heads leant forward, almost resting on the other. Sun-a looked up. She met his eyes, and nodded, and then she kissed him.

"Thank you for finding us."

A small smile graced his taut expression; he kissed her.

An American soldier reached them, tense.

"A dead Communist in there."

The American went in with his gun, then soon back out as another man skidded to a stop, to his knees, pulling the family down. She held Jeong-tae out to him as he unfastened straps on a bag.

"What happened?"

"A stab wound. Quite deep."

The American carefully teased over the fragile, injured arm in his hands. Jeong-tae cried out, and she pressed closer to him.

"He's lucky. Missed the artery."

"Yes."

"Any other injuries?"

The Medic was looking inquisitively at the blood on her sliced sleeve.

"Him first," Sun-a told him clearly.

The man took a roll of white bandage from his pack and quickly wound and secured it around Jeong-tae's arm.

"Okay, we need to get you folks to the medevac tent."

Escorted by a soldier and the Medic, Sun-a hurried south with her husband and son. They strode quickly, and she had to break again and again into a run to keep pace. Mik-uh kept his arm around her, and as they skipped across the ground it sometimes seemed that he was carrying her along.

CHAPTER 44

25th October 1950

He had been with them for almost four weeks, while his cut hands, two fractured and many bruised ribs healed. Sun-a had needed stitches in her arm where the samurai sword had staggered and cut. Now she sat with their son bouncing on her lap, and her mother and sister fussing him. Jeong-tae had suffered, and they had watched over him with concern as he lay pallid, weak and silent. But the wound had healed well, and those days seemed distant. A child of that age, he surely would not remember. Mick could imagine him in years to come, looking down at the mark on his arm and wondering, trying to recall.

The family had spent only two days at the medical unit, with its steady stream of the badly wounded, and had then stayed with relatives in Yeongcheon, a nearby town. The uncles and aunts had been somewhat surprised to meet him, but welcoming, and his Korean had improved to be instinctive again. When his hands could hold a rifle he left with the next convoy north, to rejoin with the Argylls high up Korea, to keep his promise.

***

The Chinese had fallen down in numbers from the north when the war with the North Koreans had been all but won. Mick fought with the Argylls as the U.N. troops fell back, Seoul was lost, and they held the line at Suwon. As he stood watch the first night there and looked to dark mountains to the north, he thought of once passing that Japanese ruled city, with a young woman he had found on a mountainside, hiding at night on tree covered slopes, slipping by unseen. Alongside his regiment, the Americans and the nations with them, he held those Korean slopes. As a translator he worked with the local Koreans over snow covered ridges and helped ensure supplies for that fierce winter's fighting. Though the Soviets sent planes and equipment, Mick saw Seoul won back, and the 38th Parallel hold.

***

24th April 1951

Korea had been won back, back to the border originally agreed with the Russians. He could but hope for the North, that they would one day admit their wrong.

The 27th Regiment was to leave the fighting; his battalion was to travel to Incheon, to board a ship for Hong Kong, their war over. Mick said goodbyes and thanked Captain MacCallum. Next time he was in Britain he would pay a visit to Edinburgh and introduce his Sun-a and Jeong-tae and get to meet MacCallum's Sue. Mick got a ride on a jeep away from the front line, a letter signed by the colonel folded safely behind his head, in his army bag.

He walked between the activity of a war still not yet done. Army trucks pulled up, engines loud, turning over, and soldiers jumped down, or clambered up to take their seats. Mick stopped and stood at the edge of it all, and looked south-east, across the land of Korea. Mountains fell back in volcanic, green ranks; valleys swept between the slopes of trees and the bare starkness of difficult terrain. His family were waiting for him, across it all.

CHAPTER 45

A young child paddled naturally in the moving salt waters. There was a vast gulf beneath him he instinctively knew, and yet he was safe. He would be raised up, and carried.

He laughed and moved the water with his hands, through his fingers; it splashed about him, over him in jumps like flying fish, and he cried out in a baby's delight.

He was alone in the water, his mother and father not touching him – they swam at either side, and he could see them as he tried to turn, and gurgled and blew at the water and tried to reach them. A big hand lifted him on his tummy and he felt himself rise to the very surface, become a boat. He laughed out, so happy and his father gave him to his mother's waiting hands. Her face bobbed in the water, her black hair wet, her eyes wide and looking amazed at him. She talked to him and he said noises too.

Then his father put his arms around them and they kicked to stay afloat, a happy circle, small in the sea and the waves.

***

A man stood and looked out from the Korean coast. The wind gusted past him, rushing in from the East Sea, but he put his shoulders down and held himself tall. He breathed it in, the salted air and what it had to say: he wondered how many times that breeze had encircled the globe; perhaps from the very beginning of things; what it had seen and passed over.

Waves crashed into the foot of the cliff below, sending leaping water crossing the strong rock face in clashing directions. The waves took themselves out, revealing the pebble beach he had played on so often as a child. The sea roared its honourable announcement and the waves smashed into the cliff once more.

The tide was going out now that day.

He put a hand to his arm, and wondered at the small scar there – at the things that had been before. He prayed, thankfully, quietly.

Jeong-tae nodded slowly, standing in that place. The story, and the stories he didn't know. To the truth. That was what mattered.

He checked his watch: it was time for him to be getting back. He needed to help his wife lay the table, stay out of the kitchen, maybe vacuum what had already been cleaned and generally be a presence there to help.

His middle sister would be arriving soon after her long trip from England; she'd have already landed at Incheon early in the morning, and would now be connecting to Daegu. His youngest sister would be travelling – in convoy – from nearby Busan. They were both coming with children, grandchildren and in-laws, to join he and his wife and their own extended family.

They would all return to the cliff top later that day, or the next; the grandchildren would run down into the sea in their bright swimming costumes; the parents would follow them, watching they were safe – a few courageous dads would venture far out to sea most likely; the grandparents would watch and feel glad, and paddle with the smallest grandchildren and lift them laughing over the waves' edge, or float in the buoyant waters as the waves rose around them.

He turned and walked into Korea.

The End

About the Author

Dominic Graham grew up in Derbyshire in the United Kingdom. He graduated from The University of Manchester, and The University of Nottingham.

It was when living in South Korea that he began to research, *Mothers Swam*.

He still lives in East Asia, where he lectures on English and Culture and is writing his next novel.

For more information, articles and links, please visit:

www.DominicGraham.net

www.MothersSwam.com